A
SILVER
THREAD
An adult fairy tale

JUNIA MAE

Quantum
Discovery
A LITERARY AGENCY

Library of Congress Control Number: 2024926973

ISBN
979-8-89641-024-9 (Paperback)
979-8-89641-025-6 (eBook)

A SILVER THREAD

An adult fairy tale

TABLE OF CONTENTS

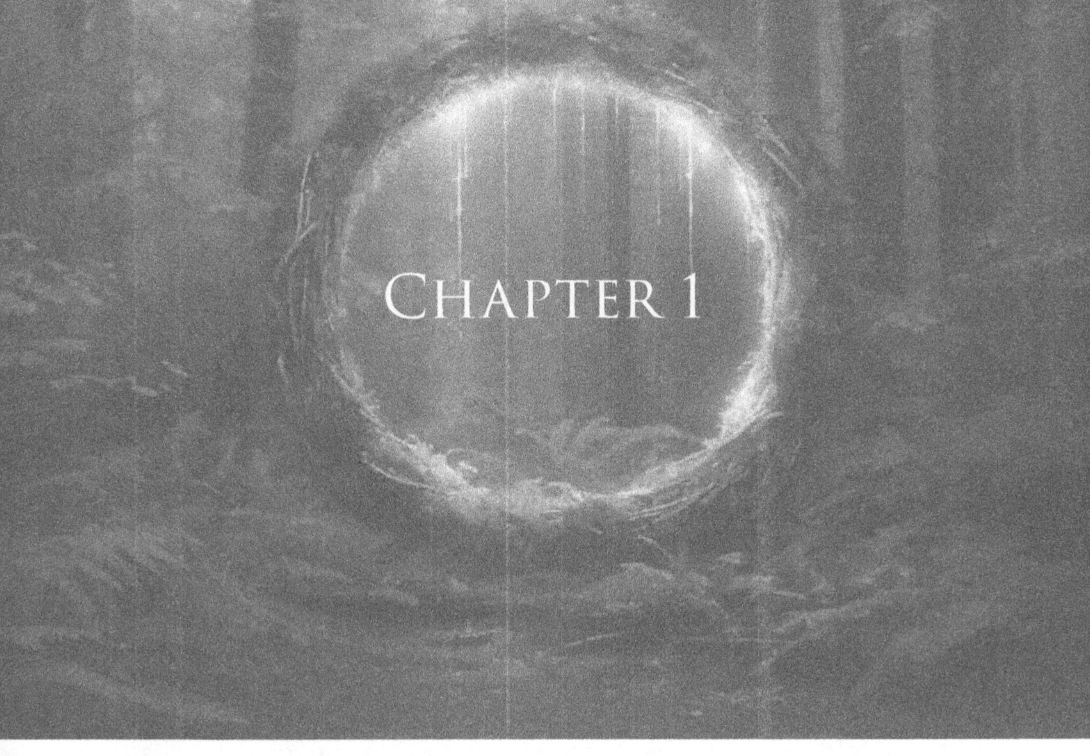

Chapter 1

Tanya Louise Gilbert opened her violet-blue eyes—eyes that darkened depending on her emotions— to a bright, beautiful blue sky with few puffy white clouds overhead, outlined against colored leaves from the trees high above. Thoughts and perceptions passed through her mind. The sky only seemed blue because people were taught the color was blue; the moss was green because that was the name given to the color of a blade of grass. But was moss any more tangible than a cloud? As she blinked up at the clouds one took on the form of a sailboat, instantly her thoughts ran along the line of a vivid imagination. How would it be to ride on a cloud sailboat through a tranquil blue sky? Could one lay her head on the billowy, white clouds and float about with them as one could lay one's head on a bed of moss without dirt underneath? The rich, pungent odor of the moist moss just beneath her head mixed with the smell of decaying leaves, dogwood, hemlock, and other piquant autumn wild flowers, like skunk weed and trilliums, were near at hand. Scanning the treetops with her eyes as the fog lifted from her thoughts, sunlight danced among the leaves like crystal gems. No, a cloud was less tangible than moss, after all. One could grasp moss, one could not hold onto a cloud without slipping through, it was but a form of moisture. The sunlight reminded her of other fairies dancing in the mist of Evald in their iridescent-colored outfits that matched their wings.

In Evald, her wings were iridescence blue, green, and purple—the colors of a river fairy. Those from the depth of the forest had darker shades of various water colors. Time seemed intensified in Evald to the point that she often had no idea how much time had passed upon returning from Evald. A day in Evald could be a week in the human realm. Each year she saw fewer and fewer fairies, elves, and trolls in her homeland; they were fading away or crossing the Great Water that led to the land of long slumber, where elves and such often go to rest in order that they may live thousands of years rather than hundreds. They would choose to slumber as fewer and fewer humans all but forgot them, for spirit folk feed off the imagination of human; without it, they fade from existence.

Her minded drifted with the clouds to thoughts of the solitaire woodland elf that resided near Gosymonity. Nateria would dress in a pale, lacy flowing gown with her feet bare when women of men would put out milk during harvest season for all the spirits who could bring a great harvest. She would wander through the fields, blessing the crop as she passed with gnomes, brownies and the like who would accept the generous offering provided by the humans during harvest. Over the course of time, Nateria had fallen for a prince of man in his youth; as he matured his eyes remained clear when it came to finding her even as the years passed, so great was his love for her.

Her thoughts skimmed through the humans she met over the years that had admitted to playing with imaginary friends in their youth, only to forget them as they age. It was highly unusual for an adult human to acknowledge seeing elves, let alone for such a pair to fall in love. Though he was obligated to marry a princess, it did not prevent him from often riding out through the fields near his castle, venturing into the tangled wood near Gosymonity and waiting for her to appear to him. More than once, Nateria had dared fate by bringing him into Evald to lie under, the great tree, Gosymonity, which was the home she shared with the fairies of Tanya's family. Neither seemed to care that with each visit he risked never being able to cross back into his own realm. It was not impossible for a spirit, but a great feat for a man. Indeed, for him to successfully make the journey was to test their love each time, long ago a wise owl had counseled him not to eat or drink the food or water of Evald, for most assuredly it would be his last trip through the mist. "Have ye not heard the tales long told of men who wandered into the wood to bowl, never to return," questioned the owl? The prince had rubbed his chin and pondered stories he had heard before nodding his head. "They drank the ale of Evald," the owl went on. "A potent magic to be sure that prevents a human from ever crossing the river again.

"So, you're saying they died?"

"Nay and aye," was the twisted reply.

The prince tipped his head to one side in thought. *Nay and aye?* He shook his head in confusion and looked about for Nateria to explain. She appeared moments later with the winsome smile he so adored. "My love, what happened to the men who came to bowl and drank the ale of Evald?"

"They remained until they lay down to rest."

"They died?"

She nodded thoughtfully, "Not immediately, but in due course." She eyed him a moment, "I suppose they died to their kind as they never returned."

"Why couldn't they return across the river?"

"The ale and food are strong magic," she replied. "Tis not allowed." They would spend what seemed to be only a few hours in Evald, but much to his surprise, as he passed over the river that separated the wood from the fields he would discover he had been gone for several days. Nateria had blessed the fields near her wood for many a season with fertile soil and abundance, and she requested in return that the farmers rest the fields every seven years. It had been so in the prince's father's time, and now it was so in his time.

While Tanya sat with a Fuath she had befriended when she was a sprig of about six or seven years of age by the name of M**** under the shade of Gosymonity. She witnessed Nateria communing with the two children of the prince of man. There are many dangers to young humans in the wood; the least of which is a Fuath. In his boy form, he was as curious to watch the children as Tanya. But she kept a close eye upon him, realizing how easily he could engage these children in a game of hide-and-seek that would lead them to the waters edge as he slipped in to resume his true form—that of a water spirit with the torso of a horse. His nature was to lead such children to a watery grave, but Tanya knew his identity, long ago she had learned his name. In naming a spirit one has control over the spirit, and with that she could protect these innocent youths from the dangers of a Fuath. She smiled as she watched the children; one was a strawberry blonde girl with a head of curls, the other a serious, sandy blonde boy with long slender fingers that could almost be half elf. Nateria gave them each a totem, a new leaf from Gotsymity, that would evolve into a colored stone over time. They were wrapped in leather to wear about their necks. "Should you or your father ever have to call for me, take these to your hearts and rub them gently. I shall hear and come," she had assured the children in her whispery, singsong voice.

The boy had taken the gift gravely; with a serious expression, he placed it round his neck. "I shall never take it from my person."

"Nor shall I," echoed the girl. Tanya estimated them to be no more than five and seven. Apparently, they were young enough to remain unblemished by the heart and selfish minds of men.

XXXXX

Hours in Evald could equate to weeks or even months in human realm. Evald, the home of spirits, was a different plane of existence altogether, a plane in which, until recently, Tanya rejoiced with her beloved sisters. A dimension that had brought such solace after their father and brother had died tragically in a car accident several years ago; when she had been but ten-human-years-old. A dimension she had imagined she would always share with her father and siblings. Each time she ventured into the wood she would look for them, but as yet she had not found them. She recalled being on a fishing expedition, shortly after they passed away, she had sat on the riverbank with a neighbor, Mr. Sands, and they chatted. He shared his belief in souls finding one another even after passing to the next realm if their spirits were truly connected.

"Kindred spirits always find their way to one another, Tanya."

She tilted her head to the left as she contemplated those words and smiled. "Hmm, I believe you're right," she agreed with a nod. His words felt right.

"Do you think family are always kin?"

With a grimace, he shook his head. "Not necessarily. Blood does not always make one family. I think complimentary souls are always drawn to one another over and over again, in this life and the next."

He turned back to the water and his pole. Somehow his words had brought her great solace; she had sensed correctness about his statement. There were people she loved in this life but did not connect with. Others she was so connected to there was little need for words. Lenora and Cecilia, her beloved sisters, were old enough to leave Lockwood, New York, and the beloved wood surrounding Mother's home far behind. Old enough to act as though Evald never truly existed. Lenora was fading from Tanya's telepathic grasp and their fairy ways, bitterness seeping to her core and if left unchecked would keep her from Evald for the rest of her days. Just as bitterness had changed their Mother and kept her from the wood, her own promiscuous nature had spoiled life for the family in Virginia. To remain a family, her Father had sought work in the southern tier of New York. The girls harbored many secrets, the one that caused Lenora such bitterness was one, which Tanya wished she could forget ever took place. It was the secret of Lenora's pregnancy and the taking of the baby per Mother's orders. Lenora had been sixteen; it was Mother's way or the highway, where would Lenora have gone? She had no where to turn once Father was gone. The baby was proof of Lenora accusations of Mother's beau having sexually taken advantage, but Mother would not hear the truth. She would not face the truth, and sent Lenora away once the pregnancy began to show. Indeed, Tanya had never connected with her older sister, Lenora, as she had with Cecilia.

Tanya consulted the owl at Gosymonity as to the fate of a bitter fairy. "Why should a sweet fairy as yourself be concerned of bitter ones?"

"Just curious."

"Ah, such pondering breeds an ill wind. Best we not concern ourselves with such a like as that."

Tanya toyed with the idea of telling her sad tale to the owl, but her conscience bid her to bite her tongue. Ill will grew when gathered in jest of such talk, and surely such a wind would pursue Lenora shamelessly until she was utterly turned, perhaps she would become a troll. Turned to what, Tanya wasn't certain, but surely she would become something unattractive that drew upon the bitterness she harbored in her heart. Bitterness brought by Mother's betrayal, which caused Lenora's fall. Mother should have protected Lenora; instead she protected her lover. It was probably as useless as contemplating why adult humans could not see the wood or the spirits therein. Surely the thick hedge near the stream slowed humans, but would it keep them at bay forever? They had such an inquisitive and yet scornful nature. Children had no difficulty in believing, but adults, they were a pessimistic lot. There was no path to the fields through the brambles. Beyond the bramble was a thick barrier of twisted, close-cropped trees before one would come to the fairies clearing near Nateria's home tree. Along the sunny side of the stream, a variety of vegetation grew: hesperis matronalis, lobella, basil, heuchera micrantha, and many others. As the years passed by, Tanya often wondered if Mother could be healed of her bitter, troll-like ways. Could she not return to the wood? Could she not reunite with Father? Perhaps she had no desire for reunification.

XXXXX

Their sense of security and any semblance of family began to come apart the January after their Father's passing, when Lenora was sent away. Since then, the two older girls seemed to distance themselves from Tanya, Mother, and all that was "the wood." Tanya had desperately tried to hold onto both sisters and Evald. She wanted to keep everything as it would have been had Father and Franklin survived, but that was her desire, one not shared by her sisters. So they distanced themselves from home and Tanya's restless heart. It was dangerous to travel "the mist through her precious wood" with her heart in a quagmire. Even though she understood why her sisters chose to walk away, she felt by walking away they dishonored their father's memory. It was like losing him all over again. She comprehended their bitterness; this world had dealt some powerful bitter blows. Rather than embrace Evald for what it was, her sisters told Tanya it was time to let go their childish urges and forget the singing and dancing in the wood. After all, where had the singing and dancing gotten them? They were three in the wood, scarcely ever seeing any others like themselves these days. "Remember how it was only a few years ago?" Tanya reminisced with a smile.

Cecilia nodded as a tight smile appeared across her face. "Hmmm, the picnics we would have with others in the wood."

Tanya nodded. "Right," she agreed, "I recall a time just before Father's accident when we were all there at a picnic."

"Sure, the time you went running toward the creek with the male fairy?"

Color rose to Tanya's cheeks as she nodded ascent. "That's the time I recall."

"No one believes in fairytales anymore, dear sisters," Lenora explained. "Fairy folk can not exist without the imagination of plain folk."

"But there will always be those who believe." she cried plaintively. Lenora shook her head and turned away. Tanya reached out to touch her sister's sleeve.

Lenora turned back with a sigh.

"Don't be so naïve, Tanya."

Tanya waited, imploring her sister with her eyes.

"Tanya, why are you blind? Father left the mountain; he left Evald so that we might survive in this realm." Tanya shook her head no. She could not accept that. Perhaps she enjoyed their time together more than her sisters. They sought the company of the sons of man, the company of the realm in which men lived. Tanya preferred the company in Evald that she had kept men at arm's length; she had few close friends in the world of men. In her heart of hearts, she felt assured there was a male fairy for her, even though her sisters believed the males had all gone across the waters. Tanya felt the tug of Evald; a tug she imagined should pull on her sisters as well. Tanya had been deeply stung by her siblings at their last meeting in the wood when Cecilia dared to go so far as to say Evald was nothing more than joint childish fantasy, similar to young girls' imaginations as they played with a Barbie. Cecilia had decided the time for such musing had come and gone. Tanya looked at her forlornly. "How can you equate Evald to Barbies? We've never had any dolls."

Cecilia shook her head. Forget all that Father had taught them of the old ways; forget their responsibility to the wood of Evald. It was simply child's play; in all the years since Father and Franklin had passed on, never had they seen Father or any of his siblings in the wood of Evald. So, he had not crossed at death. He had gone to the permanent sleep of a warrior with his son held close. It was best if they all agreed to live in reality.

That's a bygone age.

No. Tanya cried. *How can you say that in a mind link? This link alone is not something the sons of man can do.*

No one believes in fairies anymore. Lenora went on in the secret and unspoken communication of those spirits of the wood.

Evald is fading, dear child. Do you not notice the wood of Evald shrinks each year, and the farms creep ever closer to the river? If you wish to survive, Tanya, you must survive in this world. Why do you think Father brought us to Lockwood, New York? Do you image he left the mountains for his own good? It was for our survival.

Tanya had been speechless.

How could abandoning our heritage be for our own good?

She had never truly understood Father's reasoning for leaving all he knew and loved to venture to upstate New York, far from their mountain home. He must have a good reason to make such a move. His home had been in the mountains of Virginia, not the hills of upstate New York. Surely, he had found a way to continue to pass into Evald from New York. Surely she too could find a way to walk the mist even if she traveled far away from Lockwood. The key was how. Indeed, Father had sacrificed much for his family; isn't that how it's supposed to work? He had moved hours from all relations and all that had ever seemed to matter. Over the years of eavesdropping, something all children do, the girls had gleaned supposition. The move had always been because of some unforgivable sin Mother had committed, but the girls had never actually figured out what that was. Father had always said they had moved to provide more opportunities for the children. Lenora believed it was infidelity, but many people had been unfaithful to their mates before. They rarely let such antics cause them to strike out on their own, especially when children were involved. It had been hard to readjust to New York, to kids teasing them over their Southern drawl, of having no extended family to turn to when in trouble or with questions. Moving hours away from their mountain home meant isolation and a loss of a great deal of family history and folklore. It put them out of sync with their cousins and the kids they found surrounding them in their new environment. Even though they returned to the hills in the summer, they found they had less and less in common with their cousins with each passing year, and then after Father's demise, the trips ended altogether.

The girls had grown up feeling they were rootless, homeless, tethered only to Evald. That tether seemed not secure enough to hold Lenora or Cecilia. Father had always told them, "No matter what happens in life, remember you always have one another." It seemed he was wrong on that account as well. Mother had torn Lenora from her sisters, and now Cecilia had found an escape through the arms and security of a man. That was a possibility for Tanya as well, but not one she truly contemplated as a means until Auntie had tied the knot in Europe. Nothing bound them to Lockwood or the mountains of Virginia; Tanya understood why Lenora and Cecilia wanted to abandon the wood. In the joy and merriment, there was a twinge of pain, longing. Something was always missing once Father moved on. That's how M***** had become such a significant player in Tanya's life; in all honesty, he should never have become such a regular companion.

In retrospect, Tanya realized he had never bonded to either of her sisters. The few times Cecilia had been with her and spotted M****, she had shooed him away. Perhaps, Tanya should have done so as a small child rather than befriending a fuath. As she grew, she learned that fuaths were a tricky lot, never to be trusted, and yet she had remained silent and happy to spend time over the years in his companionship. M**** should have taken her long ago into his watery home, as fuaths are known to do to small children. Indeed, he should have ended her existence in her youth simply for playing with him. But that had not happened between he and Tanya as she toddled through the wood; as she grew and sharpened her mind, he came to enjoy simply appearing and sitting with her, sharing a riddle or just silent contemplation. *What be sunny on a cloudy day? What is full of merriment when the mourners have all gone away?*

Tanya furrowed her brow to think upon the question but was soon interrupted by a gnome. It was Artimis. He wished to fetch "splendidly plump" blackberries from the briar patch and requested her assistance. Tanya loved a tasty blackberry and was off arm in arm without further thought of the riddle she had been intently puzzling over. Henderson, a woodland deer, came near the stream, asking if she might gather a few sprigs of the best young birch twigs higher in the tree so that she might give it to her fawns. Of course, Tanya fluttered up into the branches to do her bidding. All benefited from a bit of pruning. Before long Tanya forgot the puzzle she had been given, as fairies tend to do. She was off here and there with her friends; enjoying a day in the wood, with a sigh she returned to her Mexican blanket in the other realm.

Tanya stretched as she passed from Evald into the world's realm. She noted that there were still a number of green leaves nestled close to the tree trunks mixed with the vibrant colors of autumn, as she scanned the area for her pets. The sweet luxury of lying out in this secluded meadow on her purple, blue, and white Mexican blanket, with her pets near at hand, her dearest friends in this world.

She had been contemplating her sister's advice before drifting off to a gentle slumber in the small escape since her father's passing—a sanctuary, a quiet place to meditate, a place to work the ancient crafts of her ancestry, such as lighting a fire without a match, levitating, or working on her gift… leaving her body and slipping into someone else's life through their dreams. Lenora had always been best at telepathic communication. Cecilia and Tanya could sense and dream, but with

Lenora, they could always hold lengthy conversations telepathically. Not so between Cecilia and herself; they could only communicate intense emotions without Lenora. Today she had received her answer; though her sisters had found it possible to forgo their heritage in Evald and shut off that part of their lives so as not to fade as so many of the fairies had, Tanya could not. In the passage of time her sister's would loose their telepathic ability, and Evald would become a faded memory. Evald was too much a part of who she was and would be for her to let go. It had sculpted her life.

Today, she had glimpsed a male fairy in the wood, one with sandy blond hair and dark roots and playful, violet-blue eyes. They had played at a distance for sometime, though they hadn't spoken, and then something had drawn her back to Lockwood. She found herself being pulled back into this realm, reluctantly through the mist. A sense of satisfaction spread through her being as she realized today she had found a mate. Surely, they would find one another again. There was a purpose for her to walk in this world, she didn't as yet know what it was, but walk it she would until it became clear. And when the timing was right, she would walk into the mist of the wood for good. It had always bothered her that Father had not managed to walk into the mist that fateful day; instead he had remained trapped in the expectations of life in this realm, the realm of her human form. Did that mean he had not faded across the Great Water? If that be

the case than she had to accept they may not meet again in this lifetime. Is that why she had never again seen him in Evald? Had they laid his spirit trapped in a human body and cremated him into an earthly grave? Father refused to leave Franklin at that crucial moment, as they were trapped within the mangled wretch of the car. There had been no hope for Franklin, and Father chose to remain at his side. Franklin had never managed the mist; he was Mother's child more so than Father's. One look at his mangled body in the wreckage was sufficient for all of them to realize there was nothing for Father to walk into the mist with. Yet Father had held the lifeless body of his son and slipped into a coma rather than walk into the mist alone. It had broken his daughters' hearts to say goodbye to them. As sadness from the memory of Father caused

Tanya's shoulders to droop she looked around the meadow, wondering what had called her back. It was time to head home for the day. It was most likely Mother blowing the car horn, two longs and a short, the signal for the girls to return to the house.

A Long and a Short

Lady, a beautiful gray and white Appaloosa, was still tethered to a broad white birch shaded in the trees at the edge of the clearing not ten yards away. Winnie, a black and white sheep dog, lay among a cluster of poplar and pine trees, her ears perked. *Hmmm.* Tanya strained her ears and subconscious. What summoned her from a blissful catnap? With inner eyes, she drank in the warmth of the sun, the pleasant periodic chirp of birds, and a sense of euphoria.

The position of the sun instinctively let Tanya estimate the time was around four in the afternoon. With a deep sigh, in her mind's eye she saw the sound calling her: two longs and a short on a car horn. Mother was summoning her girls back to her small, four-bedroom white ranch house with black trim and shutters in the hills of Lockwood, New York. The house sat up on a knoll hidden in trees, mostly poplar and pine, with a broad opening for the drive. The spell of the wood was broken. Tanya groaned and rose to collect her things. She noticed Winnie had eaten the dog food she packed for her, and Lady had munched all the grass nearby. It was a clear she had spent sometime away from them in Evald as she packed away the empty containers on Lady. Winnie rose in step, expectantly.

When Father was alive, the house was a home; now it had become a place simply to bide time. Lenora went away the previous January; Mother's arrangement to save face within the rural community of Lockwood, where they lived. She now attended a nursing school near Buffalo at the expense of Mr. Hinckley, Mother's married boyfriend. The three girls had disliked him almost from the moment they had met. The girls did not like the way he looked at them, the way he insisted on giving each a smothering hug to greet them. When the girls saw his vehicle in the drive they would avoid going inside as long as possible.

After Lenora became pregnant it was clear to all three their mistrust had been justified, but it made no difference to their Mother. She chose him over her daughters. Recently, Cecilia confided to her sisters, that she and Matthew Sands, Jr., would soon be taking flight as well. They had an opportunity to take over a farm in Wisconsin beginning March. Tanya had rushed to her school guidance counselor at Spencer-Van Etten High. Father had wanted them to live in this world, but without either of her sisters nearby, how could she remain in Lockwood?

The thought of being alone for even a minute with Mother and Mr. Pig from March to June was unconscionable. Mr. Zoltowski had been most helpful and reassuring. She had sufficient credits to graduate in January, and then she could enroll at Tompkins Cortland Community College for the spring term as a full-time student. If she chose, she could still join her classmates at year-end for graduation. Mr. Zoltowski had been helpful with a mountain of paperwork that was necessary to enroll in college and apply for scholarships. She was amazed that so much had to be done long before attendance even to a community college that basically accepted everyone. She needed to locate lodging in or near Dryden, New York, as the roads from Dryden to Lockwood could be treacherous in the winter months. Mr. Zoltowski assured her all would work out. In but a few months, her high school days would become memories of the past, left to fade with the wisp of good memories she had stored in her journal. She hurriedly tucked a well-read copy of *The Count of Monte Cristo* in her Mexican blanket and strapped it behind the saddle before leading Lady to the trail. Once the horn blew, the girls were expected to return home within fifteen minutes, Tanya had no idea how long ago she had been summoned. Mother never allowed any excuses for tardiness. Only a few short months and two more dreary holidays to spend with Mother, then she would be off on her own. *Ah, now to find the right time to tell Mother of my intentions.*

Tanya mounted Lady, contemplating the consequences of her mother's temper something she strove to avoid at all cost. Over the years, the girls sustained many a bruise, fractures, and once even a broken arm from Mother's moments. The damp moss under foot, the warm sunshine, and tempting pleasantries bid her adieu. Winnie, Lady, and Tanya enjoyed the last wisp of their tranquil afternoons together. They had stood by many a year for days while she traversed in Evald; always they would remain, awaiting her return. She would hang a bell from a nearby tree, and when Winnie was weary, she had taught her dear companion to summon her back to the woods by ringing it.

She hadn't met to slip away to Evald, not even for a short bit, but indeed the day had seeped away from her. Autumn seeped away quickly in the southern tier of New York. A deep breath of the clean air reminded Tanya of *The Count of Monte Cristo*. Few books have inspired her as much as this. Each time she read it, she was again restored with hope of a bright future beyond the limits of her present situation. The main character was not only falsely accused but beaten and locked away for ten years in a filthy, dreadful place. Did he despair? Of course. Who wouldn't? His girl was stolen from his grasp, and he was falsely imprisoned with no chance of parole. The beauty lay in the fact that he overcame his despair and all obstacles by reaching out to communicate with another prisoner and finding a way to become educated—something he would never have been able to do outside the prison walls. Time gave him anonymity, and this provided a means to escape to freedom. It also provided money beyond him imagination, and power wrapped in the mystery of his existence. That was inspiring, and the reason it was such a treasured book. The count found knowledge through his despair and in a hopeless situation. Tanya found knowledge through her loneliness, in her love for languages, in running to her sanctuary, and slipping from this world from time to time into the mist of Evald. So too, the count found a way to escape and make good— better than good. She gave an inwardly crooked smile; when Aaron discovered *The Count of Monte Cristo* was her favorite book, he had just shaken his head.

A Difference of Opinion

"That's a manly book. How can it be your favorite? I would have thought you'd have chosen a romance, like the one where the girl gets kidnapped by the Arabian nomad and taken to live in a tent in the dessert or something like that."

She laughed at the thought as she helped him with his chores around the big, red Amish-styled barn.

"You mean the one where she fell in love with her captor, and then his jealous brother helps her escape. The one where she thought he had sent her away? The brother was really using her to get even for something. That one?"

Aaron nodded in agreement; he enjoyed reading books together or over her shoulder. He liked to bask in the sun as her voice floated to his ears. He would improve his tan while her creamy completion never seemed to alter, not even by a freckle. He looked at her with that crooked, dimpled smile of his before he would stretch out and cover his face with his silly fishing hat. In their youth, he had asked her if she tanned, and she had earnestly looked into his eyes and said, "Of course I tan. Can't you see the back of my arm is two shades darker than the underside? That's a tan." Aaron had laughed and kissed her cheek playfully. He had decided there and then the fairer sex most assuredly should have lighter skin. "I don't even recall the name of that book," Tanya admitted aloud as she closed her eyes and visualized the paperback cover of the book.

With a chuckle, Aaron admitted, "I can't either, but I thought that was the sort of book a woman would call her favorite." He pulled another bail of hay down from the loft.

She gave his shoulder a gentle shove.

"Favorite? Dear boy, a lover of literature must always choose a well-remembered classic that is not an embarrassment to recall as a favorite, not a book one cannot even recall the title of. Enjoy." She shrugged, as her cheeks flushed with a memory. "Indeed, that book had memorable qualities and parts." A devilish smiled curled her lips. "It seemed to me ever more enjoyable because I shared it with you," she said flirtatiously as she came closer to him, playfully teasing. "But not overly memorable. *The Count of Monte Cristo* is a book one can reread many times, and it's just as exciting each and every time." Aaron had spontaneously grabbed hold and pulled her close as he smiled down at her. "It seems the hero gets the girl in the end, and his nemesis is the overall loser, right?"

She eyes glittered teasingly as she draped an arm playfully around his neck, his olive skin seemingly so tan against her fair, thin arm. "Did you finish the book on your own then?" she quipped.

"Grrr," Aaron growled as his mesmerizing blue eyes captured hers. "Of course, if it's a treasure to you, I would read it entirely."

For a moment, he seemed incredibly serious as his eyes searched her face before returning to rest once more in the deep pools of her eyes. He was so close she could feel the blood pulse through their thighs, desire stirring below as she melded to him.

"I've known you most all our lives"—his voice was thick with desire— "and yet when I read your favorite all-time book, I realize I don't know you at all," he whispered as his lips crushed against hers hungrily. Her arms slipped around his neck as they embraced, and she managed to pull him closer still. She always felt small and safe in his arms, like a butterfly caught in a boy's cupped hand. And like a boy with a butterfly, Aaron was always careful and protective of Tanya; gentleness he rarely displayed when they were out in public. When they were together, there was nowhere else she could imagine being. Together they were complete; apart, they were but a half of that whole. But somehow, others always seemed to pull and separate them. Tanya told herself it was always best to wait, even though they both desired far more. Thus far, Aaron and Tanya had honored their agreement to wait for intimacy, but each time they found themselves alone, they came ever so much closer to breaking their vows to one another.

Nurturing Butterflies and Fairies

Mother had taught her more than she ever wanted to learn growing up, and little of it was positive. The meadow, the books, and her studies transcended the bleakness of her current existence since her father's passing. Indeed, Mother had been a study in how not to parent your children. There was urgency to returning to Mother's house in a timely fashion. Mother was not the most patient person when it came to calling her girls. But today, Tanya didn't rush headlong down the hill at breakneck speed.

She decided she was ready to walk away from Mother if need be. In the past, Tanya had paid the price for her saucy, headstrong attitude. There was the time she'd limped to school for months after a run in with Mother. The left thigh and hip ached with each step, but she recovered and went on to return to biking and horseback riding in no time. Her sister's had been fearful of her going to the nurse or anyone and explaining the cause of her pain. Tanya had remained silent because she couldn't bear the thought back then of being separated from her sisters or the woods. But today she felt no compulsion. Today she would walk away if Mother got out of hand; today she had an inner strength she had never before known.

And so Tanya celebrated in the soft, moist meadow near Mother's house with sweets she had brought for Lady and Winnie. She entered the mist with M**** and loitered at her tree, summoning her sister fairies. A summons that went unanswered that day and many days after. She was a solitary fairy at Gosymonity. Alone with all the mysteries of Evald, of her life, of her family. Evald was a serene place, but for that moment of isolation; not even Nateria was at hand, when she so desperately wanted to share, to be joyous, she felt alone no matter where she went. M****, Lady, and Winnie simply did not suffice, she longed for the company of her own kind, and she thought of that encounter years before with the male fairy— her mate—and if ever she would find him again. She felt the emptiness Lenore spoke of when they last spoke via the phone. And she almost lost her way back to the meadow on the last day she tried summoning them; M**** had ended up carrying her. She owed him her life, for that slip of thought on her part could easily allow him to take her under. She had fallen, so by all accounts, she was his to take to a watery grave, instead he had released her.

She smiled sadly at him in the meadow as they parted that day, seeing him in a new light. She promised to tell no one of his generosity, promised never to let another hear his name from her lips; forever forward they would be able to mind link. He kissed her hand with his blackened lips in his boy form as she stepped away from the stream near the meadow and bowed her head and curtsied. They were forever tethered. *You may always find a way to me if you only consider what you've learned and through me to the wood,* he promised at their parting. For sometime she stood at the edge of the steam, staring at the ripples in the water, wondering what the fuath had meant.

XXXXX

Where would she run to, where could she hide? She could never share her dreadful secrets with Aaron, and his parents wouldn't understand if she spent all her time at their home now that Cecilia and Lenora had gone. A few more months and she would graduate from high school and go onto college. Soon she would be eighteen, old enough to live on her own. It wouldn't be right to rush into his arms simply to escape the misery of home—or would that be all right? Certainly, she loved him, had so since their first kiss in the woods near Mother's when she was a wisp of fourteen.

They had been in the wood with some of the neighbor kids and her older cousin, Ben, playing hide and seek. Aaron had taken hold her hand, and they ran into the wood together to hide. Aaron had led her to a quiet place that Ben and his friends had occasionally come to for drinking and partying or hunting small game. Under a grand spruce tree, where needles covered the earth so thickly that no undergrowth could grow, they had dragged up a few old, leather bucket seats from cars and made a pit in the center for a fire. Bramble bushes grew out a ways, making it a nature fort for the boys; they had carefully cut in openings through the bramble so they could slip in and out. Tanya had long forgotten the place, as she had so many things about Franklin.

Here, Aaron Sands sat on one of the old bucket seats and gently pulled her into his lap and kissed her quite by surprise. She had wanted to go on holding him, kissing him, but they heard the neighbor boy calling, searching the wood for those hiding. They crept quietly to peek around the base of the spruce tree at the boy on the path below as he walked along the stream. Aaron looked at her with a twinkle in his eye, and simultaneously they were off running and laughing for Steven to catch them separately.

Dreams. Dreams of shedding that way of life as a butterfly shed its cocoon. A butterfly flutters off, never looking back, so too would Tanya, except for one detail—her love for Aaron Sands. How could she ever say goodbye to this young man she had always loved? Indeed, he most assuredly was that; she compared every man she came in contact to him. He was always the one her heart would return to. Moreover, how could she find a way to remain in Lockwood for him without dying inwardly from the suffocation of memories? How would Aaron fit in her life? Could Aaron truly leave his home? Give up the security the area afforded him?

Tanya had sloughed off the afternoon, tempted by the beauty of the sun against the autumn leaves. There was a longing to contemplate every aspect of the near future and brush aside the consequences of Mother's wrath. She dreamed of riding into the sunset and never dealing with Mother's angry face or voice. So often she considered slipping off to Evald and never returning to the misery she found of this life. The only thing that ever brought her back was her memory of Aaron Sands. They were intrinsically bound; she couldn't slip into the mist without resolving her feelings for him. And for the first time, she was afraid to try. How could she resolve such intense emotions? She had wrestled with her feelings for months. Honestly, she must face it, just as she would face Mother's wrath.

It had been a beautiful afternoon when she got off the school bus at the end of the drive. She knew there were chores aplenty indoors, but couldn't bring herself to enter the house. Instead she ignored sweeping the floor, failed to prepare dinner, and took time only to put away the dishes before saddling Lady and riding off. C'est la vie. Tanya accepted she was in for serious consequences the moment she heard the call of the horn; Mother's signal to get home. She reigned in Lady and slid from the saddle at the edge of the ravine. The ravine cut deep into the old slate, far below the topsoil, exposing long slabs of slate under the water; the lush canopy of trees gave off a pungent, musty odor. Green skunk weed, lady slippers, trillium, jack- in-the-pulpit, onoclea sensibilis, and bouncing bet are sprinkled among the dark canopy that captured the majority of the sunlight, allowing little to flutter down upon the lower lying brush and wood flowers.

Tanya smiled as she remembered times past, like the time she splashed through the cool water of the ravine in bare feet or played hide and seek laughingly with Aaron, his brothers, and her sisters. Times when she and Franklin would spend hours looking for crawl fish under the rocks alongside the long, wide pieces of slate. Times when they had followed the riverbed down to the watering hole and swam for hours in their cut-offs and t-shirts.

She smiled sadly, remembering the times she would run through these woods barefoot to save wear and tear on shoes, Mother was never one to splurge. Her feet would be hard with calluses—tough enough to walk on hot coals without pain by the time spring blossomed to summer. One pair of sneakers for the year, per child; boots were expected to last longer. The downside of such antics was wide, callused feet that allowed her additional balance. Lady gingerly walked across the slate in the cool ravine; it could be slippery and treacherous for her darling horse. Portions were covered with loose, mossy stones; along the edge the slate was slippery with long green mossy seaweed. M**** rose from the ravine not twenty feet from Tanya, startling Lady, causing her to rear back and whiny as she scampered up the embankment of the other side. Tanya nodded an acknowledgement; years ago when she was still but a child, she had discovered the fuath's name. Being an elf of the Wood, and not traveling between realms Nateria was practically a queen in Evald, as such she knew many of the secrets of Evald. Such as the names of many of the spirits, the Fuath who resided near Gotsyminity for example. Tanya had overheard her speaking sternly to the Fuath one afternoon, and in so doing, discovered his name and gained his devotion.

*No time to chat, M****, Mother's blown her horn.*

I'll take Lady when you're ready to part. He responded in his whispery voice that was only heard inside Tanya's head.

She stopped still and tipped her head to one side in consideration.

How? she queried to him telepathically. *Have you found a way for her to pass through unharmed or must she…?*

The fuath nodded. *Unharmed. Yes.* He slipped back into the water, seeming to become a part of the stream, as if he'd never appeared at all. She looked up past the bank of the ravine to the hillside above Tanya knew once he disappeared from her vision she could put her hand in the water and scoop it to her lips, never knowing he lay just beneath. A fuath had the ability to become as fluid as the water that surrounded it, flowing over the stones just as smoothly as the water in which it lived. She had befriended him, because he chose to let her. The energy appeared to flow from the fuath into the stream, allowing the creature to become one with the stream. Hmm, one day she expected to have such a relationship with Aaron Sands. Would it be as simple as a fuath slipping into a stream? Becoming one as the fuath became one with the stream in which it lived. One day she wished to take him to Evald, although M**** had counseled her to reconsider such a step.

Man does not perceive Evald as you do, dear one. It is not so easy for them to cross over as it is for you. Many a man who has entered, only make the journey once. To enter he may never depart' This was something Tanya would have to contemplate for a long time; but now, she must hurry on. Lady, her cherished friend, had been a major concern. Tanya couldn't take Lady or Winnie with her to college, and she had troubled over what to do. She had shared her concerns with the fuath some time ago and had never contemplated he may have come up with a solution. Realistically, she couldn't bring herself to leave her behind with Mother, nor could she afford to board her anywhere because Tanya had no intention of returning to Lockwood for more than a visit here or there. Lockwood was not her home; though she had friends, it was not enough to keep her there. Not enough to cause deep ties that may even compensate for the heavy pain in her heart from all the sadness she felt by remaining each and every day. She had to find Lady a proper home. What did the fuath have in mind? A horse traveling through the mist was not an easy thing. She always prepared before attempting each journey into the mist. She was always careful to wear a loose, white shirt, because tight shirts would not do as her wings became visible in the mist. Tanya preferred a long dress or skirt, but there were times when she had ventured in wearing jeans. Most importantly, she had to be in the right mind frame. There was no guarantee her beloved horse would manage mentally. Horses did not see as she did. Had the fuath truly found a way? How wonderful it that could be, for surely Lady would live longer in Evald than she would on this plane.

Once Lady crossed, would she ever be able to return? It was doubtful; humans could not once they ate or drank of the food or water of Evald. Lenora could answer such a question. The older she grew, the more Tanya realized how few traveled from one realm into the other. Many who had made but one journey by accident rather than choice, those few could not travel back without assistance. Like her sisters, many of her woodland friends came to an age of decision. A time to choose between the realms; she had not chosen.

She had imagined she would choose during the summer of 1981 while traveling through Europe with her beloved Aunt and Faith. Separating herself for three months from her sisters and Evald should have made the decision easy. Instead, she was at a loss; how could her sisters forever turn away from their childhood joy? From a life few lead? She had been so fearful to go so far from the wood. Fearful she would be lost without the wood, but she had not once felt alone in Europe. She had not made a choice between the two realms.

XXXXX

Tanya recalled the daylong shopping excursion she and Faith had been on at an outdoor flea market near Pompidou Square in Paris when she spotted the shirt that caused such a raucous. The bright orange muscle shirt had reminded her of Todd, and the fact that it would be close to his eighteenth birthday when they returned at the end of the summer. She imaged the bright orange would offset his thick, long, auburn hair, and freckled biceps. It was reminiscent of an outfit in a Steve McQueen movie; Faith agreed it would look great on Todd with a pair of black jeans, so Tanya had purchased it as a return gift. After dealing with Aaron's emotions, she had reconsidered the gift many times. Aaron, nor anyone else, had any idea about the friendship she had with Todd outside of school. Nor would she ever disclose it; she was his tutor and encouraged him educationally. To her, he admitted his secret affair with a young English teacher, the reason he had sought Tanya's assistance the year before because he was struggling academically. Todd was intelligent, but even smart people struggle to comprehend the nuances in literature. He knew Tanya was helpful to others, and guessed she would have insight for him. Tanya agreed to help after reading some of his poetic accomplishments. At that time she had no idea he had become interested in English in his junior year of high school because he was attracted to the new English teacher. His poems were rough but held raw emotion and ability. With a bit of polish, they would be enjoyable reading to all. When Todd confided in her.

Tanya was shocked. "She could loose her job by getting involved with a student."

"Who's going to tell?"

Tanya raised her brow and stared at her friend intently. He was right, he had confided in her, knowing she would not betray him unless it was necessary.

Instead, she encouraged him to submit a few to the school paper; when Todd hedged, she talked him into submitting at least one anonymously.

The Lonely Boy, author unknown
He sat in a small, square, brown desk feeling out of place,
When he heard the teacher tell them to draw a picture of outside.
Other children took out their crayons and began
drawing grass, flowers, and trees.
He picked up a yellow crayon and began coloring until his entire
page was yellow, because yellow was the color of the sun, and
the sun was the feeling of being outside, bright and warm.
He was so lost in the beautiful color of yellow, he didn't
notice when the teacher came to stand over him.

He didn't notice when she asked what he thought he was doing;
he was intent on the color of yellow, of the feel of the bright sun
on his skin as he lay in the grass, gazing up and dreaming.
She placed a hand on his shoulder, and it was then
he looked up into her steel brown eyes and saw the
disappointment; he had again failed in his task.
He had promised his mother he would try this year
at school, and here he was on his first day, with the
teacher looking down on him in disappointment.
He slumped in his chair, feeling like a square peg
uncomfortably jammed into a round hole.

European Memories

As she sat in her room, in the tree roots of the Sequoia tree in Evald, her mind drifted to her summer in Europe. Her room always seemed bright and airy. A creation of her Father's nestled among the roots and ground of Gosymonity. The walls were gnarled roots on three sides, with the door being a round-topped entrance between two young roots on one side. The fourth side was a wide window from within; outside it appeared two large rocks with leaves and moss between them. She had a large canopy bed made of ivy and maple and a matching trunk at the foot, a bureau, and a night stand on either side of the bed. A cushioned bench next to her windowed wall, and a snuggle hearth on the far wall. She loved her room; it was roomy, a sense of air and her Father's touch. In all her travels about Europe, she never contemplated a way through the mist. She wasn't even certain she wanted to return to Lockwood by summers end. In Europe she had found a place that felt like "home." She missed the connection she could find in Evald with her sisters, but they would no longer be there. For the first time in her life, she had not sensed her sisters for the entire summer with Aunt June. She spent one summer truly separate—alone, but not alone, she was in the without the company of her adopted Aunt June.

Throughout the summer, even though she had not traversed to Evald, she felt she was always near to Evald. Auntie kept her so occupied she had little time to consider the separation she sensed from her sisters. However, Tanya had been kept busy, her summer full of fun.. She would only miss her sisters and Evald in passing. She was changing, up until that summer she had been a shy, quiet girl…always trying to be unobtrusive.

In Europe, she blossomed into her own. Aunt June sat back, and watched her wallflower become a gregarious daughter Franklin would have been proud of, if had he lived. Tanya basked in socializing and embracing European customs, places, and most of all, the people. Aunt June had arranged for her two charges, Tanya and Faith, to socialize throughout the summer. Instead of Fourth of July celebrations Independence Day in America on July 4th, France celebrated their independence on July 14th, Bastille Day. Auntie arranged for them all to enjoy the festivities at Versailles, overlooking the gardens and pond; it was beautiful. Additionally, they enjoyed dancing in nightclubs, hikes in the Swiss Alps, lounging on the beaches of the Mediterranean, loads of shopping in Paris and London, and lots of small places in between.

"Let's take the train up Chamonix Mont Blanc or Jungfrau," Aunt June suggested while they toured Munich with friends of Aunt June's from college.

Tanya looked at her Aunt with a heavy sigh as she looked off at the distant mountains. "I would rather not. It's cold and snow covered."

"It's an experience," her Aunt chuckled.

"One I can live without," Tanya replied.

Auntie shook her head in amusement and Tanya knew she had already booked passage on the train.

Faith sat on the outside next to Tanya on the train, Auntie was up ahead with her friend, Camille chatting intently. The night before Camille's husband, Alain had talked of his many trips up the mountains over the years. He was an avid climber, he assured the girls they would enjoy themselves. Tanya still had reservations. "I've never liked the cold," she admitted to Alain.

"Did you bring warm clothes?"

"No. I've a sweatshirt I purchased in Paris."

"You should borrow one of Jerome's." He offered, "It would be warmer."

Faith and Tanya exchanged looks at the mention of Alain's son. Jerome has made it clear he did not like American's on their first night at their town home in the suburbs of Munich, let alone for him to discover the girls took over his room, and his clothing. "We had better not." Tanya replied.

Alain shrugged. "As you wish."

A pair of handsome German Swisse took the seats facing Faith and Tanya. Before long one asked if either girl spoke German. Tanya admitted she spoke a wee bit, and they boys admitted they spoke English quite well. By the time they disembarked for lunch they were fast friends. While touring the ice caverns within the mountain they discovered they were all headed in the same direction. "We should travel together," one Youngman, Fritz suggested. After they all spoke to Aunt June it was agreed they would indeed travel together for the next three weeks or so.

During much of their trip they met up with people Aunt June knew for a meal here or there, or to visit a few days. People she knew from college, or her travel, or people she had met through those people. Some of their lunches would last two hours; several different languages were mingled together, combined with laughter, wine, espresso, and rich desserts. One man seemed to reappear through the course of their journey, Neville Longbottom, from Australia.

Fritz Fienberg and Richard Schwartz kept Tanya and Faith occupied as they journeyed together from Switzerland to Monaco and Nice. Fritz and his friend, Richard Schwartz, took the girls on moonlit motorcycle rides along the coast of the Mediterranean Sea and afternoon rides on the windy roads through the Alps. They would go for walks on the white, sandy beaches of Monaco, sharing dreams of the future. The four of them would swim by moonlight out to the sand bars and back again. What a joy to spend hours sitting with other young people on the beach as the waves crashed, dreaming of what life had in store for each of them. Fritz planned to be an accountant.

So many fond moments captured in photographs she would carefully stitch together into a storybook form scrapbook upon returning to Lockwood. Those hours on the beaches between Nice and Monte Carlo were the most treasured. Closing her eyes, she could imagine Fritz's long thin fingers intertwining with her own pale ones as they walked along the white sandy beaches at night. On the first night in Monte Carlo Fritz commented how her hair was almost the color of the sand beneath their feet, as he looked down at her long slim fingers. She smiled taking the remark as a compliment.

Auntie had insisted she take up piano as a small child because of her long, thin fingers. Mother had always thought her too small, too thin; she constantly complained that Tanya didn't eat enough. She would be pleased to see that Tanya had managed to put on ten pounds summering with Auntie in Europe. She hadn't been able to ride a bicycle or a horse all summer, and Auntie made certain they feasted on wonderful meals at least once a day, every day. The extra weight gave her a healthy appearance, as they did a great deal of walking where ever they went she remained toned.

Until Fritz called to her from the water Tanya hadn't even noticed her hair, like the white sands of the beach, almost glowed in the low light as she and Faith walked the shores at night. Even from the sandbar out in the bay, Fritz could make out her figure on the beach because of her hair. He gaily hailed her by name from the bar on which he and Richard were resting, she turned toward the waters edge and searched the waves until she could just make out the movement of his hand. She and Faith raised an arm high in greeting towards the sound of his voice. She smiled at the wonderful lilt in Fritz's voice as they sat upon the beach and he spoke of his beloved Geneva. Even after returning to the wood of Lockwood, Tanya could imagine his voice as she read his letters; she loved the German accent in his English. She had admired his ability to speak three languages with relative ease. Her French paled in comparison to his English. Even his French far exceeded her ability with the basic rudimentary German.

Fritz was apprenticing just outside of Geneva in accounting and financial planning when his holiday ended that summer they spent their time together. Tanya was in awe that at nineteen Fritz knew his course, his career path. He had no doubts; he would return to his home and work for a Bear Sterns or some other big well-known international banking institution in order to gain the knowledge he desired to successful continue his career path. The future may bring him travel, but he would live most of his life in and around Geneva. Tanya had never felt Lockwood was her home, she felt "homeless" when he spoke fondly of his own home.

She admired both young men for having such a clear direction in their life's path. She enjoyed listening to Fritz talk of the apprenticeship he hoped to get with the investment bankers in Geneva, Bear Sterns. It made Tanya wonder what was it she truly planned to do with her own life. Marriage didn't seem in the cards; even though she lived in a small farming community where marriage after high school was expected. Some of the youths in their group spoke no English, but it didn't seem to matter. Many times they found ways to communicate with others through music, when no one had a shared language. After the summer of 1981when they met, she and Fritz wrote regularly to one another through the years.

Saying goodbye at the end of that summer had been a pain to her soul. She felt torn asunder as she boarded the plane at Olio Airport in France. When the plane landed in La Guardia, all she could think of was to hurry back to Lockwood where she could run into her beloved wood and cry with delight as she ran into the mist of Evald. She had never wanted that summer to end. And yet she felt alone as the plane beaded a visual on New York City.

Lockwood is a four-hour drive northwest of New York City. It was no easy feat for her Aunt to arrange for someone to come and meet them at the airport. Her companion, Faith had parent's eager to see their daughter return, and were happy to meet everyone at the airport. Faith's parents had driven to the city to meet the plane and Auntie had arranged for them to take her and Tanya home as well. Tanya had felt torn; she had fallen in love with Europe, the atmosphere, the people. Leaving had been more difficult than anything she had done up to that point. As she sat in the back of a van headed for Lockwood, she instantly knew Lockwood would never be her home. She would have to find another way into the mist, perhaps M**** would know another way. With such knowledge she would have the freedom to live anywhere, not just Lockwood. If Aaron Sands was the man for her, he would have to be willing to leave Lockwood behind. Would he be willing to leave for her? Perhaps the answer would be clear by the time they finished their senior year of high school. That would give her more time to decide.

Of course the biggest news of the summer was Aunt marriage at the age of fifty-four to some man she had been corresponding with from Australia. The coup d'état for Aunt June in Europe was, of course, marrying while on the Mediterranean Sea just before returning to America. At fifty-four, who would have imagined her maiden aunt would be so smitten as to marry. Tanya had never seen it coming. Who would have anticipated such an event? Not only was she marrying Neville Longbottom while still in Europe, Auntie further announced she would be moving to Australia as his bride and would give up the family farm.

Tanya was happy for her Aunt, and devastated simultaneously. She felt abandoned and alone. All those she loved dearly seemed to be leaving her at the same time. She would be alone with Mother and Mr. Pig for several months before graduating high school in June of 1982.

The very night Tanya returned to Lockwood, Aaron appeared on the porch the following evening to welcome her back. She had barely recovered from jet lag, or even begun to make it through the mountain of mail that awaited her return. "T, do you think we might have a minute alone, outside?" She looked around at the few family and friends gathered and wondered what was so important that it couldn't be said inside. Shrugging with a nod, she waited while he opened the door, and she stepped through and took a seat on the front porch swing and turned to him expectantly. "I missed you a lot over the summer," he began. A rye smile crossed her features, as if she were about to laugh.

Had he really missed her? In the day she had been home her phone line never seemed to rest. 'Well meaning neighbors,' had not been able to contain themselves with the 'low down,' on Aaron's behavior in her absence. He had not missed her enough to stay home. She had heard he'd been out with Shirlene Tewksbury, Lori Peters, and Tessa Goodrich in the months she had been abroad. Now, he leaned forward and turned to look directly into her blue eyes with eyes that reminded her of the Mediterranean Sea. He grimaced. "You heard I dated other girls over the summer?" She nodded without comment. "Damn, girl, That doesn't mean I didn't miss you. I heard you were gallivanting around with those European guys and figured you might not come back."

She chuckled softly. He leaned toward her, and they kissed. As they kissed on the front porch swing as she imagined fireworks against her closed lids and felt content to be with him again.

So Aaron had heard of Fritz over the summer, though not from Tanya. Did it really matter whether he heard from Cecilia or from Faith, from the photos, or from the letters regularly flying back and forth over her summer's adventure? He boiled with jealousy, but looking into her innocent blue eyes, he knew he could trust her. She had matured, but in her eyes and manners, he knew she was still his girl, and there was no other. The question that burned in his mind, unspoken, was would he still be the man for her? He realized it was ridiculous to be jealous of a man across the Atlantic Ocean he would never know.

Still, would she save up and run back across the Atlantic to return to this guy she had "befriended" over the summer? With Tanya, he could never quite be certain. With other girls, he knew where he stood; with Tanya, he was never quite sure. Take Todd Herrington for instance. She had known Todd most of her life as well. She had long ago dated his cousin, Daryl, for a few short months. She claimed Todd was but a friend, someone she tutored, but she had thought of his birthday while thousands of miles from home. She had returned baring gifts for this guy. His jealousy toward Todd Herrington for being Tanya's neighbor and friend was a different story. He was jealous because he discovered she purchased an orange, sleeveless T-shirt for Todd in Paris for his birthday. Obviously Todd must mean something to her if she could remember it was his birthday even though she was halfway around the world. But then he thought of how she had faithfully sent him a postcard every week while there; he had never responded in the two and a half months she had been away. Aaron had kept himself busy with other women while she was off in Europe. He should have figured someone would keep her informed. Upon returning, Tanya accepted he wasn't much of a writer, or as committed as she was to a relationship. He imagined she would have been too busy to worry about some other guy, she claimed to be 'just a friend.

Her first night home hadn't seemed the time to discuss her active interest in Todd Herrington. Aaron knew it would blow up into a heated discussion, and he wasn't in the mood. She would be taken aback by his testy attitude. He wanted to simply enjoy the way she snuggled in the crook of his arm, the smell of her hair as she rested her head on his shoulder, and the swing swaying gentle underneath their bodies. He leaned back and closed his eyes, simply enjoying having her home. What would become of them? Now she had a big taste of the world, her world seemed so isolated. Is this the life she wanted?

Neither family was much for socializing or having people over on a regular basis, save for her dear aunt June, who had always enjoyed traveling, a fine bottle of wine, and dinner parties.

Tanya had come to enjoy being with others regularly while in Europe, and she often went to Auntie's for dinner parties. She knew Auntie entertained quite frequently, where would she go when Auntie moved away? Aaron looked at her now and shook his head, "I missed you, Tanya."

She smiled feeling sarcastic, but holding her tongue. "hmm, the letters you wrote didn't seem to make it to me. I had no idea you gave me much thought the summer." Rolled from her tongue before she could stop herself.

Aaron furrowed his brow as she met his gaze. "Wow, you've changed while aboard," he stated as he assessed her assertive attitude.

She nodded, "I suppose that goes without saying." She admitted. "It would be unrealistic to expect me to remain the mouse I had been after traveling through seven other countries, and meeting loads of people."

He tipped his head as he appraised her. Tanya sucked in her lower lip and gnawed at it wishing she had not spoken at all. "I'm sorry, you know I'm not one for writing."

"Hmm, I guess even one postcard all summer was hoping for too much from your busy schedule."

"You know I worked all summer."

She nodded, "Yeah. You never had a moment off to take anyone to the movies, or a party here or there." She encouraged as his face reddened.

"I heard you were enjoying yourself with the men in Europe," he accused.

Tanya smirked as she looked down at her hands. "I did indeed enjoy the company of others," she admitted as she lifted her head to look into his eyes. "But I have always been true to you, Aaron."

He was silent for some moments. His jealousy towards Todd Herrington seemed misplaced as it was clear Tanya had been well informed of his summer's escapades. He sat back on the swing and took her hand in his. She turned to meet his gaze. "I came over to tell you I missed you, T. I want you to promise to marry me after we graduate."

Tanya sat stunned to silence. This was what she had often expected, but now that he had uttered the words she was unsure if it was the right choice for her. "I need time to think on that Aaron." She heard herself say as if she stood outside her own body. He looked astonished that she needed time to think. What farm girl wouldn't hesitate to accept his hand?

"Why, cause I dated a few others while you were away? They didn't mean anything."

She shrugged. "I've done some thinking over in Europe. I'd like to go to college."

"I won't stop you."

She nodded thoughtfully. "Just give me some time."

Changes

School began the following week, and Tanya made an appointment with her guidance counselor, Mr. Zotowski. After speaking to her school guidance counselor the solution seemed to be enrolling in the community college in January and take early graduation at that time. She had sufficient credits to graduate, rather than waiting until June.

She could walk across the stage with her classmates in June with a high school diploma and a certificate in business from the local college. That certificate was transferable into most colleges, equal to a year of college credits. In making such a leap she would be away from her Mother about the same time as Cecilia and Matthew, Jr. would be moving out west to their new farm. Of course everyone assumed she wanted to move away because she missed her Aunt June, who packed up a few belongings when they returned from Europe and moved to Australia. In looking into college, Tanya learned she could sign up for a semester abroad. One of the places on the list was Australia. She would write to her Aunt and see what could be done. The more she planned for a college education the less marriage to Aaron seemed like a good idea.

"If I marry right out of high school will I still qualify for these scholarships?" She asked her guidance counselor.

He sat back in his chair and shook his head. "No. Most of them only apply if you're single and fresh out of high school."

She nodded as she looked over the stack of paperwork he had given her. There were so many options she had never considered before going to Europe.

Even with scholarship money she would need funds of her own to make ends meet. Her European photos seemed to offer an opportunity to create some of the needed revenue.

Reflections

The woods of Lockwood near Mother's house faded to a distant memory as she fingered the amethyst she wore on a long silver chain and generally kept tucked under her clothes. When Father had given her the stone as a toddler, it had resembled a budding leaf from Gosymonity; but as time passed, it seemed more shaped like an elongated teardrop with the purple color of amethyst throughout most of it, except at the very bottom where the frostiness reminded Tanya of the snowcapped mountains of the Alps on a wintry day. She often fingered the stone absently when she was deep in thought or in need of comfort. Tanya delved deeper into her repetitive dreams as years passed at college as she rubbed the amethyst. The stone was her connection to the Wood. She had carefully penned every vivid detail in her journal. To be a fairy was to often suffer long term memory loss. The amethyst gave her an ability to conjure forgotten memories in moments of reflection, but the memories were soon forgotten once she was caught up in day to day activities. Just as she carefully detailed every pleasant memory of her childhood, so too would she catalog her dreams in a separate book, holding on only to the best and releasing the pain of the past. Pain she could feel even as she forgot the cause, which was where her journal came in most handy. Most fairies simply forgot, and moved on, Tanya wanted to deal with each situation and learn from them. Her sisters were content to block out the unhappiness. The pain of loosing their father and brother. The pain of seeing Lenora pregnant by a man they did not like. By choosing to forget they felt there was nothing of their childhood worth keeping. Tanya had Lady and Winnie; her sisters had nothing. Lenora had had a pair of geese as familiars; Mother had discovered the bond and sold the pair just before she sent Lenora packing. Cecilia had a black cat with a spot of white on his neck that appeared as though he wore an I.D. tag or something. She affectionately called him Midnight.

Mother disdained cats in general, and she abhorred black ones. But Father had allowed Midnight, understanding his daughters needed to bond with a familiar; after he died, Mother banished the cat to live outside. The girls would bring him in whenever Mother was out of the house; Cecilia even went so far as to cut the screen in her bedroom window in one corner so that he could slip in during the night without Mother ever being the wiser. For Tanya, the times among the trees offset the negative and frightening moments of their youth. Tanya felt intense pity for her sisters during those algetic teenage years—tedious years that had drawn on and on after Father died. But now they had to face their past in order to move into the future. How could her sisters forget so much of their lives? There had been so much good before Father's passing. So many wonderful times they'd spent together bonding.

To erase those memories was to have never been sisters, never been family. Tanya sat back and took in that thought; they were sisters, were they not? They were family, right? Had her life to this point all been a lie?

If they were not family, how had they together in Evald? Tanya couldn't wrap her mind such a farfetched idea for any length of time; it caused her head to hurt. Instead she focused on the dreams that became more visual after Father's death. When, Tanya's repetitive dreams began, the loneliness transcended, the happy moments were few and far between. The dreams were of a dashing, young man; sometimes he would be in a trench coat and fedora at the foot of Mother's drive waiting for her. Sometimes he would be with a lovely brunette doing various activities—horseback riding, dancing, and picnics. The brunette hair was enviably thick, with the healthy shine that would reflect the sun, and as straight as it could get as it cascaded down her back to a trim waistline. She had a big, broad smile, with lots of straight teeth. Other than that, Tanya never really noticed the girl much. In her dream, the focus was always on the young man, her young man. Would he one day rescue her? Was that why she observed him through her dreams? Dreams like this were dreams she wrote in her journal, as later they became reality.

Tanya's dreams took her to specific places, specific people. How did they connect with her life? Why did she dream of the same people over and over? The settings changed, but not the people. Dreams where she assisted these people or simply watched over them. Over time, she came to accept the dreams were a part of her life; she enjoyed watching these lives play out; she stopped wondering what roll they played in her life. Whenever she interacted with the older couple—a tall reed-like genteel lady with short, billowy white hair, full of elegance and grace and a kindly faced man with great sorrow etched around his eyes, who was a bit hunched and protective of his wife—she felt a sense of peace, a sense of purpose. Without explanation, she came to understand that when she encountered them in reality she would not be surprised they would never be strangers.

Some alpdruckens, dreams others may consider to be nightmares, filled her with dread, like the one in which it was always autumn with brightly colored leaves littering a vast, sloping, manicured lawn. The dilapidated white house with Corinthian columns that were cracked, and peeling, with bits of black lacquered trim. This Southern style, with a wide wrap-around porch appeared to be from another place and time was capable of filling Tanya's heart with dread. This once majestic home set back from a rutted, thick reddish, yellow clay road was like those she recalled from childhood visits to the hills of Virginia. Here was a frightfully angry man in a stained white undershirt with dark slacks, a thin black leather belt, and malice in his heart—she could see his wild, dark eyes, his slick dark hair, the sinewy features of his biceps, and his farmer's tanned skin. Had he not been so hateful, some may find his wiry features attractive. There were three half-starved girls with dark, stringy hair; she would feel she was one of them. The smallest—she always felt a need to protect them most.

Dear Diary,

Regardless of how joyous or frightful the dreams were, they all make their way to my notebook, carefully described to the last detail. If I choose to live in the realm of men I want a past and a future that would be more vivid than that of my sisters, Tanya wrote in her journal. A fairies life was 'in the moment.' Without careful effort she would never move beyond the moment. It worked for Cecilia on the farm, she could go through the day to day routine, not so different from the wood. Lenora had struggled when she initially moved to Buffalo, but she had learned to adapt and successfully became a Registered Nurse. Tanya often wondered how Lenora had become so wise, but she knew better than to ask her older sister. Lenora was the most secretive of the three, she always had been. Tanya's dreams always seemed to play into her life in the human realm, so she took care to write them down. At times, dreams took Tanya within the walls, of that Southern house.

Sometimes in the dream the girls would be in a shabby country kitchen with walnut cupboards, yellowed, curling linoleum, a fifties-styled square kitchen table with the chrome legs and gray marbled Formica top, and four semi-matching chairs. The girls would be looking for a place to run and hide from the man hollering as he walked through the upstairs with belt in hand. Other times she dreamed they were in an old fashion kitchen, with yellowed, curling linoleum flooring; a 1950s-styled white enamel, stained yellow from nicotine; a wood-burning cook stove, a white butchers table, and heavy chairs, painted white near a window. The girls would be crying in fear. Often, the three girls were wearing nothing more than white slips, and she could feel their fright, could feel the chill on their bare skin, as they would quietly run with bare feet down the long, mahogany staircase, and around the hall to a closet under the stairs; away from a pinched faced, angry father in a sleeveless, stained undershirt, black, belted slacks wielding an axe.

She became one of the girls, feeling chilled to the bone in nothing more than short, white slips, cuddling with her sisters, too frightened to even cry out. In the dreams, their hair was long, brown, and stringy for lack of a comb and proper care; their faces elongated and thin with hunger; they were tear-streaked, fearful, as huddled in silence, scarcely daring to breathe. Instinctively sensing the dark-haired, angry, wiry man in a stained white tank-styled t-shirt, dark pleated pants, held up by a dark belt with a good three inches extra sticking out, sought them out. Always she instinctively knew this man was their father, bent on bringing them some sort of harm. These moments felt like the wee hours of the morning or just as the evening rolled in. She would be the eldest then and quiet them without a word; encourage them to breathe softly, so that he wouldn't hear them. Hatred emanated from this man's heart as he searched for the frightened sisters. For what ever reason, her dream would begin as she was leaving the house and then roll back to her observing the happenings within, just as when she road in the rumble seat she saw what lay behind the vehicle, rather than the road ahead. In her dreams she sat in the rumble seat, looking out of the rear window of a low-riding, pale green station wagon. The sky would be gloomy, as if on an overcast late afternoon or just before a lightning storm in the South. Try as she might, she couldn't wake herself before the dream unfolded. Sometimes, an wiry, angry man would run from the house toward the car as it pulled safely away; sometimes, through frightened eyes, Tanya would sit staring out the rear window as the house disappeared from view. The historic-looking home was embedded deep in her mind once regal, and perhaps full of joy, in her dreams it was always a rundown remnant of splendor of the South.

Tanya would awaken in a cold sweat in mortal fright that stuck with her for days. She would feel as though she'd been trapped for hours in that frightful place, only to glance at a clock or a watch and realize it had all happened in less than half an hour. Whenever she had such alpdrucken, she could not return to sleep, so she would rise early.

Serene dreams of standing before a white, marble fireplace, barefoot on plush, soft-colored carpet. The sense of drifting from that pale-colored living room in a white, gauzy nightgown into a cozy light-colored sunroom with a pale gray ceramic tile floor. Serenity, plants sprinkled among comfortably placed chairs, and small tables, and lamps. Here, resided a gentle, couple in their late forties or early fifties. Somehow, they could see her. They would approach or speak to her; it always seemed their voices were faraway whispers, muffled, as through a tunnel, even though they appeared within reach. They were capable of walking alongside her, but she was always beyond their touch. It was as though they were reaching her through an invisible barrier. Time and time again, they would attempt to interact with her, in a slow, calm manor. In this warm apartment, Tanya was someone to them, more than an observer who experienced emotions in the air. Here she enjoyed coming, because here she felt the warmth of love, and security she had not felt sense her father's passing.

Dear Diary,

I have such vivid dreams. I know the dream of the apartment is something I should understand, and yet it escapes me. I know not why. Perhaps the answer will become clear to me at some point in the future.'

Roy had resided in the fraternity next to her boardinghouse at 110 Thurston Avenue. Roy had been a regular face in her dream life; she had watched him picnic or ride horseback through fields, always with a lovely brunette. He had to be her soul mate; he had to be the one she walked through the mist with. Her dreams of him through high school had not been repetitive dreams; they seemed to be observant dreams, dreams of another's life. She and Roy shared no classes, yet whenever she glimpsed him in the parking lot, she wondered how he fit in her life. She felt a strong tug, drawn to this fleshly man who had walked from her dreams into her reality. For months she had carefully observed him, mostly from her window that overlooked the shared parking lot or from the front porch of the boardinghouse. Why would she have dreamed of his presence throughout high school? What did it all mean, except that he must be someone for her? Had he ever seen her in his dreams? Would he be as drawn to her as she to him?

Her dreams had always been so vivid and realistic throughout her youth. How had someone from her dreams become a part of her reality?

Once he approached her in the parking lot and cornered her by her car.

"Who are you? Why do I know you?" he asked with an utter sense of loss crossing his face.

She had shaken her head, unable to speak, lost. *How to explain?* She turned and hurried for the back door of the boardinghouse, clutching a paper grocery bag to her chest, as if somehow it would protect her. Had she actually observed peoples' lives through her dreams? How could anyone experience such a thing? She consulted Lenora, thinking she would have answers, but Lenora was silent on the matter. Rather, Lenora responded, "Have you truly given up your familiars?"

Tanya grimaced, "What difference does that make? I need your council." All imagined she had no more contact with Lady or the wood.

"If you truly gave up Evald, this would not be an issue."

"How so," Tanya questioned? Lenora was silent for so long Tanya wondered if she were still on the phone. "Please, help me."

"If you give up Evald, your premonitions would fade away. Those nightmares from someone else's life would end."

"Why? I've grown accustom to them. They are a part of me."

"To much a part for you to ever truly break free. You will fade across the water like so many of our kind if you do not embrace the realm of man."

"I have embraced it. I am as human as you. I am attending college, and doing well. I am making plans."

"You can not stand with one foot in each world for eternity. You must choose. You must set your familiars free."

"I have let them go."

"Shoo them from you."

Tanya was silent. In this she could not accept her sister's advise. "What have they to do with the dreams and this man?"

"He is a spirit as are thee."

Tanya smiled with satisfaction. "I have found a mate then."

"Perhaps not." Lenora counseled, "there is no guarantee he is the same as thee."

"We shall see," Tanya replied as a rap came upon her door. "I must fly, it's time for my study group."

XXXXX

Chris Rosen leaned back and stretched in the lab chair before the state-of-the-art computer in the lab of Columbia College. He massaged the back of his neck where he suffered a crick from being hunched forward for a long period at the monitor. A lean, handsome German guy with a cleft chin and a smattering of freckles sprinkled across the bridge of his nose and cheeks, violet-blue eyes, and summer streaks in his dark, blonde hair. He was of average height and had just finished his four-year degree in electrical engineering. With a deep sigh, he was grateful for the summer academic work-placement on campus. He was in no hurry to leave academia behind as he priced out space to move his computer equipment from the apartment so an additional cousin could move in. John was tired of walking around the computer clutter, and Chris had to agree with him. His advisor, Professor Stueben, had been quite helpful with the computer surveillance business Chris had started with his cousins while attending college. Professor Stueben had been very encouraging of the young men when Chris shared their business plan with him.

Chris was an electronic wonder who adapted readily to computers. He had spent years at the club, working the door and observing. His observations had given him insight into the security industry. John was an easy-going, likeable salesman, who didn't mind spending hours manning the systems. Steve was the intricate go-to guy. He enjoyed going out and doing the hardwiring for the clients and resolving problems as they arose. Chris was banking that more and more people were going to want high- tech security systems for their homes in the near future. They could easily take their business global if they chose to share their systems with others. For now, they were slowly expanding to cover all of Manhattan.

Professor Stueben had advised Chris to achieve his master's degree before venturing to far a field. "People will initially go with you because the three of you are enthusiastic, but you'll have a lot more weight in your profession, Chris, if you complete your master's program. I have a summer academic opening that could help you with your thesis credit."

Chris had considered the professor's offer and accepted it. He had been venturing weekly to Manhattan's financial district in the hopes of locating a suitable, affordable office space where he could relocate their equipment. Chris walked down the hall to a window and viewed a spectacular summer afternoon. It was too nice to remain cooped up in the lab. Chris realized he needed to get out among people—maybe a walk to clear his head. His mind was drifting to business plans when he bumped into a pretty, petite blonde on the street. Looking around, he realized he had drifted down to 34th Street. The girl's eyes captured his with an intensity he wasn't accustomed to seeing in the city. He had a desire to spend a few moments in her company as he glanced about looking for something to say.

"Going up today?" he heard himself ask, and he wished he could kick himself for saying it.

She tilted her head and gave him a bemused smile. "Ah, it's that obvious to you I'm a visitor in your fair city." She had a high, singsong voice.

He shrugged.

"Not particularly. It's a clear day, great visibility; the Empire State Building is just before us another block."

She turned back to the way she seemed to have come and shrugged. "It's not much of a sight to enjoy alone, is it?" She glanced back at him and seductively batted long lashes highlighted with navy blue mascara. "One needs to share such a view." She smiled playfully. "Don't you agree?"

He smiled. "Indeed, I do." She put out her hand in expectation, and he found himself offering this stranger his arm, and they set off together toward the landmark. He ventured into the line for two tickets, and they rode up in the elevator arm in arm. She was easy company; it was as if they'd known one another so long no words were necessary. He looked around the observation deck and found she had meandered to a section where they were quite alone. She dropped his arm to stare out through the bars. "Do you often go off with strangers?" he asked with a raised brow, as he gazed down at her profile, recollecting the trustful innocence she had exhibited in the street below. She sighed and glanced up at him.

"Occasionally, I find I'm drawn to them," she admitted. She wandered off toward the Chrysler Building vantage point where there were more people. The wind had picked up and blew her hair back from her face as he caught up to her. She smiled out at the city. "It's a beautiful view from up here; the air feels so…clean."

"Is this your first time up?"

She glanced at him with a gentle smile, "No. My aunt and I used to come to the city once a year. I've been up here many times." She leaned toward him and lowered her voice. "It's my first time unencumbered." Her voice was a low, sultry whisper that played on his ear. He felt a desire to pull her close, as if they were lovers, and he shoved his hands deep in his pockets and took in a deep breath of the flowery air around her presence. Slowly, with her hand on the crook of his arm, they took their time walking all the way around, standing to gaze at length wherever there was a sense of space. After a time, she turned to him, beaming with fresh innocence. She took in a deep breath before speaking, "Thank you ever so much for accompanying me. This has been exactly what I needed today."

Out of character, he found himself giving her a small bow as he again offered his arm in courtly fashion that was quite out of character for him. "It's truly been a refreshing pleasure," he assured her as they headed back toward the rampart. He stopped at one of the gift stands and purchased an Empire State Building keychain and handed it to her playfully. "To remember our afternoon together." She laughed as she rose up on tiptoes in her flats to kiss his cheek, again taking his arm.

"How sweet." The kiss burned his cheek where her lips had lightly fluttered against his skin. He closed his eyes for a moment to savor the moment before it was gone; he had been intimately touched by a fellow spirit. Once outside, she slipped away before he realized they hadn't even exchanged names.

XXXXX

17th August 1984

Dear Diary,

I should feel guilty to be sure, but I don't. I went up the Empire State Building with a handsome man who seemed familiar to me. Perhaps he's from a dream because I had a sense of déjà vu. We had a pleasant time; he gave me a key ring to remember him by, and we parted. Thanks to Rosie's advice, I went to the bursar's office. Sure enough, I can finish up in January by simply taking an additional class this semester. It will leave me with little free time to spend with Roy, but it will pay off down the road. I'll only be able to manage one part-time job, so that won't leave me with much money. I'll simply have to make good with the money I saved this summer. I should be able to manage six classes.

Roy has assured me his family can get me work in May when he moves to the city after graduation. I didn't care for his family, and I made it clear to him, I don't wish to behold them for anything. Least of all a job. I assured him it would be better for me to get a head start on the job search by finishing up by the January break. It paid off to have taken those summer courses in my senior year of high school and last summer.

Great news. I sold more photos this summer than I anticipated. That will really help me out this semester. New York tourism purchased a bunch of city shots: Chinatown, Greenwich Village at night, St. Patrick's Cathedral, the Empire State Building from the penthouse apartments down the block, etc. Then, the museum company bought a bunch of artsy, SoHo stuff I didn't even think was very good. They also bought some card stock I'd created of floral shots from Central Park and neighboring private gardens. The Metro Postcard Company was the best. They accepted just about everything I submitted to them. If I'm careful, I'll have plenty of seed money by the end of semester to get settled in the city.

Mr. White was agreeable to letting me have the same room this semester at the same cost because I offered to pay up the whole semester in advance. He's a nice man even though we've never met in person.

Until this summer I had no idea how rural Brooklyn is. It's really quite lovely. Auntie took us to Manhattan, and I imagined that was the entire city. It's only one of five burrows. Imagine. I shall be so lost come January. I'll be off on my own in an enormous place. I'm thankful I spent this summer there, and at least got a feel for the city I am about to undertake.

1 Sept 1984

Dear Tanya,

Hello. It was wonderful to receive your letter. You made New York City sound like a wonderful place to live. Perhaps one day, I too will get there. Rich and I spent out summer holiday in Romania. We had much fun hiking and biking through the countryside. It is very beautiful and old; you would have enjoyed it. Your aunt would enjoy the history and the castles, the outdoor markets, and the quaint feel of the country. Of course, we ended our holiday on the beaches of Monte Carlo, and I reminisced of our time there. Nina met up with us there, and we had great fun.

I received a letter from Natalie. She has accepted an au pair position in Stafa. Rich is very glad she close. She says the position is expected to last a year, however, au pair jobs often last longer. Have you heard from Colleen? Natalie says she has not heard from her lately. Our dear Natalie plans to return to England when the post is up. I did not ask her what happened to her marriage. It seems she took the job to get away from an unpleasant divorce. Do you know what happened? It didn't last long. Did you look Stafa up on the map? It's a suburb of Zurich.

I am thrilled to hear you will be graduating in January. Your Aunt must be pleased. Do you think you will be able to visit Europe anytime soon?

Rich's employer, Holland Advertising, is sending him to Australia next month. He contacted your aunt; she and Neville have opened their home to him. Rich is excited about the opportunity. Neville is best for her, hmm? I'm glad it all worked out. It seems things are working out for you as well. I must dash.

Love, your friend,
Fritz

1 December 1984

Dear Diary,

I went to see Mr. Kesselman, my boss at Hill's Department Store in the Oakdale Mall, today. I gave him my notice. He asked me to work days over my Christmas break. I accepted; it will be odd going in when the store is open after being locked in three nights a week for the last two years. I begin December 10th. I can always use a few extra dollars for my move to New York City. Evan's cousin has offered to take me on as a roommate until I find my own place. She lives in a walk-up in Brooklyn. I would love to live in Manhattan but loathe the cost to live there.

Cecilia invited me to join them for Christmas in Wisconsin. I love my sister and adore her daughter and husband, but I'm not into a wintry trip to a farm in Wisconsin. I really want to wrap things up here and work. I have to be out of my room by the end of the break on January 3rd. I should be on my way to Brooklyn by then. I told Barbara, Evan's cousin, I should be there by January 2nd. Wow. I'm overwhelmed; I'm embarking on real life. No more just hanging out for the summer. I'll be in a big city where I really don't know anyone. Am I making the right decision to leave without Roy?

Tanya closed her diary and lay back against the boulder where she could look up at the sky as she listened to the cascade of the waterfall down below the cliff she had chosen as a perch. The wood around her was not so different from the wood around the meadow she had so enjoyed in her youth in Lockwood. The sun warmed the lids of her eyes as memories of the past poured over her body like a velvet blanket; a deep sigh escaped her lips. Years of suppressed memories seemed to endlessly flow from her mind. Some replayed a multitude of times. How would she stem the floodgates? So much had transpired since bumping into Chris that fateful day during her summer break from college. She had moved to New York City after graduation, and her life with Roy had taken unexpected turns. Here she was once again at the edge of the Wood wondering where to turn.

XXXXX

"…Roy. I got a job with the County of New York, in their parks design and management department." She beamed at him as he scooped her into his arms and squeezed her in a congratulatory fashion. "I have a lead on an apartment in Astoria too."

Roy released her, and they sat down on the edge of her bed. He nodded. "I know Astoria. It's near my relatives in Queens. Is the place expensive?"

Tanya laughed. "All of New York is expensive as far as I'm concerned. It's a bit of a hike from my office. I got the lead from the interviewer. He says the guy is moving to Chicago or something." She shrugged. "We could go down and have a look. But I've already arranged to stay with Barbara until I find something, or until you get there." She smiled happily at him.

Roy shrugged. "We're going down on Christmas Day. Why don't we see if we can see it the following day?" Tanya nodded in agreement.

XXXXX

"If you would cut your contacts in our fantasy world and stop looking back, your life would be easier. Move into the future like Lia and me. Just let all the fantasies of our youth go. Why must you strive to keep it alive? You cannot hope to live in both worlds."

A tear had trickled down Tanya's cheek at Lenora's stinging words. Darn her sensitive Piscean nature. She shook her head and pouted at her sister.

"Fantasies? What are you saying?"

Their lives in the wood had not been a fantasy. Evald was more tangible than the shuffle she often found in day-to-day life in the realm of humans. How could her sister not understand? Lenora shook her head as Tanya brushed away the tear and confessed.

"Lenora, I want to go far from here, but I cannot abandon Evald. Father managed to traverse between the two—how?" Lenora sighed heavily and remained silent. Tanya glared at her. "Perhaps you and Cecilia can live solely in this world," she began in a soft growl. "I, on the other hand, would rather die." The anguish in her voice startled Lenora. She looked at her younger sister with wide, fearful eyes.

"Then you are lost as we move into the Age of Aquarius," she said in a stern voice. "You have chosen already."

Tanya stared at her, unable to speak, desiring to stamp her foot like a spoiled child. Why would Lenora not help her? Why would she not share her knowledge? Turning away was not an option. "What does the Age of Aquarius have to do with anything?"

"The Age of Pisces draws to a close; all will be clear in a few more years," Lenora replied. Tanya creased her forehead in disgust toward her sister, throwing her arms up in defeat.

In Tanya's journal, she shared all the questions she could not ask. Here she shared the wonders of life in a mixture of French, English, and German, so it would be difficult for anyone to translate.

My sisters believe we need never go back. I should release the past. I strive to do as they ask. How? Unlike them, rumors of the past leave me doubting who I am. I've run from the love of my life. Turned away from all that I once held dear… why? Running is useless. The past clings to my soul like a burial shroud I'm unable to shake free. Perhaps I should have remained in Australia with Auntie when I had the chance. Instead, I returned. Returned to the wood of the Southern Tier…they called me. Cornell called me back; only through them do I have access to the mist taking me to Evald. Today, I am always careful to be at peace before entering the mist, and yet it calls me… it holds me close. How can my sisters leave it behind, how can they forget?

10 May 1986

Dear Diary,

How quickly life can change. In a moment we are faced with emotions we thought buried forever. Forced to look inward, and question the significance of my life. One moment I'm out having a grand time with Lucy, my dear girlfriend from work. We have so much in common, it's as though we've known one another forever, rather that just about a year. Anyway, we're dancing, flirting with the club employees like Chris, the doorman and Jonathan, the lead bouncer, and the club manager, Frank. Or regulars, like Joe, Cheryl or Len, the next moment, life smacks me in the face. Where are my priorities?

13th May 1986

Dear Diary,

Insane. How can the trees be alive with the sound of birds and the smell of blossoms when he is gone? Truly gone? Had I pushed him more not to get involved with his family, would he still be alive? I'm sure Mark knows what really happened, but he'd never confide in me. It's so unfair. Roy was just getting his life back together; we were headed back together. There's so much I don't understand.@@@

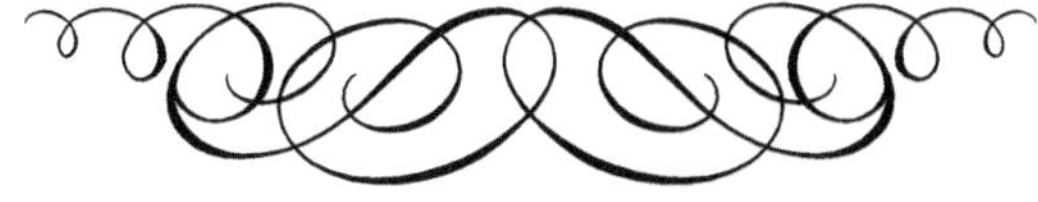

Escape to Brisbane

Imagining a semester in Brisbane would do both Aaron and Tanya good. Just as she imagined Tessa Goodrich would be a better for Aaron than Tanya could ever possibly be. She had to get as far away as possible for Aaron to forget her, as she insisted he must. If even a drop Jan had said was truth, she could never allow herself to be in Aaron's arms again. Yes, she was indeed running…running from her own inappropriate emotions, feelings, and desires. She had to go away, where she could let go her intense feelings for Aaron Sands, where she could heal and move on. If she remained, she would cave-in and confide in Aaron what his mother had insinuated. How could she spill something so devastating onto Aaron when she had no way to prove or disprove his mother's statement? How could his mother tell her and Cecilia Mr. Sands was really her father without some shred of evidence? How would Tanya be able to return to Lockwood and not reveal all to Aaron? She couldn't let Aaron suffer as she herself was suffering.

Sadly, Tanya recalled how she admired Tessa's management of men— something that escaped Tanya. Tessa was far more capable of handling Aaron than Tanya could ever imagine. Tanya had been accused of bewitching men but never with knowledge had she done so. Truly, one thing she admired about Lenora and continually sought her sister out for was her understanding of people. Tanya so frequently found herself in a muddled fog of confusion; so much about human nature she seemed incapable of grasping. Sometime ago, Tessa admitted how attractive she found Aaron. At the time Tanya had been offended, as they had been double dating, and Tanya had eyes only for Aaron. Tessa had confessed she hoped to draw Aaron's attention by dating one of his friends. Tessa went on to admit that her date, Tim Adams, liked Tanya. Tessa and Tim were curious if she would consider switching partners for the duration of the evening. Tanya was taken quite aback and clung to Aaron the rest of the evening. She hadn't spoken to Tessa since. Aaron hadn't said a word, but he seemed in agreement when she wanted to call an early evening. She'd never dared ask if Tim had made a similar suggestion to Aaron, and Aaron never said.

After Jan's accusation, it seemed only right Tanya sought Tessa out and divulged how she might attract and hold Aaron's attention. Tessa narrowed her large brown eyes at Tanya. "Why are you telling me this?"

Tanya shrugged. "Because I've come to realize he and I are not meant to be. I wish to travel the world, move far from here. Aaron desires to stay." Was it not fitting that Tanya make up a lie to push Aaron away, after all she had promised not to tell him the truth? But lying had never been something Tanya had been good at; it wasn't a part of her nature. And yet, why should she expose him to the heartache she herself felt? Aaron initially had seen through her blunder, so with a sigh, she explained that while in college it would be better to date other people. The pain found in his eyes almost matched the wretchedness that lay in her heart. She decided to make a clean break by saying she knew he would never be comfortable leaving Lockwood, and once off to college she never wanted to return. Truly, that was one of the major factors for her to ask that they date others.

After that dreadful evening, she and Cecilia had gone out drinking with Jan. She couldn't conceivably kiss Aaron romantically ever again. There would always be a shadow of doubt for her, one she would eventually share with Aaron. She had never kept a secret from Aaron in all her life, he always pried it from her. And yet her body craved his; thankfully they had never given into their hearts' desire. They had agreed to wait until they married. Yet Jan had believed her own tale since the girls were quite young; she knew how Tanya's mind worked. She had watched the girls throughout their youth. She knew their losses and heartaches and observed the bond Tanya developed with her auntie over her mother. For years she had remained silent. She had never opposed the relationship between Matthew and Cecilia; she had complained to her husband but never outwardly struck out at Cecilia for her mother's inappropriate behavior. After all it was true: her husband was a handsome man. Would she say such a thing to destroy Tanya? An innocent wisp of a girl, who'd already lost a beloved father, and brother; would she cut Tanya to the very soul purposefully out of spite for her mother? Knowing Cecilia and Tanya as she did, she knew it would be the one way to stop Aaron and Tanya for good, Jan knew to go to her boys with such an accusation would not stop them. They would not believe her, but they may ask their father in passing; he would never be certain, but she was certain what she said was truth. She had argued with Matthew after their son and Cecilia had announced their engagement. She wanted to tell the children then and there, but Matthew had put her off. It was ancient history; Cecilia had been born well before they'd met after all. Jan had no proof Tanya was Matthew's illegitimate daughter. Jan only had supposition. Jan's insinuation to Tanya and her sister would stop her and Aaron as nothing else ever could. Why would she make up such a lie? When Cecilia confided that it could be true as Matthew admitted to her that his father and their mother had at one time been rumored as being together.

Tanya considered a statement her friend and high school classmate, Stacey, had once made at school. "Tanya, are you sure Aaron is someone you want to date?"

Tanya had been puzzled at the time. "Sure. Why wouldn't I?"

Stacey had given her the oddest of looks and shrugged. "No reason, I just think there are other guys you may have more in common with."

Tanya smiled thinking at the time Kimberly's comment was made because she and Aaron traveled in a different circle of friends at school. But she nodded; Kimberly didn't realize how much time they spent together outside of school. "Like Brian Cartwright?"

Brian was a football player who mixed in the same group of friends as she. He had asked Tanya out several times, but Tanya had always politely refused. He didn't interest her, nor did she feel comfortable in his presents. Kimberly smiled impishly. "Date whomever you please." The conversation was interrupted by others joining them. Tanya forgot it and the moment quickly passed. Had Kimberly also heard the rumor? Should she dare to ask Kimberly if she knew of any rumors about her mother and Aaron's father from years ago? What if that raised gossip; could she ever bear to show her face in Lockwood again? Perhaps the best solution was to push Aaron into another woman's path and get on with her own life away from him. Honestly, would Jan accuse her husband and Mrs. Gilbert just to prevent another of her boys being linked to that adulteress's offspring or was she telling the truth?

…I ask myself; would I want to lose my sons to the family of such a woman were I in her shoes? Would I have been as gracious to those children were I her? How could she have been so kind to either of us?

Squeezing her eyes tightly closed, Tanya longed to forget that one dreadful night she had gone barhopping with Cecilia and Jan. She wished she could erase the entire incident from her mind as though it had never taken place, as if it had been a nightmare she could shake off upon awakening. She wished she could pinch herself awake, but down to her soul, she knew the night had been very real. That night had sealed her fate, had truly driven her to find away to leave the Southern Tier of New York and take Evald with her. There had to be a way because her father had done it; she simply had to find it. She knew none of them had drunk enough to ever forget what transpired. Words that had shattered her world and altered her course forever…

The Walls Come Closing In

Cecilia was visiting the autumn after Aaron and Tanya officially graduated from Spencer-Van Etten High School in 1982. Tanya had a part-time job at Hills Department Store in the Pyramid Mall, just outside of Ithaca, New York. She worked a few nights a week, stocking shelves in the men's department. They showed up to pick her up from work just before the store closed; they arranged to meet her at Friendly's in the food court of the mall. Tanya generally caught a bus back to her boardinghouse on Thurston Avenue, just below Cornell after work to save on gas money because sometimes she would go in and work through the night and get out at eight in the morning; she had tried to catch the bus in the morning, but she had fallen asleep and missed her stop so many times she found it easier to drive on those nights.

The trio dined at Mano's on Route 13, leaving Ithaca, toward Spencer. Initially, Tanya wondered if they had intended for her to go back with them for the weekend. She had explained over diner that she had a lot of studying as the summer courses were short and jam-packed. After dinner they backtracked to Kelly's Dockside Pub. The place was dimly lit and loud with a band playing in the back. They could scarcely talk over the din of music. After finishing their mixed drinks, they decided to try a place nearby that seemed less noisy—the Salty Dog, a bar near the pier on the southern part of Cayuga Lake, on a corner. It seemed a good place for another drink. Jan had never been much of a drinker—none of them were for that matter. It was obvious that Jan had something on her mind and was bursting to say it. The place had lots of windows on both walls that faced the streets; the interior was covered with blonde, knotty, stained pine and oak. Jan moved through the throng near the bar and made her way toward the back by the jukebox, where she found a narrow, quiet table. They ordered a round: Tanya, a tequila sunrise; Cecilia, a Southern Comfort and Coke; and Jan, a tall glass of dark beer. They selected a few songs from the jukebox as they waited for their drinks and made small talk. When the waitress returned, Jan insisted on buying the round. She took a long draw of her ale before looking Tanya right in the eye, as she sat the heavy glass mug squarely on the wooden table.

"I got something you both should hear," she stated matter-of-factly. Tanya and Cecilia exchanged silent glances and then both gave Jan their full attention. "If I tell you," she began as her dark eyes darted from one sister to the other, "you gotta give your word never to repeat it to anyone else. Especially to my boys."

Tanya sat back in her chair as if Jan had slapped her across the face, wondering what could be that significant. She couldn't recall having any secrets of major importance she had ever kept from Aaron. Glancing at Cecilia she could tell it was the similar for her. Neither included their family business in those secrets; after all, that wasn't their secret, it was their sister's. The abuse was a commonality that happened in many homes and, therefore, irrelevant. Even so, Cecilia had relayed some of that behavior to her husband. Tanya and Cecilia turned trusting eyes back toward Jan Sands, "Okay, shoot."

"You know, I always told my boys they got a sister out there somewhere," she began. The sisters exchanged glances and nodded in affirmation to Jan. Everyone in town knew Matthew Senior had been something of a ladies' man before a massive heart attack brought him to his senses. Jan had packed her bags at one point and taken her boys and left. Matthew had gone after her and swore fidelity if she would return. As far as anyone knew, he had lived up to all his promises to his wife since that day. Just a few days before, Matthew Senior had toasted her and Aaron's achievement with a can of beer. They had both hesitated at the toast, remembering the stories they'd heard of a different man sitting in the chair near them. They'd heard of the drinking he had forgone for his family. He smiled and assured them both it was but one beer. They clanged their cans to his and drank heartily. As always, Aaron later finished Tanya's half-drunk Michelob. She smiled to herself as she reminisced of that recent time. She and Aaron had the sort of relationship in which they could finish each other's sentences; that had often been the case throughout high school, where they would share a can of beer. Tanya had always had a propensity for hard liquor such as gin, vodka, or tequila; Aaron preferred beer, as did his friends. Not wishing to be antisocial, Tanya would accept a can but could never finish it, so Aaron would always oblige without anyone the wiser. For as long as they'd known one another, whatever she had, she had willingly shared with him, and he with her. They had never question such an unspoken arrangement, it simply was. It wouldn't be until much later in life that Tanya realize how unusual her relationship with Aaron Sands was. How fortunate they had been to have found and bonded to one another in their youth.

The jukebox was belting out some loud country song as the three ladies sat chuckling about the irony of life. Compared to the darkness beyond the streetlights, the bar was well-lit. Tanya felt Jan's eyes upon her and turned from the window to meet her gaze. Jan took a long swig on her mug, leaving less than a quarter of a mug in the bottom. She set it down, never taking her eyes off Tanya. "Well, you're Matthew's daughter." Tanya's hand began to shake so badly she couldn't even sip from her glass and had to return it to the table. She glanced at her sister, who was staring at Jan in disbelief. Jan looked from one to the other. "Neither of you ever had even an inkling?" She looked from one to the other. "Why'd ya think Matthew told you both you could call him Dad?" She shook her head. "Why'd ya think your mother doesn't come over to our house?"

Tanya opened her mouth but closed it when she realized nothing would come out. Her eyes frantically scoured the bar for a way out of her own skin. Her hand came to rest on the glass she had set down; without looking, she grabbed it and tossed the whole drink down. She spotted the restroom sign and staggered to her feet. Blindly, she stumbled toward the sign, bumping through a maze of tables and chairs as she went, as though she'd find salvation on the other side. Banging open a dark metal bathroom door with one hand, she stumbled into a narrow, dimly lit yellow walled room. The mirror was to the left with several sinks below and three stalls to the right painted dark green. The last stall was open; she leaned against the other stalls with one hand, making her way down the line, and turned in to throw up. Just making it in time, she scarcely managed to close the door as she wretched and cried in unison.

How could these people ever have allowed us to date? What could they have been thinking? I can't imagine how Jan had stood alongside Mother and Matthew at Lia and Matthew's wedding. What a screwed up family. Tanya rocked back on her haunches as a wave of nausea passed. She pulled off a swaddle of toilet paper to wipe off her brow and mouth, longing for something cool to touch her cheeks. She pulled herself up to a standing position in order to flush the bile that made her nauseous just seeing in the bowl. Her legs were shaky, and she soon sank back down on her haunches and cradled her head in her hands. The stall swam around her, as music floated in, and distantly she realized someone had opened the bathroom door.

Cecilia was calling her name softly, and it seemed she was far away… Tanya's mind drifted beyond the walls of the tiny stall, beyond the bar… beyond herself… She struggled to regain herself, to clear her mind in order to stand. Her equilibrium seemed to have abandoned her in that horrid stall. "T, are you in here?" Cecilia called as she glanced under the stalls and stopped in front of the last one. She could tell Tanya was squatting. She leaned her face against the cold metal door. "T?"

After what seemed an endless pause, Tanya responded in a tiny voice. "I'm here."

"Are you okay?"

Incredulously, Tanya stood silently shaking her head. "Are you kidding?" she responded, attempting to stand. "I'll be fine."

"T, I'm so sorry. Honestly, I wondered as much." Lia admitted much to Tanya's chagrin.

"Why didn't you warn me? I never imagined such a thing at all." Tanya leaned against the coolness of the door. "Wait, how? How could you have imagined?" Tanya rose on wobbly legs and opened the door. Bracing her arms against both sides of the stall to steady herself as she gazed into her sister's similar face in disbelief. Cecilia stepped to one side and helped her to the sink where she could splash cold water on her face and rinse her mouth out.

Cecilia sighed and cleared her throat, watching her sister in the mirror. "Because Mother has fooled around with married men." Cecilia's voice was flat, and matter-of-fact. Tanya glanced up at her sister's reflection. *Some fun night they we're having.*

"Excuse me?" She threw more cold water on her face, before reaching for a brown paper towel to dab it dry. "Not while Father lived."

Cecilia nodded. "It seems even while Father lived," she admitted. "Father knew."

"That friggin' freak. Mr. Hincley's not the first?"

Cecilia shook her head. "Mother is a fairy, dear girl. It is part of our nature unless we take a life partner."

Tanya looked at her in shocked surprise. "What?"

"Do you not know your own nature?"

"Are you saying you are such as well?"

Cecilia shrugged. "No. But I'm no angel. I had my fun before I married Matthew."

"When? You've always been Matthew's girl, since like ninth grade."

"I had two other boyfriends, and I had the summer before I married." Tanya couldn't recall the summer before Cecilia married. A vaguely imaged of another guy skittered across her thoughts; some depressing Irish guy that scarcely spoke... "Ryan? Ian? Something likes that."

"'Fraid not."

"*No.*" Tanya stated flatly refusing to believe such words. She turned to face her sister. When had she grown several inches taller than her sibling? She shook her head, imagining it all a bad dream, or that had there been something in her drink that freaked her out. She wrapped her arms about herself. "This can't be. I love Aaron, Lia. We've always loved one another."

Cecilia nodded. "What of this summer?"

"You know my heart is his. I befriended others, no more. You've always known my love for him. Now, Jan is telling me not only can we never marry…we should never have dated. And I'm to figure out a way to break up without telling him the truth." She turned back toward the stall as a wave of nausea overtook her.

"I know this sounds lame—even to myself—but T, this will work out. You've always been the strong one. You've always been able to manage far better than Lenora and I can." She shrugged, and Tanya turned away.

Leave it to Cecilia to gloss over heartache. Leave it to dear Cecilia to try to make nice out of a bowl of spilled cereal.

Tanya shook her head. "Lia, this is not going to be all right. This is never going to blow over."

"For all it's worth, I think Jan's wanted to speak up for sometime. I've seen her argue with Mother, I just didn't know what they were arguing about." She shrugged. "I figured it was none of my business."

How was this supposed to justify Cecilia's silence? Tanya leaned against the dirty stall, and looked in the streaked mirror at a ghostly pale reflection. No, it would not be all right. Every part of her felt violated, betrayed. She wanted to bolt from the dank room, and never lay eyes on any of them ever again. Did Auntie know? She couldn't imagine Auntie would keep such a thing from her, but then again, she would never have imagined her sister thinking it a possibility and never speaking up either. She met her sister's eyes as her head lolled to one side against the stall. "Give me time; I'll be fine. I'm always fine," she assured Cecilia in scarcely a whisper. Her palms felt clammy, she shook her head. "Forgive me, but I'm passing on this weekend. I'm not going down there with you all tonight. I won't be visiting Lockwood for Thanksgiving."

"T, don't be that way. Everyone will know something's up with you."

Tanya shrugged with hooked eyes; indeed Cecilia had lost her mind. There was no way she could pull off a weekend with the family after this bombshell.

"So? Maybe they should know." Tanya lashed back, all her dreams of marriage and family just went up in smokes. "Had I known she had such a secret, I never would have given my word to keep silent."

"T, we're all family. This couldn't be easy for Jan. Did you even think how she feels? After all, she wanted you to know the truth. Don't shut us out."

Tanya stood up straight and stared at her sister in disbelief. "You must be joking. There's no way I can deal with this bomb and face all of you. I'll spill it all to Aaron for sure." Briefly Tanya wondered when they had drifted so far apart. How could Cecilia be so callous to her emotions, even as she saw the aftermath of Tanya's retching? Tanya brought her hand to her face and rubbed it from the forehead down. "Lord, you had your doubts, and you allowed me to act abominably. How could you sit in silence?"

"Because I couldn't be certain."

"Doubts would have sufficed with me on this count." Tanya looked around the dingy bathroom in awe. "How could you say nothing? We should never have dated for heaven's sake. Never kissed." Tanya turned away from her sister in utter disgust and crossed her arms over her chest.

Lia grasp her shoulder. "Oh, T, forgive me. I simply couldn't speak; I couldn't destroy your relationship on a maybe. They should have spoken up sooner. Jan should have spoken years ago to us…not argue with Mother and Matthew." Cecilia tried to embrace her sister, and Tanya refused all comfort. Cecilia wanted to return to the table and talk it over reasonably.

"I'm sorry, dear sister. As much as I love you, I don't feel a bit reasonable tonight." Tanya admitted with her arms still crossed. "I'm mortified, and I'm going back to school. Have a wonderful Thanksgiving and forgive me for skipping out. Just tell everyone I had to work, or something." Tanya turned abruptly and grabbed the door handle. Cecilia rushed out behind her, grabbing her sister's jacket.

"Tanya. Please."

"No friggin' way. You two figure it out. What makes everyone think I can handle this any better than Aaron could? What makes you think I can pretend everything is hunky dory because it's your holiday?" Fury crossed her features, causing Cecilia to release her immediately. "You're all wrong. I'm not strong." Hot tears streamed down her cheeks. "I'm not going to be okay." Tanya admitted, "I will figure out how to deal. If

I never have to set eyes on any of you I'll be fine. Goodnight." She spun around before Cecilia could respond and slipped out as Cecilia regained her composure. By the time Cecilia wove through the throng of people near the bar, Tanya had hopped a cab and headed for her boardinghouse. Cecilia went back in and made her way to the table. Jan looked around for Tanya. Cecilia shook her head, "I'm sorry. She's gone. I couldn't stop her."

"What do you mean she's gone?"

"I mean she said she wouldn't come home. She bolted. I think she hailed a cab."

"She can't afford a cab. She must have gone to her boardinghouse. Why don't we just go get her?"

"She took the news quite badly. She can't understand why you didn't speak up sooner."

Jan shrugged. "I just couldn't bring myself to admit it."

Cecilia grimaced. "I've let her down."

"It had to be done." They both nodded, as Jan reached in her purse for a tip. "Let's go fetch her."

"I don't think she'll talk. I know she won't come home."

"Let's try."

XXXXX

Hot tears silently screamed down Tanya's face as she sat in the back of the cab, headed up the hill toward her beloved Cornell University. She planned to transfer to the school full-time after a semester in Brisbane with Auntie. Now, more than ever she wished to be on that plane bound for Australia... Perhaps she should forget her dreams of Cornell and hide away in Brisbane for good. How could she ever face anyone from Lockwood again? Surely Kimberly suspected, and others probably knew. Surely all laughed at her behind her back. "Driver, would you mind just dropping me off at the edge of campus on Thurston Avenue?"

"Sure…it's mighty late and dark. You're not really safe at night, and it's a bit chilly for that little jacket you're wearing, miss."

She nodded, as she looked out the window at the night sky. "I know. But I need to walk." He stopped at the walking bridge, just as she asked, and let her out. She rummaged through her purse and handed him a five-dollar bill. He gave her change and wished her a happy Thanksgiving. She wished him the same before turning to head down the path near the bridge, down toward the small waterfalls and sanctuary.

XXXXX

Jan and Cecilia turned into the long, narrow drive between 412 and 410 Thurston Avenue, to the parking lot behind Tanya's beige and brown trimmed boardinghouse. It was a rambling gambrel-styled two-story home that had the back upper porch enclosed. The back of the house was trimmed in white where as the front was trimmed in brown. Why was anyone's guess; there were twenty-four bedrooms of various sizes within the huge house, and in the center was a small open area affording outside light into the inside bedrooms, but it wasn't big enough to call a courtyard or to even grow a garden. A few of the nicer rooms hosted fireplaces, like Mrs. Krein's sitting room, and Chandler's room directly above hers. Mrs. Krein, the house matron, was allotted two rooms for herself, so she had a private sitting area where the kids could come and visit. The enclosed monstrosity of the upper porch had at one time been open, but now hung over the porch to Tanya's private entrance, and the separate porch leading to the kitchen entrance as if it were a bushy brow in need of a trim. The result mixed with the neat white picket railing and wide columns gave one the feeling the porch offered seclusion.

They found a slot near Tanya's tan 1979 Pontiac Sunbird. No lights were visible in Tanya's room, nor did she respond to the knocks on her private entrance. Cecilia walked around to the front of the house; lights were visible in the living room, but the door was locked. Cecilia didn't dare ring the bell; she knocked. Mrs. Krein informed her Tanya wasn't in. Mrs. Krein stepped back as she let Cecilia in to wonder down the hall to Tanya's room.

As usual, the door was unlocked; Tanya believed she had nothing anyone else in the house would take, so she only locked the door when she slept; as it was a fire exit. As Cecilia stepped in and switched on the light to the ten-by-ten-foot room it was immediately apparent that Tanya hadn't returned. Where could she have gone after leaving the bar? Mrs. Krein turned from Tanya's room as Cecilia thanked her. She nodded as she walked away, turning out lights as she went. Cecilia turned off the light in Tanya's room as she slipped through the private entrance. Normally such a room cost extra for privacy, there was a door to a small back porch off the parking lot, but Tanya had struck some bargain. Jan waited in the car. "Where else can we look?" Cecilia shrugged as she racked her brain for ideas.

"The campus library would be my only other guess," Cecilia admitted, as she glanced at her watch. She hadn't realized it was just after midnight already.

"Do you know how to get there?"

"I can find it," Cecilia responded skeptically. "But it's after midnight; the library closed hours ago, Jan. We should call it quits."

Jan sat at the entrance to the drive of 110 Thurston in her 1974 forest green, super sport Nova and glanced over at Cecilia indecisively. "Do you think she'll be all right?"

"I'm sure she'll be fine. She just needs some space; maybe she'll drive down tomorrow." Even as she said it, Cecilia doubted she would see her sister for on this trip.

"I don't know why she took off," Jan grumbled as they headed down the hill, back toward Ithaca.

XXXXX

As much as Tanya longed to swim to the falls and hide behind them and wish herself away, the night was simply too cold. Instead she sat on the cold stones near the water's edge and called for M**** silently into the night. If the fuath showed, she would willingly give herself wholeheartedly to the watery grave he offered so many others. She brought up her knees, and crossed her arms and buried her face for a good long cry.

A quiet, dark figure approached the sobbing figure along the shore. He pulled up short, hearing her sobs; he turned for a path and decided to leave without making himself known. He recognized the silhouette as a girl from the boardinghouse next door to his fraternity. A girl he had been interested in meeting, but thus far, the right opportunity had not presented itself. He moved toward her now, thinking finally he could get a conversation going; his ears could not doubt the agonizing sobs emitted from the depths of her being. He froze in place, not wishing to startle her. He had taken a walk to clear his mind; as he sat in the library, he'd found it impossible to concentrate. He should have gone home to Albany, New York, for Thanksgiving, but he had chosen to remain at college to study instead. Albany was just the capital of New York State. Roy had desired to get away from his Irish-Italian family and their constant bickering and badgering him to marry his girlfriend, Thea. She had become insecure, constantly calling and checking up on him and his cousin, Mark. Thea had been furious when Roy accepted entrance into Cornell University, and her discovering that to visit one had to fly or drive three hours through rural upstate New York State. "I didn't know New York was full of farm country." She whined, "You don't really expect me to make this boring trip again, do you?" How could he move three hours from her to attend a dreary university like Cornell when there were plenty of good colleges close to home? He was neglecting her, and she didn't like it. "Heavens, Roy. Why leave New York to attend college anyway?" she had asked for the umpteenth time.

He longed to become acquainted with the girl next door. A girl who had appeared to him throughout his dream life, but he found each time he approached her that the timing was always off. He would lose his nerve, and she wasn't the sort to consent to join in a fraternity party. They had had parties; he ascertained she had been invited, but she never showed. One of the guys in the house happened to be dating a friend of hers. Bob told Roy at one point she worked overnight at the mall or something. "And you would know that because...?" Roy had question

Bob had chuckled at him. "I would know that because my local babe is a friend of hers." He smirked. He did not take his relationship with Debbie very seriously; after a few conversations with Debbie, Roy knew she was thinking wedding bells. Bob had a girl in his hometown that also expected wedding bells. "Debbie says your little blonde gets locked in some store two or three nights a week."

Immediately, Roy's mind had reverted back to the childhood fairytale where leprechauns—or was it elves?—had worked on shoes for a shoemaker at night while the shoemaker slept. Why would this little blonde remind him of leprechauns and fairy tales? "Well, if Debbie's such good friends with her, maybe you could hook us up to double date sometime." Roy had suggested. Whenever he thought of Debbie, he oddly thought of pixies. Living in Ithaca around hippy professors and women who wore gauzy dresses and Birkenstocks with wool socks even in winter seemed the perfect setting for such imagination. What was it about these two girls that made him long for an altered dimension? To the magical land he shared with his beloved grandmother in California? Perhaps he would figure it out as he figured out a way to really get to know the little blonde.

Bob shrugged. "We'll see. She's crazy about her homeboy back in Pennsylvania or at least south of here."

"What homeboy? I don't see guys beating down her door. She certainly has a lot of women popping in over there though."

Bob shrugged. "Some farmer from where she grew up. He comes up sometimes; you've probably seen him. He's tall and lean, olive skin." Bob looked at Roy, who scarcely tanned at all, his arms were sprinkled with freckles, and he even had a few small ones across the bridge of his nose. Neither he nor Roy was over five ten, certainly no match for the GQ- looking carpenter Debbie had pointed out as Tanya's man. Roy was too busy keeping up in the architectural engineering program to take time to sunbathe during the summer session.

Roy shrugged with a sardonic smile. "What? You think a girl wouldn't be interested?"

Bob shrugged. "He's a lot darker than you and taller. Maybe she doesn't go for pretty white boys."

Roy gave him a shove. "That'd go for you too. Maybe the right one hasn't asked."

"Yeah, that's why I went for the unattractive friend," he admitted. "The plain girls are an easier catch."

Roy had heard of Bob's escapades, and his reputation with girls. He would use Debbie for a semester or so. Her father had money, and she had her own place, which made it easier for Bob. Bob agreed to see about double dating with Tanya. "I have to tell you, she's not keen on me," he reluctantly admitted.

"Why not?"

He shrugged. "She's heard of my reputation, I guess. Or she makes assumptions because I'm pledged to this fraternity. I don't know." He narrowed his marble blue eyes, contemplating. He told Roy what Tanya had said at their last meeting. Roy raised his brow in alarm. "Debbie must have told her we had sex or something because she came to me and said, 'Debbie's an Iccovelli; that means something in this town.' She looked furious that I'd deflowered her friend. She went on, 'She's sweet and innocent, and if you abuse her, I'll be sure her father and brothers track you down like a dog on his last leg." Bob did a poor mimic of Tanya's voice as he admitted the conversation to Roy. Roy was tempted to burst out laughing. He would have given anything to see Bob's face at that moment, because up until that point, Bob had intended to get what he wanted from Debbie and move on. "Her voice was low and venomous." Bob continued, "She looks so good natured, and then she gets this really scary look in her eyes and that low voice." He shook his head, "I wouldn't mess with her. She meant what she said. I'm sticking with Debbie 'til summer break."

Roy had seen Tanya at a distance turning guys down; she had a reputation in the house for being a snob. No doubt she would have had a glint in her eye that had turned Bob's blood cold when she'd sought him out with her veiled threat. He imagined she had heard stories about frat boys, smart girl. He considered returning to the falls and sitting next to her. Would such a girl admit her woes to a stranger? With such intense sobs he imagined another man was involved, and did he really want to hear the tale of her lost love? It was an opportunity to get close quickly. The worst that could happen was she could freeze him out. He turned back toward the path and the falls.

XXXXX

He stood just off the path in bewilderment as he watched her climb to the shore, her pale skin opalescent against the moonlight. He drew his breath sharply as he watched her redress on this cold night. The water had to feel like ice; it was no more than forty degrees on this cool autumn evening. Was this girl insane? She sat back down on the rocks with her knees pulled close to her chest; her hair limply hanging wet down her back, as she rocked slowly to keep warm. Roy stood straight and took a deep breath before daring to approach and sit quietly beside her. She turned and shot hot barbs at his intrusion as he sat down, took off his leather jacket, and offered to drape it over her shoulders. She shot him an apprehensive look before he settled the heavy brown leather on her shoulders. "Are you a twin?"

"Excuse me?" He couldn't resist reaching out with a gentle hand and brushing away the tears from her face, as she sniffed.

"A twin of yours just went to the front door of your boardinghouse. It must be a twin, because you couldn't have beaten me down here from there."

Tanya gave him a fleeting smile and nodded. "My older sister."

"Did she and your mother come to pick you up for the Thanksgiving holiday?"

"I suppose she and her mother-in-law did. But I'm not going. I told them as much earlier."

"Why not?" her companion asked. Tanya shrugged and continued to stare into the water, away from him, strands of her curls hiding her face.

"Did you come here to wash your hair in the freezing water, or are you performing some odd ritual?"

She glanced at him with a smirk. "Something," she admitted. "You ask too many personal questions."

"I'm Roy," he offered, undeterred.

"I know."

He nodded, chewing his lower lip, thoughtfully. "Want to go out for a drink?"

"Not really; it's kind of late. Thanks. Why haven't you gone home for the holiday, or at least with Bob?"

Roy shrugged. "I figured I'd stay and study. It's only a short break."

"Albany's only a three-hour drive."

"Yeah, I ride a bike. It's a cold three-hour drive. I'm not from Albany; I'm from just outside the city." He hesitated; he moved closer to her, waiting, hoping she would decide to open up as most girls would have. She remained impassive. "I've got lots of studying to do," she admitted with a nod. "You're right; it's a short break." She chuckled, and he joined in.

"Yeah, a short break," was the sum of her reply.

CHAPTER 2

Brisbane seemed like the perfect out; there was no one else Tanya desired to be closer to than her dear auntie. Certainly the thought of casting her eyes upon her mother or consulting her about the accusation seemed impossible. Of course, Cecilia had other ideas. Cecilia had dragged Tanya over to Mother's house; they'd even sat down with her at the kitchen table and shared tea. While there, Cecilia dared ask Mother about the ancient rumors. Never would Tanya forget how Mother raised her cup, looked right into her eyes, and asked, "What difference does ancient history matter now?"

XXXXX

Lord, there was such a lump in my throat, but I'd already ended things with Aaron by the time Cecilia had gotten such an idea. After all, Jan spoke to us the day before Thanksgiving; she returned for Christmas before she had the gumption to approach Mother. Cecilia said it mattered because had she known she never would have dated or married Matthew Sands Junior. "Don't be ridiculous." Mother had said. "Whatever transpired then has no bearing on you and Matthew."

"Does it have a bearing on Aaron and Tanya?" Cecilia dared whisper as we stared across the table at this formidable woman. She lifted her white coffee mug; I know there's some inscription on the side facing her, but for the life of me I can't tell you what it said. *"Doesn't matter anymore regardless from what I hear tell."*

XXXXX

Tanya desperately wanted to shout, *"Did it have a bearing on Aaron and me?"* But her throat seemed to close up at that moment; she couldn't utter a sound. She looked into her mother's eyes, eyes that dared her to ask that very question, and she couldn't bring herself to do so. How could Tanya admit to that creature why it mattered, why she had truly broken off with Aaron Sands? Because when Jan spoke that night, a picture of Matthew Senior being rushed to the hospital from a heart attack played through Tanya's mind. She saw the dreary waiting room, her mother in knickers and a white blouse sitting next to Matthew's cattle buddy, Jerry Winkler, on a cushion and metal bench. In her mind's eye, she saw a wide-eyed Jan hefting a brown leather, satchel-like purse upon her right shoulder as she crossed the doorway into the room. Both Jerry and a pregnant Mrs. Gilbert turned to face Jan. Jan and Tanya's mother looked younger; her mother's hair was dark with large curls, cut just below her ears. She looked away from Jan, and instantly Jan knew the woman was having an affair with her husband. "You were with him when he collapsed?"

"Maybe so. Someone had to fetch the fire squad," Tanya heard her mother's meandering voice inside her head as Jan found a seat across from them. Jerry remained silent; the doctor walked in before there was more of a scene. Where some might doubt such an unfounded tail, Tanya felt a sense of truth. Perhaps she wasn't the seed from an ill-fated affair, but she knew to her very bones that Jan was accurate in accusing her mother of having an affair with Matthew. She sensed her mother still held feelings for the man, though neither had acted on them in many a year. Tanya believed her mother had a different level of morality than others experienced. Why else would she have been unfaithful to her husband in the first place? What made her that way? Tanya had long been fearful of Mother and certainly never understood the woman who sat before her. Why had Father loved her so? Why had he married her? He was the very best of them all. And when he and Franklin Junior died, the family died; Mother most of all. Instead of asking anything more about the Sands, Tanya cleared her throat and informed her sister and mother that she would be leaving the day after Christmas for a semester in Australia with her beloved auntie.

December 27, 1982

Dear Diary,

Help. I'm not certain what course I should take, if any. I'm grateful I chose to remain in Australia to spend Christmas with Aunt June.

Why does he haunt me? Even though Jan's words ring in my ear forgive me I still desire Aaron with all my being. What an abominable situation. I am disgusted at my own tormented emotions, at all of those foul people who let it be. They could have spoken to me, to him. They should have. I hear, Jan actually called over to Mother's, asking if I planned to stop by as usual, she had gifts for me. I didn't want her gifts. I want no more from any of them ever again. I have given Cecilia the gifts I'd bought for them, not wishing to face them, but not wishing to be obvious either. I had considered remaining in my room at college, but I dread sympathy. I guess I dreaded one of them appearing on my doorstep even more.

All I can do is remember the last time I saw Aaron. I've avoided him since Jan's revelation in November. Aaron had showed up at my door late one afternoon. He invited me to a picnic at Stewart Park. It was a sunny autumn day, and I, being a foolish nincompoop, accepted his offer. Wow. Being at Stewart Park with him again made me realize all the wonderful times we'd spent together through the years. He asked why I was pushing him away.

XXXXX

He caught me off guard, Diary. I can't help but write down the scene, as it plays over and over in my head.

"Why won't you marry me? I'll leave Lockwood, Tanya. I know you love me. You've always loved me. What's happened to you?"

I glanced away from intense blue eyes. He took my pale hand in his large, calloused hands—so warm. Ah, such a sense of security swept through me. This man had always seemed to read my very soul. I knew if I met those eyes the whole story would tumble out before I could hold it back. "Aaron, I do love you. But I've come to realize love is not enough." I stole a glance at him before continuing. "We want different things from life, and being together will eventually bring us both misery. I don't want that; I wish only happiness for you." I faced his handsome, pain-filled face. A pain I mirrored in my own, a pain caused by my words… words that must be said. "Forget us, Aaron. It's for the best."

The cold dampness of the bench seeped through my jeans to chill my bones. My throat seemed to close, and I wanted desperately to wretch from sorrow. I forced my eyes to remain in my lap as he sat stiffly beside me.

Eventually, he spoke softly. "This past summer in Europe changed you more than I imagined. You're saying I'm no longer enough for you. That's why you push me to the arms of another. I know it was your idea for Tessa to ask me out, she admitted as much to Tim when she broke up with him, and he told me."

Hot tears stung my cheeks as I turned to reach out and run my hand down his handsome cheek. Electricity passed between us; God, I hope I never feel this way for another person again. "I realized recently we're simply all wrong for one another. You deserve far better than me."

"What's that supposed to mean?" he asked, grasping my forearm to still my hand. I couldn't meet his eyes because I had to make this break final. "Whatever it is you're hiding, we can work it out."

"No." I hadn't realized I'd yelled until it was out of my mouth. He looked at me bewildered, as I dropped my hand, and he released my arm. I couldn't recall ever having raised my voice in his presence before. "I'm sorry," I began again in humility. "Aaron, I know you don't understand…I'm

not certain I can explain. But I know the life I want is different from the life you've always imagined we'd share. I'm not ready to settle down, I'm not certain I ever wish to marry. I know I don't want to live near either of our families, not even my sisters." Wetting my lips, I searched his face; he turned away to face the lake. With a sigh, I rose and headed slowly toward his orange Dodge pickup in parking lot. He caught up with me and opened the passenger side and helped me climb up. I leaned back into the seat and closed my eyes, knowing I had embarked on a lonely, worthless path. A path I had no heart in traveling. How foolish I'd been to accept such a promise. Aaron had every right to know all I knew. Lord, so many secrets have destroyed my life, and it's only just beginning. Aaron was talking again; I couldn't understand initially. I was caught up in the soothing, musical rhythm his voice had always held for me... "I imagined that if you discovered I was dating others you'd come back to me. I got drunk one night, lonely for you, Tessa was there. The next thing I know everyone's making plans and arranging a wedding. If you'd marry me today, Tanya, I'd go wherever you liked."

I opened my eyes and turned to him sadly, reaching out again to touch that incredible cheek. I shook my head, still resting on the back of the seat. "No. Aaron, I know Tessa's far more suited for you than I shall ever be. I love you enough to admit that."

He shook his head and turned to start the engine. "I don't believe you, T. I never thought there would be a day you'd lie to me."

XXXXX

How can I admit this to anyone? I was so grateful to Auntie for a way to escape. A way to spend time in Australia. Brisbane awaited me at the end of December. I had encouraged Aaron to see his marriage proposal through. I had to believe the words I spoke were true. Why else would it come to this meeting? How else could I be assured he'd never second-guess his vows? I had to turn him toward her.

As much as I love Auntie, how can I truly forsake Evald to stay with her in Australia? So kind and loving of her to offer to arrange for me to remain at Brisbane University and avoid ever returning to upstate New

*York. There is urgency in my veins to return to at least as far as Cornell, one I can never explain. I've spoken to Lenora over the phone; she thinks she's come up with a way for me to traverse to Evald no matter where I go. She says when I return she'll come to Cornell and show me. Perhaps, I'm fooling myself into imaging I can actually put Lockwood and the wood behind me. Lenora said if I could just let it all go it would be the best thing for me, as I'm only a halfling and she is full-blooded, she cannot understand why I hold so tight. I asked her what she met by that, and she said it didn't matter so much; she wouldn't quantify such a thing over a phone. Cornell is not so far away from there; Aaron could easily find work in Ithaca and travel to Lockwood to visit. What am I saying. We can never be. Besides, according to my last letter from Cecilia, he's proposed to Tessa. I long to leave the area of Lockwood, in fact Ithaca too for that matter, for good…but I'm torn. If I leave, I must also leave Evald, and never see Lady or M**** again. I've not even admitted to Lenora that I didn't forsake my familiars Lady is content in Evald near M****'s stream. She lives on a farm, a kindly couple that owns a farm; they're gnomes, M**** says. I don't know this farm you speaks of; it's a ways down stream from Gosymonity, but if Lady is happy and well- cared for there, it is enough for me.*

*They open their farm to anyone who comes their way and knew my father many moons ago. Just talking to them of Father caused me to choke down my tears. I still miss him so; he could have offered so much guidance and knowledge, and I still fail to understand why he had to go. They open their door to all weary travelers and allow them to stay as long as they like; why did Father stay with Franklin when he could have at least made it to the farm? Lady is tended by friends or some strange relative of M****'s, called a Kender, that frequently visits the farm. M**** says that the Kender took to Lady, and Lady to him; I am content that she is happy. The last I saw of M**** was at Christmas, I didn't venture to Evald because I feared I'd never wish to return from there, and I sense there is a purpose for me in this world. Winnie is with Aaron. I saw her at Christmas too, and she looks content with Aaron and his parents on their farm just outside of VanEtten. I longed to ask Mr. Sands if all Jan says is true, but I cannot bring myself to be so forward. My heart is torn in two, and I've done it to myself. What would it matter if I did ask, and he affirmed? Even if he were to deny her* *allegations, would I ever be able to look at Aaron the same again? I must move on, and yet I'm stuck in quagmire. Though we are now apart, my dear familiars are still a part of me. Lord, help me, even though I've accepted Aaron and I could never be, it cut me to the core to hear of his wedding announcement. I should be happy for him. Happy he could forget me and love Tessa. But a big part of me is devastated, I can't even bring myself to leave my room and attend to my studies.*

Auntie is wonderful, and she sensed my heartache. She cannot understand the depths or the cause. She said it's to be expected from time to time, and I need to get out and mingle with others. Honestly, that's the furthest thing from my mind. Neville's invited some of his students in the engineering department over this afternoon for a barbeque. The last thing I need is to be among a group of chipper, dull, engineering students. I'm the furthest thing from a practical, engineering mind one could be. Thankfully, Auntie bailed me out by inviting over a girl from her history and ethics class, Jamie Tucker. She and I got on from the first time Auntie introduced us. Jamie's planning a jaunt up the coast, and today she invited me to join her. Sounds exciting, just what I need. Jamie's from Sidney; I'm a bit surprised she chose to attend the University in Brisbane. She admitted she wanted a change of scenery. I'm certain there's more to it, but I've no desire to explain myself to anyone, so I felt it only fair for me to do likewise to another and simply accept her statement. In my spare time, I've dug out all the photos I brought with me of Aaron and had them copied. I couldn't bear to give them up, foolish as that may be. I even wrote to Tessa's parents and requested a few photos of her to add to a small album I put together for Aaron's wedding. I documented some of our best childhood memories into a storybook format.

Like the times we used to watch the baseball games at the diamond near his house, and he would invite me over for lunch. We would dine on frozen bread spread with peanut butter and jelly, or his Mom might be home to serve up something interestingly undistinguishable. Or our jaunts in the woods, the picnics we enjoyed in wine county around Seneca Lake, haying by headlights. Hanging out with friends at Park Station or Stewart Park. Tessa's parents were wonderfully accommodating, even going so far as to write a few misadventures of her childhood on paper, which I cut to fit into the book around the pictures. I tried to weave the stories together, so their parallel lives were twined together and now will knit into one. She had also spent a lot of time at Park Station with friends, so I used that and school as a focal point of the book. I hope they both enjoy it; I poured all my love and pain for Aaron into that simple little album. I am so thankful to be halfway across the world as an excuse not to be anywhere near their wedding. May he find happiness and love with her, a love greater than what we seemed to have had, a love I should never felt or been permitted to feel toward him. He's a great guy; she's very fortunate to have caught his eye. I wonder if she saw that way back when we double dated. I mailed it off to Cecilia in ample time for this day. Aaron's wedding day. My heart is so heavy, the last thing I want to do is smile and pretend to be having a grand time among a group of engineers in the making. All I want to do is lock myself away in my room and cry a river of tears.

Oh, Dear Diary,

*Often I've considered slipping into the mist of Evald, not to look back, leaving this world and all the sorrows I've experienced here behind. But M**** and Gosymonity tell me I have unfinished business and cannot yet remain indefinitely in Evald. They refuse to explain themselves; all they'll divulge is that I cannot remain in Evald alone. I am to find something here that is to come back with me. Sometimes their riddles make me crazy. They refuse even to point me in the right direction. Instead, they assure me I'll know when I find it. How? As much as I love Evald, as fond as I am of both of them, I'm torn…frustrated, they know something I don't. Everyone seems to be in on a secret, and I'm left in the dark. I sense they are correct; there is something for me to find in this world, but I've no idea what or how I might find it. Even worse, without Aaron, life now seems so pointless. How can I admit* *that to another living soul? How could our families ever have stood by in silence if Jan is telling the truth? If I run to Evald, I'll never know what I'm searching for. Would I fade, as others have? Can a fairy live endless days alone and yet not quite alone? I will be in the company of M**** and Lady, but they are not of "my kind." Ironically, I would have given up Evald for Aaron…but now that is not a choice for me to make, I have no desire to marry any other human ever. Is that how Auntie has been all these years before finding Neville? Is that why she willingly relinquished her farm, her country, and her life as a professor of English at the college in Scranton, Pennsylvania, to travel to Australia as Neville Longbottom's wife? Would I be content living in Gosymonity without my sisters filling the rooms in the great sequoia tree? Since returning from Europe last summer, visiting Evald was peacefully lonely, even in the company of M****. It seems something important was missing, I had imagined it was my sisters' companionship, but perhaps it's something more. Something I have yet to find.*

It's not so difficult to walk away from most of the people I know, save for Aaron; truly the wood binds me, the streams…I long for them desperately. I'm overcome by a sense of isolation here in Australia, even in the company of Auntie…this is not "home" for me. It never will be. At Cornell, I felt such a peace listening to the falls. Of course if I were to slip into Evald and remain there…I would not miss…what? I come to the wood to connect to Evald, when in Evald all around me is the wood, past the stream, and down in the valley below are farms, farms I have never ventured near. In the wood of the Southern Tier, I found tranquility for a time; when I sit under the falls of Ithaca, I'm washed in peace I can find nowhere else in this world. While in Australia, it seemed I am unable to truly… breathe, I cannot connect to the mist, just as I could not connect in Europe, being separated from the mist is a death unto me, I cannot bear to be apart from it long. As much as I enjoy meeting people, learning, and traveling… seeing the ocean, the mountains, and cliffs, it is all with heaviness on my chest that I cannot explain. How insane is that? My fear is should I leave the wood of the Southern Tier I would lose my way to Evald, as my sisters seem to have lost theirs. I can scarcely wait to see Lenora and see what she has devised for me to traverse the mist.

<h2 style="text-align:center"><u>XXXXX</u></h2>

I've received the oddest letter from Cecilia. In it she writes…

Dearest Sister,

It is good to be on our own, but the holidays are difficult to be apart from family. Ah, the price we pay for our choices. Have you heard the news? Mother is no longer seeing Mr. Pig. I'm not certain why. I believe his health fails we should all forgive the past, dear sister, for our own sakes. I know that in my heart and have spoken to Lenora at great length. If she is able—and she certainly has been the one most effected through the years. Surely, you and I can forgive as well. Her response is inconsequential. What say you?

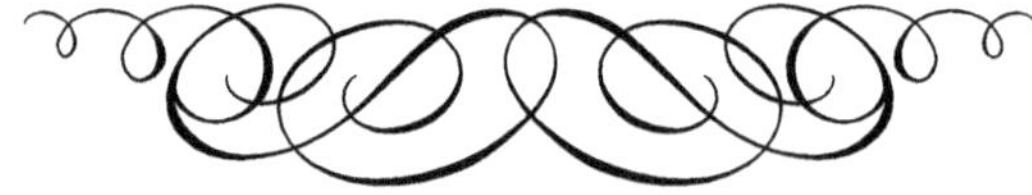

XXXXX

What is this?

How much simpler my life would be if like my sisters I could devoid the past. I cannot omit its existence…it would be to omit our existence and where would I be then? I adore Auntie; she's always been a loving mother figure to me. Even so, graduating from the University of Brisbane would be as good as graduating from Cornell University, but I must return, not for Cornell so much as for the falls that take me to my escape, to a sense of serenity… to a means to breath in the fresh, clean air of the wood. I could not remain with Auntie in Australia; it's too far from my precious wood. Brisbane holds emptiness for me. I should return to Ithaca, New York. To Cornell University, once again to smell the wood to lose myself in the tranquility brought on by sounds of birds high in the tree and waterfall cascading, enwrapping my senses, restoring my sense of order and security. While away, I imagine things would somehow work themselves out. Silly girl.

XXXXX

Of course Auntie knew best. Tanya had a wonderful afternoon, which spilled over to many wonderful evenings in the company of a handsome pre-med student, Jerome Audier from South Africa. Neville found the striking pre-med student intriguing; he had such a fascination and talent for engineering. It seemed Jerome was bound to be a physician because his father was a physician, but Jerome's passion was for engineering. Jerome seemed to be the balm Tanya needed to get beyond Aaron's speedy marriage; the more time she spent in his company, Auntie felt the less she thought of Aaron or of Lockwood. After all, he was a strikingly attractive man, with thick, black hair, dark penetrating eyes, and tan skin, and that striking South African accent. Many female students were envious of Tanya. What was not to find appealing? He had name, reputation, exemplary social etiquette—what more could an Aunt or mother hope for her daughter? She encouraged and cultivated the relationship for Tanya, as Tanya seemed incapable of mustering much enthusiasm in anything since Aaron's wedding announcement. Auntie even felt confident enough to write to Cecilia:

17th April 1984

Dearest Niece,

How are you? As I promised I'm writing with news of our dear Tanya. She has blossomed and has agreed to remain for the summer. I'm delighted. You and Matthew need not worry. I knew she created an album for Aaron. I thought it a wonderful way of mending the divide between them. She is still a bit to innocent and green, but she will be fine. It still breaks my heart to hear they did not marry.

My dear, I promised never to speak of why we left Virginia. Why, when all our kin and history remained behind? Some things are best forgotten. Your mother is a difficult woman, made bitter by happenstance, but I can assure you when they married moons ago, there was love. It was a happy day. I cannot say what drove your mother to change, but change she did. But, for you lovely girls, I could forgive her and love her. My love for her allowed me to be there to assist the three of you. I am sorry I was not a greater part of your lives. Sorry that Lenora has had many misfortunes already at your mother's hand. I have made every effort to prevent such things. I failed.

You will be glad to know that shortly after she arrived, Neville and I hosted a student reception in our home. Tanya made fast friends with a girl from my history classes, and the two are touring up the coast at the end of the semester. She's emotionally strong. She's attached to a handsome, young, prosperous, and talented student she met at the reception we held for her arrival. All is well, Tanya is like a cat, and she always lands on her feet. Keep in touch.

Much love to all,
Aunt June& Neville

Neither Aunt June nor Cecilia were aware that Aaron had acquired Tanya's address and wrote to her after his wedding.

Dear T,

Hi. You know I'm not much of a writer. I never had your talent. I guess you're having fun with your aunt. I just had to tell you how blown away I was by the album you put together for me. You once told me you gave such albums away as gifts of love, thank you. I had no idea you even had all those pictures tucked away. I imagine you spent a lot of time on it; I struggle to understand you, T. When I looked through that album and read your memories, it brought tears to my eyes. You of all people have betrayed me. You were not honest when you broke off with me. Why? I must know. You cannot run or hide forever, T. 'Til then, I await an answer.

Aaron

Dear Lord,

What have I done? Now he knows I lied. I am so foolish… in letting go I've caused him to hang on. This is very bad indeed. This is probably the longest letter Aaron's ever written. Distance does not protect me or dull the emotions. I've locked myself away in my room to cry away my broken heart.

Lord, I'm abomination. How can Aaron or Jerome find me attractive when I have such mislaid intense emotions. My entire life is a lie. Even my dating Jerome is only to appease Auntie.

How pathetic is that? Here's a gorgeous, intelligent guy that chooses to be with me when there's lots of other women interested in him, and I date him to please my aunt. Right now, I hate Mother, I hate Mr. Hincley, I hate Jan Sands, and most of all, I hate myself. Hate myself for who I may be, hate myself for hurting the love of my life. Hate myself for living in the web of lies others spin around me.

Through all this…I don't hate Mr. Sands; he's always been so kind to me. So…fatherly and yet I should hate him most of all…if it's true… He of all people surely should have spoken. How can I ever return? How can I survive without a way into the mist? I've no desire to live without Evald…without at least seeing and hearing of Aaron from afar. He is the only reason that keeps me from traversing the mist never to return.

I've heard from Lenora… shocked as I am, she has completely forgiven Mother and Mr. Pig. She writes she spent a week at Mother's. She confirms Cecilia's statement that Mother is through with that man. Perhaps she looked at herself. Lenora says she's in some sort of religious study group with her neighbor, Mrs. Cole. I can't imagine Mother attended a study group regularly, let alone a religious one. Good for her.

XXXXX

True to her word, Tanya went through each day smiling as if life were good. She led Auntie to believe that she had moved on from Aaron. Even when Auntie tried to feel her out, she brushed it aside and found more and more time to spend with Jerome. She and Jamie spent hours planning out their trip up the coast. After her trip, she would catch a plane to France where Tanya planned to rendezvous with Fritz and some other friends in Monte Carlo for a few days.

XXXXX

Dear Sister, I'm grateful to be far away from Lockwood, from my problems I left behind there. Thankfully, some things work themselves out. By the time I return, Aaron will have been married a few months, Tessa's grasp on him should be firm. I'm so grateful to be in Auntie's company and guidance. Happy to have my camera with me to grasp hold such incredible opportunities. I've focused on scenic beauty here. Human ingenuity blended with God's glory is incredible. Simply astounding—imagine creating your own coast. They did in Brisbane. It's a horseshoe shape. As Brisbane is inland, they brought the coast to the city, as well as imported white sand. Is that not incredible. It's really a joy to partake; the water is warm and wonderful.

Dearest Cecilia,

How are you and yours? I've not heard from you lately. Your mother sent a brief letter; it was a surprise to hear from her the other day. Apparently, Aaron's wedding went well. Your mother seems to have had a delightful time because you and Matthew were able to attend. Whether you believe it or not, dear girl, your mother loves you. Both families are so pleased when you returned for visits.

You needn't worry about our little dove. She's the outgoing girl I enjoyed traveling throughout Europe with. In fact, she's met a wonderful young man from South Africa. Jerome Audier III, no less. He comes from an upstanding family. Of course she chose a man that's handsome, a bit too cocky, and quite intelligent from what Neville sees of his work... I'd say dashing is an appropriate description. Neville enjoys having him in philosophy classes.

Honestly, Tanya tried to hide her emotions. She locked herself away in her room the day of Aaron's wedding. But Jamie's quite a sport and not one to let a friend remain down in the dumps.. She found a way to lift Tanya's spirits and off they went. There is sadness in our dear girl's eyes I never saw before she arrived here and admitted to being quite finished with Aaron Sands. I had never imagined such a day would come, but she is quickly returning to the bubbly girl of old. You have this Jerome Audier to thank for getting her laugh back. He's the best medicine a girl could have at hand. It's joyous to have our house filled with all these young minds and helping hands. I admit I'm trying to coax her into finishing out her last few years of university here. I'll miss her dreadfully when she leaves.

I hadn't realized how much I missed all of you until she came to stay. My house and heart bubble with joy and contentment. With her under our roof, we have all we need to complete our home, a family, is that not why you married? Tanya has always kept me feeling…young. Should she ask for your guidance in her decision, I hope you will support my suggestion. I think it best for both her and Aaron to have much distance between them.

Ah, time flies. I must run along, take heart in my request. I close with much love to you and your beautifully growing family. You have done well. Honor your path you've chosen for your own life, dear girl.

I've asked Tanya to remain with me, but I sense she longs to return.

Love to all, Aunt June& Neville

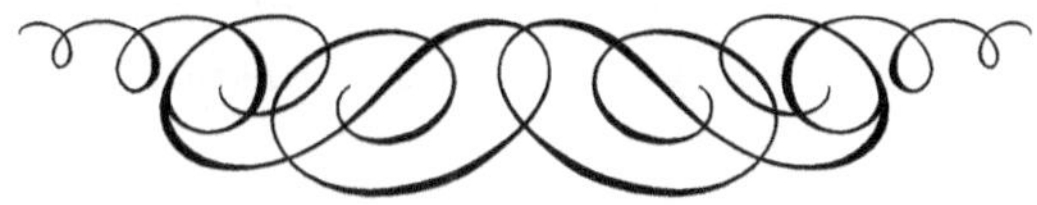

XXXXX

"See," Matthew assured Cecilia as she sniffed and stuffed the letter back into the envelope. "I knew Tanya wouldn't mope over Aaron for any length of time. You worry over nothing; that girl's always been a survivor." He grimaced at his beloved, wondering why she cried. "After all, if I remember correctly, Tanya dumped my brother, not the other way around."

Cecilia crossed to the desk in the den and bound the letter with the postcards she received from Tanya. The fact that Tanya hadn't sat down to actually write told Cecilia she was avoiding her emotions altogether. Knowing her sister as she did, that could be a mixture for disaster. This was the first Cecilia had heard of Jerome Audier, but it brought no surprise. Yet, another indication that Tanya was pushing the past under the rug. Better still, pretending the past had not happened as it unfolded; especially their evening out with Jan Sands. Tanya usually mentioned people in letters once she had decided to keep them around.

The fact that she hadn't mentioned Jerome was an indication that he was simply a distraction from her emotions. Matthew lacked definite, relevant facts, which would prevent him from seeing the situation from Cecilia's perspective. Tanya was right; it was horrid of Jan to extract a promise that forced her to have secrets from Matthew. It built a wedge between her and her husband. Could she allow Jan to do that? Had it been a part of Jan's plan all along? Cecilia turned toward her husband, and the words began tumbling out before she had a chance to stop them.

Matthew dropped to the couch and listened without interruption. When Cecilia finished, he remained in silent contemplation for sometime before daring to speak. He rose without response and crossed to the kitchen to grab a beer and offered to prepare her a scotch and soda. Cecilia gratefully accepted with a deep sigh. Handing her the tumbler of liquid, he nodded, "That explains quite a lot." He sighed and remained standing, resting his free hand on the mantle. "I'd heard your mother had an affair with Father. That was ages ago, I had no idea a child had come of it." He pressed his lips and rubbed his chin thoughtfully.

"So you doubt your mother's story?"

"That Tanya is my sister? No. She looks so much like you, how could it be true? You're definitely your father's daughter." He shook his head. "Still I can see the doubt from Mother's perspective." He glanced out the window for some moments. "If Aaron knew, it would devastate him." He shook his head not wishing to say more of his brother's depression. "Mother's gone too far. How could Tanya do anything different with such an unfounded allegation.?" He slammed the mantle with his fist. "What proof did Mother offer?"

"None. We went to our mother; she neither admitted nor denied the allegations. She simply asked why it mattered... That's why Tanya broke up with Aaron."

Matthew nodded. "I'll talk to Father; perhaps I can get something out of sight."

Cecilia sighed deeply; she hadn't realized what a heavy weight a secret from her husband had been on her. It was a relief to let it go. Matthew's father was a wonderful man, now in the later seasons of his life. Had he always been a good husband, the present predicament would not even exist. Still everyone had problems and growing pains.

The Sands had managed through some difficult times and raised a pair of wonderful sons. "Matthew, I don't want to go back there when you go. Do you mind visiting your parents alone?" He looked at her with a deep understanding of her sensitive nature and respected how difficult it had been to break her promise to Jan. He nodded, his father would understand once they had time to talk.

A Window Opens

Mrs. Gilbert changed under the guiding, supportive group she had joined with Mrs. Cole. She felt loving acceptance she had long ago forgotten. She contacted her brother via post and began a dialogue with him and his wife. She volunteered for meals-on-wheel two days a week after getting home from her factory job. She no longer found a desire to waitress at the local bar and fraternize with the patrons as she had once done when her daughters were at home. She enjoyed listening to the memories of her elders as she visited with them and delivered them food. Some would invite her to come just to visit. She became friendly with a gnome-like man twenty years her senior. He had her read to him from Homer, and he talked her into playing checkers with him and bird watching. She began to laugh again and see the beauty of life as he saw it. He told her tales of the old country—Aachen, Maastricht, Heerlen, Kerkrade, Genk—towns near his beloved city of Luxembourg. Towns he had known well as a young man. Places he had not been since the end of the last Great War. Places he kept alive in his mind. Places still rich in folklore and superstitions. He enjoyed reminiscing about the old stories, the land, and the people. He had been a peddler and antiques dealer once he migrated to New York City. He had enjoyed his shop, his business in New York. It had afforded him visits back to the land he loved after the War. He was happy to share stories rich in folklore with all that would listen.

Chapter 3

I've overcome my fear of holding my head under water for any length of time in order to go snorkeling this afternoon with Jamie. We planned a trip to the Great Barrier Reef. I figure if I've but one life and cannot have one love, I shall make my life worth living. Auntie encouraged us to visit the beach in Hervey Bay; she says it's really neat. It's not as rocky there as much of the northern coast tends to be. We're also considering venturing down to Sydney before I leave, but we've not made any permanent decisions yet. The coast, the rocks, the wind, and the sound of the surf have an incredible soothing sense for me. It's just what I needed to regain my focus and clear my head. Here again I feel close to Evald, even though I cannot walk the mist.

I am focusing on my studies this semester as much as Auntie would have me focus on other things…like Jerome. Auntie is so happily in love with Neville. He makes a splendid husband for her, very attentive in all her needs. I'm jealous he took her so far away, but she deserves this slice of heaven on earth. She deserves all the love and doting he has to pour upon her. She of all people encourages me to get out and socialize, and not worry so about my studies. This is a woman who wrote in her diary that she needed to study more, even though she was top of her class all through school. This is a woman who was valedictorian of her high school class. Obviously, now that she's found true love, she believes everyone should find it. How can I admit I found it and had to throw it away? How can I admit my feelings and thoughts disgust even me. That if I can't have Aaron Sands, then I truly prefer to have nobody. Instead, I agree to accompany guys out on dates. Nothing of serious interest, after all I'm only here for one semester. Auntie reminds me, I don't have to return to Cornell. I can remain with her and Neville and graduate from Brisbane. Such a thought is indeed tempting.

I'm submitting a few of my coastal shots to some calendar companies. You never know. If I get published, that could pay for another semester of school. I realize I have no one to help me through; I have to live the rest of my life on my own. I might as well get used to it and begin saving now.

XXXXX

Dear Diary,

I am so shallow at times. I came here to escape Aaron, escape men and the problems they encounter. Yet, here I am with a perfectly delectable male that Auntie quite approves of.

Jerome Audier, is a British subject from South Africa. Seems a lot of British subjects in Africa send their children to Australia for university. When Jerome speaks of South Africa, I close my eyes and imagine what its like to be there with him. He makes it sound absolutely gorgeous.

Jerome's almost too handsome. I know he's arrogant, but he makes me groan inwardly, an ax andiron with dark, curly hair—almost black—and intense brown eyes. Imagine, a rich, tanned skin, hmmm. Dark curly hair on even his arms and legs and cleft chin. He looks more Sicilian or Eastern European than a British subject. So trim and fit, other girls simply drool over him. Ahh, he even has dimples when he smiles. At six feet and that incredible physic of his, I feel perfectly safe in his company. When we're together, he makes me laugh, a quality I've always found attractive, and yet he has a serious side that draws the admiration of Neville. For example, he's intensely excited with the career of chiropractics. I had no idea how involved and demanding that internship could be. A chiropractor actually has more school hours than any other doctor, save for a veterinarian. Can you imagine that? A chiropractor tries to assist a patience's body to heal itself, with a few adjustments; whereas most doctors turn to medication to heal a patient.

The more I learn of chiropractor practices, the more I'm inclined to choose one over a regular physician. Until meeting Jerome, I had not given the practice any thought. I enjoy simply listening to him speak for hours on end. He has a deep, rhythmic voice, thick with that high English accent that simply makes a girl moan with delight. When he talks of his studies or his family, and especially of his African homeland, you can hear the passion in his voice. He truly loves Africa. It makes me realize what Auntie so often talks about, the opportunity that life offers each of us. Where one door closes, another will open. Painfully, I can say, it may be for the best that Jan stole away my world. Had she not, I would never have been willing to extend my wings to their full expanse and dare fly.

Dear Diary,

Ah, it had to end. I did consider remaining in Brisbane. It would resolve so many difficulties I face in returning simply by distance and time. But last night on the beach, I saw Jerome for what he truly is. A racist. I can't imagine myself spending another moment in his company, much less the next few years. We were all having a nice time at the beach, he had to ruin a wonderful evening by making fun of a couple of blacks that happened to have made a fire near ours. Why couldn't he let them be? Perhaps he would have had not the two pretty brunettes joined the blacks, that really seemed to set him off.

He would make my time miserable if I broke off with him. I've seen what a sore loser he can be. Lord, how embarrassing. Just what I didn't need on this trip. He always has to win, even in a sporting race along the beach with one of his buddies. When he didn't beat Leif in a dash, he insisted on beating him out to the reef and back. Again Leif won. So Jerome couldn't stop. He made a complete jerk of himself by knocking Leif from his surfboard and causing Leif to be taken to the hospital with his neck in a brace. I don't know how bad it is, yet.

I'll never forget how embarrassed and inept I felt for not speaking up about the blacks. I never expected him to be outright cruel. He's so tan, surely someone as dark as he has Moor blood pulsing through his or her veins. His good looks couldn't come from a pure blue-blooded English lineage. It was all I could do to hold my tongue and not get up and run as far from him and the rest of the group as possible. I was so ashamed.

What a mealy mouth weasel I've become. I should have confronted his bigotry, at least in private. Instead I said not a word. Would my speaking up have made any real difference? I'll be leaving in a week; I suppose I should simply leave things as they are. Jamie and I go up the coast, and then I'm bound for Europe before returning to New York. So it's not as if I have to spend more than a day with him, now. Can I hold my tongue and bear him for even a day?

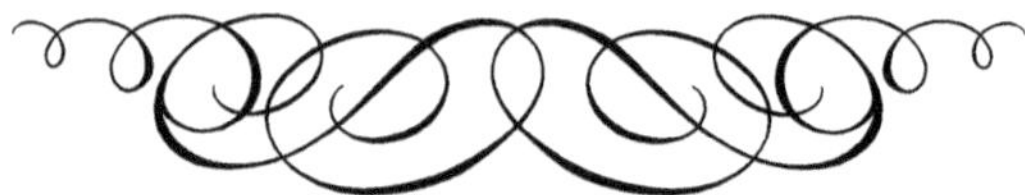

Enduring Strength Comes from Within

Tanya had been in touch with Mrs. Krein to secure a room in the boardinghouse; her room had already been assigned to another, but she could have a room next door. It was a relief to know she would have a place to return to. All she owned fit in her car. It was parked at her mother's while she had been away. She would have to arrange for a ride from the airport to Cornell, and then another out to Mother's to retrieve her belongings. Mrs. Krein wasn't able to pick her up at the airport on the day she was due back, and Debbie was unable to leave the city of Ithaca, due to her phobias. Against Tanya's better judgment she phoned the Sands to ask someone there for a ride. Jan answered and assured her someone would meet her at the airport.

XXXXX

Dear Diary,

Foolishly, I hoped the darkness, which had seeped into my life, would some how dissipate or be exposed as lies and be banished. Of course that was not to be. How can I solve such a riddle when it means I must confront Mother? How can I keep Aaron at bay when I long to be in his company? How can I arrange for him to fall into the arms of another and go on without him? Returning to Cornell from Brisbane has caused a festered wound to be freshly opened. I fear this self-inflicted wound will not easily mend.

*Distance has not faded my feelings, nor has any lingering doubts been lifted. Distance didn't change who I am. What I dream. Memories that had driven me to run… memories haunt me and forever bar me from being with Aaron. M****, of all creatures, speaks of my sorrows. "Aaron was a deep and desperate love that can never be, anymore than you and I could ever be," he admitted to me. I had never considered M**** in that way.*

"Dearest Tanya, you live. Embrace life and you will find all you seek." What on earth can a fuath mean? A memory of what was, what could be. Memories of a… I'm a washed in emotions…sadly, I am alive…even if those very emotions cause me horrific pain. Heartache and self-loathing are part of life, perhaps the only emotions I shall ever know. How could it be different unless I find a way to disprove Jan's accusations.

XXXXX

Closing my eyes and letting the rush of the falls stream over me, cooling my senses, I'm lifted from the heartache of this life. Through a dream, I reach a plane where I can focus, were these visions or dreams? How does a man walk out of them into real time? Is he to be my focus, a way to draw myself away from shadows? Recently, in rehashing an odd conversation, I discovered some of my dreams of him were really parts of his life. I never used to question such occurrences; they were regular happenings. I imagined everyone had similar experiences, but now that I'm in college, and actually confide in others, I'm not so certain. Truly, Roy thought it was freaky that I knew details of his life as if from the vantage of a bird. Would it be acceptable for me to develop feelings for Roy Wilson?

How could Aaron's mother have dumped such a bitter pill and expected me to swallow it? Never will I forget that dreadful night, a night that drove me to run to Auntie in Australia. A night Jan sent me packing. Even now I run. I can't even bear to put my enduring shame to paper.

Oh Dear Diary,

Help me.

*Roy, the man so frequently in my dreams…dreams he admitted were his realities with his high school girlfriend, Thea Rivera. Quite by accident, at least I believe it was by accident, he caught me down at the falls alone. I must believe it was an act of irony, I knew he had followed me that night. Yes, I believe he has followed me in the past, and this time he knew where to find me. Even though we talked, I am afraid at how I'm drawn to him, like two magnets polarized. I fought to slip away from his polarity; his questions I have no answers for. How had I observed his life in my dream state? Of course, M**** refuses to answer me in this question, though I sense he could.*

When Roy and I met in the parking lot behind my boardinghouse, it was like greeting an old friend. Just as it had been when I first encountered that other guy from my dreams on 34th Street in New York City. What an odd chance meeting. That moment, as we stood in the elevator rising up to the top of the Empire State Building…it seemed surreal, as if I expected meeting him in such a way. Sometimes it is difficult to separate dreams from reality. My dreams seemed to constantly unfold, pouring out into the real world. That man spoke to me, but I couldn't find my voice to respond... I was aghast.

At least in this world, none carries into the mist, but can a dream become reality? Am I insane? Did I imagine that night with Jan and Cecilia? Was it a miserable dream that felt like reality…? Perhaps I should call Cecilia and ask. I've come to realize not everyone lives in this manor, so why do I? That night couldn't have been a dream—maybe a nightmare—but certainly no dream. The night my world was shattered forever into minute bits and pieces. The night Cecilia followed me into the bathroom just after I had expunged my soul into the porcelain bowl of cold self-contempt and dared asked if I was okay. No. I wanted to shout. No, I'll never be okay. Instead, slowly I gathered enough strength to open the stall door and tell her I was fine. Fine. What a joke. I was far from fine, and yet all I wanted was to run to my college room and be alone.

Never would I admit my sense of self-revulsion, enmity. Never again did I wish to expose my heart to the world. How could I hide? I'm not independently wealthy. I have to find a way to provide for myself, both in this world and Evald. As much as I long to be alone, alone surely I will die. What I guess I truly seek is anonymity. Where can I find that?

XXXXX

The hills around Ithaca, New York, beckoned her. The Cornell Alma Mater ran through her mind, "…on the shores of Lake Cayuga…," as she wandered upon a wooded path near the Rosen's lodge, hours away from Cornell into Rensselaer or Columbia County, she wasn't certain which. Her mind was adrift; there were similarities to these woods, and the woods she loved, foothills to the Adirondack Mountains. Virginia and the Southern Tier of New York offered foothills to the Appalachian Mountains, as well as the Adirondack. Until she found herself walking alone among these woods near the Rosens' lodge, she hadn't realized she had been so homesick. In contemplation, it was a longing for what no longer existed.

Ithaca sat down in a valley with colleges on two hills. She smiled as fond memories of her college years popped into mind. Tears rolled freely down her cheeks as the good memories melted with the moments of intense heartache. She let it all flow freely; so many years had passed since college. It was time to let go. It was time to move forward.

XXXXX

She let her thoughts wander back to the city of Ithaca, where she discovered a semblance of acceptance she desperately needed. A city satiated her appetite for knowledge; a city that unified her to Roy Wilson. Now, that was all gone. With a measured deep breath, she accepted the memories in the hopes of an overlooked clue. Even back in their time in Ithaca there must have been something she had chosen to overlook. The memories may hold the key as to why someone had wrecked her home three years later and sent her running off with

Chris as her protector. Did it matter who killed Roy? Yes, for Roy was definitely the key.

With all that happened, his grandmother had only told Tanya, "You've moved on, child. Thank you for being willing to change course and reunite with him again, but it was not to be." Beatrice had shaken her head; little got by her. Slowly her relationship with Roy had seeped away. Almost from the moment she and Roy married on the edge of Buttermilk Falls and moved to New York City, it seemed to come undone. New York City, the city where she met Chris Rosen and realized he was more suited to her than Roy ever would be. Not that it mattered; she had married Roy before a pagan minister and would honor her vows despite everything that had transpired upon their moving to New York City. They had no legal documentation of their marriage, but they exchanged vows nonetheless, and that was all she needed. Had she not said as much in the hospital, as his broken body lay in that cold room in a coma?

XXXXX

She thought back to happier times of their lives. Had those college days really only been a few short years ago? It was difficult to focus on the present as her mind drifted back. They had wed the weekend she finished college, back in May of 1986.

"Hey. I have a surprise for you." Roy smiled at her from his bike. Tanya grabbed her helmet and hopped on the back. At Buttermilk Falls, they joined up with fellow students. Ethan Talbot was a certified pagan priest; he loved his black leather biker jacket trimmed with silver zippers and matching boots even in the warm summer. Tanya had never seen him in any other color but black. That day, his long dark hair was slicked back to reveal a V hairline that accentuated his black goatee and mustache. An ancient soul, that belied his nineteen years. He smiled as he took her hands and kissed both cheeks in greeting. "Splendid day for a white wedding."

She smiled at the reference to a Billy Idol song they both enjoyed as she returned the greeting. Tanya happened to be wearing a gauzy white, ruffled, off-the-shoulder peasant top and jeans and black dress boots; Roy was dressed in a white polo and jeans and biker boots. The small assembled group knew Tanya and Roy were bound for New York City. This gathering was full with joy and sorrow, the joy of anticipation, the sorrow of farewell to friends. She and Roy would be moving to Queens within two weeks of Roy's formal graduation form Cornell, thanks to one of Roy's cousins, Mark.

Tanya had roomed with another girl, Rose, in a small one-bedroom in Brooklyn since her early graduation in January. May was a great time to hang out in Ithaca; the trees were blossoming and the sun was bright against the cascading falls. Roy took Tanya's hands in his under the shade of nearby trees as Janice placed a wreath of blossoms around Tanya's head and John snapped a photo. Ethan opened some book of poetry and began reading, "…some people go from…," and then turned to Tanya as he finished. "Tanya, we come together today to witness the profession of love between yourself and Roy Joseph Wilson. Do you solemnly swear to love and honor him as you embark on a life together?"

"I do."

"Do you swear to stick together through thick and thin in the years that lie ahead?"

"I do."

Ethan turned to Roy and asked if he had a token of his love. Roy produced a silver golden band he slipped on her finger as Ethan repeated the vows. "With the powers vested in me as a pagan priest, I do hereby announce you husband and wife," Ethan announced as he beamed at them. "Roy, you may kiss your bride."

Start Again

The first apartment Roy and Tanya shared had been a small one bedroom. A place where Roy taught Tanya to traverse to Evald without the wood or water; he was her leprechaun, and he willingly shared his treasure with her. His talisman was a tiger's eye pendant around his neck. She smiled sadly at the memory; she remembered how amazed she had been at his gift. The gift had been as simple as the amethyst she had long wore around her neck. Lenora shared with Roy something she had never imparted on her younger sister. The talisman each had been given in their youth could be called upon to transport them to Evald now that the talisman was fully formed. Roy had shown her how the talisman worked. She recalled every inch of that dreary place—a gloomy, ugly apartment that Roy had brought it to life. It was dark, cramped, ten-by-twelve-foot bedroom with the galley kitchen opening to a small living area not much bigger than the bedroom. There was scarcely space between the two areas to squeeze in a kitchen table for four, and the bath was just big enough for a full-size tub. The windows in the kitchen and bedroom offered only a brick wall and a thin slit of sky far above as a view. The living room had no window at all. Tanya felt she had entered a dark cave when they went to see the squalid apartment that was affordably priced. She had turned to Roy and whispered they'd both surely die in such an environment. Roy asked her to give him an opportunity to prove her wrong. He had been certain he could coax the place into a haven she would be comfortable to call home. She conceded to give it a try. Under Roy's hand, a tiny, viewless, Queens apartment had been transformed into a palace she enjoyed calling home. Even the super had told Roy if they ever moved out, he could leave his mural as it was. Roy had created a beautiful wall mural for her in the living room, one in which he'd framed into a false French window. He and Mark even hung curtains around it. Roy hid ascent lights behind the curtain rod to give the painting the feel of sunlight. It was a mural of the wood of Evald, near the stream they both adored. Her dancing-eyed leprechaun was quite an artist. The mural felt like a real scene, and when they sat before it with candles lit, Tanya could imagine the wood beyond the glass was three dimensional, not a painting.

Roy's cousin, Mark, lived in Queens as well. He had shown up at their apartment, shortly after they moved in, offering his assistance. Tanya didn't find the slick, sweet-talking Italian very handy when it came to helping Roy fix up the apartment, but he lent a hand from time to time when it came to heavy lifting. He was always the gentleman in Tanya's presence, tall, well-spoken, well-groomed, and dashing with his slicked- back black hair and dreamy blue eyes. "Most women go for

Mark," Roy observed when Tanya confided she felt uncomfortable in Mark's presence.

Tanya shook her head. "I'm not most women. There's something sinister about him, he's…I don't know…sly, gangster-ish."

Roy chuckled as he guarded his thoughts. Darn that discerning heart of hers; it always saw through people. How many times had she ignored it, only to later discover how right she had initially been? He wrapped an arm around her shoulder as they sat on the sofa. "Mark's all right; I've known him all my life." Tanya nodded and let it go. Dearest Roy, how she adored this leprechaun. She leaned over and kissed him as they fell back into the couch. She could never get enough of him. True to his nature, he often made rash decisions that had long-term consequences, like arranging their wedding at Buttermilk Falls.

"What say you to christening every room in our new apartment?"

Roy's eyes were gleaming, mischievous green as he smiled at her. "We could begin right here."

"Sounds delicious." She would tread lightly and keep Lenora's warning regarding the character of leprechauns closely tucked away. What did it matter if she didn't like Mark? That she didn't trust him? He was Roy's cousin; she would accept him. She grimaced. "I guess, he's just too Italian mobster feel for my taste."

Roy smiled and squeezed her to him. "Am I too Irish?"

She smirked. "Never, my little leprechaun." With Roy, she felt protected. Her feelings toward Mark were an ungrounded, unfair.

Roy assured her it hardly mattered. "It's not like we'll have a lot of contact with my paternal family anyway."

She had wanted to believe him. Initially, the contact had been light, though she knew that Roy spent a great deal of time with his family without her. As time went on, he desired to spend more time with his family, and he dragged her into the mix. It became a bone between them, to the point where Roy would trick her into accompanying him.

"You too good for my family," Leo yelled at her one evening.

Tanya's brow rose in shock, as she shook her head. It was near Christmas, and Roy wanted to go for a ride, only to show up for a holiday party at Leo's. Tanya hadn't wanted to go in. "I'm not properly dressed." She was casually dressed in a pink sweater and white corduroy pants.

"You're beautiful, T," Roy claimed from the driver seat. "You don't need any makeup to visit my family."

"Right. Your cousins and aunts wear big hair and have perfectly manicured nails twenty-four hours a day."

He shrugged. "You don't need to impress them. They don't work."

She sighed. "I just wish I looked my best. I could have put on some makeup."

He leaned over and kissed her as he squeezed her knee and smiled. "If I mentioned this party, you would not have come." He was dressed in a pale blue dress shirt, khakis, and his brown bomber jacket and brown loafers. His Sunday casuals gave her no clue that tonight was any different from any other night. His cologne made him delicious enough to eat.

She smiled. "I would be here for you." she assured him as they looked into one another's eyes. "Roy, I love you. I just wish you'd said something."

"So we're here."

His dictator uncle embarrassed her. Never had she imagined herself too good; it was more her sense of danger that kept her at a distance. If Roy saw them through her eyes, he would understand her fear. She saw through the smiles, the made-up hairdos, the layers of makeup. She saw women who were black and blue. Other, women who starved themselves to remain thin. Sadly women who stayed for the money and luxury, not love or devotion.

She saw a reflection of herself alongside these divas in photos; she was "au natural." Simple, a plain, thin country girl, living in the city, not fitting their mold. Leo's daughter, Stephanie, rushed to Tanya's aid and defended her from Leo like a tigress protecting her young. Tanya looked at her in shocked surprise. Stephanie took her by the shoulder and moved away from her father into the game room where the rest of the young people gathered. "Don't mind Daddy," Stephanie assured her as her friend, Dawn, came up along Tanya's left side.

Everyone gathered around and made her feel welcome. "Don't mind Leo," Stephanie's boyfriend, Tony, assured her. "He yells at me all the time."

"Yeah, he doesn't think any guy is good enough for me," Stephanie gave a reassuring smile to Tony. He seemed the prime specimen of a hunk. Thin, brown hair just past well-built shoulders that rippled through his brown, a silk tunic that was opened part way down his chest revealing a well-defined, hairless chest, dark passionate eyes, thin waist, and muscular legs that attested to his hours at the gym. Leo didn't think he would be able to provide for Stephanie in the way she was accustomed. With a body like Tony's, Tanya was pretty certain he would be successful in body building and wrestling. Languidly, his eyes ran over her body as though she wore sexy silk lingerie under her sweater and corduroys. Tanya blushed at the intensity of his gaze. Looking at him, she knew he could have any girl in the room, except for the fact that he was with Stephanie.

Being a country girl wasn't enough for some of Roy's family. "You're enough for me," Roy assured her, "and that's what matters." But he changed over time; she suspected the drugs even before she found them. Marijuana and beer she had always been okay with. After all, one grew in the wild, and the other was a legal substance, but Roy was into things far more serious than either of those. She knew he was in deep with Mark, what she didn't know was how she could hope to get someone out of a situation they were content to wallow in.

Change in the Wind

When Fritz came to New York on business, Tanya confided in him; he was a terrific listener, and she ended confiding all her woes to him. "I'd really like to get out of Queens. Away from Roy's family." She admitted, "With or without him, I like a place closer to the mid-town Manhattan office. I'm up for a promotion there."

Fritz agreed to help her search, and through a work associate he found her a lovely two-bedroom condo just across the bridge, in Brooklyn, on the third floor of a nice five-story brick walkup. Lucy thought she was out of her mind to move anywhere but in Upper or Middle Manhattan. "That may be so," she stated calmly, "but I can't afford a decent place in Manhattan, and I don't want to rent forever."

XXXXX

"My dear American friend, Tanya…the one I've remained in contact with since meeting her several summers ago in the Alps, is in need of my assistance." He wrote to his sister back in Switzerland: "It is well that I took the internship with Shearson Lehman and can spend some months with her. This marriage of hers seems not to be working out. She admits they were never legally married, no licenses. Yet, she is still married in her heart. Even as she contemplates leaving him, it is clear she has much love for this man."

XXXXX

She purchased the condo in Brooklyn and ironically served Roy with separation papers. She had consulted a lawyer, as they had lived as husband and wife and the apartment lease was in both names. Roy had cleaned out their joint savings and checking accounts in retaliation. But she had been ready for such a move and had already moved the bulk of her money to new accounts. Even changing over her direct deposit before serving him. Somehow in his twisted, drugged mind, he believed he could stop her from leaving him by taking the money from her. She shook her head when she received a call from the checking department of her bank. He was out of control.

"Tanya, this is Marlene over at the Queens branch." There was hesitation on the line. "You have a flag on your joint accounts with Roy. I've confiscated his debit card, he left here quite steamed, and I imagine he's headed your way." There was a heavy sigh over the phone. The situation had been unavoidable, as Roy had refused to hear the words "we're through" from Tanya.

"I'll cover any outstanding debts from my personal account, Marlene. Thank you for taking his checking card and calling me."

"Any time, Tanya."

<u>XXXXX</u>

Aaron had shown up and offered to assist Tanya in her move. "How did you know?"

"Mother mentioned you bought a place of your own."

They chatted while he built bookshelves in an alcove off the living room. Aaron redesigned the counter separating the small, galley kitchen from the dining area, an area that openly led into the living room. By raising and widening the counter and purchasing a couple of bar stools, he transformed the counter into more efficient space. He built her a double waterbed frame with a bookshelf headboard. She listened to his woes of married life as she painted his handy work. She encouraged him to work things out with Tessa.

After all the years since that fateful night out with Jan and Cecilia, during times like these, Tanya still longed to open up and divulge the truth to Aaron. Let him know that despite their mutual attraction for one another, it could simply never be. If she couldn't confide the truth to him, she should cut the connection between them. She thought of all the times, she had tried to cut contact over the years; somehow they always made up. Looking through her journal it was clear she had traveled half the world away to hide from Aaron, who was the first person she saw upon her return? In truth she desired his companionship as much as he sought her out. Neither seemed able to live without some contact with the other. They were bound together as if a ship was tethered to an anchor. How could she sever the ties without damaging them both? How would Aaron take it if she could bring herself to share the secret and break her promise to Jan? A promise she should never have given in the first place.

Aaron laughed. "Do you ever take your own advice? You believe marriage is sacred, and I should work things out, and yet you're separated."

Tanya nodded thoughtfully, blushing ever so slightly. Should she admit to him what she had not confided before…that she had never legally married Roy? "I'm in danger by staying with him," she admitted with a grimace.

"Danger?" Aaron furrowed his brow. "He's hurt you?"

"No. Roy would never physically hurt me. It's the people he runs with I fear; it's his drunken mouth that gets him into trouble more and more frequently. I fear his drunken escapades. I fear the drugs he's taking. I fear his paranoia and his binges." She frowned. "He's embarrassing to be around when he drinks." She confessed shaking her head, "He never realizes when he's had enough. He's detrimental to my career. He's dangerous to drive when he's drunk." She hesitated, should she confide to Aaron how Roy had tried to climb out of the passenger seat of her Mustang as she drove to Mark's garden-styled brownstone apartment in Queens a week ago? Her shoulders slumped, as she recalled the trip to Mark's a week ago. Roy had screamed out the window he was being kidnapped late into the night as she drove through empty streets. No, he may not be physically dangerous, but he was cause for alarm.

XXXXX

"Lordy, Mark. You've no idea how embarrassing it can be to drive with him so drunk in the car." Tanya admitted breathlessly as she leaned against the doorway to Mark's apartment. It had been a struggle to get him to Mark's door and ring the bell. Mark stepped forward and took Roy from her arms as he fell forward into a beige living room. Dumping Roy unceremoniously on the sofa, Mark turned back to the door as Tanya turned to leave. "Hey, T. Wait up," he called as he rushed down the hall after her. She planned to leave Mark to manage his pathetic, drunken cousin.

She glanced back over her shoulder, wishing she had made it to the door. "I'm always afraid he'll climb out while I'm driving," she confessed. She turned away and wiped a tear from her eye. Mark reached out and grabbed her upper arm. She stopped short and turned to gaze into his liquid brown eyes. "What's the rush?"

"I can't deal with Roy like that. Why does he have to make such a spectacle of himself anyway? Why doesn't he learn when to stop?"

With a sigh Mark shrugged. "He's a drunk, T. Didn't you realize that before now?"

She shook her head. "No. He never got like this at Cornell. He drank, but not to the point that he made a fool of himself and everyone else." Mark grimaced as he put a comforting hand on her shoulder to guide her out. "I'll call you tomorrow."

She nodded and moved to the door.

As she drove back to her apartment her mind drifted to her relationship with Aaron. It had been tenuous from the day she returned from Australia. Their feelings were always in check with a smoldering desire just below the surface. Both clung to frivolous excuses to maintain contact. She should never have allowed the relationship to continue. Her mind raced to Lucy's advice that she should get him out of her system. Of course she had never shared her secret with Lucy. But Lucy was right; she needed to put distance between them if she was to have a life with anyone else. Never should she have given him money for a down payment on his house in return for the room over the garage. It was simply a means of antagonizing one another under the guise of generosity. Did they enjoy causing one another misery? Neither seemed willing to sever connection, it seemed inconceivable as they had family ties to one another and a history of friendship that seemed to endure.

The man she had fallen for in college had understood that. Roy had been so sweet, so understanding, and accepting. She recalled the night she had run to the falls from Jan and Cecilia. He hadn't pressed her; he had offered his warm jacket and strong shoulder to lean on. Roy had warned her so many times about seeing Aaron; both marriages suffered a barrier caused by unresolved sentiments. She and Roy had even broken up in college over a visit from Aaron one weekend. Ironically, it had been the weekend she talked Aaron in to returning to his wife, giving the marriage a real shot by opening up with his wife, as he opened up with her. She and Roy had made up.

"Oh Roy, forget Aaron. I know it seems there's something between us, but believe me, there never can be."

"What's to stop you?"

"Lord, Roy. We're related. Aaron's more like a brother than a suitor."

"I don't think he knows that." She smirked as she kissed him and moved around to massage his shoulders. "He exudes charisma around every woman he knows." Roy leaned back to stare into her eyes, as she moved her body into line with his as they kissed. He reached to caress her thigh, and soon Aaron was all but forgotten. Even so, slowly, that man she had fallen for in college, the Roy she adored, disappeared as he became entangled with his New York City relatives. The man she often came in contact with now was a total stranger. More often than not, this man was someone she chose not to be around. She knew she was equally responsible for that distance between them. What seemed uncertain was how could they resolve the growing distance between them? When would he see it had nothing to do with Aaron?

She should reveal to Aaron the true reason she broke up with him all those years ago. Why she had thought half a world would be enough distance to make Aaron forget her for another? If she could bring herself to share the ugly innuendos with him, surely he would understand. Understanding would set them free. Free of the hope and desire that had bound them together and threatened all other relationships they would cultivate with others.

Roy begged her for a second chance. "Come on, T. Don't shut me out."

Her heart swayed with his pleading for another chance even as she sensed he was high on some drug she was unfamiliar with. "Wow, this is a two-bedroom condo. How did can you afford it?"

She shrugged. "I'll manage. If it gets tight, I can take in a roommate,"

He smiled. "Could I be your roommate? I'll take the extra bedroom if that's what it takes, hon. Give me another chance."

"I'll think about it, Roy," she promised with a serious expression.

"Aaron's been here, I see. Did he help you pick this place out?" He tried to contain his paranoia. "Did you buy this as a love nest with him?"

She grimaced. "I bought this place on my own, Roy." She turned away as her face blazed with color.

"Right." His jealousy flared as he looked around. "I see his handiwork, T." She could hear the pain in his voice when he spoke again. Pain she caused by continually interfacing with Aaron and keeping her secret from both men she professed to love. "I would have built shelves for you if you'd let me, T," he pressed.

Lord, he was too clever for his own good, she thought to herself. In a flash, his face darkened as their eyes met. In taking the promotion, she would be spending more time with her friend, Lucy. Lucy and Roy seemed to vie for Tanya's attention. From the moment they met they seemed to antagonize one another. Lucy would want Tanya to spend a Saturday afternoon horseback riding, where Roy would want her all to himself for a Saturday afternoon. He didn't like the thought of the two girls going out dancing while he worked the late shift. He realized she had taken the promotion in Manhattan. "So now you'll work in the same office as Lucy?" He gazed at her as if seeing her for the first time. "You took the promotion to Manhattan?" He shook his head. "When were you going to share all this with me?"

Eyes flashing, she faced him. "When you pull yourself together and return to the man I fell in love with." She cried. Shaking her head, she continued, "Lucy has nothing to do with this move. Neither does Aaron. For your information, Lucy and I will be on the same floor, in separate offices." Why tell him she had a corner office to herself on the fourth floor? Taking a position in the mid-town Manhattan office on 3rd Avenue was definitely a step up for Tanya. Should she mention to Roy that it would have been foolish to pass up? Why mention the raise that afforded the condo in Brooklyn?

He shook his head as disappointment crossed his face. "She doesn't like me. The more you're with Lucy, the less we get along." She grimaced as she realized he would not accept responsibility for the problems that had developed since college were between them and had nothing to do with other people.

"Lucy has nothing to do with our problems." Narrowing her eyes, she hissed at him, "I don't know you anymore."

He stood staring her down with a face full of anger for a moment, before crossing to the refrigerator, looking for a beer and finding only water. She didn't even have a can of soda. From their first meeting at college there was always someone between them. Before Lucy, it had been the close proximity to Aaron. God only knew how she wished to be done with those tempestuous feeling. She had to force those emotions away and build a life without Aaron in it. He was a proud man, not one to take rejection well. Still, he was Tessa's husband, she acidly reminded herself for the umpteenth time. The down payment money she had given him for his house had been a gift, just as his coming to fix up her condo had been a gift in return. Over the years, it seemed natural to pick up the phone and chat and sort out life's curve balls via long distance. They advised one another on relationships, investing, and where to go hiking or fishing. Sitting back on her heels, she suddenly found it ironic they should bounce relationships off one another. She truly wanted his marriage to work; it let her off the hook.

Had she not recently encouraged Aaron on ways he might show his affection for Tessa in a meaningful gift? No, Tanya never honestly intended to use the room over the garage of Aaron's home. It had been an excuse for her to give him money. At least Matthew and Cecilia and even Lenora would have a place of their own to stay should any of them choose to visit Lockwood in the future. She had found the condo in Brooklyn with Fritz's help, not Aaron's. Aaron hadn't seen it until she actually had the new locks put in and the keys in her hands. She loved it especially because it was away from "the family" in Queens. Proof to herself she could make it on her own, without a man or family near at hand. Tanya leaned against a doorway, remembering why she and Roy were no longer together.

XXXXX

Recalling how she came to be alone—truly alone—she had grown tired of Roy's family connection, drugs, and mostly, of his drinking. Now she had no husband or lover to share her life, no family to have over for a cup of tea and bemoan her problems. No familiars like a cat, dog, or horse to comfort her when she felt isolated. Here in this big city, she had few friends, lots of acquaintances, and a calendar of social events. It was meaningless. Her emotions were buried deep beneath the smiling surface. Roy had been the only one really close.

Chances were good, now that Aaron knew the truth he would simmer down,, but nothing would ever be the same again. So much had happened in so short a time. Still she hadn't imagined the relief she now felt in simply disclosing her long-held secret. She had freed them both. Now that he shared her burden, he would seek answers. She had fractured the invisible barrier, cementing it into a permanent wall. Now, she could see him as she never had before, a childhood sweetheart. Someone she no longer had much in common with outside of family. Civility would be easy, after a fashion.

XXXXX

The accident happened within days of Roy's decision of reconciliation with Tanya and separation from his family. Who could guess it would be an accident he never recovered from? That one incident led up to a chain of events that brought her hiding in Chris Rosen's apartment, altering her life's course. Leading her into hiding with Chris, first at his apartment and then at his family's "cabin." It had been the catalyst in her final break from Aaron Sands. Would she ever have broken her promise to Jan had she not been under stress? Tanya doubted it; the intense shame and self-loathing she had carried for years now seemed to have been washed clean. And yet those very emotions had maintained her silence. Once the feral cat leapt from the bag, there was no recapturing it; it was done. As she watched Aaron walk down the street, she realized she should have released him long before he married Tessa. The knowledge she had just dumped on his shoulders would have made a difference for him and his wife. Was it too late for him and Tessa? Tanya had no way to know. Perhaps now he would no longer hold back; she had made it clear they could never have the sort of relationship he desired. She stood at the rail for sometime after Aaron was long gone. A sense of peace she had not known since moving to the city settled over her.

XXXXX

Looking honestly at her relationship with Roy, she had to admit the last year had been marred with drunken escapades that left her dreading ever becoming emotionally entangled with a man again. She had not chosen well. She laughed bitterly at herself as she thought, *A childhood sweetheart who was perhaps a half-brother. A college sweetheart obviously imbalanced and now very dead.* Perhaps her girlfriend, Cheryl Towne was right, "One-night stands and goodtime friends were the safest way to go." That was Cheryl's philosophy: "Never let a man weigh you down." She was forever coaxing Tanya to cut loose and let the past go. "Nothing too seriously intimate to leave ones nerves and emotions painfully raw," had been Cheryl's advice.

Cheryl was no bones; she would do whatever it took to get to the top of the corporate ladder, and no relationship would get in her way. Tanya admired her honesty and moxie; she was certain Cheryl would indeed be a vice president or CEO at some point along the way. All of her efforts and good looks would definitely pay off. "You just need some great sex, girl." Cheryl would insist. Tanya smiled; great sex was Cheryl's answer for most problems.

"Really, Cheryl, and how does one experience great sex without attachment?" She didn't want to feel so deeply again. Tanya considered attempting to experience Cheryl's lifestyle. She wanted to forget Roy. Forget the embarrassment of Martha's party. All those business acquaintance who had been on hand at her moment of embarrassment. The party that had been the topping on a toppling cake. She had gotten Roy into her Mustang and drove him to Mark's brownstone. She squeezed her eyes closed tightly, not wishing to dwell on the memory, the embarrassment. She wanted to forget her pent up desire for Aaron Sands. Forget the frustration she experienced when looking into Roy's glassy, drugged-up eyes. Forget his paranoid voice when he thought someone was following them or when he yelled from her car windows that she had kidnapped him. How could meaningless sex help her forget?

Cheryl was speechless for a moment. Then she laughed, as if she had had a few to drink. That slow, smothering smile that wrapped men around her finger in a teasing manner. She had had nothing to drink during their lunch together. "Oh, T, you slay me." she pronounced patting her on the back. "Surely, you've had sex just for kicks." She laughed. "This is New York."

The last was stated as if sex were a pre-requisite to some business class Tanya had forgotten to sign up for. How could she admit to this worldly woman? "No. I'm not a native New Yorker."

Cheryl threw her head back and laughed. Sitting back in the chair at the outdoor café, Tanya raised her brow and looked surprised. How many times had Roy cautioned her she used the term friend too loosely? She had associates, or acquaintances, but in the city one had few friends. As she looked across at Cheryl, she suddenly understood what Roy met. A friend would stand by you, not laugh at you. Cheryl was an acquaintance. In the two years they had worked together, Cheryl would rattle about her escapades constantly. Tanya would occasional share an event in her life; they had talked at length in her effort to find a place of her own. But as Cheryl met her eyes, Tanya accepted just how different they were.

So much changed after the department party at Martha's home. Roy had gotten so drunk; he and Martha Ames had been, arguing over something so trivial no one could even recall the point. He had gone to the bathroom and come out, into the middle of a room full of her business associates without his pants. He was spouting to Martha, who sat on a sofa in another room. Jonathan Hardy and Lucy Scandura had recently arrived. Normally, their arrival would give Tanya a sense of joy and relief. Two dear friends she felt herself with, dear Lucy… the small Italian princess, who managed to whip people into their place with her take-charge attitude. Tanya adored horseback riding with the petite, trim, and muscular beauty who had curly red hair, doe-like brown eyes, and a sincere, wide smile. When Lucy smiled, her face lit up and made those around her smile as well. With Lucy, she was certain to have an enjoyable time, no matter what they decided to do together. However, this day would be an exception; there could be no joy for Tanya at this particular party.

The house felt as though it would close in upon her. She couldn't breathe from the heaviness on her chest. Her eyes met Jonathan's as she saw the door just beyond him and bolted. She'd successfully made it to the safety of her red 1984 Ford Mustang convertible. Roy found his pants, followed after her, and pounded on the passenger window until she relented and let him in. She took him to Mark's apartment and left him there. That moment was an eye opener for her; she never wished to feel so mortified again as long as she lived. If that was the life Roy offered, she wanted no part of it. The following day, she began her silent search for an alternative place to live. For his alcoholic binges alone, she should have declined his pleas for a second chance. She had wanted to believe he had dried out. That he wanted to be given a second chance. Perhaps had she stood firm on the separation, no one would have trashed her beautiful home, and she wouldn't be in hiding. She had little doubt Roy would not have altered his path had they reconciled or not. She had passionately loved the man she had met at college. She had lost that man when she agreed to move to New York City; he had buried that aspect of himself to return to the "family fold."

The life Roy desired was a life of acceptance, a life apart from her. The life he desired had not been one she had imagined existed beyond the realm of books and TV shows. It had been the reason she had moved away from him and their Queens apartment. She had moved away from the lifestyle he offered. Roy had been livid when he went to clean out their joint accounts only to find they had low balances. She had been making minimum direct deposits for months, just enough to pay her share of expenses. Why had she agreed to let him move into her condo just days before his accident? She had been willing to take him back.

After Aaron's visit, it seemed fitting to give Roy a second chance. If she thought Aaron should work on his marriage, shouldn't she rekindle the love and passion she and Roy had shared? Roy seemed excited to join her in Brooklyn, away from his family, away from the lifestyle that had destroyed their relationship. How could she deny him? Did they not share a fantasy world of their own in Evald? A world he sought out less and less, but still a world they shared. Was that not something most people only found in fairy tales? People of the twentieth century didn't really believe such a place existed. They no longer believed in fairies, elves, and wizards. These were all stories of old. She listened to his worries as he cried; she assured him even as he claimed he couldn't escape.

"Is this not the land of the free? Are you not your own person?"

"You just don't walk away from family."

"You mean you don't walk away from Leo," she clarified. He nodded.

"Your mother did. She took you away from them years ago. I know you say she's crazy, and I admit she's a bit off, but she kept you away for a reason." She continued her argument but saw his face hard with decision. "You have your mother's relatives. Your paternal grandmother, she shared with you the wood. That sets you forever apart from these people." Roy looked into Tanya's soul as she spoke, for a flash they again touched on mutual terms. "That's the part of you that attracted me, held me." The conversation faded away as the phone rang. Roy lifted the receiver when he heard Mark's voice on the other end. In reflection Tanya wondered if Roy would still be alive had he not insisted on a second chance. Had he not pushed to move to Brooklyn with her? Tears swam her vision as the weight of responsibility descended on her slim shoulders. Was she the cause of Roy's death? How could she ever be certain she was not, and if she were the cause would the Wilson/Ceiro's family come after her as well?

Walking Backward

Closing her eyes, she lowered her arms as exhaustion overcame her. She lay face down on the boulder; the stone was cool against her cheeks. She was thankful Chris had taken her to the Adirondack's for a few days.

Until arriving, she had not realized how much she missed the wood. Still, she was miffed with Jonathan for having packed her off with Chris for her own protection. Surely, there were other options they could have come up with. She didn't want to recall the incident at the club that had brought her to the Adirondack's with Chris. Looking around, she realized the day was slipping away, but she was too weary to move. Here she lay in hiding from the world as she sorted through the recent past. Chris knew these woods well; surely, he would find her if he chose to look. He seemed to understand she needed space, and thankfully, he had some work to occupy his day. Her thoughts were still jumbled. Her tossed condo had not been a welcome sight to return to after her dreary trip. The trip was meant to offer answers and a semblance of peace within her soul, but it had provided little of the solace she had sought. She had kept busy with her sister's children, and helped out where she could at their farm. But she had found little time to sort through her thoughts, emotions, and journals for answers, signs warning her of such and outcome while visiting family. She simply hadn't been as ready as she imagined she would be to resolve Roy's death in her mind. Would the nightmare she had entered the moment she gazed at Roy comatose body lying in that cold, comfortless-looking bed never come to an end? When she memorialized Roy only a week ago, she had imagined all was over, finally she would be truly free of his problems—his family.

Now she would have to sort through her life and continue on truly alone with no husband to share her secret life. There would be no sisters to romp through the wood of Evald with, as they had turned away as if that life had never existed, no parents to offer guidance and comfort, no dear maiden aunt to lean on, no dear Aaron to turn to, no familiars, and no fuath. Her father and brother were long gone. Her sisters and aunt, even Aaron, had lives of their own apart from her and apart from Evald. Could she go on without equals, without love? Earlier in the day, M**** had denied her passage into the mist of Evald.

"You must clear up your life in the realm of humans before entering Evald again," he had said as he stood in human form upon the path.

What life could there be solo in any realm? She cried aloud in a voice full of self-pity. *What purpose does my life have if I'm to walk alone? I'm not an elf or a fuath. I'm a fairy, and fairies live in groups.* She longed to understand M****, but his riddles no longer made sense. It was as though her trauma had caused her to lose the ability to even communicate with a fellow Evaldian. Was she losing her mind? Or simply had she lost touch with herself?

Had it only been a week ago that she imagined Chris Rosen had been a captivating boy toy? Chris had been a man to flirt with in passing, someone to hug and kiss on the cheek, not someone to consider introducing to your family—not Prince Charming riding to her rescue. She sat up, as straight as if an arrow had hit the boulder from underneath her, as she realized a contented, faithful wife would not audaciously flirt with other men. Alas, she had not been a contented, faithful wife for sometime.

Lord, forgive me. Roy, if you hear me, where ever you've gone, forgive me. I lied even to myself. I'm so sorry I never truly committed to you. It had been a slow death for their marriage, the straw being Martha's company party. He had known of her sorrow. Known her attachment to Aaron. Too attached to truly be completely Roy's, and he had accepted that. He had loved her more than she had ever deserved to be loved. She recalled him once saying that it was a fairy's nature to love more than one. She had not argued with him, simply filed it away. Had that been her mother's case? Were male fairies different than female ones? She now understood Aaron; he had been right. Roy had never truly been her equal, and yet he had been a match. Certainly, a more appropriate match than Aaron Sands. Alas, she and her sisters would not be the first fairies to fall or to mate with a human. Many a fairy did mate with humans, and of those, many were faithful throughout their human's life. But then fairies aged slower than humans and lived longer lives. She, like her sisters, was but half-breed; some were faithful after a fashion, but all had a propensity toward nymph like behaviors. She had always curtailed her own sensuality as she had grown up around religious-minded people and did her best to honor their beliefs.

XXXXX

Hesitation

Mark stood in his father's dimly lit office next to Stan, "the Mouse," Lemowitz, with his hands clasp behind his back, facing his father. He recalled being a young boy, no more than twelve, and his father catching him and the neighbor girl playing "show me yours." This wasn't anything like that time; why did it pop into his head? Leo sat back in his crimson-colored leather chair behind his oversized, mahogany desk with a half-smoked cigar in his mouth. He was clearly angry at their failed attempts to recover his "misplaced assets."

"Lemme get this straight…my son failed in his attempt to recover the misplaced merchandise so you thought you'd *chat* with the girl, and she'd confide in you?"

The Mouse cleared his throat nervously and nodded. Leo chewed on the cigar and rolled it around his mouth, clearly in disgust. Mark had laid a key on the edge of his desk and believed it held the answer to the lost disk and money. Leo nodded thoughtfully and then rose to his feet and leaned over the desk to stare into his son's eyes—eyes so like his own and yet not.

"What good is a key without the box it unlocks?" Mark didn't respond. If he did, surely his father would go after Tanya with unexpected force. Mark was certain Tanya was innocent; she had no idea what Roy was involved in. Leo turned to the Mouse," and in that instance, the Mouse was grateful for the dim lighting and fearful of the dark wainscot woodwork that covered soundproof walls, and the fact that this office featured no windows. He only knew of one entrance and that was blocked by two of Leo's soldiers. "What did you imagine could be accomplished by daring to confront her on her own turf with a cop bodyguard friend hanging around?"

"If I had managed to get her outside, I know she would have talked." The Mouse assured Leo.

"She doesn't know anything. If she does, she doesn't realize the significance," Mark insisted again. Leo narrowed his gaze in disappointment of his son.

"Being sweet on your cousin's wife isn't helping your cause."

Mark took a deep breath, forcing the color away from his face and gritting his teeth to keep from breaking his father's nose. In his mind, he saw his fist impact with that arrogant face he had once so respected and had recently come to loath. Despite his thoughts, he stood military straight, looking past his father at some unforeseen spot on the wall behind Leo, his face devoid of all expression. This bothered Leo more than a physical assault would have. Leo sucked on his cigar and glanced down at the key. With a heavy sigh, he rocked back on his feet. What were they to do now? The girl had gone into hiding; he would go with his son's instincts on this one situation.

"Forget the girl. Bring me the merchandise, I don't care about her."

Mark glanced into his eyes, a nod that equated to a bow, and grabbed up the key. "Thank you, Father." He backed away from the desk; it would be detrimental to fail his father now. He dare not turn before reaching the guards, who stepped aside to let him and the Mouse' exit.

XXXXX

Dear Diary,

Lenora warned me that the difference between Roy and my nature would eventually have a negative impact on me. I guess I always knew. It didn't matter at college, but once I began climbing the business ladder, it did matter to me. Our imbalance hurt us both. I wanted Roy to change, but I was never willing to release Aaron and commit to Roy. I never accepted I had to change. How horribly unjust I was to Roy. I ignored his leprechaun nature, where he saw my flaws and accepted me despite the fact I didn't accept him.

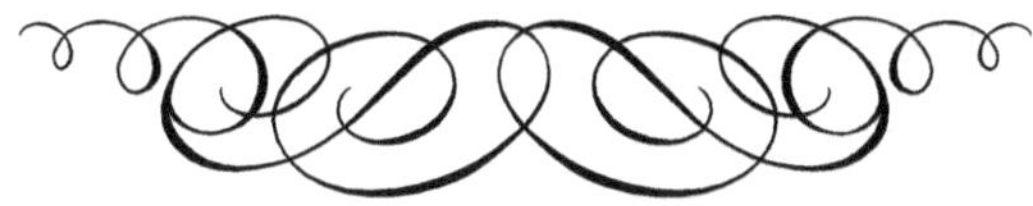

XXXXX

Until the night after Roy's death, she had held out on the hope that she could somehow disprove Jan's accusation. She gave herself a rye smile and hit her forehead with the palm of her hand. "Lord, I've been ignorant." she said aloud. "I had as close to equal in my grasp, someone like myself, and I misused him under the hope of being permitted to love a human.

A human." Bitter laughter emitted from her lips, as she recalled her conversation with Lenora.

She recalled her own scorn for her sister when Cecilia had chosen to marry Matthew Sands Junior. He was a dear but still only human. It had been a time when she claimed she couldn't give up the mist, she couldn't forgo Evald without feeling she would be betraying their father. "I would have had to give it up for Aaron Sands." She now admitted to herself. "After all, he is a human. A man who would never accepted that part of *me*."

She sat and looked around, beckoning M****, but he did not appear. How could she have deceived herself so completely for so long? What a *fool* she had been. Jan had done her a tremendous favor that night so many years ago. She had made Tanya's life's choice for her, and Tanya had been too stubborn to accept the choice made until this moment, alone in contemplation far away from it all.

Now, here she sat daydreaming of captivating Chris—her rescuer. Once again she had needed saving, and happenstance provided a man willing to whisk her to safety in a remote family lodge. Now, she would be sleeping under the same roof as Chris for who knew how long. Was this man father material? Marriage material? How could she even consider such a questions. Her mate wasn't even considered cold yet. Ironically, through Lenora's urging, she and Roy had agreed from the very beginning to never have children. Until now, she had imagined she never wanted children. It hadn't seemed right; Lenora had been correct in her statement: a leprechaun should not sire the children of a fairy. Roy was not her equal. They came from the same dimension, but they were not of the same kind. Now, she had been barred from her true home until something changed. Even her perspective of Chris was skewed.

How could she trust her emotions? They had led her to Aaron and then to Roy. Neither man had been a proper match. So how could she be certain it would be any different with Chris? Suddenly, Chris took on a whole different light. He had offered her shelter and safety in his beautiful family lodge while Jonathan did his best to sort out her troubles back in the city. He would certainly be better off if she remained hiding in the wood, away from him and his beautiful lodge.

When had everything gone awry? The more she learned about Chris the more appealing he became. A few days ago, she may have agreed with Cheryl about simply needing sex, but somehow she knew she couldn't have sex with Chris without emotional strings. He had admitted in his apartment the strings would be mutual. Was she truly ready for that? Unsure, she had escaped to the serenity of the woods; she feared the intensity of her emotions, feared the answer that came to mind even as she thought of the question.

XXXXX

After Roy's service, she boarded a plane to Chicago with Beatrice and Roy's ashes; she packed up several years' worth of journals and called Cecilia and arranged a visit. His family had been furious when Beatrice insisted on cremation so that she could take his ashes back to Sacramento with her. Tanya didn't see the harm, but she didn't share their religious beliefs that seemed to forbid cremation. She couldn't recall Roy ever stating he had been against the practice.

From Chicago, she bid Beatrice adieu as she took a connecting flight to Wisconsin. She needed a place to reflect as to whether or not she should remain alone in New York or move closer to her sister now that Roy was gone. After all, what ties did New York have on her? A job, no family, few friends. She could find employment anywhere. She imagined by sifting through the past journals that she would have a perspective on her life and from that she could glean a direction for her future. By week's end, Tanya had found no clear answers in her journals or in her heart. She had been unable to focus. She was restless at the farm, and realized she enjoyed the interaction she achieved from living in the city. Wisconsin was too flat, the wood seemed too thin, and it was a different sort of quiet. Perhaps, she had been away from the country too long, at least long enough to realize she had no yearning for the farmlands of Wisconsin despite her affection for her sister. She enjoyed the city almost as much as she enjoyed the wood of Evald.

May 15th, 1986

Dear Diary,

Admittedly, I'm a basket case blowing in the wind. So pathetic. Finally, I've pushed Aaron away for good. That's probably one good thing I should have done ages ago. I dream of Roy nightly… In my dreams, we've made amends, and he's quite alive. I'm losing my mind. One minute I'm dreaming of picnicking in the woods with Roy, then he fades into Chris. I never anticipated Chris. What a wrench in the spokes at the wrong time.

Cecilia wishes me to stay at their farm for a bit. I can't imagine what I'd do for employment. I can't live off my relatives. What life could I carve out here as a single woman? I've no desire to wed a farmer in this clear-aired country. Honestly, I missed the hustle of city life in just the few days I've been here. I have a life of sorts in New York, a place of my own, friends, and a decent job. Now, that Roy's gone, Cecilia thinks I should consider starting fresh. She hopes I'll settle here. I don't think so. Of course there are no memories to cloud my vision here. This is wonderful country, but I feel no connection…it will never be "home." So what should I do? Where should I wonder? Evald seems empty. I need a mate or a clan. I know Roy was not my kind, but loneliness breeds strange companions. What my sister must think of me with a fuath and a leprechaun. The only companion they did approve of was the owl. Why should it matter to me? Have they not turned their backs on our ways, our heritage? If they were in Evald with me, I would not have sought companionship elsewhere.

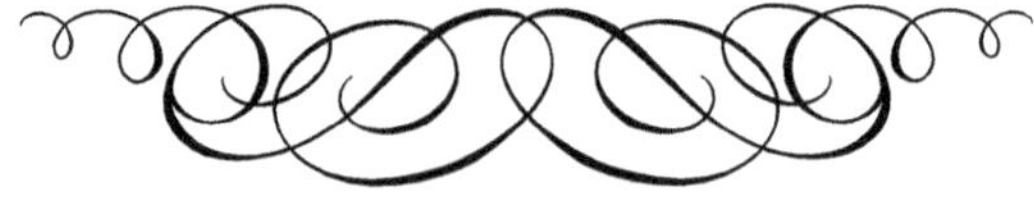

For her, if there were no other fairies in Evald, she would just as soon remain in the city life of New York. What difference would it make if she were to live alone in Evald or alone in New York City? Either way her life would lack purpose as she had once had, no longer did she look forward to the dawn of each new day. In both places, she had a place to call her own. The city offered her a job she enjoyed, friends, and acquaintances. Evald offered a similar situation. But what mirth could there be without sister fairies to sing and dance and flutter about, companionship? Ah, that was the key to her life. Cecilia seemed sad to say goodbye on the porch of her rural, white farmhouse. Matthew was kind enough to drive her to the airport, through miles of fields just beginning to flourish with the spring wheat and vegetables. As they drove the narrow, windy road through the vast farmland, Tanya realized the land was much like the farms in Evald that she enjoyed gazing at from a distance. She rarely crossed the river near Gosymonity to wander through those fields and look into the small farmer's cottages or drift down to the music of the small village. Sometimes, usually during a harvest moon, men would play their fiddles in the moonlight. The raucous of dancing and singing would draw her and her sisters into the torch light to dance with drunken men and laughing maidens. Ah, those rare occasions when few could recall accurately the days that followed. Those same farmers would leave slices of fresh bread on the windowsills or a bowl of fresh milk on the back stoop for the brownies who assisted in caring for the farms. They would leave small bundles of wheat or fresh vegetables near the river for Nateria at harvest time, thanking her for a good crop. The owners of these vast Wisconsin farms did not believe in brownies, pixies, fairies, elves, and fuaths. They did not leave offerings on the back stoop. They believed all their successes and failures were their own. No. Wisconsin was not a place Tanya could see herself calling home.

Facing Facts

Now her thoughts turned to her latest dilemma; having her condo trashed while she had taken a few days at Cecilia's farm after Roy's funeral. Whatever someone had hoped to find, they apparently hadn't. Or perhaps the scary man at Cahoot's was unrelated to the break in. Perhaps, he was a freak who took interest in her for his own sadistic reasons. Cahoot's had been a place where she had felt safe, now anywhere she turned could be invaded. The recent past seemed interwoven with her life, and all roads led to her current predicament. Had Jan not taken her and her sister out that fateful night, never would she have fallen into Roy's comforting arms. She raised her fist in frustrated injustice. Had she been foolish to finally unload Jan's secret on Aaron? Or should she have done it years before? Aaron could be so unpredictable. He had caught her at a most vulnerable moment. A time when she felt it all had to come to an end, her future unclear. Darn Jan Sands. Tanya could be living a ho-hum life similar to Cecilia's had Jan not thrown that wrench in the works. Had that one event never happened, Tanya would never have waded into such an emotional and mental quagmire. Contentedly, Tanya would have been bound to her high school sweetheart, living this moment as his wife, a life similar to that of Cecilia's. A life being lived by someone else, ironically, someone who did not fully appreciate what she has. Was it truly considered separation when one never legally married in the first place? Was she considered a widow? Not really—even if the lawyer had drawn up separation papers. They had never bothered to get a license to legally acknowledge their vows.

XXXXX

How was Jan living with her innuendos now that Aaron knew all that Tanya knew? Had Aaron run straight home to let on that Tanya had spilled the beans? It was a relief to realize there would be no more games of cat and mouse with Aaron. No longer did she carry the heavy burden of an ugly secret. He finally understood why she ran halfway around the world years ago. Why she had encouraged another woman to grab him in her absence. Why she ran off to the big city after to college. Why she hid in the arms of another. No, she no longer needed to run from Aaron. In that respect, her conscious was clear. Perhaps he should have been told before; it would have been easier on his marriage. Until she had spilled the ugly mess at Aaron's feet, she hadn't realized what a burden it had been to carry for almost a decade. Now, in retrospect, she could see how it had affected her life choices. It had been wrong to have maintained the secret as long as she had, wrong and unfair to both herself and Aaron. Now, they were both free of its poisonous effects. Had fear alone shoved her into the arms of yet another man? Was it another fateful mistake? She shook her head and sat up. No. It had not been a mistake, she realized as the vision of M**** barring the way to Evald came back to her. What was that all about?

Certainly, the situation had spun out of control, she and Chris seemed much too comfortable with one another. Yet it had not been too fast for M**** to bar her way alone through the mist to Evald. He hadn't forbidden her entry, she suddenly realized—he had forbidden her to pass alone.

An Unwelcome Homecoming

The flight from Wisconsin had been long and tedious with a long delay in Chicago, and then a harried cab-ride to her condo. From the moment she stepped into the airport, she had imagined how wonderful it would be to soak in the deep tub and forget all her troubles. Instead, she entered her condo, rooted at the door as she gazed at the havoc in the main room.

Instincts took over, as she stood frozen in place.. She couldn't bring herself to cross the threshold of her own home. She picked up her suitcase she had set in the hall and turned around, retracing her steps down the hall. Around back she found her car unscathed, and popped the hatch for her luggage, then she slid into the driver's seat and left. It was too early for Cahoot's to be opened as she stopped at a payphone in the lobby and called Jonathan's house. His father didn't expect him back before his shift at the club. Tanya decided to go through the kitchen and see if he was around. She found Chris and Frank taking inventory. One look at her, and Chris turned to excuse himself with Frank, and he ushered her into a booth near the bar of the club. "Wow, T. I've seen you look a lot better," he said shaking his head at her disheveled hair, loosely pulled back in a brown ribbon. She was shaking in a wrinkled knit purple and brown floral top, baggy brown slacks, and brown flats.

She couldn't help but smirk. "I'm looking for Jonathan. Do you know where I can find him?"

Chris shook his head as he glanced at his watch. "He should show within the hour. Can I get you a bite to eat?" Raising his brow. "Help?"

She shook her head. "I just need Jonathan," she repeated urgently. Chris leaned back in the booth, his arm across the seat, casually. He narrowed his eyes and really looked at her.

"Okay. How about I get you a sandwich and a drink, and you tell me what's up." He waited expectantly. She glanced around the empty club, subconsciously folding her arms across her chest and rubbing them as though she felt cold. She barely nodded Chris getting up and leaving, until he returned with a turkey club on fresh-baked rye bread and a cranberry soda water with a lime twist the way she liked it.

She took a sip and smiled at him. "Thanks." She pressed her lips and looked down at the sandwich with the dark green lettuce peeking from under the edge of the bread; she couldn't eat. She expounded a long breath before beginning. "Someone tossed my condo." His interest was piqued. So much for the newly installed security system he and his cousins had installed in her absence. How had it happened? "I just got back from Wisconsin this afternoon and took a taxi from JKF straight to my condo. I opened the door…" She shook her head, staring down at the plate as tears welled in her eyes. "My place is a mess. I couldn't bring myself to go in." She added as she fingered the sandwich. "I picked up my suitcase from the hall and walked away. Thankfully, my car was untouched around back in my parking space." She smiled at the irony of her car having no alarm being unscathed. "I hadn't even covered it while I was gone." She shrugged. "I didn't know where to go." She seemed so forlorn; he slid around to her side of the booth and put his arm around her. "I drove straight here." She looked up into Chris' eyes expectantly; he sat thoughtfully for sometime afterward.

"Excuse me." He slid from the booth and went out back to talk to Frank. Frank phoned the police; they would send someone down to talk to Tanya. He put in a call to his apartment and left a detailed message for John and Steve about checking out the security system on her place. He narrowed his eyes, as he looked her over, she had been so stressed from Roy's accident, and subsequent death that she had probably forgotten they had installed the security system just before she left. Later, Jonathan accompanied her back to her condominium where a couple of local police met them and walked her through the disheveled rooms. After taking a cursory inventory and finding nothing missing, Tanya went back to the club with Jonathan in silence. He bought her a stiff gin and tonic and left her at her usual table with several of her coworkers. While at the condo, she had changed into a sapphire blue dress that gathered on the hip on the left side, and captured the blue of her eyes, and her small feet now encased in navy sling-back pumps. She would look stunning despite her frazzled nerves. Jonathan stopped speaking to a police officer in mid-sentence as she entered the living room where they stood. A shy smile played across her face when she saw him gape as he gazed in her direction.

She apologized. "I hope you don't mind. I've been in that outfit since early this morning. A fresh outfit always energizes me with a different perspective." She should have chosen a less attractive dress for an evening at Cahoot's after the trip and break in, but it seemed a great way to put the situation in her control.

The Walls Went Up

They had slipped into his place quietly one night a lifetime ago. She had been in a stress-induced fog getting out of the cab; the last few hours had sent her mind in overload. As she trudged up flights of stairs behind him; his hand firmly tugging her upward, ever closer to his third-floor apartment in lower Manhattan. Her emotions had been on overdrive all evening. By the time they climbed out of the cab outside his apartment building, she was numb, drained of emotion, and cold to the core. Her mind couldn't envision anywhere safe; she simply followed instructions. First Jonathan's instructions, then Chris whispered instructions. They had climbed in a taxi; Chris leaned forward and spoke to the driver in a low voice before leaning back to put a warm, protective arm around her. She had slid, shivering with fear, against the warmth of his body. Pushing aside his leather jacket, so she could feel the warmth and security his presence offered through his crimson-colored, linen dress shirt. She had needed the heaviness of his arm around her shoulders as she pressed closer for warmth for security. She remained silent as the taxi sped to lower Manhattan to an area she was unfamiliar with. Her mind was in a fog of confusion. He slid out ahead and paid the fare before reaching in the backseat to take her hand and pull her from the cab. He ushered her across the street, whispering something encouraging in her ear, as if he were explaining something to a child. "I have two roommates. You must be quiet, and you must stay in my room." He guided her up three pale stone steps next to a storefront, which was flush with the sidewalk; she had glanced at the thirties-styled storefront without registering where they were. This was supposed to be her shelter from an emotional storm? Why did it feel as if she jumped from a flaming oven into a boiling pot? Stay in a bedroom with the object of desire?

Glancing up at him, something like panic registered on her face, she pulled slightly away only to catch the cab's taillights as it turned to the left and out of sight further down the deserted street. Numbly she registered what he had said in the cab. "Spend the night in your room? Where will you be?" She looked fearfully at the gothic building made of stone and plaster six-stories high. It was a narrow building meshed between a high, rectangular brick building on one side that hosted a restaurant, set back away from the side walk to provide a wide portion of sidewalk covered with a green-and-white-striped awning. The place acted as an outdoor cafe on nice days. On the opposite side was a wide cement structure that appeared two stories higher than his building and appeared to be all apartments.

He smiled as he took her arm. "I'll be right beside you." She hesitated as he opened the lobby door and ushered her in to the small, dimly lit foyer, and opened another door into a wide hall. The place had a bank of mailboxes to the left of the door. The floor was in serious need of a good cleaning but appeared to be spotted black and white tile; the walls were equally as dirty. Tanya longed for a bucket and rag even to dare touch the door handles or rails.

"I can't spend the night with you." she said pulling free from his grasp with a painful cry as she, belatedly she clenched her side as she winced. Chris turned and grasped her upper arm, supporting her as she doubled over due to the shooting pain. They stood still for a moment in the small foyer as if she had slapped him. He raised his brow.

"I didn't realize you'd find the idea so revolting." He seemed to be genuinely insulted by her response.

Blushing she sputtered. "I'm sorry; I didn't mean to sound that way. I'm grateful, really." She glanced around looking for words that would not come. "Do you think Lucy or Jonathan will come get me?"

He shook his head. "Not tonight." Chris searched her face, "T, you'll be safe here," he raised his hand as if a boy scout, "honest."

"Safe? How can you say that?"

He shrugged. "I have two male roommates, and I'll be right beside you." She felt her face burn betrayal as she imagined spending a night next to this enticing man. She stepped back, slowly shaking her head. Chris looked past her out into the wee hours of morning and sighed. It had been a long night. "Look, Tanya, it's really late, or very early." He glanced at his watch. "It's nearly four in the morning. Would you like me to get us a hotel room?" She pressed her lips and shook her head. He nodded. "Right, it's not a time to be looking for options." He placed a reassuring hand on her arm, and the other on the handle of the inner door, "You're safe. Jonathan knows that."

She looked up and searched his eyes, nodding. Through the door she found herself in a short, narrow hall with trash barrels lined up down one side. He led the way up the dimly lit stairway, the upper half was painted dark beige, and the bottom half was painted a glossy, bubbly brown. She did not dare touch the rail. Each floor sported four doors down a short hallway, two doors on either side. On the forth floor there were only two doors, one on either side of the landing. Chris explained as he stopped outside a purple door to pull a set of keys from his pocket and place one in the lock. "This floor and the fifth floor have only two larger apartments each, where the lower floors had four small apartments. The top floor is a huge apartment." He raised a finger to his lips before opening the purple door to his apartment.

She managed to smile and shrug. "My dad always told me every rain cloud has a silver lining…sometimes we just need to look," she whispered as they stood in the hall.

"Where does your dad live?"

"He's dead."

"I'm sorry."

She shrugged. "It's okay. He's been gone a long time."

"And your mom?"

"She lives in Lockwood." When Chris raised his brow curiously, she added, "It's a small town upstate."

"It's in New York State?"

With a smile she continued. "Have you ever heard of Watkins Glen?" He nodded. "Lockwood's about an hour southwest of there," she added as she scanned the walls and threadbare hall carpet of some nondescript dark color. There was dirt along the edges of the walls and the runner down the middle of the hall, the floor was painted brown lacquer that should be shiny but seemed dull. It appeared someone damp mopped the edge at some point, but on a whole, the place lacked a through cleaning. The lighting was poor at best, perhaps a 55-watt bulb where a 75-100 watt was needed.

"Ah," Chris responded as he opened the door. She wondered if anything was ever replaced or maintained well in his dilapidated building. Did he notice it was in desperate need of a good cleaning? Maybe it was simply not as important to a man as it was to her. Still she couldn't imagine Roy living in such squalid surroundings; the two of them would have committed a few Saturdays to cleaning the passageway if nothing else.

"Do you have reliable heat in the winter?"

He looked puzzled and smiled. "Yeah. We don't complain."

She smiled. "Nice door," she remarked as Chris stepped through the dark purple door. He smirked as he realized she meant the color, the only dark purple door in the building. At least her sense of humor was intact.

He shrugged. "It helps when you've had a bit much to partake and forgotten what floor you're on." It was good to hear her chuckle softly into her hand; he smiled at the sound of her stifled laughter.

"I really enjoyed the solitude and tidiness of my Brooklyn condo," she admitted as her face crinkled as if she would cry again. "I don't know if I'll ever feel safe there again." She managed to keep her voice down as she lightly stomped her foot on the thin carpeting of the hallway. Alarmed he reached out for her waist as he glanced across the narrow hall and down the stairs. They were so close, she felt his breath on her face as she noticed his long, beautiful dark lashes; she glanced down at his other hand on the doorknob. She held her breath against him as she imagined counting the slight sprinkling of freckles that graced his nose or running her hand through his blond highlighted, spiked hair.

She drew in a sharp breath. "Chris." His eyes riveted to rest in her large, intense blue orbs; her face was filled with apprehension as her tongue slowly wet her lips, and her breath was uneven. He forgot the code to the alarm as his eyes followed her tongue. He cupped her chin gently in his hand. "It's okay," he assured her softly, as he pulled her inside, and she leaned back against the wall and closed her eyes. He was drawn to her lips; they melted against his own hungrily, as his mind exploded with a sensation of her jumbled emotions. Alarm overtook his senses, how was it possible for him to feel her emotions? Instinctively, he wanted to break free from this embrace he had initiated.

The emotion he felt from her reminded him to set the alarm code; he pulled away to punch in the numbers with the door still ajar. His attention was riveted to her; as they kissed again, he pulled her so close they seemed to meld together as they sank into the kiss. His heart almost stopped beating as long-buried images and feelings awakened within his very soul. He never wanted to be apart from the woman in his arms again. He guided her into a man's lair with his lips locked in passion that was met with an equal explosion of fervor on her part. Reluctantly, he released her from an embrace that had scarcely allowed either to breathe.

Tanya's mind was reeling with a sense of yearning she had never before experienced from a kiss. Her emotions were making her lightheaded; it was difficult to focus as she brought a hand up to shelter her eyes from the light. As she took in the room, Chris doused the light and released her hand to cross the room to the bathroom. She felt so unbalanced when he released her she almost sank to the floor. Brown, marbled Berber carpet covered the entire floor, and an old gold-colored sofa and chair faced away from the door toward a large black television on the entertainment center between two large, high windows. The windows faced the sofa, and provided ample daylight, when the heavy, dark drapes were open. She smiled at the shelf above the valance, laden with dusty trophies from various sports. The sofa and chair separated the living room from the kitchen counter and stools and left a sufficient space to maneuver to the bathroom from the doorway. A brown recliner and end table were parked before the hallway to the bathroom, directed toward the television, and past a small round wooden kitchen table with four chairs to the right of the door was a wide counter, which led around to the kitchenette. A A large bowl of half-eaten popcorn, magazines, and debris that appeared to be discarded clothing tossed about here and there. The place needed a good once over, Tanya thought as she looked around for a place to leave her shoes.

, She turned to whisper to Chris, "I can't imagine anyone climbing all those stairs to break into this place."

Chris smirked and took her hand. "Neither can I. I'm part owner of a security systems company," he admitted. "I might as well test my own product line." She was taking in this revelation as he led her down the hall to his bedroom. *Why hadn't he told her this before her trip*, she briefly wondered. His room next to the bathroom. To the right of the hall were two closed doors; the one directly across from Chris was practically covered by a full-length frontal view of a voluptuous, brunette pin-up poster with a lavender background. Chris' door held a view of the Swiss Alps in a white plastic frame. The third held a poster of Mickey Mantle of all things. Tanya shook her head in amused relief.

"I have to use the facilities," she whispered after stepping into his neat but crowded room. He nodded, as he brought a finger to his lips. "Do you have something I could sleep in?" Chris opened the narrow closet behind the door to his room, and emerged with a roomy red cotton single-pocket t-shirt on a hanger. Tanya took it thankfully, glancing at him in surprise as she estimated the shirt would be loose even on his frame and slipped out of the twelve-by-twelve-foot room. She could scarcely move inside that room. A twin bed was tucked below a high ceiling with gelded crown molding painted white against spring green walls. Halfway up the wall over his bed was a shelf mounted to the wall; floor-to-ceiling bookshelves covered the wall to the left of the door, and a window seat past the closet was covered with books and papers. It felt like an overstuffed library. He had black speakers mounted in two high corners of his room, and a big white fan-globe light suspended from the center of the ceiling. Chris turned the fan on low to circulate the air; he stood back and watched her take in the confines of his room as he hung his blazer up in the surprisingly large closet.

Tanya slipped from his room to change. When she didn't return Chris padded down the hall in bare feet and tight, black cyclist shorts with a navy blue t-shirt that fit him snuggly. He used the bathroom without completely closing the door. Tanya sat on the sofa with her feet up, her head resting on her arms across her knees. No chance he would forget she was there.

She had considered sleeping on the sofa, but it was lumpy and uncomfortable. She wondered how long he had been standing over her, the light from the bathroom outlining his silhouette. The painkillers the doctor had given her at the club had begun to allow her exhaustion to take over as she leaned back into the sofa. Her limbs felt too heavy to move.

She managed to smile up at him sheepishly, a flutter of color to her cheeks. He held out his hand, Tanya weakly lifted a hand, glancing about the darkened room as he pulled her gently to her feet. She gasped as she entered his room, as it was a blazed in candles. Her eyes scanned the room, nervously in the gentle candlelight. Familiar volumes of books on the shelves: Piers Anthony, Tolkien, Creighton, Jakes, Asimov, Clancy, Demille, Dickens, Shakespeare, and Dante, just for starters. Names that made her feel at home, beloved friends. Her eyes fluttered across the golden letterings of the spines. She glanced at Chris as he leaned against the doorframe watching her, watching the way the candlelight played in her hair.

"I never would have guessed," she admitted. The soft music from speakers fluttered to her ears— "you wanna man with a slow hand…"

"I'm a multifaceted man," Chris responded with a nonchalant shrug as he stepped into the room and quietly closed the door. She ran her tongue seductively over her teeth, unconsciously, as she glanced toward the shelf over the desk. Grimacing as he crossed his arms, he was almost certain she had no idea of her own attraction.

"I thought you once told me your only job was the club." She moved back to the window seat again.

He shrugged as he stepped near her. "It's my only job. The security business I own with my partners"—he shook his head— "it's not really a job." He smirked; as he stood so close, her senses were overwhelmed by the scent of his cologne.

"You must do okay."

He nodded, pulling her away from the window seat toward the bed. She tried to ignore how tight the black biker shorts were so form-fitting to his body. How intoxicating she found his cologne. Could she restrain her desire to caress the sandy hair that curled on his legs when she lay beside him? She closed her eyes and imagined lying next to him in a bed of leaves, the sun glistening through the tree branches above them. How soft the sandy blond hair on his freckled arms would be under her fingers. *Ahhh.* "You wanna a man with an easy touch…" belted out from the speakers.

Oh, she recalled past moments in her car, just how easy his touch was. *No.* she told herself, as her eyes flew open. At present, she was in the wrong frame of mind. The t-shirt he had offered her fit like one of Lucy's miniskirts. She hadn't really considered before tonight how much taller he was to her. It seemed he was just the right height for her to wear heals, and still look up into his eyes, a good two inches taller than Roy. Not as tall as Aaron, just shy of six feet she guessed. *Captivating Chris,* she thought. She and Lucy enjoyed coming up with names for men Lucy dated—Delightful Dalton, Dancing Drew, Jovial Jonathan. Even though Lucy hadn't dated him, they had deemed Chris "captivating." Chris leaned past her and pulled back the blankets and spread, Tanya glanced behind her and stifled a desire to cackle.

California Raisins danced across the sheets lighting the electricity between them. Chris smirked as she dropped to the bed. "My sister, Stacey,, bought the sheets as a gag," he explained.

She nodded. "Your string of conquests must find them amusing."

He sat down next to her, narrowing his gaze at her. "Actually, women usually take me to their place," he quipped. She realized instantly she had unintentionally offended him.

"Chris, I'm sorry." Tanya pressed her lips together. "I'm honored to be here. Really, you've gone above and beyond tonight." She blushed, deeply, feeling off balance; she had always imaged him a playboy. She thought of the times they had gone to after-hours bars; he had always been a teasing, tantalizing flirt. Once Lucy had joyfully announced all too loudly among their group of friends at Cahoot's that Tanya and Roy had separated, Chris made it clear he wanted her, but he had never been too pushy. He nodded, as he moved the covers back further and removed his shirt. She closed her eyes, swooning over the desire to run her hand through the tempting sandy blond hair at the nape of his neck; she dared to reach out and run a cool hand over the muscled shoulder blades as she imagined how it would feel to have her lips buried deep in his throat; she felt the heat of his chest against her cheek without even touching him.

"Chris, I…" Her eyes cast around the room looking for words to conquer her desire. Clearing her throat didn't seem to do any good; the emotions stirring inside were beyond her comprehension. Would anyone believe she had not really known any man before she had partnered with Roy? How could she tell Chris she felt incredibly guilty? Additionally, she was afraid to rush into the arms of another man. Surely he, like Lucy, would expect her to have been more adventuresome, more experienced. He would be sadly disappointed, better she not give him the opportunity to find out. She was embarrassingly naïve for a woman living in New York City, having Roy was like having a protective blanket. From the moment she had reconnected with Chris Rosen, she had struggled to keep him at arm's length.

Admitting only to herself, she used Chris' buddy, Jonathan, to keep a wedge between herself and him. She introduced Jonathan to her Suisse friend, Fritz, when he visited New York. Jonathan knew Fritz had assisted in her home search and in fact had found the condo for her. Fritz's business associate that had sold her the condo simply assumed she was Fritz's girlfriend at the time. Neither had bothered to correct the man. Jonathan had also met Aaron, her high school sweetheart when he helped her move into the condo. The guys had gotten along so well, Jonathan had offered to stay and lend Aaron a hand with the entertainment center, which left Tanya time to organize her bedroom. Lucy had assumed Aaron enjoyed coming for more than lending Tanya a hand, and Tanya had never deterred her thoughts. Was the knowledge of other men in her life a deterrent for Chris?

It had been far simpler for her when she had thought of him as the club doorman. Perhaps it was snobbish, but she couldn't bring herself to date someone who didn't earn as much as she did. At twenty-four, she still imagined she would eventually like to marry, and when she had a child, she desired to stay home. That objective had always swayed her in whom she chose to date.

Now, here she was with "Captivating Chris"—the club playboy. Chris smiled as his hand rested on her cheekbone; he read the apprehension in her face as he bent close, their lips met as her nostrils delighted in his scent—masculine sweat mixed with cologne. Her tongue hungrily sought out his as she lay back and felt him slide her gently against the wall as he moved beside to her. They fit so naturally together. Tanya could simply let one step lead to the other, uncomplicated. Instead, her mind cried out for her to move away from him. For her to stop.

Her body and her emotions told her to go with the flow. The twin bed adequately accommodated them; she was weak with desire, for the scent of him she had no desire to be separated from even an inch of him. She relaxed as she lay beside him, her leg intertwined with his. She delighted in the feel of his silky leg hair against the smoothness of her skin. Still her mind cried out as she pushed against his shoulder with the heel of her hand. He pulled back to meet her gaze. His reputation preceded him; should she ignore it, even though he seemed incredibly sincere? She saw desire burn in his eyes, the desire enflamed them just as if he had ingested a narcotic. She knew her own desire burned as intensely as his, a desire that had been there since the first moment her eyes had rested in his. She reminded herself men were ruled by the physical. She didn't sense any insincerity, but what about his reputation. Did it matter? Even as her mind cried out for her to stop, she had been lost to him the moment they had reconnected in this incredible city—a most unlikely place for her to find such a man.

"Your eyes are incredibly blue in this light," he whispered as he kissed her. She closed her eyes for a moment after they stopped kissing. Phooey with her emotions; the emotions of a fairy would always give her away. She knew from glancing at herself in mirrors in the past that her eyes were ablaze of unnatural turquoise blue from desire. It seemed this man could read into her soul.

In retrospect, the odds had always been piled against a lasting relationship with Roy. There were barriers between them from the start. He was a leprechaun and she a fairy, causing a barrier in Evald. Aaron had never left them alone, even when he had married another. A foolish man who believed he should have cake and pie on the side. Finally, she was done with Aaron Sands. And now this man who was so tantalizing to every sense she possessed. Why this man? He raised his brow in surprise, and she realized she had spoken aloud.

"Are you okay?"

She forced herself into a sitting position, and sensing the shelf just above her head, the music flowed over her and through her. "I'm hot blooded, check it and see…I gotta fever burning inside of me… come on, baby, can you do…" He reached up toward her shoulder and rubbed gently, moving his hand across her narrow blade, she felt the warmth of his hand through the cotton material, as if there was no material at all. She moved into his touch, as he had rolled over on his back. "Come on," he urged, softly, his voice filled with desire. She shook cobwebs from her head, as she ran a hand through her hair, dropping back against the pillow, a part of her longing to run. Run from the desire this man stirred inside of her. Beside her, he took a long, deep breath, his hand resting on his diaphragm, exhaling slowly. "Okay," he said, opening mesmerizing dark, passion-filled eyes to the ceiling. "You win."

She waited and watched him a moment, scarcely breathing, before slipping down beside him and turning on her side to take in every inch of his profile. Her hand naturally came to rest on his chest, feeling the thump of his heart with the gentle rise and fall of his breath. Without thought, she pressed her lips to his cheek. He smiled and turned his face toward hers, something about her seemed as innocent as the other side was flirtatious; she closed her eyes, nuzzling his neck, almost purring as she did so. He rolled on his side, scooping her into his arms, smelling the shampoo in her hair and the lingering scent of her perfume. His right hand glided down her side to rest on her hip. He smiled as he gazed into her resting features she had fallen to sleep, snuggled against him. Exhaustion had won out.

XXXXX

Tanya freaked as she opened her eyes in a strange room with Chris snuggled beside her. It was difficult to breathe; it was as if a stack of old dusty hardbound books lay on top of her chest. Nothing seemed familiar; her left side had a dull throb to remind her of the previous nights events. She glanced in disbelief at the clock on the corner of the bookshelf as she sat forward, gasping from a shooting pain up her side. *Ten in the morning.* The night's events came tumbling back into focus as she rubbed her eyes and looked again. *Lord, it had not been a dream.* Here she was in bed, half-dressed with Chris. Gazing down at him, she felt herself calm; she felt secure rather than embarrassed. A chill ran over her, she wanted nothing more than to snuggle up against the man who had been so chivalrous the previous night.

She recalled having promised she would not to leave his apartment. Those painkillers must have been potent because she never imagined sleeping away an entire morning. Glancing down at the man beside her, she tentatively ran her hand through the blond curls on his chest as he sleepily stirred and rolled over on his side, throwing his right arm over her thigh. She was drawn to him, desiring to slip back beside him and nestle against the warmth and security his body offered. He smelled so delicious last night; it had been difficult to deny their mutual desire. His eyes fluttered open, and he sat up and gave her a sleepy kiss before rising to pad to the bathroom. When Chris returned in nothing more than his biker shorts, she could have leaped on him and devoured him where he stood stretching just inside the door. Instead, she rose to slip past him and headed for the sanctity of the bathroom. "Hurry back. I have two male roommates," he growled. "T, you don't want to be in the living room with nothing more than my t-shirt on."

With a sigh, she examined herself in the mirror. She was tempted to remove the neat, white wrap around her ribs, but the pain prevented that move. Chris had been sweet; as she glanced about the bathroom, she realized at some point during the night he had brought her wet clothes into his room to hang on the door to his closet and doused the candles and the stereo too. While he had been in the bathroom the night before, she had cleaned off the window seat with the idea of curling up there. Chris clearly had other ideas. She quietly went back to his room. She had slept well and felt better than she expected, but she could easily take in a few more hours of rest.

He opened one eye to gaze at her in the dim light streaming in threw a crack in the thick red velvet drapes. "Good morning," she whispered, sitting on the edge of his bed. *No, it would not be a good idea to snuggle up next to the lion.* He rolled over on his back and pulled back the cover, encouraging her to climb over him. He couldn't resist reaching up to assist her as she slid across him. She paused as she straddled him; she smiled down into his eyes, as he wrapped his arms around her. They kissed good morning. It was chilly in the room, and he felt so warm and snuggly. She felt his body respond through the nylon, biker shorts. He smiled at her as she slid gracefully across his body. He rolled over to face her, his eyes lit with passion, as his hand slid up her arm and moved to her breast. She closed her eyes as she ran her hand up his thigh not thinking, just responding to his kiss, his touch. She rubbed her foot through the curly blond hair of his calf as she moved closer. Her body desired nothing more than to be one with his.

The sun peaked through the slit in the heavy crimson drapes of his room and felt over his handsome features. She swooned as the caresses stirred up unbound emotions and responses from her body. Then her mind took over, and she pulled back.

"Chris, it's after ten in the morning. We've missed the best part of the day."

"Tanya, it's Sunday. And we're enjoying the best part of any day."

Her eyes widened as she got his meaning and smiled. "I can't lie around all day."

He gave her a devilish smile. "We can have a lot of fun right here."

"Chris. You're incorrigible."

"So?"

She looked away, he could feel the flutter of her heart, feel the heat of their mutual attraction. She forced herself to steady her breathing before she dared speak. "Do you have a pair of sweats or something I could wear around the apartment? I promise I won't leave, but I can't stay in bed with you."

He rolled off of her with a sigh. *What an impossible woman she could be.* "Why?"

She took in a deep breath and shrugged, "I…" She pressed her lips together, her eyes searching the room for words she couldn't grasp.

Chris flopped onto his back. "I'm rushing you," he moaned.

She sighed and nodded. "I'm rushing myself. I'm the one who kissed you. Sorry." She felt foolish for desiring him and then pushing him away. How many times had she been angry with women at the club for teasing guys and leading them on? Here she was doing the same thing to a guy she had been into for sometime, even if she had refused to admit it.

He turned his head to look at her and smiled. "I liked it. Want to try some more?

She chuckled softly. "Honestly, yes. But do I dare?"

"Tanya, we didn't even get to sleep until after four this morning. Stay. Rest."

Shaking her head. "I've had enough sleep."

He stared up at the ceiling. "Four hours? That's not enough for me." She smirked.

He knew she wouldn't relent without coaxing. "Okay." He rose and rummaged through his bureau to pull out a pair of gray sweats with a drawstring. She smiled at him as she reached for them gratefully. Then in one swift motion he had her in his arms, pinned under him on the bed. She felt the crush of his lips on her mouth; the sweats fell from her grasp and slid to the floor, forgotten, as she was swept up in his warmth against the chill in the air and delighted in his kiss. Her tongue trailed along his jaw, to his ear, and down the soft hair of his neck, as he rolled next to her. Pain shot through her side, alerting her mind, as she felt the heat of his kisses trail down her neck, she pressed the palm of her hand against his shoulder as she took in a sharp breath. He pulled back in alarm, seeing her curl in pain. Shaking her head, she gasped for air as she felt the cool, hardness of the wall against her back.

He winced and dropped back against the pillow. "Sorry." She forced herself to uncurl and lie next to him as her hand traced the light, sprinkling of hair on his chest.

"Chris," she whispered his name as she faced him, her breathing labored. Hot tears stung her eyes and dropped onto his stomach, he looked at her with frustration, his eyes so dark they were almost black, and he slowly exhaled.

He reached up to push the hair from her face. "The pain?" She nodded, as she breathed shallowly for a moment.

With a sigh, she moved to look into his face. "I'm just not ready." He rolled over away from her as she extricated herself from his bed and stood on wobbly legs. She retrieved the forgotten sweats as Chris watch her clumsily tug them on.

"You're a tease." He hissed angrily, his eyes flashing.

She closed her eyes to him, shutting him out. "I don't want to be. I'm so confused." She wailed softly, dropping to the edge of the bed beside him, shaking. "God, Chris. I'm so sorry." She slid to her knees and knelt next to the bed, facing him, reminding him of being a small boy. His grandmother coming into the boys' room at the cabin, having them all kneel and say their prayers before going to bed. Tanya reminded him of the land around the cabin. The smells of the woods seemed to linger in his memory whenever she was near. She looked beseechingly into his eyes, bringing him back to the moment at hand. She seemed so forlorn, he felt almost guilty he had pressed for a part of her she wasn't willing to share. He reached out to touch her cheek with gentle fingers. Would she believe the only other girl he had ever brought back to this room was his ex-girlfriend, Rita Schultz? He knew his reputation held her back. Admittedly, he had slept with to many women for his own good.

He had gone through a spell where he had wanted to treat them all as Rita had treated him. But that had changed since Tanya, watching her at the club, spending time hiking or horseback riding, his thoughts had changed. He recalled a conversation he had with Lucy.

XXXXX

Chris recognized Tanya after the first few times she came to the club. He wondered if she had made the connection. He had a difficult time understanding her friendship with the playful Princess, Lucy, she often accompanied to the club. She and Lucy couldn't have been a more unlikely pair. Lucy was all city; with that hard city attitude, and sexy attire. Tanya was soft, lady like, trying to fit into a city she was clearly not born in.

"Tanya doesn't seem like your sort of girlfriend," he admitted to Lucy.

Lucy shrugged as she smirked at him. "Why?"

"She doesn't look like a clubbing sort of girl."

Lucy tossed back her full red mane and laughed. "She's not." She admitted, "But she will be. Do you think she's too conservative?" He nodded with a smirk. "She's great once you get to know her," Lucy assured him, and she had been right.

He nodded doubtfully. In retrospect, he admitted he would not have let Tanya in without Lucy. But as she adjusted to the scene, she came dressed for the part to the point where Lucy borrowed her clothes. He and Lucy had been riding side by side on a trail in Central Park at the time of the conversation. Tanya was farther ahead, chatting avidly with another girl from work, Linda. The two women didn't seem to notice they were well ahead of their companions. Linda had always reminded Chris of an accountant or attorney. Short, bleached blonde hair, with dark roots—big lips, heavily rouged, that sorority girl persona. The sort of girl who wore braces throughout high school and often still had bad breath. She had been quietly having an affair with a married local radio disc jockey she and Tanya had met at a Halloween party the year before.

Lucy laughed when he had asked if Linda was an accountant. "She does work in the accounting department of our office," Lucy admitted. "She and Tanya get on well for some reason. They enjoy talking about investments and how to best build up their next eggs or something." Not something that would interest Lucy; she left those things to her father to manage. She turned to him with a flirtatious smile. "T always makes a person feel accepted." Narrowing his eyes, he thought about her comment before responding. Tilting his head to one side, he realized she was right.

"That she does," he admitted, thinking of his surprise when she first agreed to join the gang after hours.

"When I'm down, I talk to her and come away feeling things will work out."

He nodded, completely understanding Lucy's sentiment. It had been clear a number of times that Tanya didn't like something Roy had done, but she stood by him. She didn't like watching her friends leave the club with strangers, and yet she accepted their decisions and their friendship. He recalled times when others around her would verbally bash someone; Tanya would usually find something positive to say about the person. How often had she silenced him for making fun of some poor slob? Last night she had really been afraid. For the first time, she admitted a guy seemed creepy.

XXXXX

Coming back to the present, he looked into her eyes as she knelt next to his bed. "I hate admitting I need anyone." She seethed through clenched teeth, as she laid her head on her forearm. He thought again how different she was from Rita or any woman he had dated. Someone he had picked up from the club and could not even recall their name. He recognized their faces as patrons of the club, but he really had no interest in getting to know most of them. "I need you, Chris." she whispered as she buried her face in her folded arms. His anger melted.

She glanced over her arm at him, trying to hide the tears.

She hid away from him again in her forearm and mumbled, "I want you." He was speechless and still half a sleep. She shook her head, sitting back on her heels to dash an angry hand across her face. "That's so wrong, Chris." She licked her lips, daring a glance his way through her golden mane. "Having you right now will not be enough." He reached out to stroke her cheek with the back of his hand, his anger traded into yearning.

"We all need someone, Tanya." He heard his own voice filled with tenderness he wasn't certain he possessed. She stared straight into his eyes. *A vision of a teenage girl full of wonder on a New York City sidewalk filled his vision. They were heading up in the Empire State Building together.*

"I've wanted you since the first time we met." she confessed in a hoarse whisper. He had an instant realization she meant from that odd first meeting, from that crazy ride in the elevator. "That's all wrong." she continued as she wrapped her arms about herself as a chill ran through her. She realized what she feared was her own emotions. She again pressed her forehead into the mattress for a moment, lolling from side to side. The coolness of the sheet felt refreshing against the heat of her face. He watched, lying supine on the bed, as she struggled. He scarcely recognized the muffled agonized voice as she spoke without raising her head. "I can't handle a one-night stand with you, Chris."

"Who said this would be that?" he responded softly. She lifted her eyes, her hair falling forward, partially hiding her face, as she met his gaze intently. It was as if her eyes were burrowing to his sole. Her face was etched in pain and yearning. Why did she fight her own desires? He felt incredibly moved by the raw emotions played across her features. "Your reputation," flowed simply between her parted lips. She could have slapped him, and it would not have stung as her words did.

"Give me a break, T." He rolled away from her and blew out an angry breath. "I never said you would be a one-night stand." He glanced over his shoulder at her kneeling form through narrowed slits. His nostrils flared; she lowered her head, blushing, as he turned back toward her to stroke her thick mane with his left hand. She moved; he slid back and lifted the blankets, inviting her to lie in his arms. The room was chilly; she slid in next to him feeling confused and apprehensive. He felt her tears on the side of his neck as he pulled her close, his cheek resting atop hers. His hand rubbed her shoulder and arm, feeling the coolness of the room all over her body and longing to warm her. She snuggled in, and then their mouths met. He was gentle, loving in his kiss, in the touch of his hand caressing her. Time became meaningless, lost in the passion and warmth of their embrace, kissing, caressing. He slipped his hand under the t-shirt and over the bandages and stopped to open his eyes and stare intently into hers. Her hand found him and stroked to the point he stopped her and simply held her close. He was dozing with her wrapped in his arms; she had fallen asleep. *It's a wonder the painkillers hadn't kept her out longer,* he thought. He turned over on his back and drifted off. As he dozed, he heard her sigh softly; he was lying on his side with his right arm draped over her thigh. He smiled at her without opening his eyes, as she strummed his exposed shoulder, he had her pinned, but he knew better than to keep her.

"Don't clean the place too much," he whispered as he released her. She kissed him quick and bounced joyfully off the bed.

"You're a dear." she claimed breathily, a voice sounding so overjoyed, it made him smile, despite his own desire. He looked up at her joyful face and shrugged at her delight. She glanced at the clock, it was almost noon. She had fallen back asleep for some time. He smirked as she bounced quietly from the room. Leaving him thinking of Rita Schultz, his long-time Greek-German squeeze. She had broken his heart, and he had still been willing to marry her. He recalled her raving temper and prima donna attitude in comparison to Tanya's playful, sometimes innocent personality.

Rita would never consider hovering over a discarded lover's bedside as he clung for life. She would not have pressed those ruby red lips to non- responsive, cold cheeks, in an intensive care unit and promised to reconcile if he would simply open his eyes. Rita was a dark beauty with long, luscious black hair; the opposite of Tanya's enigmatic, pale beauty. Rita's eyes were dark and secretive, where Tanya's were large, chameleon blue, and open. He knew Tanya craved him because her eyes took on a vibrant intensity when she felt passionate, just as they had done while she was in his arms this morning. Tanya certainly gave, where Rita had only taken. How could he have fallen for such complete opposites? Tanya would never be a pampered princess; he could placate by showering with gifts. She would be far more emotionally demanding of his time. He had never imaged a woman expecting a guy to wait. And yet he had agreed to wait for her.

XXXXX

After a shower, she couldn't stop herself from cleaning the common areas. Had she not promised to remain in the apartment, she would have given the hall the good scrubbing it desperately needed. She wanted Chris to be happy with her effort. She had not forgotten his warning of two roommates, and she cleaned as quietly as possible. The gray sweats hung on her loosely, drawn tightly at her narrow waist. They were more appropriate than walking about the apartment in Chris' red t-shirt. After cleaning the coffee pot, she brewed up a pot after mentally inventorying the cupboard and not finding any tea. Apparently, the aroma awakened a tall, lanky man with stringy, sandy blond hair and hazel eyes. He emerged from the room next to the kitchen while she was cleaned and straightened the kitchen. He sported nothing more than a pair of white cotton boxer shorts with cute red hearts all over them. He stretched and looked around the kitchen as he scratched his bony chest absently, before his sleepy gaze came to rest on her. "Hello?"

She smirked at him as he dropped onto a barstool. "Good morning," she responded in a soft singsong voice and bright smile. "Or should I say, 'good day'?"

"Are you the cleaning fairy or something?"

Tanya laughed. "Not quite. Why, have you left a bowl of milk for a brownie?"

He looked at her a bit confused. "A brownie?"

She waved the comment away. "Mythical, magical creatures that would actually do your cleaning. Some farmers leave fresh milk as payment." She explained with an easy smile. "I'm a friend of Chris'." She grabbed a cup from the cupboard and offered him the first taste of coffee. "Tanya. Tanya Gilbert," she stated as she handed his the cup across the counter.

He bobbed his head as he accepted the cup. "John Bloom," he said taking a deep drink of the black coffee and eyeing her speculatively. He sat down his cup. "I live here." He looked at her as he swallowed another drink. "Did you lose a bet with Chris or something?"

She smiled as she stifled a playful laugh and instantly liked this guy as she leaned on the counter between them. "No. Why?" When she had wondered from Chris' room the whole place had cried out for a good going over, and she had the energy to give it a go. "You're cleaning our place." He observed with a gulp of coffee. Tanya shrugged and pursed her lips thoughtfully.

"I couldn't make proper-tasting coffee in a dirty pot, so I needed to clean the kitchen first." She shrugged. "I promised Chris I'd be quiet and not wake anyone. I'm sorry if I failed." She sipped a weakened cup of coffee and longed for a cup of sweet-tasting tea.

John shook his head. "No, you're mighty quiet. I smelled the coffee; it tastes great too, by the way." He nodded as he looked around hesitantly. "Are you planning to clean the rest of the place?" A smile broke across her lips.

"It's generous of you to offer your assistance." She responded as if it had been his idea to help. "I'm certain you're allowed to run the vacuum cleaner, as that would be making noise, it's something I'm not allow to do."

He looked at her and chuckled. "Right. You promised to quietly clean." She nodded. "What's in it for me?" he asked, looking her over as she stood behind the counter in Chris' clothes that fit her quite loosely.

Tanya blushed to the roots of her hair as she recalled Chris' growl about not sleeping in the living room. "I'll prepare you a delightful breakfast when we're through," she promised.

He gave her a skeptic look before smiling. "Deal." He looked around. "Where's Chris?"

"Still in bed," Tanya replied matter-of-factly. John nodded as he walked about the living room gathering up laundry and making piles near the door. "You all do have a vacuum, don't you?" She dared wonder aloud as she wiped down the counter and refilled his cup.

John smirked. "It may shock you to know we have a great Electrolux."

"Do you happen to have gloves and bathroom cleaners?"

He stopped in mid-motion with a perplexed look on his face. "Bathroom cleaners?"

"You know, Soft Scrub, Comet, or something like it, a bathroom sponge, or brush, or something?"

He nodded. "I use the stuff under the kitchen sink."

"You use the same sponge, and the jar brush for the toilet, with Comet?"

John shrugged. "Honestly, I don't think any of us clean the toilet."

She nodded. "Do you all have bleach?"

"Sure. I keep it with the laundry soap," he said opening the closet and pulling it down from a shelf above the coat rod. She glimpsed the blue canister vacuum on the closet floor; her aunt had one just like it.

"Will the vacuum bother your other roommate?"

"Steve's not here. He went away for the weekend," John supplied.

"Steve's big into hiking and bicycling."

"My kind of guy," she muttered.

John laughed. "Then what are you doing with Chris?"

"Who said I'm with Chris? We're friends." Nodding, he narrowed his eyes at her wearily. "Chris doesn't bring girlfriends home." He admitted giving her the once over. "And I don't know any of his girlfriends that would walk around in his clothes, cleaning our apartment."

"Maybe we have a bet," she suggested.

John shrugged as he blushed. "Some bet. You're cleaning his house. You're wearing his clothes." He looked skeptical. "Got any of your own clothes by the way?"

Tanya blushed. "I rinsed them in your bathroom last night, and they're hanging on his closet door," Tanya laughingly admitted. "I asked myself that same question this morning as I was emptying your cupboards before cleaning them."

John chuckled, as she grabbed the cleaning supplies and headed for the bathroom. He vacuumed before checking the refrigerator and realized he needed to run to the store in order to have something to eat. When he returned, he found she had moved the furniture and had vacuumed underneath everything, as well as under the sofa cushions. He watched her dust as he put away the groceries. "No one looks underneath the furniture or cushions," he offered. She looked up at him and shook her head as she pushed the furniture back in place.

"It still should be done."

"But you promised to clean in silence," he reminded her.

She smiled as she headed back toward the kitchen and winked. "Yeah, but you already had the vacuum on. I didn't think it would matter if I turned it on again because you said your other roommate was out."

They chatted about him and Chris growing up together as she scrambled up some eggs, bacon, and toast for his efforts. She discovered they had been roommates since entering college, and both Chris' roommates were also cousins. "Whoa, slow down. You are all cousins?"

"Yeah, all our mothers are sisters. That's why we have different last names."

"Do your parents live nearby?"

"Nah, they all live in Jersey." He replied as if it were far away, rather than across the water. "They all live within blocks of one another," he admitted as an afterthought.

"Okay, so you all are related and family oriented?"

He shrugged as she offered him coffee. "Yeah, we found this place after finishing college. We wanted our business in Manhattan," he explained the apartment had initially been office and residence. Now, they had an office in mid-town Manhattan, near the financial district. She realized without speaking aloud that his office was near her own. Did Chris know that? He hadn't mentioned it, just as he had never mentioned he owned one third of a successful security business until he had offered to install an alarm system for her after Roy's death.

XXXXX

She recalled him once confiding early one morning in the parking lot of Len's Bar and Grill that he had wanted to work at GE.

"You have an associate's in electrical engineering? What were you planning to do with that?"

"I always wanted to work for General Electric," he replied with a nonchalance he didn't actually feel. Not that it mattered any longer, but he had never been accustomed to being turned down. Not being accepted at GE had been a hard blow, but it became a blessing.

"What happened?" She pressed, looking for dialogue with him to steer him away from his obvious desire to sit and make out in the parking lot. He shrugged and looked down at his lap thoughtfully. "I applied, but they didn't hire me."

"So you gave up? You didn't apply somewhere else, and then reapply to GE or go back to college for your four-year degree?" She seemed incredulous that he would only apply at one place after graduating from college.

He shook his head casually. "No. GE was the only place I wanted to work, and they didn't hire me." So he had not been completely honest, leaving her to believe he was content as the doorman at her favorite club. When faced with disappointment, he had created a job. Why had he attempted to make himself less attractive to her?

Chris made an appearance as Tanya served John a plate of breakfast. She smiled at him from the kitchenette as he headed toward the bathroom with a yawn and rubbing his stomach. He stood looking at himself in the bathroom mirror; the place looked as though someone had scrubbed the edges clean. The whole apartment smelled great. He decided to have some fun with John, he was pretty sure Tanya would play along. As he came out he looked around the place and padded toward the kitchenette, smiling. "Hmmm. The place looks great, and it smells delicious." he said as Tanya handed him a cup of coffee just as he liked it, extra cream, and no sugar.

"So we're square on our bet?" she said with a wink. He smiled, realizing she had been up to some fun of her own.

Chris took the coffee in one hand and wrapped the other around her waist and kissed her cheek. "Hmm, thanks, babe. We're square."

He turned toward John's stunned, gaped-mouth expression, a fork of egg frozen in mid-air. Chris raised his brow. "Behaving yourself with my woman, bud?"

"Ah, do I have a choice?" John asked with raised brow.

Chris chuckled, giving Tanya a squeeze. "She can be pretty pushy, hmm?" As he released her and headed back toward the bathroom and turned back toward them, "Babe, you joining me?" He enjoyed the blush spread across her face at the thought, as she shook her head.

"I'm not finished yet," she confessed. He grimaced and shrugged as he closed the door, as John turned back toward Tanya.

"Okay, honest, how long have you two been dating?" John prodded again as the shower came on.

Tanya blushed. "Hmm." She laughed. "Honest, we're friends." She felt herself blushing. "He's just playing. We hang out. I don't date. We met about a year ago." She fumbled for the right words. Sighing looked toward the bathroom. "Last night was…" She was at a loss. How to explain last night? "Ah sometimes we go out after the club closes or get together with other friends." John's brow shot up and bobbed his head. "Right. Right." He finished his breakfast and sat back to enjoy a second cup of coffee as Tanya ate a slice of toast with butter and jelly. When Chris re-emerged, he was wearing a purple polo shirt with the collar up and tight black Levi jeans. He slid onto the stool next to John as Tanya offered him a refill on his coffee and breakfast. John smirked at Chris with a nod. "So is this the girl you've decided to marry?" Chris nodded taking the bait. "Hey, babe, I thought we agreed you'd let me tell my family," he said to Tanya's back. She glanced at him over her shoulder quizzically but remained silent.

John choked on a gulp of coffee, as his eyes traveled from one to the other. "What?"

Chris clapped him on the back, as he sputtered on the warm liquid that traveled down the wrong way. "Hey, I knew she was perfect, but she's a tough one to convince." He smiled as he continued. "I could get used to waking up to a clean house, a nice meal, and fresh coffee. Right, man?"

"Umm, sure," John agreed, wiping his mouth with the sleeve of his shirt. Hesitantly, he sat back and looked seriously at Chris.

Chris nodded, "I'm glad you agree, because I cut out from work early last night, we drove down to Atlantic City and got hitched." He sipped his coffee calmly to hide his smile. Tanya didn't dare turn to face them as she struggled to stand nonchalant at the stove and dished up Chris' breakfast without shaking too noticeably. "We just got in a few hours ago," Chris rambled on. "She couldn't wait to get up and dig into this place for a good cleaning." He shook his head. "She wanted to clean when we got in this morning, but I wouldn't hear of it."

John's face turned red as he sputtered and chocked on his coffee. "What? No way, man. Your mother's going kill you." He leaped from the stool and backed away from the counter.

Chris pressed his lips and nodded. "Yeah, Tanya's got her own place, but it's being remodeled, so we'll be crashing here for a few days. Do you mind?" Tanya quietly set a plate before Chris as she watched John's reaction with a sheepish expression. John set down his cup with a bang and looked at Chris seriously.

"You're joshing me. No way would you skip out and marry *this* chick without telling any of us." John waved toward Tanya, as he glanced again at the ring on her left hand. His brows went up in recognition as he froze on the balls of his feet and rolled his eyes toward Chris and back to her ring before daring to meet her eyes.

The humor on Chris' face disappeared as he read the expression on John's face. "Who says I didn't take a family member with us?" Chris' voice was low and cautious. John shook his head, pointing at her ring finger, color draining from his features, as his eyes were round with shocked surprise; he struggled to speak. "Sh-she's th-th-the one. The one you mentioned."

Chris sat up looking from John to Tanya, and back at his plate, shaking his head with knitted brow. "Okay, John, I'm joshing you," he mumbled as his face reddening. Clearing his throat, he glanced up. "What's with you, man?" he asked as he picked up a piece of crispy bacon.

Tanya swung around to fully face them both, quietly taking in the interaction, wondering exactly what they were discussing. She felt as though she had lost a thread of the conversation somewhere. Why was her ring significant to John?

"Whoa, man." John put his left hand over his heart, as Tanya refilled his cup. "You had me going their f-for a minute." He sat back down, his eyes still lingering on her ring. She felt self-conscious and abruptly turned away.

Chris smirked. Tanya whirled from the sink after washing John's plate. Her eyes resting directly on John. "Really. I'm sure a good-looking guy like Chris has a hard time pulling one over on you." John raised his brow and shook his head, as his eyes sought out the silver band, with a black oval onyx, and a quarter-karat diamond cut in the center that she wore on her ring finger. He gulped his coffee and sat down the half-empty cup.

"You're the girl he dumped Rita for," he announced. Chris' head shot up as he stopped chewing to turn and glare at his cousin. Pressing her lips together, Tanya dared glance down at the ring on her left hand. The ring she moved from her left hand to her right after Martha's party when she had separated from Roy.

It was the ring she had been given by Jan Sands for Christmas years ago while she was in Brisbane. Jan had mailed her the ring with a note, "Sorry to break your heart and shatter your dreams. It had to be done. Please understand. Love, Jan."

She looked from John to Chris and back to John, too stunned to speak. Chris set down his fork and slid his hands to his thighs in silence, meeting her eyes as she narrowed hers in thought. A flash of a lovely, polished, raven-haired beauty not much taller than herself, thin and delicate looking, swirled through her mind. She recalled an evening when the woman came to the club wearing an almost sheer, cream-colored, long-sleeved blouse and plunging V neckline, tucked into an A-line black skirt, and black pumps with trim ankles. *It appeared she and Chris were having an intense conversation*; Tanya clearly recalled the incident.

She had been at his side, catching the look in his eye when he had glimpsed the girl. Tanya had moved back to her usual table and observed them from her seat. The woman walked away, stopped, and then turned back, her dark eyes flashing. She yelled at Chris as she stormed off toward the hotel lobby. Tanya hadn't been close enough to make out her words over the music. He had abandoned his post at the door to pursue her, calling after the beauty. Following after her into the hall, he had reached for her arm. She never looked back or slowed her step.

Chris was staring down at his plate in silence, the remainder of his breakfast untouched as Tanya came back to the present. He seemed so forlorn; she resisted the urge to reach out to him as she leaned against the counter. Her cool, soft hand reached out to gently caress the back of his right hand, which rested next to his untouched plate.

"I didn't break up with Rita over another girl," he denied again softly, his head bowed. He stole a glance up into her eyes, steadily meeting her gaze before tuning to John. " John. Rita was a witch.. She moved on." He ran his free hand angrily through his hair. His thumb moved over Tanya's fingers for more contact. Gaining reassurance from the weight of her hand he sat up, focused his eyes on the counter, and spread his fingers so hers slipped easily between. "Forget her," he growled.

Clearing her throat, she managed, "Is Rita that beautiful-looking Greek or Italian girl that used to come to Cahoot's?"

"Yeah," John replied.

"She would never lift a finger to make your breakfast." Chris shook his head in anger. "She wouldn't lift a finger to help anyone."

John's Adam's apple was now working up and down as he sat silently. Chris looked sharply at Tanya and shook his head. "We broke up over six months ago, for the last time, but certainly not the first time. End of story," he explained.

Tanya nodded, her throat felt dry. "That night at the club." She closed her eyes; her voice was soft and low. "She came in yelling."

"Stop. It had nothing to do with you." he insisted. She remembered they had been holding one another when he had glimpsed the other woman over Tanya's shoulder. Now, she opened her eyes to stare into his eyes and knew he wasn't being truthful, but this wasn't the time to discuss it. He turned toward John. "I was joking about eloping with Tanya, but not about her staying for a few days."

"What?"

Chris shrugged. "Her place was broken into." He sighed as he forked at his food. "Didn't you check the messages?"

John shook his head. "I took yesterday and today off."

Chris nodded. "Well someone bypassed the system we installed. Her place needs a few repairs before she can move back in," he explained. "Is that all right with you?"

John shrugged. "I'm not sure how Steve is going to feel about it."

"Yeah, well, the alarm system failed. Tanya won't be a problem for any of us."

She smiled across the counter, leaning toward him; as the ice seemed to fade away, she kissed his cheek. She noticed John watched her closely. The two guys were discussing security when Tanya slipped away, relieved to leave them chatting amongst themselves. She scanned the bookshelf and randomly pulled down a sci-fi to bury her nose into as she curled up on the window seat.

Chris returned. "What did you find?" he asked, leaning over her shoulder. Tanya glanced up at him with a shrug. She had not really been able to focus on the book. She couldn't even tell what the initial chapter had been about.

"Why'd John say that about me while looking at my ring?"

Chris shook his head with a grimace. "Who knows? Forget it." She saw his eyes smolder with a fleeting temper as he spoke. He leaned over and touched the book in her hand to see the title. "*Cathedral*."

"Is it any good?"

Chris shrugged. "I think it was okay." Squinting slightly as he tried to recall the thread of the plot. He couldn't quite recall it, something about bringing someone to the future to save them from their own timely demise at the wrong hands. He handed her a cup of tea. She looked up at him in surprise.

"There was no tea in your cupboards this morning," she remarked with raised brow. Chris shrugged as he pressed his lips together.

"I went down to the corner deli and grabbed a small box for you." She smiled up as she accepted the cup, desiring nothing more than standing up and throwing her arms around him and kissing him passionately.

"Thanks." She sipped and smiled at him for his efforts. How thoughtful. She tasted just enough sugar to sweeten the tea before setting it down on top a pile of books she had moved from the window seat to the floor. Rising to her feet, she wrapped her arms around his neck and kissed his cheek, he turned into her kiss, and their lips met. Tanya closed her eyes, giving into the embrace, allowing him to realize her desire, before stepping back and lowering her head, as she licked her lips and waited, her arms resting against him. She wanted to know the truth about Rita. Did she dare press? "Chris…"

Chris sighed as if he expected her questions. "I have to go out for a while."

She looked up into his eyes with panic, as he took her hands and moved to sit on the edge of the bed. She sat next to him. "Is this about Rita?"

He furrowed his brow as he searched her eyes. "No."

"You expect me to just wait here?" She seemed angry and hurt. What was she to him? She looked expectantly into his face; he remained silent. "How long will you be gone? Why do you have to go out?" He shook his head in exasperation.

"Yeah, I am expecting you to sit tight," he stated flatly, before meeting her gaze. His eyes were smoldering with flashes of emotion. He gave her a questioning look, "Promise you will stay, T. My place is the safest place for you at the moment."

Pressing her lips together, she leaned back on her elbows and glanced up at his ceiling, already feeling stir crazy. "Why should I stay?" She sulked. "I won't feel safe if you're not here."

He couldn't resist the urge to reach out and stroke her nose. "I won't be long."

"What do you imagine you'll accomplish?" she asked. He remained silent. "Chris, I honestly never saw that creep before last night." She shook her head. "I don't even know why I'm hiding. This is foolish." She sat forward, feeling overwrought. "I want to go for a morning jog to clear my head. I want to go home. I want to take a long hot shower and change my clothes. I hate hiding."

He shook his head. "Just give it some time, T. I'm just asking you to lay low for a few more hours." He watched her profile; he could tell she was stir-crazy. She and Lucy were whirlwinds, always in motion. That's one thing the two had in common.

She narrowed her eyes as she turned to glare at him. "Tell me I'm not the reason you ended a long-term relationship with that beauty." The question took him off balance, and he hesitated for a moment, not certain he had heard her correctly. She waited staring at him intensely; he knew he couldn't avoid saying something.

He shook his head and huffed. "Why do you care?"

She shrugged. "I just do."

"I can't say my sister, Stacey, approved of Rita. She was elated I'd come to my senses when we broke up this last time." He looked away. "Rita always had someone else to fall back on, T. She hated me working the club; she was insanely jealous because she had never been faithful to me." He shrugged involuntarily. "She'll never be alone." He met her gaze with incredible sincerity in his violet-blue eyes. Tanya wanted to reach out to him, touch his cheek, nuzzle against him, and forget this woman John spoke of. She wanted to leave her problems behind; her condo would never be the same again. He wanted to assure her there was no one between them.

Instead, she pressed on. "Why did you break up? It was that night she came to the club yelling, wasn't it?" He looked deep into her eyes and nodded. "Then it was because she saw me in your arms. It's my fault."

He shook his head. "You may have been the catalyst, but it was bound to happen." He admitted. "Rita and I just used each other for years; we weren't meant to stay together."

"You almost married her."

He nodded. "I realize I came close to a *huge* mistake. Stacey talked me out of that." He shook his head. "When Rita saw us, she and I were already on shaky ground. I knew I'd never marry her. Forget her. Let's focus on you," he said effectively, turning the conversation back to the moment at hand. "Where do we go?"

"Mark has answers, but he won't be forthcoming." She narrowed her eyes. "If only I knew why my place was searched. I'd gladly provide whatever to Mark. Whatever someone's looking for, it probably cost Roy his life." She rose. "Chris, it's best I go, not hide out in your home and put you at risk."

"No one knows you're here. I'm not at risk. Just let the police have a chance to do their job. Let me secure your place with a security system."

Hesitantly, she nodded her agreement. "I know Mark could straighten this out, Chris." She looked at him with despair. "I can't hide forever." She wailed. "I should just call him." He brushed the hair from her face tenderly; fleetingly her mind swept back to how tender Roy had been as Chris looked into her eyes.

"Don't call," his voice was comforting. She wanted to cling to him; her eyes begged him to stay with her. She didn't want to be left alone in this cramped apartment that held no view. She desired to run through the woods hand-in-hand with the man beside her, laughing, playing, enjoying the smell of the wood and the sunshine through the trees. "I'm not asking you to hide forever, just a few more hours." He sighed, tender like Roy had once been, but not Roy at all. "Can't you just give Jonathan time to do his job?" He exhaled slowly and narrowed his gaze at her. "Honestly, T. I'd like to know how that guy found us at Len's." Tanya chewed the inside of her cheek and nodded. So he voiced the real reason for his concern. The reason he wanted her to promise to stay put. She glanced toward the window seat, thinking back to the previous night, it was such a blur as she reached to run her hand through Chris' hair. He was right, after they left Cahoot's for Len's Bar& Grill, the stranger was still dealing with the police, how had he been released and able to catch up with them? Someone had followed them; someone had tipped the guy off and bailed him out. No way was he working alone. Chris entwined her fingers with his. She knew it was sensible to stay out of sight, but she couldn't fight her own desires for Chris if she remained in his bed. Chris released the fingers of her right hand to take hold of her chin and tenderly turn her face toward his.

Oh, Lord. This is torture. I want to devour every inch of this man. Not be a goody two-shoes. But if I give into desire, how can I expect him to respect me? She pressed her lips together intensely lowering her gaze. *Maybe Cheryl can have casual sex. But I know I can't. At least not with this man.* Raising her eyes, she looked into his intense violet-blue eyes; they were almost black with emotion. She cleared her throat and dared ask, "Chris, what does my ring mean to John?" The question had the desired effect, throwing him off guard so she had time to collect her emotions. She chewed her cheek, fearing his answer. He flicked his eyes away, toward the bay window. "Why did he ask you if I was the woman you…you were planning to…?" She pressed, sensing a nerve. He shrugged; she perceived a change in his demeanor as he stiffened. She squeezed his fingers that rested between her own, as she sat up and rested their hands on his knee. "Please," she whispered.

Facing her with dark eyes that flashed with anger he met her gaze. "Tanya, you're as attracted to me as I am to you." He brought her fingers to his lips before releasing them; he rose from the bed. "I don't know why John was looking at your ring, talking like that." He shrugged and figured it must have been something Rita had said in John's presence or to John when Chris wasn't around. Tanya reached out for his waist, not wanting him to leave her. His voice was low. "John still runs into Rita from time to time. Maybe she said something to him about seeing you at the club wearing that ring. I don't know." She let it go, as she pulled him back beside her.

Their mouths met in an intense kiss as their hands roved over one another. Chris moaned as he pulled away from her and rolled to his feet. She sunk her teeth into her upper lip as he moved to the door. "Chris. I…" She shook her head and pressed her lips as she stood. "I'll be here."

"I know."

"Everything is moving way too fast. I can't catch my breath." She took in a deep breath. "You read me right." She dared to glance at his face. "I've been attracted and afraid for months. Even more so now." She turned to face the window, to hide from Chris' gaze. Her emotions were in turmoil.

He crossed the room to kneel before her. "Stay. Wait for me, and we'll continue this conversation when I get back," he whispered again, running his hand through her hair. She closed her eyes rising in unison with him, pressing against his chest. She felt his arms embrace her, as she wrapped hers around him and held him tightly.

"Go," she whispered at his throat. He felt the warmth of her breath, and the beat of her heart.

They melted together to the edge of the bed. "Trust me," he whispered as their foreheads touched. Hot silent tears ran down her cheeks.

"Okay," she agreed, her mind brimming with thoughts and questions, hot with raw emotion. She clung to him, as if to life itself. Her back was seared with the heat from his palms, as she tilted her face toward his. She enjoyed the hot, crushing kiss of his lips hungrily seeking hers. She raked her nails across his shirt as she moved so close a slip of paper wouldn't have fit between them, her legs overlapping his. "Don't leave me." She panted. "Stay." She breathed into his ear as desire heated her body.

He groaned as he pulled away. "I have to go. I promise it won't be for long," he whispered against her ear as she nibbled his neck. He reached for her arms and clasped her hands to her sides as he kissed her again, moving from under her legs. He rose and stepped away before releasing her. She stared at him, and he smiled at her playfully. "Hold all your thoughts for my return." She took a deep breath, never taking her eyes from him as she let it out slowly. He backed away toward the door, holding her eyes in his own.

XXXXX

It was so much easier to think of the recent events of the morning, rather than the night she had spent in Chris' bedroom. The night. Had she only returned from an emotional week in Wisconsin at her sister's farm a day ago? Had it only been a little over a week since Roy's death? Had it been yesterday morning she cleaned Chris' apartment? Or had it been the day before? Events were merging together, and she couldn't keep the days straight in her mind. Where was her head? Obviously, she hadn't reflected sufficiently to realize she was still in danger even though Roy was dead. Why? She thought of her suitcase still in the hatch of her car parked in the underground garage at the club. She went to the living room phone and called Jonathan's home phone number from memory. He wasn't there; she left a message with his dad and then called his office. There she reached him just as he was leaving.

"Jonathan?"

"Hmm."

"I have a suitcase in my car at the club parking area. Could you bring it by Chris' so I can have a change of clothes?"

"Why do you have a suitcase in your car?"

"I just got home yesterday from my trip," she reminded him. "When I saw my place, I picked up my suitcase where I set it down in the hall and left in my car."

"Okay. I'll swing by later."

"When can I go home?"

"Soon. I have to run, but we'll talk about that when I see you."

"Okay." She flopped in the window seat thinking back over what she recalled of her journals. She had scanned her journals and her college scrapbook briefly in Wisconsin. True, she had been looking to sort through her feelings then, not for clues as to the cause of Roy's demise. She had been looking at clues of the past hoping they would lead her to make better choices. She had hoped to figure out if she should remain in New York City or strike out for someplace else. Everything had been too recent, too raw to reach any decisions. Cecilia had told her she just needed more time to mourn.

"You're dealing with a lot of loss, not just Roy's death." Great, here comes the speech Tanya had expected from her sister. A speech she didn't want to hear. Should she play dumb?

"How so?"

"You're grieving his loss. A part of you was willing to make amends. And let's not forget Aaron."

How she wished she could forget Aaron.

Tanya sighed. "Let's do."

Cecilia shook her head, with a sad, serious smile. "You're reeling from dealing him a crushing blow you had hoped to avoid forever." Tanya smiled sadly as she nodded. Her sister was all too accurate.

"It's really better that he knows," Cecilia had assured her many times over her stay. Tanya hadn't been so certain.

"If it is better, why didn't Jan ever tell him?" Tanya asked. "Why come to us?" Cecilia shrugged.

"I can't speak for Jan. Maybe she didn't think he'd listen. Maybe she didn't think he could handle it. He's always been moody." Tanya nodded; she knew better than most how moody and dark Aaron could get.

"Maybe she was right not to tell him." She looked into Cecilia's eyes as her heart filled with anxiety. "Maybe I should call Jan and tell her he knows. Someone should keep an eye on him."

"T, he has a wife to keep an eye on him," Cecilia counseled. "I'll call their house and talk to Tessa." Tanya nodded her agreement.

XXXXX

Of course she hadn't spent as much time as she should have reviewing the last few months. Guilt over spilling a tawdry tale to Aaron days before had clouded her thoughts. Belatedly, she had confided in Cecilia she had told Aaron of their evening out with Jan years ago. She had confessed all to Aaron. To her surprise, Cecilia expelled a long breath. "Wow. You held out a lot longer than I ever imagined. I wondered when you would get around to confiding in him so that you could both get on with your lives."

Tanya was stunned. "Why didn't you ever say anything?"

Jan had been right years before; Aaron was sensitive. She replayed the look of betrayal on his face over and over in her mind's theater. What could she have possibly done differently? She knew if anything had happened to Aaron the farm would be notified. Cecilia assured her, "It wasn't my place to tell you what to do. Don't beat yourself up. You had to tell him. What choice did you have?"

"To gently send him packing."

"For how long?"

Tanya shrugged. "I should have cut ties with him ages ago."

Cecilia nodded with a smile. "That would have been easier were I not married to his brother." They both laughed at the irony. Tanya focused her waking hours assisting her sister in day-to-day chores around the farm and running oneself to exhaustion chasing after children. Daily menial task at the farm had been balm on an open wound. When she confided in Lia, Tanya expected recrimination, instead she received understanding.

"I was so emotionally raw when he showed up after Roy died," she had admitted when Cecilia pressed. "Tessa called, blasting me over the phone." She grimaced and went on, as Lia nodded. They were in the kitchen; Lia was whipping up a berry pie for dinner. "When he arrived to console me, I asked him to leave." Tanya shook her head as she struggled to get the telling right. "I told him not to come. I had that phone call from Tessa fresh on my mind when he showed up. He thought it was 'our time'." She looked plaintively at Cecilia. "I just wanted him to know it could never be 'our time.' I had to squelch that hope." She wanted her sister to understand.

Lia reached out, covering her hands with her own in comfort. Their eyes met. With a deep sigh, she said, "I figured it was you Tessa spoke to when she called here yelling not too long ago. I'm sorry to say; I told her I hadn't called." She shrugged. "She must have figured her mistake and called you back." Tanya nodded as she remembered unplugging the phone. Lia shook her head. "Tanya, I don't know how you ever kept it from Aaron for as long as you did and still managed a relationship with him and Tessa. I told Matthew when you were in Australia."

Tanya clutched the counter to remain upright, as the world seemed to turn topsy-turvy. It felt as if icy cold water had been poured over her head by the buckets when she heard her sister's confession. Her sister, the "keeper of secrets" in their youth, had confided in her husband seven years ago. She, Tanya, had kept it from the two men she loved, against every grain of her body, to everyone's determent. And yet as she looked at her sister a slow smile sprang across her lips. "You're a smarter woman than I, dear sister. You realized long before I did how incredibly destructive such a powerful secret can be." Cecilia nodded and patted Tanya's hand. "Matthew said it could be possible." She grimaced. "He'd heard rumors about our mother and his father. That much seems true enough, but he doubts Jan's accusation is true."

"No doubt they had an affair though?"

Cecilia nodded. "That much seems unmistakably true. But I think the timing for you to be their child is off." Tanya drew in a deep breath and exhaled slowly, throwing up her hands. It no longer mattered. They were free. She had set herself and Aaron free. "It doesn't really matter anymore. It's too late to take back the telling."

XXXXX

Truly, the reason she was steamed at Jonathan Moyer for pushing her into Chris' realm when she was at an intensely vulnerable point in her life. Jonathan and Lucy both knew how drawn she had been to Chris. What of Chris Rosen? What of his family? She knew his coworkers and their mutual friends that went hiking or horseback riding in the group. The attraction was mutual, and yet there was no attachment. Of course she had made it clear she was not available even after Lucy let him know practically the moment she and Roy had separated.

XXXXX

Dear Diary,

Lucy gleefully let Chris and Jonathan know Roy and I have split. Why? At least having Roy kept me at arm's length from any other guy.

I wonder about Chris. Is his family so different from Roy's family? Would the connection with Chris be just as tight as it was initially with Roy? Or am I simply drawn to the wrong sort of guy? How can I be sure Chris is not involved with the "family," as Roy was? How would I know if his own family was any more functional than mine or Aaron's? What do I know of this man I've had a flirtatious relationship with any way? Honestly, it was fun flirting because there never seemed a chance at anything else; now, that has changed.

It really throws me to meet up with a mystery man I chance to meet on the sidewalk years ago. It took me forever to place his familiar face when I finally placed him. I haven't asked him if he remembers our first meeting; that might really freak him out. What are the chances of us ever coming in contact again after that one afternoon at the Empire State Building?

XXXXX

Since becoming more friendly with Chris and Jonathan it had become commonplace to venture to an after-hours bar after Cahoot's closed on a Friday night; they often regrouped at one in the theater district. There they would enjoy a drink and some breakfast before calling it a night. She would often be out until 5:00 a.m., shower, sleep for a couple hours and then go to work on Saturday for four to six hours before going out again Saturday night. A good night's sleep for Tanya since she and Roy split up was four hours; she knew Lucy usually needed six to eight. She and Lucy generally appeared at Cahoot's at least once a week between Thursday and Sunday. If Lucy wasn't around, Tanya felt comfortable enough to show up at Cahoot's on her own. There was always someone she recognized to hang out with for a few hours, and she didn't mind dancing with strangers because she knew Chris and Jonathan had her back. She gave herself a sour smile; at least she was certain he was in no way related to her, they were from different communities, different walks of life. A life she now embraced and lived within, and yet she had never quite become a part of this city. People were forever asking her, "Where are you from?" The accident flooded her thoughts in unwelcome fashion. Her mind's eye reenacted a scene she never actually saw. The screech of tires, a big, brown 1974 Mercury Marquis clipping the front tire of Roy's bike. Roy being thrown in the air, hitting the top of the car, and sliding from the trunk, catching his boot-cut pant leg on the rear metal bumper of the car. She saw his rag doll body being dragged down the street behind the car. The nurse in a white uniform flailing her arms and crying out for the driver to stop. Someone screaming.

XXXXX

10th May 1986

Dear Diary,

How quickly life can change. In a heartbeat, we are faced with unexpected emotions we thought were long buried. In a gasp, we turn inward and question the very significance of life. One moment I'm have a great time with Lucy, dancing, flirting shamelessly with other men; the next life smacks me in the face. I'm a married woman. Why am I living as if I'm single? Did I not promise to love him for the rest of my life for good or bad? If he chooses to come back to me, must I not honor our vows and try? Have I not always assured him a piece of paper wouldn't make my commitment any deeper? Because, I'm the one who didn't want to get the license, not him, I feel obligated to stand by him now. He was always more committed than I. I can't walk away now.

13th May 1986

Dear Diary,

How can the trees be alive, the birds singing, the smells of spring in every breath I take, and yet he is now gone. It seems so unfair. Like he was cheated. Gone as my father and brother. He was getting his life together. We were going to give marriage a go. This should never have happened. At the hospital I still felt a sense of danger emanating from his uncle Leo and in Mark as well. Perhaps his death was not an accident. The nurse says there were two young boys in the car…they took off on foot, and she didn't get a good look at them, but to her recollection the driver was so small he looked through the steering wheel, not over it.

XXXXX

He lay in critical condition at St. Vincent's Hospital's ICU; Tanya stood looking through the windowed wall of his room at his still form, as he lay broken and bandaged on a slightly elevated bed. A respirator assisted his breathing via a breathing tube, fluids hung nearby attached by a shunt in his right hand. The doctor seemed to have no real answers; he talked around her with his mumbo jumbo. Lucy had been at her side; perhaps Lucy made heads or tails from his words, and Tanya had been unable to focus on the words her ability to comprehend seemed to have abandoned her. The whole event from the moment she received the call at work took on the feel of stepping into a twisted soap opera that no one ever admitted watching. Lucy had been near her office door; Lucy had spoken to their boss and driven her to St. Vincent's. It had all been a hazy blur. As much as she tried, she couldn't find her way off the set of this soap opera. She looked around and wanted to shout, "I'm not an actress, and you have the wrong person." But nothing escaped her lips. She turned and walked down the hall to the payphone and stood for some minutes simply staring at it blankly.

Lucy came up beside her. "Hey, girl. What are you doing?"

"I've got to call his Uncle Leo."

Lucy nodded. "Do you need a quarter?"

"No. I have change."

"Did you forget his number?"

"No."

"Do you want me to dial?"

Tanya turned to meet Lucy's big, brown eyes and nodded stiffly. Lucy dialed and handed her the phone. Afterward, she took out her address book and placed a personal call to Roy's father's mother in Sacramento. Beatrice thanked Tanya for the call at the end of the short conversation. Tanya heard herself offer to pick Beatrice up at the airport. She invited her to stay in her Brooklyn condo. Lucy stood off to the side with her arms folded.

"What are you doing?"

"Being hospitable." Lucy nodded. She stepped up to the payphone after glancing through her address book and called someone. "Hi, Mark. It's Lucy. Roy's at St. Vincent's ICU. He was hit by a car. I don't know all the details. Uh huh. Okay."

"You have Mark's number?"

"We dated a few times, remember?"

Tanya nodded. "Thanks."

Lucy nodded. "We can't stay any longer. Visiting hours are over until this evening.

Tanya didn't question; she simply followed in Lucy's spiked-heeled footsteps. She looked down at Roy's brown leather bomber jacket in her left hand. A nurse handed it to her when she'd entered the room; she hadn't realized she'd never set it down. It was all ruined; he wouldn't be able to wear it again anyway. His room had been so noisy with the bank of monitors, all the noise from the ICU desk floating in through the open doorway. No privacy, he lay with lights shining on him as if on display. There had been a hard lump in her throat as she had entered his room. They had partially shaved his feathered, light brown hair and bandaged his head and left arm. He was left-handed; he wouldn't be able to write for a while. His collarbone and left arm were broken. His left leg was in a cast, slightly elevated; the other leg had been caught on the bumper. Had the doctor said a coma was the body's way of healing? His face was partially bandaged, his lower lip was swollen, and his cheek was bruised and scraped. The only emotions she felt as she looked down at that handsome, bruised face was love and pain and an undoubting desire for him to open those incredible, dancing green eyes of his. She longed to hear the timbre of his voice as he assured her all was well. Her hand reached out to clasp the fingers that protruded from the bandage of his left arm, as she leaned down and brushed his cool cheek with her lips. He seemed more a mannequin than her estranged husband. Normally, his hands were always warm, gentle, long fingers, like her own. He kept his nails bluntly cut, his hands were calloused from landscaping, something he enjoyed doing. She looked around and told herself she'd need to bring him a change of clothing.

She leaned over him and spoke ever so softly, closing her eyes and blocking out the room around them, seeing the meadow in her mind where she had first observed him in a dream. "Roy, a reverti moi. All is forgiven; work with me. We'll go away from New York; we'll begin fresh." Her face was just inches from his; she waited, trying to sense him, but his body seemed lifeless. She could not feel his presence. All the petty disagreements—his drinking, his family connections—all seemed irrelevant as she sat cradling her head. Her thoughts drifted back to the past Labor Day weekend. It had been a warm September evening, she'd delivered him an ultimatum and left. He entered rehab shortly after, but he slipped several times since then. Just three weeks ago, she had served him with separation papers and told him she needed to move on with her life, she couldn't be his crutch. Now, here she was, willing to be his crutch if he would only open his eyes.

XXXXX

12th May 1986

Dear Diary,

I wonder…what if I find a way to slip Roy into Evald?
His grandmother should be able to help me. If I could get
him there, surely he would mend. He could live there even
though he would be gone here, couldn't he? I feel so helpless
holding his cold, lifeless hand in ICU. He's so pale, I hardly
recognize him. Can we really die in this world, and just
like a human, be gone forever?

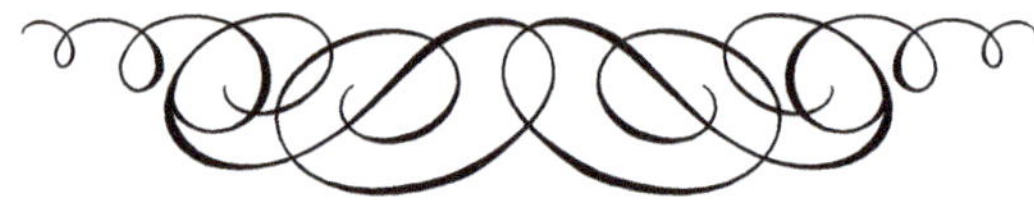

XXXXX

At Martha Martin's party, where he had completely humiliated her with his drunken behavior, she had realized his alcoholism was detrimental to her career. From that day on, she had drawn an invisible barrier between them, she had been mortified beyond words. The memory still brought a sense of dread to her heart, and yet she had taken a vow to stand by him. This was in sickness, he needed her, perhaps even the party had been in sickness, and she couldn't bring herself to recount that day again. He should be surrounded by familiar people, hear their voices, and look into their eyes when he awakened, not into the eyes of a stranger in a cold glass hospital room. Her mouth turned up in a sad smile as she stroked his thigh through the thin, white blanket. The room seemed chilly. Tanya wished she could take him home and tuck him in a warm cozy bed. She and Roy had separated eight months ago when she moved into her condo in Brooklyn. All their problems seemed insignificant now. She liked Brooklyn so much better than Queens.

It seemed a world away from Roy's extended family and yet only a twenty-minute train into mid-town Manhattan where she worked. Some of her coworkers thought Brooklyn was a world away, but she enjoyed the train ride early in the morning and late at night. She enjoyed the solitude of going home to a place of her own at night. It had become a haven. Here was an opportunity to make amends of their marriage; Roy would need her now. He wouldn't need his uncle Leo or his cousin Mark. And in his present state they would certainly have no need of him.

Tanya couldn't keep away from the hospital; she went to work early to leave early and rush to his side. Someone from his family was usually somewhere nearby when she'd arrive. They had never been so attentive when he'd been well. Nonetheless, she would sit at his side and talk to him softly or read to him as if he could hear her. She watched the nurses come in and periodically change the clear bags suspended from a pole by his bed. She would hold his cool hand and pray he would pull through and open his eyes. She prayed for everything to be as it had been at college. Tanya gazed down at his restive face and longed to feel the strength of his freckled arms as he held her close. Would she once again gaze into those incredible, merry green eyes of his?

"Hey, babe, you're not looking your best today," she whispered as she leaned forward to kiss his pale cheek. "Gosh, you were on the right track before this little calamity. But I've been thinking we can work through this. If you want, we can up and maybe move to California near your grandmother. I can sell the condo, and we can start fresh somewhere else. You mentioned maybe giving Canada a try. Personally, I think it'd be too cold, but I'd try for you, babe." She folded her hands in her lap and let her mind drift a bit before rousting herself and chuckling, "Thanks for leaving me as your emergency contact. Can you imagine anyone in your family calling me had you changed it to one of them? I suppose Mark or Stephanie might have thought of me. As things turned out, I'm going to pick your mother and grandmother up at JFK this evening. Go figure." Her eyes wandered around the tiny, cramped cubicle and wondered when he would open his eyes and assure her this was all a tasteless prank. "Hey, I invited your gram to bunk at my place while she's in town. I'm surprised she accepted. I didn't really figure she'd be gong ho to hang with your mother's family. I suppose she could stay in a hotel, but I don't image she's accustomed to traveling alone."

She sensed a presence at the door, and without turning, she caught a whiff of Mark's cologne, Dakar. She stiffened where she stood next to the left side of Roy's bed. The cologne suited him and his slicked-back hairstyle, dark brown, neatly cut hair, his preppy outfit, right down to the pleat in his slacks, and the tassels on his loafers. She turned to meet his gaze. "Hey," he acknowledged as he sauntered into the room, his trench coat draped casually over his left arm. He was dressed as if he'd just come from communion.

"Hi, Mark." She glanced through the window. "Have the doctors said anymore about his condition?"

"Not that I know of. Mom's with them now; Dad's parking the car."

Tanya nodded, glanced at her watch, "I'll be off then."

Mark grabbed her elbow. "Stay, T." He surprisingly implored her. She glanced down at his hand on her arm, before meeting his warm, brown eyes.

"I really have to run." She shrugged away from his grasp. "A girl's gotta eat, and then I'm off to the airport to pick up Beatrice and Janet."

"I'll come with you," he offered. She shot him a quizzical look at the offer. "You shouldn't pick them up alone," he clarified.

Tanya shrugged. "I'm not. Lucy's going with me. Thanks just the same." Tanya hesitated. Mark seemed to have something to say. When Mark remained silent, she slipped from the cubicle and headed down to the main lobby to meet up with Lucy. While Tanya waited on the black, faux leather cushioned bench in the lobby for Lucy, she leaned back against a half wall and let her mind wander. She found herself, in her mind's eye, at Cahoot's, the friendly faces she had come to know so well. Chris Rosen's face flashed through her mind's eye—he had seemed familiar from the first time she had seen him at the door. It had taken her sometime to place where they had met. As she sat in the lobby, flashes of memory played through her mind. Chris was the guy in the elevator of the Empire State Building years before. She smiled to herself as Lucy came to stand before her.

"Hey, girl, what are you smiling about?"

Tanya shrugged. "Memories." Tanya seemed more upbeat as they headed out. At the airport, both mother and grandmother wished to dispense with their luggage as quickly as possible and head straight to the hospital. Tanya gave Beatrice Wilson a spare key with her address written on the attached tag. She and Lucy stopped at an upscale bar and grill near St. Vincent's for dinner. Over grilled white fish and Chardonnay, as she watched Lucy eat fried chicken strips and sip at a beer, Tanya acknowledged how drained she felt. In the past two or three days, she hadn't gotten more than two hours of sleep at a time. "Luc, I'm beat. Do you mind if I rain check tonight?" Lucy looked at her with concern and nodded as she shoved a piece of chicken dipped in bleu cheese dressing into her mouth.

In the city, she developed a strained, flirtatious friendship with Chris Rosen almost from the moment she'd moved to New York. Another man from her dreams—would the interaction between her dreams and life never come to an end? Hiking in nearby state parks, mostly in New Jersey, had familiarly acquainted them with a group of friends. There was horseback riding on weekend afternoons around Central Park with Lucy and Jonathan, which occasionally ended in a dinner together. She had come to realize through shared trips that she and Chris shared a love for the waterfalls.

> *Excerpt from Tanya's diary,*
>
> *...who would ever image it possible to enjoy a slice of the country in the heart of the BIG Apple. That's how I feel when horseback riding through Central Park. It's fun getting wet in the falls and streams. It's a wondrous place to picnic with Chris, Lucy, and whomever. Am I treading dangerously?*

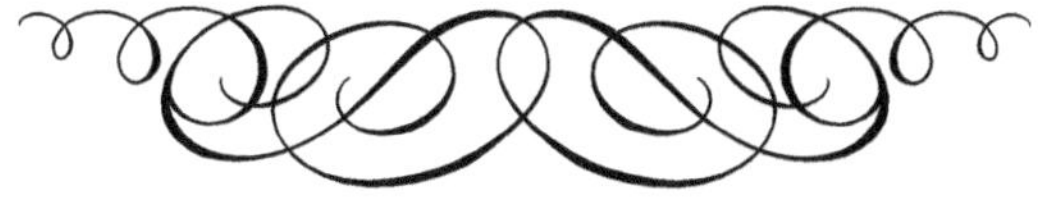

XXXXX

It never occurred to ask him how he could afford to accompany them on these excursions on the salary he drew at Cahoot's. They loved the same music. She enjoyed dancing at Cahoot's,; he enjoyed watching. The club had a big screen behind the dancers; the cameras around the dance floor displayed the dancers up on the screen. Roy worked many nights, so Tanya became a regular at Cahoot's along with Lucy and a number of other coworkers as it was near their Manhattan office. Roy hung out with his family in Queens even when he wasn't working. Tanya didn't want to hang out in a small Queens apartment alone; she didn't enjoy hanging with Roy's family. "Hey girl, why don't you hang with Roy and his family?"

Tanya shrugged, "I don't have much in common with them."

Lucy nodded as she pursed her lips, before breaking into a smile. "I didn't think we had much in common when we first met," she offered.

Tanya smiled at her. "But here we are." She shook her head, "Honest, Lucy, I don't see that happening with his family."

Lucy nodded acceptance and dropped the subject.

She didn't enjoy going to wrestling matches.

Tanya was no fan of boxing or wrestling, however, she was Lucy's friend, and wanted to support her in her endeavors. If Lucy wanted to box, she would tag along with Lucy to the gym around the corner from their office, where Lucy worked out and sparred.

"So, why don't you like boxing?" Lucy asked one afternoon as she jabbed a medicine ball.

Tanya looked around the dimly lit, dingy gym and envisioned the bright, clean Bali gym she held membership too. "Boxing and wrestling are loud sports," she began, as she wrinkled her nose, causing Lucy to chuckle. "This place smells of sweaty men even when it's clean," Tanya added.

Lucy nodded her agreement; "You get use to it."

"I joined Bali, and I like the quiet, sedate early morning atmosphere," Tanya admitted.

Lucy nodded as she moved to a small swinging ball that forced her to make quick, short rapid jabs. "Wanna go dancing tomorrow night?"

"Where?"

"A club near the Manhattan main office."

"Sure."

When she and Lucy danced at Cahoot's, they would feel the spotlight and then see themselves up on the screen. She had grown accustomed to it and no longer gave it any thought. It was the one place she didn't feel shy and out of sync; on the dance floor she could be herself. She enjoyed dancing, even with strangers; there was no need for conversation, just movement to the music.

Tanya hadn't been in the emotional state of mind when Aaron came to New York after Roy's accident. Roy was dead. She'd felt weak and vulnerable, not the strong shoulder she'd been for Aaron in the past. Death had dealt her another crushing blow, and Aaron came rushing to her side. Too convenient. She needed to break from the past to properly grieve for the man she had loved enough to call her husband, despite the fact they had lived in separate places for the last eight months. They had maintained contact, discussed reuniting. Roy had been in detox; he was faithfully going to counseling, working out in a gym not far from her office in mid-town Manhattan. She had met him near there several times for lunch in the weeks preceding his death. Looking into Aaron's eyes, she knew Tessa was right. Aaron imagined he and Tanya could carve out a life together.

XXXXX

Dear Lord, what can I do? With Matthew, Sr. and my father both being dead, I spoke to my doctor about a paternity test between Aaron and I. She said they couldn't be conclusive between siblings even it we each had a known sibling participate. I guess I should have asked, Matthew, Sr. for such a test before he died. I never could bring myself to ask him.

"Be honest with thyself."

Years that had brought her to this point with Chris' family lodge in the Catskills. For the first time since she could remember there would be no Aaron Sands to turn to. She had closed that chapter forever. She had run to her sister in Wisconsin to sort it all out—not that any progress was made before her return to New York. She hadn't even give Aaron any thought as to why she had found her condo trashed. It wasn't something he would have done; her place had been searched for something. Now, here she was in hiding, hours away from the city, from all she knew…away in a cabin with Chris Rosen. She had finally closed the door on Aaron for good. She sat squeezing her knees to her chest, feeling freer than she had in years. Reflecting without internalizing. A huge burden had been lifted from her.

Now that she had time to reflect, she realized she should have done it long ago. She never should have honored her ill-gotten promise to Jan Sands. It had been wrong of Jan to extract such a promise from the very beginning. But what was done was done, and now she had to decide how to go forward. Where did she wish to live? For the first time in her life, she was truly free to make her own decisions and to know they bore little consequence on anyone else. She felt adrift with the knowledge. Did it truly matter where or how she lived if she were to be alone? She knew she wouldn't want to live in Wisconsin near Matthew and Lia; she wouldn't wish to prevent Aaron from visiting them. He would need them more than she would.

XXXXX

Closing her eyes, she saw them both clearly on her balcony in the wee hours. He had asked, "Does Lia know?"

With a nod, the whole scenario tumbled from her lips. "Your mother took us to dinner at Mano's; then we all went out for a drink near the wharf," she began, as the story spilled from her lips. In the end, she asked for his forgiveness with a lowered head. "I'm so sorry, Aaron. I couldn't tell you, so I encouraged Tessa to pursue you, and I went away."

She couldn't bring herself to meet his eyes; he strolled to the rail. She risked a glance in his direction from her seat. Silently lamenting, but knowing in her heart he needed to know. He had whirled to face her with such intense emotion.

"You couldn't tell me then. Why are you telling me now."

"Because your marriage could be salvaged. Roy is *dead*, Aaron. Tessa is alive. She's waiting for you." She rose as her whole body shook. "I'll never have another chance to make things right. But you, you do have that chance."

He turned away from her clutching the railing so tightly his knuckles were white. Without another word, he stormed from her condo and her life. Nothing tied her down; her condo was just a structure. A structure she called home, but it held no family member, no pet. Just stuff; stuff could be replaced. Here she was twenty-six years old, and what had she to show for herself, her existence?

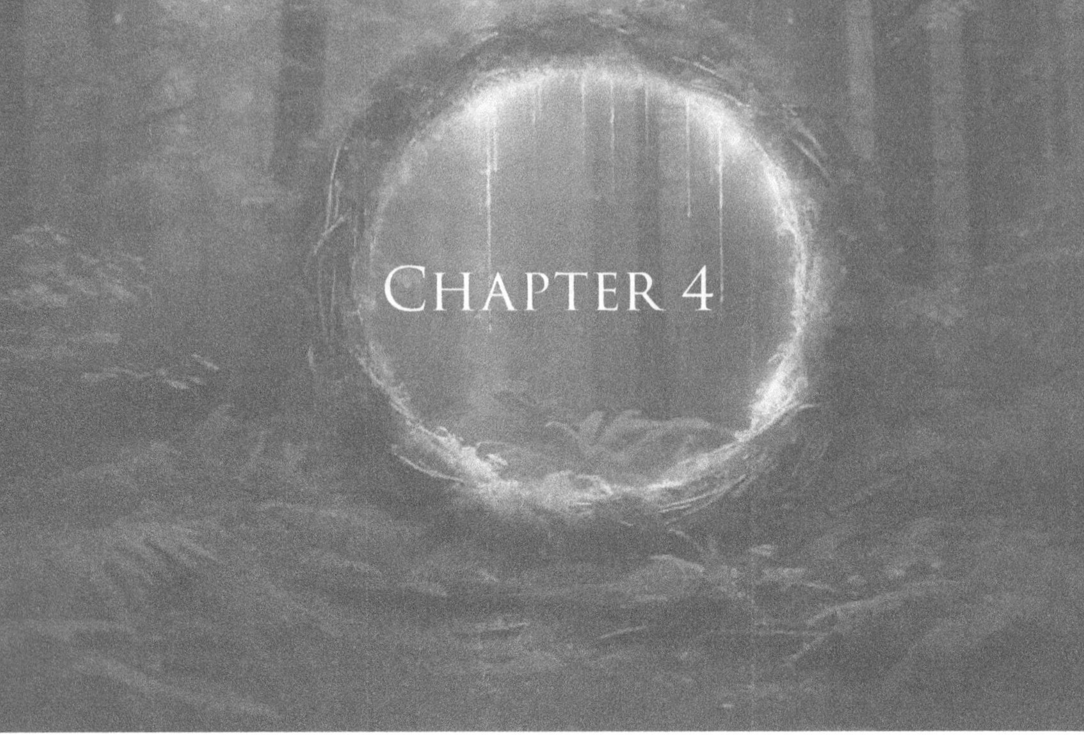

CHAPTER 4

The course of her life appeared to have built up to the present situation, as if it was all preordained by some unseen force. A force that sent her to run and hide from all she knew. Just as she had run to her aunt in Australia after Jan had made her accusation. Just as she had moved to New York City after completing her four-year degree in horticulture to get further away from Aaron. But this time it was different. Never before had she felt her life threatened as she did this time.

Dear Diary,

I'm not sure what day it is any more, does it matter if I do not know? Is it a sign I've lost my mind?.. What does matter is that I'm sitting here in reflection, and I've come to a tough conclusion... It's time I stop running. Running hasn't solved any of my problems. Running didn't get me permanently away from Aaron. I have to face facts. Somehow I found the courage to face Aaron and send him packing for good. Honestly, I never imagined I would feel relieved there are no secrets between us. But I do. I can stand on this bolder and twirl about in relief. It was such an incredible burden I had carried for too long. I didn't even realize its weight until it was gone.

I'm not certain if I know the facts where Roy is concerned. So, here I have run. I hide in a beautiful lodge with a delicious man, waiting to see if someone can explain what I should do. My gut tells me to go to Mark and tell him whatever I know. The trouble there is that I don't know what they think I know. So, I play a waiting game that leaves me in a lair with a tantalizing protector. That's why I've decided to camp here in the woods away from Chris and his house. I can't hold out if we are both staying in there together. I am so incredibly weak.

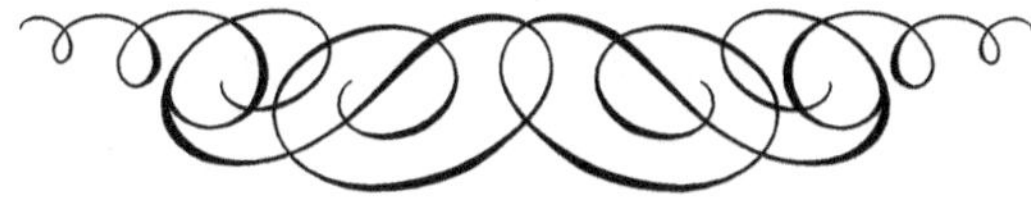

XXXXX

What had she ignored in Ithaca that she should have seen? So much she had ignored over the years due to shame or embarrassment. An inability to dare ask pertinent questions of the people who would have been able to answer them…Mother…Mr. Sands. Aunt June, like her sisters, would undoubtedly not have answered her questions; Aunt June would have glossed over the past. She would have chosen not to know any innuendoes or discover her niece's questionable parentage. What of Kimberly? Did she know anything, or had she heard rumors from her parents? Most likely it had been rumors that had sent Tanya's life into turmoil. She mentally sifted through rumors. What she sought now were the facts she had glossed over. As she wracked her brain, and scoured her journal she sat back. Until Jan's announcement that one evening way back in college Tanya had never doubted her parentage. Even now when she considered who had taught her to walk through the mist, to practice mind linking with her sisters. Who had been a loving mentor until his death, she should never have believed Jan's wild accusations. In her heart she knew who's daughter she was. It had not been her that had been Matthew, Seniors child from the affair with her mother, it had been Franklin. Now, it made sense why her brother had never been able to walk in the mist. Why he had no gift to mind link with his siblings or his father, he had not been a full fledgling. Of course. Why hadn't she seen it before?

What had she missed in her inexperience that she should have realized for truth? Perhaps Mother had been right—she lived too much in fantasy and not enough in reality. Isn't that what her sisters had said in different words? She should have chosen but didn't. Her mind was sometimes fuzzy, especially after returning from Evald. It took days to and see this realm as it truly was without the aurora of Evald giving life a euphoric haze. Living on the cusp by not choosing her world, she had missed something significant. Something about Roy that led to her beautiful home being ransacked, led to her feeling she was not safe there or in her favorite haunts. She dared not involve Lucy any further for fear of endangering her as well. If she had seen Roy clearly, she should have realized the danger before it had invaded her space and sent her running into hiding with a man she found incredibly delectable. She had never been able to decipher what Chris' role should be in her life because she had been too busy sorting out the quagmire her life had become. In running from ugliness, she had run into quick sand of her own making, and now she had to force herself free to see clearly into the future. Inadvertently, she had dragged another man into her mess, a man that admittedly sent her heart into a tizzy at his touch. Her emotions were all over the page. Everything was moving way too fast. Part of her wanted simply to move with the flow and forget Roy and all that had happened. She wanted to allow herself to become entangled with the sumptuous treat she and Lucy referred to as "Captivating Chris." Had they both not found him delectable for over a year? And here she was with him. She had been leaning more and more toward him for months, so much so it had given her an excuse to keep Roy at arm's length, rather than ready for a quick reunion.

XXXXX

With a sign, she lay back and closed her eyes, letting memories of recent evens pour over her in the hopes of piecing together the puzzle of Roy's demise. In her mind's eye, she plopped down exhausted in the center of her cream-on-cream textured camelback sofa and leaned back into the cushions. The accident didn't make sense; the more she thought about it, the less it rang with truth. The peel of the phone dragged her from her reverie. Cecilia's soft, loving voice drifted through the line. Tanya found herself pouring out all her troubles on her unsuspecting sister.

"Oh, honey, I'm so sorry," Lia cooed. "I wish I could be there for you."

"Me too," Tanya admitted. "Oh Lia, I'm sorry to burden you. What's up?

"Oh, I was just thinking about you."

Tanya smiled into the phone. "Thanks Lia. That really means more than you know. I've really been thinking a lot lately. Maybe too much."

"I can understand that. T, this accident shouldn't change your decision to separate from Roy. He was headed down a path you didn't want to follow; it had nothing to do with your feelings toward him. It had everything to do with the choices he was making. Please keep that in mind."

"I will. But now that he's lying there in a coma, none of that seems to matter. Earlier this week when we had lunch, he wanted to move in. He wanted to reconcile and leave his family in Queens. When he pulls through, I've decided to bring him home and start over."

"Tanya, this may or may not change things for Roy. Please give this decision a lot of thought. You may need to wait until he's a wake and you can talk it over."

"He'll need care when he wakes up. While he's on the mend, he can stay here. After that, we'll see what he decides. Before this accident he was making progress. He'd checked into rehab and everything. We had lunch together several times a week."

"Just promise me you won't be rash in your decisions out of sympathy, T," Lia said into the phone. "Please think it through. Your problems never stemmed from lack of affection for one another, but rather from his dependency on his family."

"Okay. I hear you."

"Just keep in mind why you bought that condo on your own, T. Think about where the two of you have been for the last eight months. You were beginning to move on with your life. He wasn't the one."

"How could I really move on? We made a commitment."

"You never got a license."

"So what. We were considering doing just that only a week ago."

Tanya admitted, thinking to herself, *At least that's what Roy was pressing upon her just before his accident.* Cecilia sucked in her breath but didn't speak while Tanya's mind reran the lunch date with Roy where he had pressed her to get married. He wanted reunification with her, and he wanted to make everything legitimate; she had been the one to hesitate. She had moved on, but was she headed in the right direction?

"This accident could be the deciding factor for us."

"Just promise you'll take things slow."

"Yeah, okay."

"I'll call tomorrow."

"Okay."

"Love you."

"You too. Goodnight."

"'Night."

After the call, she found herself too restless for the much-needed sleep and changed into one of Roy's old navy blue t-shirts, a gray pair of sweats, and jogging shoes to go for a jog through the neighborhood. While she jogged, her mind replayed her last conversation with Roy. Had it only been days ago over lunch? "Roy, I'm sorry. My dad drank; I won't tolerate living with an alcoholic for a husband. It's embarrassing the way you don't control yourself. I can't handle that behavior."

"I know, hon. That's why I'm in rehab. I want to work things out."

"Can we?" She had reservations. Since moving to the city with him, so many things had changed. He had a side to him she didn't want to know. "I know your family means a lot to you, but I don't know if they're a positive influence on you." He nodded as they sat at a sidewalk eatery on Platt Street near her office. "I know we still love one another, Roy, but I don't know that I can accept the life you offer." His eyes brimmed with tears. She shook her head. "Oh, Roy. I hate to say you have to choose me or your family. But honestly, it's more I'm asking you to choose to be the man you were when we first met then the addict you've become."

"T. I'm clean. I want to stay clean, the way I was when we first met. Forget my family. You're the girl I married; you're my family."

She so wanted to believe him, and so realized how much he desired to be accepted by his extended family. A family his mother had the good sense to run from after his father died. She sighed.

"I want you to succeed, Roy. You'd have to stay clean for a year for me to really believe in you again. Can you manage on your own that long?"

"I won't be on my own. I have the support group from rehab to help me." She nodded. She so wished she could believe him, but she wasn't ready to trust him again. "Gram wants us to move out to Sacramento with her. She invited me to stay with her while I work through rehab, a change of scenery and all that."

Tanya nodded. "That sounds like a great idea. You could go ahead, find a place for me. I could sell or rent the condo and join you."

"Would you really do that?"

She shrugged. "Roy, I have no ties here; just a job and friends. You're my family." As she looked into his handsome, finely chiseled face, she imagined he'd meet someone out there; maybe that would be for the best. Someone who liked him where he was at the moment, not the man he'd been. Tanya stumbled as she jogged, bringing her back to the present. Exhaustion bested her, as she saw her condo building ahead in the distance. She paced herself the remainder of the way back and imagined how nice her bed would feel after a long, hot shower.

The answering machine on the corner of the kitchen counter was blinking as she walked in the door. She kicked off her sneakers by the door before walking to the counter on the muted gray low pile carpet. Mrs. Wilson had arranged to spend the night at the hospital; Leo had made the arrangements for herself and Janet. She would see Tanya tomorrow. A long, steamy shower was just what Tanya needed. The only thing missing was a stiff martini and a massage. She sat down on the sofa and drifted off into a restless sleep without finishing her drink.

In her dream, she was the nurse, watching in horror as Roy was struck and then dragged down the street by his pant leg by an old brown Cadillac Seville. She opened her mouth to scream, but omitted no sound it seemed stuck in her throat. Tanya awoke in a cold sweat; she sat up and showered again. As dawn broke, she grabbed her keys and headed for the sanctuary of her office. By lunchtime she was ready for a break and hurried to the hospital to check on Roy. She stood by his side holding his hand, chatting away nonsensically. His aunt Elaine cleared her throat as she entered the room. The woman always looked and smelled perfect; Tanya had always admired her poise under any situation. Tanya turned with a brief smile. "I just dashed over on my lunch break," she explained.

Elaine nodded. "It was kind of you to offer Mrs. Wilson a place to stay."

Tanya nodded, as she released Roy's hand and stepped back from the bed. "It's the least I could do to help out." She shrugged.

"Sleep is a wonderful panacea for the body," Elaine agreed kindly.

"So I'm told," Tanya replied as she drifted toward the door.

"Tanya?"

Tanya spun around to face Elaine's back. "I know you don't see eye to eye with my husband or my son, but I am grateful you're devoted to my nephew."

Tanya was stunned as she stood in the doorway to his room. She pressed her lips together and numbly nodded. "Thank you," was all she could manage.

XXXXX

Days later, she had confided in Lucy about her intentions of reconciling with Roy when he woke up. "T, are you insane?"

"He'll need someone to look after him."

"The guy's still affiliated with the mob. You don't just walk away from that." Lucy glared at her with her hands on her narrow hips, as if Tanya were planning a trip to Mars. "Don't act crazy. This changes nothing. Think this through."

"I've given the whole situation a lot of thought over the last few days. It's the right thing to do; I'm still his wife. I took a vow."

"He's got family. His gram is talking of shipping him to California to live with her. The woman has the money to provide him with the care he'll need. You don't have to do this."

"It's my job."

Lucy shook her head. "No, Tanya, it really isn't."

"Luc, we were together for three years. That has to count for something." Lucy chewed on her cheek and remained silent. Tanya offered her a ride home. Lucy accepted; she had a car she rarely drove. It was easier to grab a train to work in mid-town Manhattan from her up-town penthouse apartment on the East Side near Lenox Hill Hospital. She shared the sumptuous home with her parents and two unmarried sisters.

"Stay for dinner," Lucy offered once they reached her apartment.

"I'm really not feeling social," Tanya admitted grimly. "I'm beat."

"You look awful," Lucy agreed, examining her closely. "You have to eat."

"Luc, I'm fine, really."

"Right. When was the last time you got in a good four hours?"

Tanya shrugged. Lucy nodded thoughtfully.

As she pulled behind the four-story brownstone walk-up she lived in, Tanya was grateful her condo came with its own parking space. Most places in the city offered on-street parking if you could find it. And garage parking was pricy. That's why she often took the train into the office; lately she drove so she could dash to Roy's side. But usually she only drove in on Friday's if she was not planning to stay at Lucy's. She stretched as she got out of her red convertible Mustang and popped the small trunk where she kept a canvas car cover. It was a nice afternoon for a walk around the neighborhood. Tanya looked around as if seeing it all again for the first time. This was a pleasant neighborhood; how fortunate she was to have afforded a condo of her own. It was great having the convenience of a corner grocery store, with fresh fruit and vegetables on the sidewalk in open crates just down the street. She liked the look of the brownstones mixed with the white cement buildings near the corner store. She was fortunate to have the view of a small park across the street from her condo balcony and the narrow driveway leading to the small parking lot, where everyone had an assigned slot. The streets were lined with neat, little trees, and it was kept reasonably clean year round. It was a daily track to her mid-town, Manhattan office from across the river, but this slice of peace had made the trek worthwhile. When she entered her condo she saw the answering machine blinking madly. Aaron's strong, masculine voice flowed from the machine, like a refreshing burst of air. She picked up the receiver and dialed from memory.

Tessa answered on the second ring. "Hey, Tessa, is Aaron around?"

"*No.*" Tessa gave a drunken yell. "Mind your own damn business. Why can't his family leave us the hell alone." Her words were slurred but came through loud and clear. "Our marriage would be fine if you all would butt out. Aaron doesn't need any of you nosing around, and putting in your two cents every time he turns around. I'm all the family he needs. I know you wish he'd married Tanya, but he didn't."

"Um. Sorry to bother you, Tessa." Tanya tried to back away, realizing Tessa mistook her for Cecilia. "I was returning a call. I'm sure we'll catch up later."

"F— you. Your sister is the only problem in our marriage. Every time we hear from you, it makes him long for her all over again."

"Whoa, Tessa. If you have problems, Tanya's not the one to blame."

"She doesn't need to. He married me because he couldn't have *her*."

"Listen, Tessa, Aaron married you. He loves you, not her."

"Like hell he does. I think he just married me because he wanted to get back at her or something."

"Um. Tessa, I have to go. I'm probably not the person you should be talking too."

"You can't take the truth? Your sister slept with my husband, but she wouldn't marry him, I did. She's still sleeping with him."

"Whoa girl. That's a major accusation. You need to work this out with your husband."

"*Like hell.* I double-dated in high school with your innocent sister and Aaron. I know how far they went." Tanya's hand shook on the receiver. She recalled the prom night when things went a little too far with Aaron. They had not had sex, but they came close. Too close. "Tessa, you should be discussing this with Aaron, not me." She hung up the phone and sank onto a bar stool, sobbing. Moments later the phone rang; she reached over and turned off the machine. She couldn't bring herself to talk to anyone else.

She called Cecilia later and never mentioned her conversation with Tessa. They talked of Lockwood and how lucky they were to have left the small community where they had grown up. Cecilia laughed. "You got that right. The best either of us could do was leave." She sighed heavily into the phone. "I'm glad we got out."

"Me too," Tanya admitted. "But did we really escape? Or are we scarred for life?" She asked the silence that followed.

"Lia?"

"Hmm?"

Tanya moved on.

"It's been such a stressful day, I'm wiped out. If you don't mind, I'm going to call it a night."

"No problem. Keep in touch. I've got wide shoulders."

Tanya chuckled as they signed off. The phone rang again as Tanya headed down the hall without any intensions of answering it. She shook her head as Tessa's unmistakable, angry, drunken voice yelling through the machine. "*I know you're there. Pick up. I got something you need to hear.*" Tanya moved close enough to the machine to turn down the volume. Tessa could use up the tape and then Tanya could simply erase the message without listening to it. She would talk to Aaron about considering the money she had lent him for the down payment on their house as a gift. She would never use the room over the garage. She had liked the idea of having her own space if she ever returned to Lockwood. Matthew and Cecilia had at least used the place. Undoubtedly, it was a problem that Aaron wouldn't let Tessa's family use her apartment.

Nor would he allow anyone to rent the space out. Tanya knew she would never use the in-law, apartment over the garage. How had she been so blind to Tessa's feelings? Suddenly she understood how Roy felt; she recalled his jealousy toward Aaron. Tanya had assured Roy on numerous occasions her relationship with Aaron was platonic. It would take an idiot not to see their emotions for one another ran much deeper than normal friendship or extended family relations. She had spent too many years lying to everyone, even trying to convince herself.

The phone continued to ring. Stop. Ring again. Finally, Tanya walked over and lifted the receiver without listening to the person on the other end. "Tessa, I'd be happy to chat when you've calmed down. At present, my plate is full. Please refrain from calling again tonight." With that she hung up and unplugged the phone. She decided to shower and tumble into bed.

Tanya awoke to find Lucy standing over her. "Come on. I plugged your phone in, girl. You've really had an exhausting day."

Tanya sat up and grabbed a shirt from the foot of the bed; she pulled it on and raked her hand through her mane. "Did you listen to the messages?"

"I erased the messages from some ranting lunatic." Lucy shook her head. "Want to tell me about it?"

Tanya shook her head. "I'm really not up for company."

"I bet. But you need it." She had noticed Roy's Grandmother, Beatrice, seemed to have popped in and out again. With a deep sigh she looked into Lucy's excited face, with a shrug she agreed to go out for a drink. "As in one, Lucy." She got up and padded to the closet to pull out a pair of dark, pressed jeans and pulled them on.

"Surely, you're not going to wear that t-shirt."

She looked down at her pink and white Garfield bed shirt and smiled at Lucy and looked into the closet. She pulled out a blue and white horizontal striped quarter-sleeved, square-neck sweater and replaced the t-shirt. She slipped on a pair of knee-high, black patent leather pumps. "Okay. I'm ready."

Lucy shook her head as she shooed her toward the bathroom. Lucy applied eye makeup, teased her hair into submission, and handed her a bottle of Gucci perfume. Tanya sprayed a little on, brushed her teeth, applied mauve lipstick, and smiled over at Lucy's approving smile.

The moment she stepped into the familiar surroundings of Cahoot's, she was thankful Lucy had brought her out. She hadn't realized how much she needed the interaction until she arrived. "Captivating Chris" took her hand and kissed it before stamping the back. She smiled at Lucy, chuckling inside. Happy she had come, happy she realized who Chris was after all such a long time. Unfortunately, Chris knew he was attractive, and he cultivated a flirtatious relationship with several girls. Lucy swore he looked at Tanya differently. "Sure, I'm safely married off. Strings to someone else and no worry for him." Tanya assured her.

"Everyone knows you've been separated for close to a year," Lucy reminded her.

"Thanks to you."

Lucy smiled with a shrug. "Roy made a lot of bad choices, T. You're willing to forgive them because of this accident. I think you should give that some more thought."

"Luc, Roy and I were talking through our problems, even before this accident." She shrugged. "I may find other guys attractive, but I love Roy. We have history."

Jonathan greeted her with a bear hug before she'd walked in the door. She and Lucy never had to stand in line. She and Lucy got their drinks from the bar before Chris and Jonathan got them out into the hall. He assisted Jonathan in lifting one girl on either bicep. Tanya never felt comfortable on his arm as he moved around in a circle as a free show for those awaiting entrance into the club. Lucy loved the attention. Jonathan was in his bodybuilding glory until he growled for Chris assistance. He looked at Tanya, as she was lowered to a chair. "You've put on a few pounds since the last time I lifted you both."

Tanya felt her cheeks burn. "I hadn't noticed. My apologies." He nodded as he flexed his arm. She managed to smile up at him as she rose. "Does this mean you'll have to find an actual dumbbell for your exhibition?"

He shook his head. "It means I just have to lift more weights."

She leaned over to kiss his cheek affectionately. "Thank you, Jonathan, you're such a dear."

Lucy was at her side with drinks in hand. Tanya gratefully took her tequila sunrise and sipped through the stirrer. Chris had already returned to his post at the door. Tanya wondered why people chose to hang around outside; did they really imagine getting in? It always amazed her how people would hold out.

As she watched the dancers from a seat at their regular table, Tanya reflected why it had taken her so long to place Chris. Maybe she had been too caught up in work and life with Roy. How strange to meet yet another person from her dreams, a person she had once fleetingly spent an hour or so with at the Empire State Building was absolutely ludicrous. Did he remember? Is that why he was so flirtatious?

Lucy broke through Tanya's reverie. "Keys?"

Tanya dug in her pocket for Lucy's car keys. Lucy leaned toward her ear. "I'm putting my purse in the hatch. Need anything?" Tanya shook her head, as Lucy turned away. Lucy hadn't returned by the time Tanya's glass was empty. Tiffany, one of the waitresses, came over to offer a refill. Tanya stifled a yawn. "Just cranberry and soda, please," Tanya practically had to yell to be heard over the din of music and conversations. She laid some money on the table as she stood up. Joe, from her office glanced up at her, questioning. "For my drink," she explained as she headed for the restroom. He picked up the money and handed it back to her. "Thanks."

She made her way toward Chris as she returned, still not spotting Lucy. Chris wrapped an arm around her waist as he collected money from a group of four. She leaned her head on his shoulder as he stamped their hands. "Chris, can you call me a cab?" His wide, black leather-banded, big-faced watch proclaimed it was eleven thirty on a Friday night. Things were just beginning to pick up at the club. Thankfully, she would not be going to work tomorrow. She had decided to cocoon herself away for the rest of the weekend. She loved the smell of Chris' Cool Waters cologne as she snuggled against the soft linen of his light, black linen suit jacket.

"Where's that fancy convertible tonight?"

"I came in Lucy's car." She didn't notice Chris signal Jonathan because her eyes were closed as a guy stepped up to the door. Tanya opened her eyes to see a smirk on the stranger's face and a comment from his mouth about even the help getting lucky. Chris ignored him, as Jonathan appeared at Tanya's right. Chris glanced down at her. "I'll give you a lift."

"Thanks, but I don't want to hang around until closing."

Everyone who knew her couldn't mistake the haggard look under makeup. He kissed her forehead. "Bad dreams?"

Tanya shrugged. "I'm fine. Just weary." Jonathan moved to converse with Chris for a few moments. Tanya attempted to wiggle free from Chris, but he held firm to her waist. Tiffany appeared from nowhere and took Chris' place at the door as Chris released her waist to take hold of hand. "Come on," Chris said firmly in her ear.

She pulled back. "Chris, thanks for the offer, but a cab is fine."

"No problem," he assured her, as he guided her through the throng and out the front door.

"I'm not good company tonight."

He smirked as he gave her a sidewise glance. "That's okay."

Down in the underground parking lot he opened the passenger door to Jonathan's green Gremlin hatchback. Tanya slid in without further protest. He adjusted the driver's seat as he climbed in beside her and started the engine.

"Chris. Do you know I live in Brooklyn?"

He nodded; she knew he lived on 2nd Avenue in lower Manhattan somewhere. Jonathan had once mentioned he lived near Central Park when they were horseback riding. "I know where you live. It's not far from Jonathan's," he admitted. They drove in relative silence over the bridge into Brooklyn. Chris had the radio on low to some easy listening station. "I just closed my eyes tonight...dream weaver...if I can just reach the morning light..."

"Hmm, I love this song. Gary Wright is great," she stated as she leaned her head back against the headrest. He swung into the narrow drive of the brownstone as if he had been there many times before and pulled into one of the few visitor parking slots. Tanya sat up as he turned off the engine. They walked up the stairs quietly. Tanya kept looking over her shoulder at him curiously.

Chris slipped into her place as she removed the key from the door. She stepped out of her pumps and shoved them into the closet behind the door. Chris took off his black sneakers and smiled as he realized for the first time just how short she was. She and Lucy favored stilettos; even their hiking boots had heels. The open floor plan of her small condo gave the appearance of being spacious. A galley kitchen and extra-wide counter doubling as a bar was lending space for the dining area and living room. The dining area yielded a small, center claw-legged, oak, oval table with four matching high-back chairs, covered with a white tablecloth that appeared to never having been used, save as a rest for the centerpiece of fresh-cut black-eyed-susans. The dining area was separate from the living room by a sectional cream-colored sofa. He noticed the pale earth tones of peach, tan, and blue brushed and blended across the walls, highlighting the cream-on-cream sofa. The carpet yielded flecks of the same earthy colors with ecru sheers between the same muted tones in darker colors. The colors reminded Chris of the seashore, of sand and water.

The dining area sported a built in corner cupboard, painted a high-gloss white, with decorative glass doors in the top half, displaying a set of Nortaki floral china with the gold trim. The display was balanced by a set of oriental porcelain vases with gilt gold hands in the shape of a ladies white lace-up boots with a pink floral pattern rounded out the display. The bottom half of the corner cupboard yielded a wide, beaded country slat wooden door to hide treasures behind. The narrow wall, which separated the cupboard from an alcove near the French doors, sported a glossy white chair rail that separated a creamy white upper wall from the salmon colored lower part. The crown molding and the ceiling were painted high gloss white. He glimpsed the built in bookshelves beyond the arch of the alcove, and a desk, with a large brown office chair tucked neatly away in front of a long, narrow window in the small alcove.

He nodded. "You know a talented woodworker, or was this place like this when you moved in?" Tanya was putting a kettle on behind the counter. She glanced at him over the counter as he sat down on a cushion covered milk canister. "A friend from home. How can you tell?"

Chris shrugged as he moved toward the glass doors to the balcony. "My older brother's a carpenter." He stated as he stepped out into the cool night air. Her steps were so light; he smelled her perfume rather than hearing her step onto the balcony. He turned to smile down at her. "This is a nice place," he admitted. "I see a lot of you here." He glanced at the plants sprinkled around the balcony suspended in pots and hanging over the railing in metal plant boxes. They effectively created privacy from the neighbors on either side. A small round cast iron table and chairs were painted a deep green to blend with the plants; she put indoor/outdoor fake grass down on the floor of the balcony. Here Tanya had created seclusion three stories up. The lights of the big city seemed far away from this tiny oasis. He heard the whistle of her teakettle.

"Would you care for some tea? I think I have a few beers in the fridge if you prefer."

"Tea is fine." He wandered over to the alcove while she busied herself in the kitchen. He scanned the titles on the book bindings with a raised brow. She was a vicarious reader with a number of familiar sci-fi authors. Isaac Asimov, Piers Anthony, along with classics like Robert Frost's poetry, Emily Bronte, Dante, Longfellow, *The Road Less Traveled*, *What You Should Know about Condos*, *The Riches Man in Babylon*, *The Black Arrow*, *The Count of Monte Cristo*, *Gulliver's Travels*, among many others.

"Did you read these adventure books?" he called to her from the alcove.

"I wouldn't have them if I didn't enjoy re-reading them from time to time." He smiled as he continued to browse through her collection. A shelf of colored cloth bound eight-inch-high books with no titles along the spine caught his eye. Curious he drew out a teal-colored book and randomly opened it. He was drawn into Tanya's eye for a shot and her love of travel. The pages were filled with breathtaking views and neatly calligraphic captions or titles. Brief, journal entry boxes were sprinkled among the shots, along with memorabilia, dating, recording where and when. He glanced through another and realized each book represented a year or event in her life. Flipping through, he found few photos of friends or family members. She enjoyed landscapes, nature shots, and portraits. Tanya sat a tray on the low, black, oblong coffee table, and moved aside a dark brown, leather-bound calendar journal. A crimson ribbon marked a page within the gilded cover.

Chris glanced up from the album in his hand. He smiled at the tray with what appeared to be fresh-baked peanut butter and chocolate chip cookies on a plate. Tanya blushed. "I love to bake," she admitted, as she poured herself a cup of tea. Chris watched with interest as she opened a large, five-pound bottle of honey and add a heavy dollop into her tea before stirring it and taking a sip. Jonathan won another bet. Tanya was a domestic little Betty Crocker.

"Do you eat all that you bake?"

She laughed. "If I did I would be as wide as I am tall. I give most way to friends, people I know in the service, etc." She handed him a cup of tea. He accepted it and added cream and sugar as he glanced around the room as he tried a peanut butter cookie. "How do I make your list?"

"Consider yourself added." He wandered over to the photos on the wall near the entertainment center. Nodding to himself, it was an easy bet for Jonathan, who made sure Chris knew he had been to her place many times. He had warned Chris, Tanya was a country girl at heart, a nester, a girl groomed for motherhood and farming. He didn't see much to indicate either in her pristine home. Most of the photos were scenic shots taken from all over the world, framed in matching plain black wooden frames. He recognized the black beaches of Australia, the Suisse Alps, unfamiliar, white sandy beaches, clear turquoise blue waters, and odd rock formations near a sea.

"Are all these photos yours?"

"Mostly," she admitted as she sipped her tea.

"Nice place." He observed. "Your photos look like postcards."

She smiled. "Some of them are," she admitted with a shrugged. "Some are calendar covers." She gave him an amused look. "You seem surprised."

His gaze rested on her for a time as he shrugged. "This place is bigger than a lot of studios in the city. I figured you for a studio girl."

"I bought this place almost a year ago; it has two small bedrooms."

"Really. Have you a housemate?"

She cocked her head. "I'm separated. I don't really need a roommate."

He nodded. "I remember." He moved near. "Jonathan and Lucy helped you move in, right?" She nodded with a sigh. "Still, it's surprising you haven't found a roommate."

"At present I do happen to have a house guest. She's out visiting family."

"Where's she from?"

"California."

"A relative of yours?"

"No. An acquaintance."

Chris put on a cassette of mixed music. "Sea of Love" came resonating through the speakers.

"No TV?"

Tanya smiled as she walked over to the bottom cabinet of the entertainment center, inside was stashed a small thirteen-inch color TV. She turned toward him. "I'm not a TV fan. I only have whatever you can catch from an antenna on the roof. This dial adjusts the antennae from here."

Chris nodded; it seemed to figure this wisp of a woman loved books more than television would practically have no TV at all. He knew she and Lucy went to football parties or to bars for the big games; it never dawned on him what sort of TV he might find in her home. Glancing around, it didn't look as if she truly lived here. "I guess you don't spend a lot of time here?"

She shrugged. "Actually, a fair amount. I enjoy the solitude." He nodded. She stifled a yawn and set down her cup. "I suppose Jonathan will be expecting your return. I'm exhausted. Thanks for the ride."

Chris glanced as his watch as he turned on the TV and played around until he found a channel. He grabbed a combo peanut-butter-chocolate- chip cookie. "Hey, these are really good."

She nodded as she leaned back against the sofa. "Chris, I'm really tired." He nodded and brushed a wisp of sandy blonde hair back from her face, as he reached behind him to turn off the lamp on his side of the sofa. She grimaced. "I've been set up, is that it?"

He shrugged wrapping an arm around her shoulder and pulling her closer, as he turned toward the TV. She never meant to drift off to sleep, resting her head on him, but that's what she did. When she shifted, he moved so she could lie down, and he took the tray into the kitchen and turning off all the lights save the light over the sink. He went back to the sofa and picked up the leather-bound journal and sat near her head, randomly flipping through.

It seems another lifetime ago when I worked here and stayed with Rosie. Imagine laying eyes on that guy again after all these years. This is an amazingly small world. It reminds me of meeting a couple from Syracuse, New York, in Germany while traveling with Auntie. Chris probably doesn't even remember the incident, let alone that I'm that girl.

Tanya stirred and opened her eyes. Chris quickly flipped toward the beginning in an effort to seem nonchalant as his heart raced. He looked over the cover as she sat up.

"Who's Aaron?"

"Hmm? Oh, a friend from back home. Did he call?" she asked looking around disoriented.

Chris shook his head as he glanced at her answering machine and noticed the blinking light. "No. But you have a message." Her eyes moved to the machine, but she made no move to get up. He smiled and read aloud from her journal:

> *I put the sink stopper in upside down to mop the floors.*
> *I wanted it to be clean for the new carpet. I've never had*
> *a place with a garbage disposal before, and didn't think*
> *much about how snugly the stopper fit into the drain until*
> *I couldn't get it out. Aaron went knocking on the neighbors'*
> *doors. He borrowed some tools and had to remove the pipes*
> *to pop out the stopper. What was I thinking. Can you*
> *believe I put it in upside down? C'est la vie. He didn't seem*
> *perturbed at all he's accustomed to my craziness.*

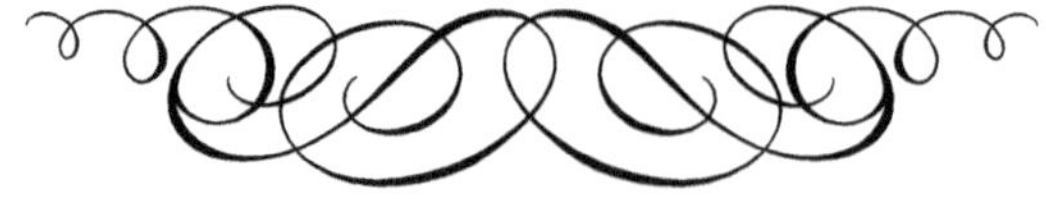

Tanya burst out laughing as Chris glanced at her with a smirk. Chris joined her boisterous laugh as he closed the book; she wiped tears from her eyes as he sat it down.

"Sorry, I didn't mean to pry."

She waved him aside. "No, that's why it's there. It's my 'happy book.'"

Chris smiled at her. "Your 'happy book'?"

Tanya shrugged. "Yea, ya know, a place to write down funny thoughts or incidents. That way when you're down you've got something to pick up and give yourself a lift." From her lips it sounded as if every table in America carried such a book rather than just her coffee table.

His blue eyes flashed with merriment as he gazed at her in amusement.

"Get down much?" He couldn't picture her really depressed; she was too vibrant for such melodrama. "I always see you smiling." Glancing at the book, she had a lot to smile about.

"I prefer a smile," she admitted. "Who wants to be around a whining person for any length of time?" She shrugged. "I am normal; I do have moments when I'm down." She insisted, "That's why I leave that book laying around." She gave him a coltish grin. "Anyone's welcome to read from my 'happy book.' If you can't laugh at yourself, whom can you laugh at?"

He shook his head in wonder. "You're a strange girl, Tanya Gilbert." His eyes drifted from her eyes to her lips. Tanya caught a whiff of his cologne as his mood changed; she closed her eyes and imagined allowing herself melting against him. Her eyes flew open playfully.

"Did you enjoy delving into my silly pleasures?" she asked, mischievously alluring. His face reddened as if he'd been caught looking through her underwear drawer. She brightened at the thought. "I suppose I'll have to add this night."

"How will it go?" His face was flushed with color.

"Hmmm, rescued from loud, undulating club by a dashing, captivating prince, and whisked off to my humble abode on a silvery thread." They both burst out laughing. He caught her off guard as he leaned in and brushed her lips with a kiss.

"Why the silvery thread?" he whispered against her cheek, as she pulled away, her cheeks a blaze as she turned to a commercial on the TV and attempted to focus; she managed a slight shrug.

"Must be the adventure books you asked if I had read," she offered. Why had she thought that? What brought out a sense of the wood whenever she felt intimate with this man?

He cleared his throat. "Have you considered having a security system installed?"

Tanya gave him a quizzical look. "Why would I do that? I've little of value." She absently ran a hand through her thick, unruly blonde curls and gently tossed her head to one side. Had she any idea how the unconscious movement seemed seductive?

"You live alone in a big city." He looked around. "Securities systems are protection." They turned in unison toward the door as they heard a key slipped into the lock. Lucy and Jonathan entered. Chris turned back toward Tanya and in a low voice. "Lucy has a key to your place?"

Tanya shrugged. "So does Jonathan. He doesn't live that far from me, should I ever lock myself out." He held out his hand expectantly, she gave him a quizzical look. "What?"

"Where's mine? I'm feeling left out."

She smiled and pushed against his upper arm playfully, as she called out a greeting toward the door.

"What'd I miss?" Lucy asked walking toward the sofa.

"Besides my ire at being set up?" Tanya asked looking into Lucy's eyes. Lucy blushed as Tanya added, "Just Chris looking for a way into my 'happy book.'"

Jonathan gaffed. "Oh, like he's not already there," Lucy remarked slipping onto smaller leg of the "L" of the sectional. Jonathan mixed her a drink before sitting down next to her with a soda for himself. Chris noticed how at home they both appeared to be.

Tanya glanced at the clock on the entertainment center in surprise.

"Oh Chris, I'm sorry, I must have dozed off for a bit."

Lucy waved her hand in the air. "Think nothing of it. Chris has been known to have such an effect on ladies."

Tanya blushed as she watched Chris grimace. "I'll keep that in mind for the future," she assured Lucy with a smirk.

XXXXX

Lucy slipped into the office off the kitchen of Cahoot's to chat with Frank Smith when she had seen how frazzled Tanya looked and had run to him for ideas as too how to help her friend. Frank was the manager of Cahoot's and a relative she had always admired. Frank and Lucy sent Chris to take Tanya home and get her to relax. Beautiful young women attracted the crowds, and Frank aimed to keep them happily returning. Who didn't enjoy Lucy's happy, playful persona around? He had often imagined Tanya a bit too prim to hang with a wildflower like Lucy, but they generally went hand in hand. Maybe Lucy needed Tanya's stable influence; Lucy's state-congressional-appointed mother ensured Lucy's entrance into most Manhattan hot nightspots. The whole club knew of Roy's tragic accident and Tanya's vicious predicament. Little wonder the girl wasn't sleeping. Frank knew of Roy, and like many local businessmen, he knew Leo Cicero. It didn't take a genius to guess about what really happened to Roy, but who would voice it?

Lucy confided in Frank, "I think that if Tanya was distracted for a few hours by someone she finds attractive, she'll remember she dumped Roy in the first place."

"If he's still her husband, isn't it her choice?"

"Lord, Frank. They never married legally."

He shrugged. "That doesn't seem to matter to Tanya."

Lucy strutted about his small office like a cage leopard. "She's not thinking clearly at the moment." She shook her head. "She's planning to reconcile and take care of the guy." Lucy looked at him, "Frank, They just had a friend marry them near the falls in some state park in upstate."

Frank burst out laughing. "So, no problem; they're not legal."

Lucy pressed her lips together. "Not yet. But Tanya is talking of redoing their vows when he wakes up. Tanya doesn't realize who his uncle is or how dangerous that man can be."

Frank shrugged. "How can she not know?"

"She's a sheltered country girl. She fell for Roy when he was away at college. She doesn't understand how things are really run." A smirk played on Frank's lips as he poured himself a brandy and raised the decanter to offer Lucy one. She declined with the shake of her head. "Come on, Frank."

"What do you have against this guy?"

"Don't get me started."

"Remind me not to get on your bad side."

She laughed at him playfully, as she tossed back her wild red curls.

"Don't be foolish, dear cousin. How could you ever get on my bad side?"

He shrugged without desiring to give the idea much thought.

CHAPTER 5

Tanya woke with a start. The ringing wasn't part of a dream; it was the phone. She didn't even remember going to bed, as she realized she was clothed under the covers. Vaguely she remembered people talking softly, strong arms lifting her and carrying her to bed. She reached for the phone on the nightstand as she glanced at the wind-up clock that no longer operated as an alarm but still kept good time. She had never really needed an alarm anyway. "Hello?"

"T," came Aaron's concerned voice over the phone. "Hey, you didn't call me back the other night."

"I did." She sat up and brushed the hair from her face. "I caught Tessa at a bad time, so I gave up. She thought I was Lia."

"You okay?"

"I'm fine. Roy's in a coma at St. Vincent's Hospital; even so, I think I may be doing better than you are, my friend."

"Forget Tessa. What happened to Roy?"

"He was hit by a car, while on his motorcycle. His foot caught the bumper, and he was dragged quite a ways."

"How bad is he?"

She shrugged involuntarily. "I don't really know. But I contacted his family, and they've all flown in to be supportive." "I'll grab the next flight down your way."

"No, Aaron." She lowered her voice and tried again, realizing Beatrice may be sleeping in the next room. "I'm fine, really. You've got problems of your own."

"There's nothing I can do for Tessa."

"She's your wife."

"Don't remind me. I'm done with her, T. You're not going to talk me back to her this time."

"She needs you."

"It's okay for you to walk away from Roy, but not me from Tessa?"

"Aaron, I never legally married Roy…we don't have a piece of paper. You do."

"We'll talk when I get there." The line went dead before she could argue.

By the time Aaron arrived, Tanya's life and emotional state were in a different place. She felt adrift and vulnerable. In her mind all would work out, she would take care of Roy, and they would work things out. She hadn't allowed herself to prepare for the worst. She hadn't expected the call she had received from the hospital. Roy had some sort of seizure and died without regaining consciousness. His grandmother and mother came by, taking over. His grandmother wanted him to be cremated so she could take him back to Sacramento with her. Tanya's head was spinning, she hadn't had a moment to really grasp Roy's death, and these two women were discussing how to best handle the final resting place of his body. Tanya sat utterly lost, scarcely able to respond to their questions. She wasn't capable of following their complete conversation. How did they manage? Were they not in mourning?

"Did Roy express a desire either way, Tanya?" his mother asked her. Tanya felt as if she were sitting in a classroom in a Charlie Brown, *Peanuts* comic strip with the teacher going, "*#$@.***?" She couldn't concentrate, and she absently raked her fingers through her mane and looked around for help that did not appear.

Instead, she nodded her agreement with his grandmother. His grandmother took her hand and stroked it comfortingly. "It's all right, dear. He spoke to me. He believed cremation was best. Do you remember?"

Tanya nodded absently, and it was agreed he would be cremated and his grandmother would take his ashes back to Sacramento for burial.

XXXXX

By the time Aaron arrived, she had felt completely drained. "Now that Roy's gone, I'll move closer. This can be our time, T." He walked about the condo thinking out loud until she put up a hand to stop him.

She shook her head. The time had come for him to know why she really left Lockwood all those years and had clung so tightly to Roy.

And we all fall down…

The earth-shattering news had come to her in the form of a tearful phone call from Beatrice.

"*No.*" She hadn't recognized her own voice screaming into the phone. "I was just there for my lunch break. He hadn't changed a bit. This can't be."

"I know, dear. I can't believe it myself. He started convulsing; the nurse came in and ordered me out. I'd only been there a second after Leo… anyway; he had some sort of seizure. That's all there is, dear."

"I'm going to call the nurses' station. Call me back." She hung up and took a scrap of paper from her purse and dialed the number. "Is Nurse Bechtel available please?"

"One moment, ma'am."

"This is Nurse Bechtel," came the kindly voice Tanya had spoken to almost daily for almost a week. Tanya found a lump in her throat when she tried to speak.

"Um." She struggled for a moment. "This is Tanya Gilbert Wilson," she managed to choke out.

"Oh, dear."

"His grandmother called."

"Ah, I'm sorry, dear."

"What happened? I don't understand. I was just there."

"It happens sometimes with head injuries. We really can't explain why."

"I see. Thank you very much for all your help."

"You're welcome. I'm sorry for your loss."

Tanya leaned back against the leather of her chair and swiveled to face the window trying not to cry. She couldn't fall apart at work. Lucy came through the open door. "Hey girl, you day dreaming?" Tanya swirled around to face her with red-rimmed eyes. Lucy dropped into a chair in front of the desk. "What's going on?"

"Beatrice just called." Tanya controlled her voice as she shook her head. It was difficult around the lump in her throat. "He's gone, Luc," she whispered.

Lucy raised her brow, uncertain if she heard right. "What?"

Tanya nodded not able to speak. She grasped the arms of the chair until her knuckles turned white.

"Holy cow. How?" Lucy stammered in surprise. Tanya slumped in the chair she had been gripping as Lucy came around the desk. "We have to get you out of here." Tanya nodded. "Let me go talk to Mr. Kessel," she said as she flew from the office to locate their direct supervisor. Even though he had been in a coma, Tanya had not prepared herself for such a possibility as his dying. Once again, a loved one had not crossed over to Evald. She should have asked Beatrice to help her get him out of the hospital and to the tapestry in their living room so that she could take him into the mist of Evald. He may never have been able to return to this realm, but at least he would be alive.

XXXXX

Death could be so very stressful; Roy's grandmother was a blessing of strength and organization. She and his mother had made all the arrangements.

"I really should shop for an appropriate dress for the funeral," Beatrice said in passing to Tanya as they sat in her living room on the evening of his death. Tanya looked at her blankly for a moment as the words seeped into her brain. She couldn't bear the thought of leaving her sanctuary.

"I've a friend who sells 'Weekenders,'" she offered.

Beatrice knit her brow in thought. "I believe I've heard of that."

"Nice clothing. Shall I phone Teresa and have her bring a selection over?"

Beatrice nodded absently, and Tanya rose to cross to the phone. "How do you know this woman?"

"We work together," Tanya admitted.

XXXXX

The funeral had all seemed surreal to Tanya; Beatrice had insisted on cremation. So much had transpired in so short a time. Beatrice had arranged for the family to go through Roy's things. They were spread between Tanya's condo and his uncle Ryan's trailer in the woods of Queens. Tanya hadn't even realized there were woods in Queens. Mark offered to come over to Tanya's to gather Roy's clothing before the memorial service. He suggested returning for Roy's bureau and any other furniture she wanted removed while she was gone. "Okay, you can coordinate with Jonathan or Lucy to get the bureau while I'm in Wisconsin," she agreed. Mark nodded.

Roy's family had arranged a formal service; they insisted on a viewing prior to cremation. Tanya lay out his blue-gray pin-stripe suit he had last wore at a business dinner a year before. He had left it in her closet. Mark offered to come by and pick up the outfit and take it to the mortician. Beatrice assured Tanya that Roy would looked fitting in the suit.

"And what of you?" Tanya asked before leaving. "He was more like your own son, was he not?"

Beatrice nodded. "That he was, my dear. I shall make certain his family here remembers that."

Tanya acquiesced, grateful for the older woman's presence and strength. Grateful that Beatrice blessed her with the tapestry. She had seen it mounted on the living room wall when she had first entered the condo and remarked how well it looked there. "It seems to have found a new home," she had commented as she set down her suitcase in the foyer and slipped graciously out of her black pumps.

Tanya had turned and stared at her intently, "By all rights, it belongs to you.

Beatrice shook her dark, perfectly coiffure head. "No my dear. My beloved grandson gave it to you for safe keeping, and keep it you shall."

Lucy accompanied Tanya to the church in Queens for moral support at the funeral service. They were surprised to see so many in attendance.

On the way to the funeral home she and Lucy had time to chat. "Lucy, I think Roy was murdered."

Lucy moved closer on in the subway seat they shared as she glanced around. "T., why would you say such a thing?"

"What caused him to have a seizure in the hospital? Why were those kids driving a car?"

"You have to have more than that to go on."

Tanya shrugged. "It's a feeling I have."

"You don't like his cousin or his uncle. You don't like the family business."

"True. But it's more than that."

"Enough to talk to Jonathan about your accusation?" Tanya looked into her eyes and shook her head. "Then let it go. That sort of talk is dangerous."

The rest of the ride was relatively quiet. It surprised them both to see so many black cars lined up outside the funeral home, as they walked up the side walk to go in. Tanya glanced about and realized she only knew about half of the people present. Were his killers there?

It was an overcast morning as they entered the church; somehow the chilly wind spitting icy pellets seemed a fitting day for the memorial. The family had been furious the day before because Beatrice wanted Roy cremated so that she could take him back to California. Uncle Leo said he died in New York, so he should be buried in New York. Roy's mother, Jan Platt, calmly stated her decision. "Let his grandmother have him in death as she raised him in life." Still all agreed to a service at the family crypt after the church mass. A gentle arm braced Tanya's shoulder as they all stood out at Roy's small family crypt. Tanya glanced to her right to see Mark standing beside her. It was he who had braced her so kindly. She would have shrugged his arm aside except for the fact that she actually needed it to remain standing upright against a gust of wind. She felt so weak against the wind gust, as if perhaps it could have blown her away. It seemed odd to have a graveside service without a burial.

She and Beatrice were leaving around lunchtime the following day; Beatrice had arranged to pick up his remains on their way to the airport. Mark offered them a ride. Tanya would have taken a cab but Beatrice accepted his offer, knowing he would borrow his father's Lincoln Town car for such a trip.

"Why not go in comfort?" Beatrice had suggested. Tanya was speechless. She only stayed briefly at Leo's home after the service, long enough to be courteous. She had not wanted to go at all, but Lucy told her it would be expected and offered to go with her. It was only fitting to acquiesce. It wasn't as bad as Tanya had imagined, but she couldn't eat a bite, and people kept encouraging her to eat. She played with a plate of food until she was able to slip it untouched into a garbage bag. Mark was unbelievably kind. He brought her a glass of white wine and didn't push any food at her. He and Stephanie came over and talked of when they were kids.

"Do you remember the dirt bike you had?" Stephanie said smiling up at Mark.

He smiled in reflection. "Yeah, that ramp Roy built and insisted on sailing off. He wanted to be Evil Kevel."

"He broke his leg."

"Yeah, but man…he flew." Mark turned to Tanya. "I know you and I have our differences, but I just want you to know I think you were the best thing that ever happened to Roy."

Stephanie raised her glass and nodded her agreement as tears streamed down Tanya's face at the unexpected compliment. Lucy took that as their cue to leave a short time later. Mark and Stephanie would vouch for Tanya.

The Arms of Friends

Mark drove them to Lucy's Manhattan home, where Lucy changed and grabbed her car from the garage. She drove back to Tanya's in relative silence. Around five Jonathan and Chris appeared at the door with pizza and drinks in hand. Tanya looked from them to Lucy; she was not really in the mood for company. They ate pizza and played cards, but Tanya's mind kept drifting. Others wandered in, and Lucy entertained all. She longed to be alone, but she knew they all met well.

The phone rang, and Lucy lowered the volume on the stereo for Tanya to answer. It was Beatrice. "Hello dear, I just heard that Mark is collecting some of Roy's things while you're out of town."

Tanya breathed a sigh it seemed such an effort to speak into the phone.

"Yes. I told him to coordinate with Jonathan or Lucy."

"Do you think it wise?"

Tanya held the phone away to glance at it in surprise. Did Beatrice suspect Mark as well? "Well, is it not best to feed the lion, so that it no longer hunts?"

"Do you have a safe place to store the tapestry, dear?"

"Is it in danger from Mark?"

"I believe all is, dear."

Tanya looked about and her eyes rested on Lucy. "Yes," she stated flatly. "I'll take care of it tonight."

"Thank you, dear child."

"I'll see you tomorrow then?"

"Indeed." Beatrice hung up. Jonathan and Lucy reminisced about things Roy had done, like when a group of them went miniature golfing at Lake George.

"Why were we up near Lake George anyway," Lucy asked.

Tanya smiled. "We went up for the annual Saratoga Jazz Fest." She chuckled at the memory. "And Roy wanted to retrieve his ball from the water over the fence." Lucy laughed at the memory of Roy climbing the fence and rustling through the reeds in his jeans and black sneakers just to find his blue ball as the sun began to sink.

Tanya slipped behind Lucy and asked her if she would take the tapestry home with her until Tanya returned from her trip. Lucy looked at her puzzled. "Why would I do that?"

"Beatrice would rather not have Mark see it here while I'm away."

Lucy looked perplexed. "And that didn't strike you as odd?"

"Should it have?" She wet her lips and looked at Tanya as Jonathan walked to the wall and removed the tapestry from its rod. He rolled it up and assured Tanya that Lucy would take it home.

Lucy turned the music back up; some people danced around the apartment, Tanya drifted out onto her balcony as more people arrived. Roy hadn't been so popular in life; he wouldn't have liked having so many around at any one time. Chris drifted out to the balcony as well. *He always smelled good*, she thought. Roy had worn Bruit or Polo when they met. He had always been judicious with money until he had become entrenched with his family. Closing her eyes, she leaned on the railing, letting her mind drift away. Chris came up behind, engulfing her in his cologne, handing her a vodka and soda; she gratefully accepted, imagining drinking in those violet-blue eyes if she whirled around into the strength of his arms. The melodic music drifted out with the sounds of laughter. "They all mean well," Chris offered, lifting his glass toward the wake going on within her home.

Tanya nodded as she turned to lean back against the low railing and face the building, glancing through the doors past Chris, seeing coworkers and neighbors in her small home, hearing their chatter over the music. "I know. I'm just not good company. I can't bring myself to celebrate his passing just yet."

She realized Chris and Jonathan must have taken the night off to hang out with her, as it was Friday, many of those in attendants of the services complained they had held the viewing on a Thursday evening after work. Why not wait for the weekend? It was apparently customary in New York City to hold funeral and wakes at the convenience of the living. Roy's mother, Jan had to return to work in Chicago, Illinois, initially by Sunday morning. That had been the main reason for holding the services so quickly. She had a big fashion show coming up and feared her designs not being finished correctly without her there. By holding the viewing on Thursday evening they could have the remains by Saturday afternoon. The graveside service would be in name only. The remains would go to Beatrice. Beatrice and Tanya decided to fly out on Saturday, Janet had decided to wait and take a later Saturday flight so she could visit with relatives.

Chris nodded. "All packed for your trip?"

She took a deep breath and nodded as she sipped the drink. "Pretty much. I don't need much; I'm going to spend a week with my sister on their farm in Wisconsin." She grimaced. "I need some place peaceful to do some serious thinking." He nodded.

"Tanya, it's not my business, but right after the death of a loved one isn't the time to make life-altering decisions. Are you considering moving to Wisconsin?" He winced. "You don't strike me as a farm girl."

She smiled with amusement at his tone. "Indeed." She smiled. "Such irony. I grew up on a farm," she admitted. Shaking her head at his surprise. "I'm afraid I traveled too far and perhaps too much for a farmer to have me. Wanderlust, my mother would say, has ruined me."

"Or improved you," he replied, toasting her as he drew on his beer. She drank along with him. "Will you move back to where ever you came from, T?"

Tanya shook her head vehemently. "I'm considering a lot of things. Returning to the home of my youth is not an option," she admitted with a grimace. "I'm not sure I should stay here either." With a heavy sigh, she looked around bitterly. "Honestly, I'm unclear where I should go, or what to do." She glanced into his handsome face, knitting her brow. "Perhaps I shouldn't be too hasty to decide."

He moved closer. The scent of his cologne, something she couldn't identify, overpowered her senses. "Stay," he whispered as he bent and dared kiss her neck. "You were willing to stay when you bought this place after leaving him," he reminded her softly, his hands felt warm, strong through her clothing. "You didn't run to Wisconsin then; you came to the club." His caressing voice reminded her. "You ran to your friends, to me." His kisses traveled up to her cheek and next to her lips as she titled her head, their lips met. His lips were warm and inviting, and she struggled to turn away and move to the small wrought iron table, placing her back to him. He took a deep breath as he set his bottle on the table. "I'm sorry," he said softly. Shaking her head, as she glanced back toward him. He shrugged. "You left him, T. You've been separated almost a year. Were you really going to take him back?"

Tears brimmed in her eyes as she looked into his all too handsome face and nodded. "I don't expect you to understand, but yes. Yes, I was willing to care for him, to see him recover." His brow knit as his eyes roved her face, searchingly. She was right to get away and sort out her feelings. Tears streamed down her cheeks unbidden as she reached for his hand. "My mind is all jumbled," she admitted shaking her head. He eyes met hers as she fell against his chest and cried softly. He held her, one hand on her hair as she just cried in silence. Lucy came to the open doorway and looked out; seeing Tanya crumpled in Chris' arms, she turned to the reverie and encouraged people to wrap up and leave.

XXXXX

Entering her bathroom the next morning, she closed her eyes and leaned against the doorframe enjoying the lingering scent of Chris' cologne. He had a powerful effect on her, and she should be thinking or Roy. Where had they gone so wrong? Could she have done anything differently? It had been a tremendous mistake moving to the city, being so close to his family. Lenora had been so incredibly right all along. How had her sister known after meeting him that first time? Even though Lenora had discouraged Tanya about remaining with Roy, Lenora had spent a lot of time with Roy before moving away from Ithaca. Initially, Roy hadn't liked Lenora, but as he sought her advice, he came to respect her wisdom. Tanya's relationship with Lenora had always been tenuous at best, but it pleased her to see Lenora warm up to Roy. Tanya wondered what the source of Lenora's intuition was. It was incredibly accurate. Once in the city, Roy pulled her further and further from her family, and they were increasingly drawn into his. He had been angry when she had wanted to go to Wisconsin their first year for Thanksgiving. In the end, he had remained in New York to spend Thanksgiving with his family, and she had gone to Wisconsin alone. Roy had been angry that she would spend it with Aaron's family. She reminded him that Aaron's family was her family. She and Aaron shared a beautiful niece in Wisconsin. It was clear that first Thanksgiving when she had married him at the falls he had expected she would choose him over her family from that point forward. Tanya wasn't willing to do that.

A Fairy's Survival

Forget that Roy had been murdered. Tanya had no proof, but she had always relied on instinct, and her instinct told her the condo had been tossed because of Roy's death. As was the frightful man with the narrow, chiseled features and cold, gray eyes who attempted to kidnap her from Cahoot's connected with Roy's death. She had no idea why she drew such conclusions, but it felt…right. Someone thought she had something or knew something. Tanya wished she had some idea what exactly it was. If she could figure it out, she could make it available to Mark, and he would certainly take care of things. Mark could solve her problems whether he trusted her or not.

XXXXX

It was her time in Ithaca and conversations with Lenora that had lead her to an alternative path through the mist. Through Roy, Tanya found an alternative path into the mist. And that very fact had drawn her to Roy, sealing their fate, uniting them as nothing else could have. In many ways, he was very different from Aaron, not simply due to the fact that he was shorter, a loner, and a rebel. Roy indulged in a wild and dangerous side; that side enticed Tanya. That side drew Roy toward unsavory characters that caused Jonathan to be alarmed for her. Once Tanya discovered Roy could also travel the mist…all was lost. It was uncanny. His faults didn't register; she had found an equal in this danger-loving guy.

XXXXX

His grandmother in Sacramento had bestowed to Roy and Tanya a beautifully, hand-woven tapestry that would carry them safely through no matter where they took it as long as they followed the poem Roy had learned as a child. It was Roy's connection to the tapestry that had led her to take him on as a lover and companion. She imagined if she ever found a man who understood the mist and believed in Evald, she would become a part of him. Lenora skeptically accepted Roy, far more than Cecilia and Matthew. Cecilia was disappointed Tanya chose to settle for a man simply because he was a leprechaun from Evald. "They're a tricky lot, never to be trusted," she warned.

"As if our family is any more trustworthy because we're fairies," Tanya scorned.

Cecilia grimaced. "Not for that reason, no. Simply because, dear sister, you're settling. Don't hang onto Evald. Don't let mother's promiscuous behavior sway you to think less of yourself. Perhaps you can't bear to live near us because of your shame, but you are just as good as any of us. You never asked to be born of questionable parentage, and I don't believe Father loved you any less." They both had tears in their eyes as they embraced.

She sighed heavily as they embraced. "I've thought a great deal of the situation with Mother. It seems certain she and Father were both from Evald." She sat back and shook her head, "Mother is what can happen if a fairy turns away from her heritage. I fear that could happen to any of us."

Cecilia shook her head sadly at her younger sister. "It won't happen to us. We're aware and cautious." Tanya knew that Cecilia meant well, such a dear sister.

Lenora was the family genealogist; Tanya wondered how a leprechaun could relate to a fairy, why should they not unite? It satisfied her to have at least one sister's approval of her choice of life companions. "Of course there can be no children," Lenora announced after they wed.

"Why not?"

"Because he's a leprechaun, of course." As if Tanya should know that for herself. Tanya was speechless; did Lenora mean it wasn't possible? Or was she being prejudice? The look upon Lenora's face made it obvious she expected Tanya to understand. Was there some unspoken rule about such matches? Fairies married humans; elves married humans at the sacrifice of their own immortality. Why not a leprechaun and a fairy? Now, as she sat quietly alone reflecting, Tanya realized Lenora expected her to consider the tales of leprechauns: of their nature for being tricksters and dishonest to protect their worldly possessions. Why had Tanya not seen it then? Not understood her sister and M****'s warnings? Roy was the first man since Father who knew anything of the mist. It mattered not that M**** warned her away from Roy, that he was not the one according to M****. What made M**** an expert on who she should and should not promise herself to? She smiled at M**** with angry flashing eyes. *And what makes you the expert?* she said through their telepathic conversation.

M**** shrugged and shook his head. She continued to press: *Ah, my dear friend, what does it matter? He can travel the mist, nothing else matters to me anymore. If I cannot be with the love of my heart, then I will settle for one who shares my land and has taught me a new way to access it. Through his knowledge I can now travel where my heart leads me. Can you not rejoice in that?"* M**** remained silent in her query. His eyes conveyed more than words ever could; Tanya never imagined a day when she would disappoint a fuath. What did a fuath know anyway?

He refused to assist her through the mist to Evald beyond the surrounding wood of Ithaca. Roy Wilson had done that for her. Lenora had no trouble talking to the intelligent and secretive young man who lived in the fraternity next door. He lived in the same fraternity as Chris Rosen before Chris gave into his families desire to have him back near his hometown of Union City, New Jersey. He transferred into a Manhattan College after Tanya returned to Ithaca from Brisbane. They had only lived next door to one another and shared a large campus for a semester to short a time of her to remember him.

As Tanya spent more and more time with Roy during her college years, she dreamed less and less. For Roy's assistance in leading her to an alternate path into the mist she would marry him. She gave up on the notion of disproving that Aaron was not her half-brother. What did it matter now that he was married? So when she and Roy had completed college, marriage seemed the next course of action in order to begin their life together anew. Should ever she find a way to prove she and Aaron were not related, they would cross that bridge, until then she would live on as best she could imagine. A friend of hers was an ordained pagan minister. They worked together for Ritz Camera on the Ithaca Commons. Alvin agreed to unite them next to Buttermilk Falls, where they all frequently gathered for picnics. It had been a beautiful, breezy April afternoon when they promised to share their lives as one.

After moving to New York City things had begun to unwind; her life seemed to spin out of control, and she had found herself running hand in hand with Chris Rosen. In her mind's eye, she could see Roy's casket floating behind them.

My life is a map of The Road Less Traveled. *I stand at a crossroads; to the right there lies a wide, well-paved path; to the left is rutted and narrow, grass has grown over parts long unused. Instinctively, I chose the rocky, narrow path. Why be a bass swimming downstream with all the other fish, when you could struggle with the salmon to swim up stream to tastier water? Would the West have been settled by bass? It seems doubtful to me. Even the Native Americans had to be the hardy salmon varied of humans in order to survive. The adventuresome spirit has been a barometer in my life, inherited from my father, or so I'm told. So much of Father has faded from my memory as the years have past. That's why I journal; after all, it is my nature to forget.*

Yes, the rocky, narrow path seems more interesting than the wide, paved road. After Franklin's birth, Father drifted from state to state, seeking opportunities he knew he would never find in the hills of Virginia. Ironically, he thought he'd found opportunity in the Southern Tier of New York State. Fourteen hours from the hills of Virginia through the Cumberland Gap must have seemed a world away from his beloved mountain home, far from the life of a poor coal miner. To him, a factory job was safer, and therefore… better, or did he simply not feel qualified for more? What irony life has to deal those trusting enough? I should laugh at Father's efforts… where did his efforts get him and his beloved Franklin? Both went to an early grave… just as they would had we remained in the mountains of Virginia. The coalmines didn't take either one; as Father feared… instead, fate took them. The result was the same—a young death. At least they did not suffer a slow, painful death, as many a miner experiences with Black Lung. After researching, the factory Father worked at in Elmira, New York, was little better than the coalmines of western Virginia. Neither was it conductive to the body, though I doubt either affected the soul.

Father sacrificed so much for us… leaving his mountain home, leaving his family and friends. In going back and visiting, I realized how difficult that must have been for him. As poor as my cousins are, they would not leave their mountain home or family; its amazing father did. Turning away from all he knew, leaving inclusion for the exclusion. A life based on essentials, such as a shotgun for rabbit hunting, a patch of black earth for a garden, a pole for fishing from the nearby rivers. As foreign as that life is to me, sometimes I think of the closeness among my cousins and long for just such a simplistic life myself.

Mother often commented how she could kill a weed by looking at it, and Father could coax it back to life. Father had loved the wood, had loved nature, and shared his love with us girls. Through Father we learned the art of concentration, the ability to call out to one another in times of need. Would we ever use that ability now that he's gone? Who can know?

Surely, her being with Chris endangered him as well; she shouldn't have sought out Jonathan's help while he was at the club. Would either of them safely be able to return to New York? Belatedly she realized she should have dared venture into her apartment and gathered up her passport and bankbook. Had she given it more thought, she would have simply tapped her savings and flown the coop. It would have been easy for her to fly to Australia and stay with her aunt June for a month or even move there should she desire to do so. Or she might have slipped into Evald if she could pull herself together long enough to cross safely. She simply hadn't been able to think clearly since she had opened the door to her disheveled condo. It had chilled her to the bone, and all she could do was to close the door and run away from the shambles her home was in. Had she placed Jonathan or Lucy in harm's way?

No, she had to think. Why had her home been vandalized? What would it take to be rid of Mark and his ilk? If she could figure out what she had overlooked, she could return and straighten things out. Somehow, she had to be truly free of these people.

Squeezing her eyes closed tight, the last thing she wished to recall was the cause of her running off into hiding with Chris. Saturday night now seemed a blurred memory. The Saturday crowd had the club rocking and all the bouncers on their toes. The DJ's dance rhythms kept the lights and the people gyrating to popular beats. Tanya allowed herself to be whisked onto the dance floor by associates from work and regulars alike. A guy at her table took her by the hand just as her gin and tonic arrived. She took a sip before following his lead; she hadn't recognized him and hadn't even paid him much attention. She simply figured he was an out-of-town guest of a coworker. Why else would he be sitting at the table with them? Jonathan watched as he stood next to Chris.

"She seems in rare form considering her welcome home."

Chris nodded. "Where's she going to spend the night?"

"I have a call into Lucy, but I know she's on a date with Mike this evening." Jonathan began. "If she doesn't show, my dad won't mind having Tanya over. I'll have a locksmith at her place tomorrow."

"Okay." Chris nodded. "John and Gordon are supposed to check out the security system I installed while she was away tomorrow as well. Could you coordinate with them, so you're there if they come after the locksmith?" Jonathan nodded his agreement. They both turned to check out the dance floor. Chris nodded his head toward Tanya. "Who's the clown dancing with her?" he asked Jonathan as they both watched the man's hand travel down her behind.

Jonathan furrowed his brow as they watched Tanya gracefully pull away from the guy and move toward the edge of the floor near them. The man reached out to grab her arm as Jonathan stepped forward and intervened. Tanya expertly slipped around Jonathan, putting him between her and her assailant as she stepped off the floor. He looked at Jonathan as he drifted back and melted into the crowd of dancers. "Who was that guy?" Chris asked, furrowing his brow.

Tanya shook her head. "I've no idea. He was at my table and asked me to dance." Chris nodded for Anita to cover the door as he led Tanya upstairs to the quieter lounge. "How are you doing?" he asked, guiding her away from the rail toward a plush, white leather low-backed lounge chair near a table.

"I'm fine."

"Is Lucy joining you?"

Tanya shrugged as a playful smile turned the corners of her mouth. "She might. She's on a dinner date with Mike." Mike was Lucy's on-and- off boyfriend since high school. Tanya never quite figured out what held them together. He was wrong for Lucy, but her parents liked him. "I'll be fine. There are plenty of people I know here."

"Jonathan says I'm buying you breakfast after hours."

Tanya smiled as he pulled her into his lap. "Hmm, sounds too tempting to pass up," she agreed, as he rubbed her shoulders as her eyes trailed down his nose to rest on his lips.

"I like the way this dress looks on you," Chris said, meeting her eyes. She smiled into his. "It really sets off the blue of your eyes." Tanya flushed at the compliment as he leaned in to kiss her. He glanced at his watch and rose to his feet. "Come on, I have some guys I'd like you to meet at the bar."

He led her by the hand to the bar and introduced her to a group of five guys to occupy her evening. The Mouse slipped in unnoticed and took a seat at her table; he had her routine down after previously observing her. Mark had informed him when she would be returning from her trip out west. The Mouse narrowed his eyes as he reflected on his last conversation with Mark Cierros. He was certain the guy had a thing for this particular mark. Perhaps Mark needed to be reminded they had a job to do, or his head would roll, even if the boss was his own father. Mr. C was no one to disappoint. The Mouse shook his head in reflection. Mark was an imbecile; he had worked with idiots like him before. The guy was soft on this girl, and it interfered with the job. Mark was sore because the Mouse had trashed her home. Did Mark realize he wasn't the only guy interested in her current status? It seemed the doorman and one of the bouncers had their eye on her as well.

"Couldn't you have non-intrusively searched her home?" Mark had demanded when he found out what had been done.

The Mouse shrugged. "You did that without results."

"I don't see where you turned up any more than I did. At least I found a key in the lining of his winter jacket."

"Not much use considering you don't know what it goes to."

"Yeah, but Tanya just might have recognized it, had you not spooked her."

He was brought back to the moment at hand and scanned the room for the mark. He caught a glimpse of her as she descended the open, winding staircase hand in hand, a step behind the doorman. *Please. No one would actually believe a woman like her would be interested in the doorman of a nightclub. Really.* The Mouse sipped his Southern Comfort; he could afford patience. A burly Irishman a good head taller than Tanya monopolized her attention on the dance floor while four other jocular guys from the bar occasionally stepped up for a spin around the dance floor with her. She had a friendly smile and playful, melodic laugh that sometimes carried off the floor toward his table. A slow number came up, and the Mouse decided to make his move. He elbowed his way into her arms just before the number ended. Tanya attempted to turn back to the burly Irishman he had elbowed from her grasp as another song began. She agilely stepped from his grasp and headed for her table, where she still had a gin and tonic. He had waited long enough; it was time. The Mouse pursued and took up a seat near her.

She glanced around the table; this man certainly didn't fit in. He had a western flavor to his black outfit: black button-up, trimmed in silver and clear rhinestones, a bolo around his skinny neck in place of a tie, black jeans, with a gaudy, large oval buckle, and black cowboy boots with silver tips. His aquiline features somehow reminded her of an underfed mouse. He had pinched cheekbones like David Bowie. Icy gray eyes, long, bony white fingers, and a porcelain complexion that foretold he rarely ventured out during the day. She disliked him immediately and wondered who at her table would have invited such a person. She glanced around but saw no sign of Lucy as she rose and glided around the railing separating her from Chris. She had the sudden urge to touch someone she knew well, someone who seemed to care about her well-being. He distractedly wrapped his left arm around her thin waist as she rested her head on his shoulder and waited for him to stamp the hands of two women with one guy.

"What's with admitting a cowboy?" she whispered into his ear. He smirked recalling a time she had brought an out-of-town client to the club dressed in a cream-colored cowboy suit, trimmed in brown thread. He had been rather huffy and snobbish to see her on the arm of this older guy he didn't know. She had called him a snob and asked Jonathan where she could show such a gentleman a nice evening in New York.

Chris shook his head as two guys approached with cash in hand. "I didn't," he replied, glancing toward her table. "Anita must have let him in." He was stamping the guys' hands. "Is he bothering you?"

She shrugged as Jonathan came over to stand on the other side of him. "Not really, he gives me the heebie-jeebies." They both looked at her and chuckled. She looked from one to the other and grimaced. "Forget it. I'll hang at the bar with your buds, as they talk basketball scores or something equally boring." Jonathan gaffed at the thought of Tanya faking interest in basketball. She sighed. "I think I'll check in upstairs for the night, and go home in the morning to clean my place up."

Chris shook his head as he glanced at his watch. "No way. You promised me breakfast. Now you're trying to cop out on our date?"

Tanya chuckled. "Dome date. Along with how many others?"

"I'm game for one on one if you are." He flashed his brow at her, and she laughed as she shook her head.

"I'm not ready for that." He reached out to brush a lock of her wild, golden mane from her face. It reminded him of a lion, thick and soft, filled with sunrays.

He leaned into her. "Say you'll stay, or I'll show up at your room after we close."

She smiled, as she blushed up at him. "You win." She spun out of his grasp as Len stepped away from the bar and put out his hand toward her. With a smile she gratefully accepted his offer to dance.

Len was a correction officer at Green Haven Correctional Facility. He'd known Chris since high school in Jersey, just over the bridge in Union City. She relaxed and fell into the beat of a Hall& Oats number that faded into the Eurhythmics: "Would I lie to you, honey?…My friends know what'd in store… I don't need to be here anymore… I've packed my bag…"

"Mr. Bolo," as Tanya thought of the odd, western-wearing dude, cut in against Tanya's wishes. He took a firm hold of her hand and trim waist as he whisked her away from Len. Len drew Chris and Jonathan's attention with hand signals over the undulating music. Tanya frightfully glimpsed herself on the big screen that covered the back wall; the soundman had her covered via cameras. Would anyone realize she was in trouble as she struggled to extricate herself from the man's grasp? Images of *Peter and the Wolf* popped in her mind, as she dared glance into those steely gray eyes. She imagined running through a dark, foggy forest as they gyrated, out of step across the dance floor. Tanya realized he was attempting to maneuver her toward a side exit. She was determined to fight him at every step as waves of panic cascaded over her body. She forced herself to remain focused to prevent herself from hyperventilating and losing her head. He spoke with an odd lilt. "You're lovely, my dear. I simply wish to enjoy a quiet chat."

"I'm sorry; I've made plans with friends for the evening. Perhaps another time."

He shook his head. "See your friends another time, dear. We need to chat."

She shook her head, unable to speak beyond a lump in her throat. A chill running down her spine; this man was dangerous, her instincts warned. "Come, come, love. Your friends won't miss you if we're just gone a bit."

"I believe they will," she replied.

"Please, don't insult my intelligence by thinking I'd believe a girl like you would really be interested in a doorman."

She turned away from his gaze. "Things are sometimes as they seem." She winced with pain as he tightened his icy grip. She caught a whiff of alcohol on his breath. She glared back at him. "But of course you don't know me, sir," she managed to hiss through clenched teeth. Her side began to ache where he continued to tighten her against him in an effort to control her movement as she continued to struggle against his grasp. The music slowed: "…could I have this dance for the rest of my life? Would you be my partner every night?" Tanya wanted to laugh at the irony of the melody as she struggled to break free from this madman. The Mouse slowed to the music, scanning the area between them and the exit. She continued to struggle against him, preventing him from reaching the exit in a timely fashion. His slender fingers dug in like a cold iron wrap; she would not break free. Bile rose in her throat as she tried to comprehend his babble, rushing water filled her ears, and the room began to whirl from her vision.

"Relax," she read on his lips as she opened her eyes again. Those lips curled into a cruel, icy smile, as she glanced into cold, malicious eyes. The room spun out of control and her entire body went slack in his grasp. What had he done? She felt herself slip from his arm; she could not open her eyes, her face slack, leaving him to drag dead weight as Jonathan and Len moved in. Chris jumped the rail, maneuvering through the low tables, chairs, and people to head the man off. The Mouse whirled around with her limp body in his arms to face his pursuers; placing his back toward the exit, Tanya slipped from his grasp to the floor. She caught a whiff of Chris' cologne as the man cried out in anguish. Fluttering her eyes as strong, masculine arms lifted her from the floor where she had banged her head on something as she fell. Instinctively, her hand reached for her aching side as she stared up into Chris' concerned face.

A small smile played on her lips as her other hand reached for her aching head. "Ah, my knight to the rescue," she gasped despite a sharp pain in her side. She pressed her side with her hand, as Chris helped her to her feet, forcing her trembling legs to sustain her weight.

Seeing her struggle, Chris scooped her up in his arms. She pressed her lips together and put her arm around his neck. He steered through the crowded tables, toward the bar, halfway across the room. She glanced over his shoulder toward the side entrance, several bouncers had restrained the man and were now ushering him out. The bartender followed Chris to Frank's office with a shot of peach schnapps. She tossed it back, and color returned to her face. Chris' face was full of concern. "You okay?"

"My side hurts," she admitted still clutching it.

"Frank's sending a doctor to look you over." He glanced at the open door where a group had gathered. She asked if Linda was still at her table, and if so, could she come to Frank's office with the doctor. Chris spoke into his mouthpiece again; a short time later, Linda, a coworker of Tanya's appeared, full of concern. She occasionally joined Tanya and other co-workers at Cahoot's for an evening of dancing.

While alone with Chris in Frank's office, she clutched Chris' hand. "Chris, I've never seen that man before tonight," she managed in a hoarse whisper, as she sat on the leather sofa, pressing a hand into her side. "Why'd he want to hurt me?" She shuttered involuntarily. "He sent chills down my spine."

Chris listened intently, not knowing how to respond. She turned to Linda and the pair dismissed Chris without further ado. Linda was as curious as Tanya. *Why would anyone go after Tanya?* With a sigh, Linda decided it was necessary to get in touch with Lucy. She would know more about the situation. She picked up the phone on Frank's desk and dialed Lucy's home number. She reached Lucy's Mother and softly spoke into the receiver. Doctor Andrews entered the room and closed the door. He was in his late forties with brown hair that was just beginning to gray at the temples and gentle brown eyes. He had a confident, reassuring disposition. His confidence immediately put Tanya at ease. "A bruised rib as far as I can tell." Doctor Andrews informed the threesome after examining her. "And a solid bump on the side of your head, but it doesn't appear to be a concussion. Take it easy for a few days, and you should be fine." Tanya pressed her lips together, and he offered to wrap her ribs with a bit of gauze. He handed her a couple of large white pills for the pain as Linda got her some water. "Lucy's Mother is sending one of her brother's to let her know you're here and injured," Linda offered as Tanya accepted the glass of water.

"Oh, Thanks, Linda. But I wouldn't want to cut in on Lucy's date."

Linda smirked down at her, "Like she would forgive me if I hadn't called." She shook her head as she placed the glass in Tanya's hand.

Tanya hesitated before taking the pills. "I've had a drink."

"It's okay. This is like Tylenol. This is a sleep aid to take when you're ready." He handed her a small white envelope containing two Valiums. "You'll only need one at a time."

Would I lie to you?

The gang agreed to reassemble at Len's Bar& Grill in lower Manhattan for after hours-drinks and breakfast. Chris led her in via the back door and directed her to a corner stool at the bar. Jonathan, Linda, and a number of others meandered in via the heavy oak windowed front door, singing out greetings to the owner/bartender. Chris stood next to Tanya with his arm draped on the back of her stool as he placed their order, and Lucy slipped onto the stool to his right. Tanya leaned forward so she and Lucy could chat as Chris stood back to chat with Jonathan and a few other guys. As Tanya sipped her soda, she glanced casually up at the mirror running behind the length of the bar. The front door opened and color drained from her face as she reached out and sunk her lacquered nails into the tender flesh of Chris' free forearm. He stopped in mid-sentence to glare at her. "T." Concern crossed his face as he followed her gaze to the mirror behind the bar. He heard Jonathan curse under his breath as he and Lucy caught sight of the recent arrival. Jonathan pulled his police radio from his pocket and attached it to his jacket shoulder holder as he pressed the button and spoke directly into the mic. The stranger at the club smiled toward the mirror as he took a seat behind the door in the front plate glass window facing the bar. "Mr. Bolo" smirked at Tanya's frozen image as he calmly placed an order with a waitress. Chris turned to Tanya in shock. "How could he know we'd be here?" He growled under his breath. She couldn't manage to even shrug; her body felt frozen to the barstool, as she struggled to take her eyes away from the reflection in the mirror and loosen her grip on Chris forearm. "T, this guy knows you. He knows us." Chris breathed in her ear. She shook her head.

"Impossible. I've never seen him before tonight," she insisted hoarsely before tossing back her cranberry and vodka.

Jonathan exploded as he growled into his shoulder radio. "Get her out of here through the back." He barked at Chris, as he whirled to face the man. Chris offered Tanya his injured arm and hustled her back the way they had come. As he pushed through the backdoor, he took hold her hand and pulled her along the alley toward Fifth Avenue. A patrol car picked them up at the end of the alley and headed toward the station, where they were transferred into an awaiting taxi. Chris leaned toward the screen as they slid into the backseat and barked an address to the driver. Tanya shot him a curious look, not recognizing the address. He sat back next to her and swung his good arm about her shoulders, drawing her near so that he felt her shivering with fright.

"Where are we headed?" she managed to whisper as she glanced at into his eyes.

"My place," he responded.

"Oh, no. I couldn't." She tried to pull away from his grasp. He smirked and glanced at his watch.

"T, it's almost four in the morning." She looked out at the sky high above the crowded buildings. How could anyone gauge time in such a jumbled place, so many streetlights, blotting out the early morning sky? "Too late or too early for a respectable hotel," he continued. "The locks are busted at your place. Jonathan's diverting that weirdo; Lucy's with him. You got any other ideas?"

She glanced at his profile and remained silent. He shrugged. "There you go, then. I have two male roommates. You'll be safe at our place."

She sighed and leaned against him, pushing aside the side of his leather jacket near her and snuggled closer to his warmth, too exhausted to argue further. He felt her shaking uncontrollably beside him as he pulled her close. She felt his hand in her hair, as she rested against his shoulder. Both her sides ached, and she had a headache as a reminder the events had not been a dream.

CHAPTER 6

gain her life completed yet another circle. As she sat on the cliffs near the Rosens' lodge, she looked back to the trail that had led her to this moment. The lodge itself was incredible. Chris had expertly driven Frank's 1970 blue with white stripe, Dodge Charger up an old logging road in the wee hours of the morning. Had it only been yesterday or earlier today? She had walked admiringly around the vehicle inside the underground parking lot of the hotel that housed Cahoot's. She had seen it parked there many times in the past, but she had never ridden in the pristine automobile. What would Frank say had he known they would drive it down an old logging path, not even a real road.

Chris had patiently awaited her inspection of the vehicle; he seemed awed that a woman would ogle over a car. It was apparent Tanya admired a finely-kept classic as much as a good bottle of white wine or a hike through dense woods. Climbing into the passenger seat, she leaned back into the smooth, white leather, bucket seat, adjusted the headrest, and sighed. He had turned to her as they drove and asked if she was hungry. Once asked, she realized she was quite hungry. With a grimace, Tanya acquiesced to a McDonald's drive-thru. He smirked. "Don't tell me you don't do McD's." "Okay, I won't tell you."

He laughed. "T, for real?"She nodded as she glanced out into the darkness; it seemed the only thing available at 5:30 a.m.. She squinted over the menu. "Can I get a breakfast sandwich without meat?"

He smiled at her and ordered. "Can we have three breakfast sandwich meals, one without meat, a hot tea, and a coke?" He purchased breakfast sandwich meals and a coke for himself.

A short time later, he turned onto Route 301 and headed toward Feura Bush. Tanya had never heard of the place and consulted the map that lay on the console between them. Chris flashed her a sideways glance. "There's not much there," he conceded. Pressing on. "That's why it should be the perfect place to stow a damsel such as yourself." She flashed him a chipper smile. "How'd a prim girl like you become enamored with vintage cars?"

She hesitated as she ate her cheese and egg croissant. "Maybe this 'prim, citified girl' wasn't always so prim," she admitted as she sipped her tea. "Lockwood is near the Chemung Speedway, Watkins Glen Race Way, Shangri-La, and Green Mountain," she explained. "Ever hear of any of them?"

He nodded as he shifted back up to speed, "Watkins Glen is on TV, right?" She nodded with a bemused grin. "I grew up around cars and horses," she explained. "So did my interest. One should be interested in the things that interest those around them."

"Which speedway is closest?"

"Chemung Speedway is about eleven miles from Mother's place." She glanced at his profile, "Ever been to the Carlyle Car Show?"

He shook his head. "Never heard of it."

Tanya grimaced and furrowed her brow. "It's a week-long annual car show just south of Scranton, Pennsylvania, on Interstate 81." She raised her brow now, "Are you sure you've never heard of it? I know I've seen signs for it in and around the city."

"A lot goes on in and around the city." He shrugged. "You can't expect a guy to keep up with all of it." They turned onto Route 443 as he finished his soda and shook the ice.

"This isn't anywhere near Selkirk," Tanya admonished him as she consulted the map. He shrugged unconcerned. "It's between New Scotland and Selkirk." He slowed to a snail's pace after passing a barbed wire fence, she thought he was watching out for deer, until he turned left onto a narrow logging trail, and traveled on for about a mile. Turning to the right, the path opened to a small meadow, and Chris pulled up to park near the edge by a prefab storage shed she hadn't even noticed from the trail. Chris cut the engine and dropped back in his bucket seat, reaching in the back as he did so, pulling forward two throws. She looked at him expectantly.

"Might as well take a nap," he suggested, as he handed her a throw. "We can't attempt the trail until it's light out." He put a ball cap over his eyes; Tanya stared at him in disbelief before she followed suit.

The poor man had to be exhausted. Closing her eyes, she managed to get comfortable enough to nap in the leather, bucket seat. *How could anyone have ever imagined making love in a drive-in in such a car?* she wondered as she drifted off.

Sunlight streamed in through the windshield, bringing her alert and awake; she stretched and sat up cautious, not ready to disturb Chris. Turning to look out the passenger's window, she glimpsed several deer on the far side of the meadow, rising with the sun to move on from their slumber. Chris startled her and the deer as he opened his door and sat up simultaneously. A flood of memories flashed through Tanya's mind as Chris walked around the shed out of sight. Flashes of times spent at the Sands' hunting cabin, laughing, playing cards, and drinking hot cocoa before a roaring fire. Of silently moving through the woods, sitting with Aaron in a deer blind for hours of silence, watching and waiting. She was stirred from her reverie by his return to the car after unlocking the shed door. Surely he had slept poorly for a few hours in the cramped leather bucket driver's seat. Driving up that logging road had not been any rougher than the dirt roads that led up to the mountain homes of some of her western Virginian relatives. When Chris mentioned a family hunting cabin, Tanya had envisioned an old shack of a place, without paint or porch. The lodge was anything but. They parked in a clearing that offered nothing more than a storage shed near the wood line. Chris opened the shed to retrieve a sled and wheel barrel, and faded green canvas; he used the canvas to cover the car after they had unloaded. Silently she thanked Jonathan for retrieving her hiking boots she stored in the hatch of her Mustang, along with the suitcase she had packed from her trip to Wisconsin. What a relief to have washed her clothes at her sister's the night before she left. Chris offered to stow Tanya's Tamarac camera bag among the provisions as they donned their hiking boots and dropped their shoes into the bottom of the wheel barrel.

When had he packed enough provisions in the trunk and back seat to last a good two weeks? she wondered as they dispersed them between the sled and wheel barrel. "Thanks, but I can manage my camera bag." He shrugged nonchalantly. She gratefully handed off the suitcase to be jostled along with Chris' large gym bag; he slung his computer over his shoulder.

"Where are we going?" she dared to ask, getting behind the wheel barrel.

"The cabin's about a quarter a mile up the trail." He responded taking up the rope of the old-fashion wooden sled. She lifted her brows in surprise. "Great," she half-mumbled as he took the lead. Looking at his back, she couldn't picture this city boy with his soft skin and teased hair as a hunter in his youth taking down a deer or rabbit for dinner. On the journey, Chris confessed he preferred shooting animals with the lenses of a camera to a gun, but his father had insisted his boys learn to hunt.

"It must have been great coming here to hunt in your youth with your dad," Tanya remarked as she looked around.

"In truth, I've never been much of a hunter," he confided as he wrinkled his nose. "Are you?"

She smiled as she sized him up, "not really. I prefer photographing the wildlife. But I do enjoy eating it as well."

He chuckled. "I enjoy fishing," he admitted with a wry smile. "There's a nice stream nearby."

"Oh, I like to fish," she admitted.

He nodded. "I'll show you to the stream then." The trail grew steep, and Tanya concentrated to maneuver the wheel barrel over some large rocks and sharp turns. She drew up short with a gasp as the cabin came into view. She had expected a cabin like the Sands, with a large main room, a picnic table in the center, a stone fireplace off to one side, a galley kitchen, functional bath, and a dorm-like bedroom upstairs equipped with four sets of bunk beds. She stored many fond memories of times spent snowmobile riding, three-wheeling, or simply hanging with Aaron before the fireplace on chilly evenings. So much of her life had been woven intricately into his over the years. There was a painful tug at her heartstrings as she shrugged off. The Sands' cabin had been rustic and cozy, with Aaron's parents' bedroom off the common area being the only private bedroom in the house. The greatest feature of the Sands' cabin had been the wide, wrap- a-round porch; they had all enjoyed hanging out on in the late afternoons. What stood before her took away all thoughts of Chris as a young man, or of the Sand's rustic cabin.

The cabin was a beautiful two-story country lodge, with the top floor being centered and smaller than the first floor. It was nestled among the trees near a ledge of the foothills, offering an awesome view of the valley. She imagined such a place in a *Better Homes and Gardens* magazine or perhaps *Architect's Digest*. It was stained a dark brown cedar to blend with the trees. Younger trees stood century around the yard, backed up to older trees of the forest. The front of the two-story house seemed nestled in a clearing, with older trees behind and on the other side of the pond. To the left of the lodge was a small pond and the faded remnants of an old logging trail. Tanya couldn't believe her eyes. This lodge was far superior to anything Tanya had envisioned as she reached out to stroke the workmen ship of the siding. She walked over to the ledge to look down at the view in awe. Rensselear Valley seemed far away in the distance below them. It was a sheer face below her feet that would give even a seasoned rock climber like herself a run for their money. Chris quietly came up behind her; she sensed his presence without turning.

"What's that long white structure down there?"

"GE Selkirk," he announced matter-of-factly. She glanced at him and back at the monstrosity off in the distance below. "I told you it was nearby. That's the only place I ever wanted to work," Chris confessed, softly, as he stuffed his hands into his pockets.

"What stopped you?"

He shrugged. "I started the security business in college; then I applied to GE after graduating, with my degree in computer engineering," He took her hand as they stared down into the valley. "They offered substantially less than what I made running a company I co-own with John and Steve." He shook his head. "It no longer seemed so attractive by the time I was ready for the job."

She smiled soberly, glancing at his profile. Pressing her lips and absently wetting them she turned away in thought. "Why didn't you tell me about your company before?"

He shrugged. "Does it really matter? You were no less attracted to me when you thought I was just a night club doorman."

She chewed her lower lip and glanced at his profile. "It certainly helped keep you at arm's length."

He smirked but remained silent. The more she learned about him the more attractive he became, and she was struggling for ideas as to how she would remain at arms length. When exactly had her life had spun out of control? The moment Roy had collided with that car? No, perhaps before then, she simply had not realized she had lost control. "… Ground control to Major Tom,…can you hear me, Major Tom…. count down commencing…. Put your goggles on…." The words of a David Bowie song wound their way through her thoughts. The words to the song clouded her carefully constructed threads of thoughts, jumbling everything together. How was she going to manage in the company of "Captivating Chris" without a chaperone? Lord, she wanted him more and more, not less even though she tried to find fault. Why was she finding it difficult to be judgmental? Skeptic? Those judgments she had created in her mind of him were crumbling, like a sand castle against the incoming tide. It had been easy to flirt when she was committed to the possibility of reuniting with her husband, and she thought Chris was just a glorified bouncer. Rapidly all that was changing, this was a successfully businessman who stood at her side. Was he an equal in other ways? She understood why he still worked part-time in a pick-up place. He enjoyed the atmosphere and people. He had worked in the club on and off since his first year of college, when the drinking age had increased from eighteen to twenty-one. Jonathan had cast her in this man's arms just as all her protections and carefully constructed walls were stripped away.

She shook her head. "I don't understand why you work at the club," she blurted out to stop her mind from racing.

He gave her a voracious smile and wiggled his brow. "You don't?"

She laughed. "You could hang out like the rest of us."

He shook his head. "I like working the door. I like getting to know the regulars."

"You like watching the dancers," she teased, thrusting her chin out toward him.

He gave an appraising look as he tilted his head thoughtfully to one side. "I enjoy watching some of the dancers," he corrected mischievously. The big screen behind the dance floor flashed through her mind; it had been her saving grace. Was that last night? She recalled herself up there, bigger than life; was Chris a voyeur of some sort? Who knew what might have been her fate had Chris or the DJ not been watching. A chill ran through her as imagines of that man's cold, calculating eyes, and his wiry, icy grasp on her arm. She looked at Chris as she struggled against the raw memories. Her savior—a playboy from her favorite hotspot—stood beside her on a ledge looking down into a valley early on a clear Monday morning. They walked back to the lodge and quietly began unloading onto the porch. Chris stowed the sled and wheel barrel underneath the porch by sliding back a section of the latticework near the five steps leading to the porch. The visage of the lodge was a two-story A-frame with large windows squared on either side for ample morning lighting. Trimmed inside were energy-efficient French doors sweeping across the bottom, and the upper part held a designer fitted triangular window. From the ledge, Tanya noticed the large-paned window running along the side facing the pond, sheltered by the wrap-a-round porch. She chuckled. "I expected to stay in a shed, and you've provide a palace."

Chris laughed as he slipped off his hiking boots on the porch before hefting a large box of supplies in his arms and opening the front door. Tanya's eyes followed the sunrays as she stepped inside the house; she scarcely noticed the hooks mounted above a runner to the right of the doors where people hung their coats as her eyes adjusted to the dimmer interior. A few rain slickers hung there on a regular basis. Tanya padded across the floor to the left after Chris with a box in her arms. They passed through the dining area, which held a huge oval table with two thick scrolled center legs holding it up; it easily sat twelve people comfortably. A counter, with three old milk jug stools separated the dining area from the kitchen. The kitchen had a warm, country feel with solid light oak cabinets and flooring. Country blue curtains with white geese in quilted bonnets and small white polka dots covered the windows, complete with a matching floor runner and hand towels hanging from the yellow stove handle. The refrigerator matched the stove and offered an icemaker in the left door. One could stand at the sink and gaze out into the woods beyond while washing dishes.

With each load, she passed a large stone, open fireplace almost in the center of the downstairs, effectively separating the dining area and kitchen from the living room. Jonathan had been thoughtful enough to venture to her condo and retrieve all she would need for an extended visit in the woods. He had gathered up what he deemed necessary, having forbid her to returning to her own home or her job. He insisted he needed time to effectively do his job. And that meant to tuck her away somewhere for a few days. So here she was in a lodge with Chris Rosen. The fury Tanya felt toward Jonathan would have to remain buried for the time being. She had decided not to take it out on Chris. She would make the best of a tentatively volatile situation. How could Jonathan call her a friend and place her with a man she found so tantalizingly attractive.

The stone fireplace was so large she only had to duck slightly to pass through the hearth into the living room. Standing within the hearth, she noticed a niche on either side of the chimney. "Chris," she called from her vantage point. Chris padded to the hearth from the kitchen and ducked to look in at her. "What are these holes for?" Chris stepped back and handed her a black, metal bar that leaned against the fieldstone on the kitchen side. She slid one end into the slot nearest her as he slid a cast iron pot on his end, and reached in to slide his end into place.

Tanya stepped out of the hearth and nodded, "Ah." She acknowledged realizing they could heat water or soup in such a fashion. She smiled, imagining young boys running through this house, enjoying playing in the hearth with glee. She looked up the open rectangular staircase and hallway. There was a wide landing halfway up to turn into the hall, the foyer of the room opened straight to the second floor ceiling and the point of the triangular window. The whole house had to be closer to three thousand square feet than the nine hundred or so she had anticipated. Sock-footed, they made several trips from the porch to the kitchen before they had everything put away. Tanya noticed he and Jonathan had stocked enough to last her and Chris for over a week. She realized Jonathan had said it would only be a few days, but he must have anticipated keeping her hidden away longer.

When they were through, Chris smiled at her. "Would you like a tour?"

"I'd love one." Her eyes had already taken in the two-toned blue and white bathroom off the kitchen through the open door. She smiled at him as she moved to have a better look. Drawing a deep breath she took in the beautiful, deep, old white claw tub, with piping all round above the shower head to hang a white shower liner and country blue ruffled curtains tied back on either side of the wrap-a-round curtains, exposed a sunken window, where potted plants would love to perch. The bathroom overlooked the pond, and she leaned against the door frame as she imagined lying back, and soaking in such a tub filled with bubbles as she gazed at the pond and woods beyond. A basket of rolled up towels, a small tray of scented soap and a fake fern occupied the deep well of the window. She admired the cool white and blue ceramic tiles beneath her feet, across the short hall off the kitchen she discovered the laundry facilities, and a closet sheltering the furnace and hot water tank. Yes, this was a place built for self-sufficiency.

"You heat with gas?"

Chris nodded. "Natural gas. We have mineral rights with this land, so it does cost much." The walk in pantry took up the rest of the room on the left of the hall, and bathroom on the right, with the back door straight ahead. The hall widened, near the door just past the bathroom. There was a rug before a bench, and a coat tree near the door that led around to the pond via a stone path. Inside the pantry, Chris pulled a shelf of canned food forward and opened the wall to a cleverly hidden narrow staircase that lead to the upstairs back bedroom closet.

"It must have been wonderful playing hide and seek in this place growing up."

Chris smirked. "My dad loves the game." She nodded, as she looked up the steep stairs in disbelief. "Shall we?" Chris encouraged. She shrugged as she stepped into the narrow passage, and up the worn, wooden stairs. She moved in semi darkness, as Chris held a large flashlight below her. She entered what appeared to be a long, narrow closet by pushing back a board. Chris came up and reached out to sweep aside the clothes on hangers and opened a door before him. Light streamed in from the windows of a generously proportioned master bedroom. There were two large windows with lace curtains and floral valances adorning the far wall, a third window faced the pond. The curtains were drawn back with bronze buttons, mounted to the wall. A cherry, queen-size, four-poster bed, with gathered brocade curtains pulled back against the posters and matching valances sat at an angle away from the windows, giving the room a cozy inviting feeling. The room was complete with matching cherry nightstands and a vanity near the door and a thick crimson oriental rug adorning the hardwood flooring. Two winged back chairs and a round cherry table with a heavy Tiffany lamp resting on a coquetted doily situated between the two back windows. A dark, polished wooden trunk ran the length of the foot of the bed. A handmade quilt with colors to match the room lay carefully folded at the foot of the bed over a brocade coverlet. Chris walked to the hall door and stood waiting for her to follow. The hallway was open to the right with a rail running the length to the front staircase. It opened to a square staircase leading to the great room below. "Oh, Chris, this place is incredible."

Tanya stepped up to the railing to look down at the front door, and the dining area just beyond. She turned back to see a bathroom next to the master. This bathroom had cream-colored speckled linoleum from the 1970s, the area rug and toilet cover were peach colored, as were all the accessories in the room. A small wooden pine magazine rack separated the toilet from the shower. There were three oval antique white pictures frames mounted diagonally on the wall across from the toilet, picking up the peach colors of the room and holding simple, decorative eight-by-ten oil paintings. The next two rooms were of similar size and features; the first had steel blue carpeting and a masculine feel. Two pair of handmade bunk beds, with captain beds nestled in the bottom bunk, dark maple, shaker dressers, with an oval mirror mounted above it on the wall, and an amber colored lamp sat in the corner of the dresser on a yellowed crocheted doily. A mounted trout and fishing poles in a rack adorned the wall on either side. The other wall held a large old world map with a handcrafted model boat mounted in the center of it on a small lacquered shelf.

"My older brother, Simon, made the ship when he was ten," Chris explained as Tanya stepped up for a closer look. "I caught the trout and Dad had it mounted because I won the area fishing contest that year."

"How old were you when you won?"

"Twelve."

Tanya nodded and moved to the next room with an amused smile. The next room had plush, peach carpeting and light yellow paint on the walls and ceiling. On the dresser lay a linen, hand-embroidered scarf with a lantern in either corner. The closets separated the two middle rooms, half-opening to either room. This room also held two pair of handmade bunk beds. The landing, hallway, and stairs were covered with a thick, crimson oriental wool runner to muffle footfalls. Oil lanterns were dispersed with wall mounted light scones along the hallway. Tanya turned to Chris. "Do you frequently lose power up here?" Chris nodded, as Tanya went to the door closest to the stairs. This doorway was wider than the others, and opened to a large, sparsely furnished corner room with windows on two walls. Rich, sapphire blue insulated drapes hung to the floor, pulled back with silver tiebacks, to leave a bright, airy feeling about the place. A walnut queen size, four-poster bed occupied the center of the two windows on the east wall, with matching nightstands on either side. The closet ran the length of the inner wall, separating this room from the neighboring room. A small walnut vanity, stood angled in one far corner, the opposite corner held the matching six-drawer dresser. The area carpet was a muted midnight blue emboldened with muted, pink flowers. Tanya peeked in the closet to find neatly stacked extra bedding on the shelf above the clothes racks. The handmade quilt captured the rich blues, and dark purples in rings and trim around a white background. Tanya sat on the edge of the high bed and felt at peace.

"Hmm. Who's the woodworker in your family?"

"My grandfather and my older brother, Simon." Chris smiled at her, as she seemed reluctant to move from the bed. "This is my grandparents' room. Is this your pick of the rooms?" Tanya nodded.

"It feels so inviting."

"You're spring, like my grandmother," Chris decided.

Tanya blushed. "How can you tell?"

Chris shrugged. "The watercolors attract spring people." He came to stand near her, his cologne was overwhelmingly tantalizing. It would be so easy to simply fall into his arms on his grandparents' bed; she closed her eyes.

"My grandmother's room is the same colors of your own bedroom, Tanya," he stated softly into her hair.

Tanya nodded slightly in response as she imagined what his parents would say should they drop in and discovered them in his grandparents' room on top of the grand bed coverings. She blushed slightly at the thought.

What would they think of Chris with a widow, whose husband wasn't even cold in the ground? What would they say to him hiding such a woman in their home after discovering her husband murdered, and her home tossed while she was out of town? And topping it off with some scary, thin man who tried to kidnap her from the club their son enjoyed working at. Oh, that would be a glorious meeting Tanya looked forward to postponing. She stepped away from Chris and ran her hand over the quilt on the bed. She considered sitting on the high bed to test the firmness, but she knew it would be just right. Closing her eyes, she thought of resting her head on his shoulder, of his arm around her, of his lips. She leaned against the bedpost for a moment, pushing away her dangerous thoughts. Had she not pushed him away? Should she not be in mourning?

"Hey, do you need to rest?" Chris asked as she rested her head against the sturdy bedpost.

She shook her head. "I'm fine." She turned toward him with a tired, half-hearted smile. Could she tell him she had gotten caught up in reverie? After all, had she not decided to work things out with Roy? Roy had been enough when they were in college. He should have been enough despite his problems, and choices, had she not vowed to accept him as he was?

She felt Chris move beside her; placing his arm around her shoulder, his free hand was so warm and reassuring as he slowly moved it up and down the arm closest to his body. She found herself leaning into him, keeping her eyes closed, and simply living in the moment—living in the touch of his hand, the scent of his cologne, the atmosphere of comfort, and love in the room. She turned toward him, her heart beating with desire as her lips parted, hungrily seeking his. They kissed as she placed a cool hand against the warmth of his cheek. He pulled her close, and they fell on the bed, before she pulled back, biting her lower lip.

She smiled at him coyly. "And what type of person is a hot-blooded male such as yourself, Chris?" she asked moving to a sitting position and glancing down at him as he propped himself up on one arm.

He smiled playfully at her. "You haven't yet guessed?"

"Hmm, you seem passionate like someone born of fire. Are you winter?"

He shook his head. "Taurus; spring, like yourself."

She nodded, as he reached to pull her back beside him, her legs dangling over the side of the bed as he kissed her some more. Tears streamed from beneath her closed lids, he groaned and took her hand, pulling her to her feet. She opened her eyes, Chris opened the door, and stepped into the hall, she let him lead her down the stairs with the thick, high-polished, rounded handrails, toward the front door. Her mind was swimming—how warm and reassuring his hand was; how comfortable it felt holding hers. This man she had imagined as a playboy had saved her life. She angrily wiped the tears from her eyes as they moved quickly down the stairs. How could she keep him at arm's length when she wanted to devour him?

She shook herself, as her eyes scanned the great room it was broken into areas by the set up of the furniture. The L-shaped cream-colored sectional sofa, and matching recliner half circled a large, tree trunk polished table, with a round glass top held a brown bearskin rug before the hearth. The rustic look was completed with an eight-point buck's head mounted in the fieldstone over the hearth. Off to the far corner of the back wall was a cherry colored executive desk with black leather chair by a wide, slated window. Filled matching bookshelves were built into the wall on either side of the desk.. Above the bench by the door, a space had been built to hold a modern stereo system; Tanya would have to stand on the bench in order to use the system. She looked around and noticed the speakers were mounted high on two walls of the room. Next to the bench was a cabinet that held a rack of records, and cassettes. The bench opened to provide ample storage space they used as a tender box. Completing the room was a nook under the stairs, covered with a blue oriental rug, with a pair of reading chairs directed toward the window. A square, wooden game table rested between them, and a floor lamp nestled to one side.

"Chris, this place is magnificent." Tanya breathed as she took in the room. "Thank you for sharing it with me."

He smiled down at her with obvious delight. "You're most welcome." She pushed herself to keep up with him despite her fatigue from her bruises. After the tour and carrying their personal items upstairs and settling in, they finally napped. Chris put his duffle bag in the middle dorm room that was obviously for the boys. Tanya took his grandparents' room. He asked her if she wanted to shower. Her shoulders were tight from the last few days of tension; she glanced at his watch and smiled as she realized it was after twelve in the afternoon. She strained her ears, wondering if the local fire department sounded a noon whistle as they did in Lockwood. Was it customary in all small towns? She decided she had to be sure to listen at noon tomorrow. A shower would be a welcome relief. She suddenly felt as if she had lived in her clothes too long. She smiled playfully and requested the use of the old-fashion claw tub in the downstairs bath.

"You got it." He agreed as he bowed and left the door to her commandeered room open as he padded off to his own room. She went down and began the bath, testing the water, and adding bath oil before heading back upstairs to finish unpacking and finding a change of comfortable clothes. She could hear Chris in the upstairs shower, as she walked back downstairs to enjoy a long soak.

She slid down into the bath and leaned her head back, letting her whole body finally relax. The last few days had been a blur. Returning to a trashed condo. Let's not forget, Roy's death, her spilling the beans to Aaron, and his taking off. He hadn't gone home; he hadn't checked in at work, except to say he had needed a vacation via a phone call to his boss. She reminded herself again that his choices were really not her business. Aaron had a family; he had a wife. The scary man at Cahoot's with the icy gray eyes and bolo ran through her mind. How did he fit in the mess? The funeral followed by her trip to Wisconsin. Too much, to close together. It all whirled through her mind like a run away train car without an engine. Why else would she have relied on Jonathan to come up with a game plan?

XXXXX

Before the trip in the darkness of night with Chris, Tanya had spent the night with Chris after a harrowing experience. The following afternoon she had been left alone in his apartment. Now she found herself sequestered with the object of her desire for at least a week. She hadn't even dared call her sister to discuss the incident or her current situation. She had been afraid to call anyone, to go anywhere. John had left shortly after Chris; that hadn't been long after she prepared their brunch. She had cleaned up the kitchen and Chris' bedroom before running out of things to do. Throwing herself on the sofa, she flipped through the channels, as she found herself unable to focus on the pages of the book she had chosen. She couldn't read, the apartment was too confining, and yet she feared even to open the door to the hallway. She paced the common living area like a caged bobcat filled with nervous energy and hunger pains. Lucy wasn't home when she called. Jonathan had been on his way out of the office when she had reached him. She felt left in the dark everyone knew something she did not. They were free to go and she was not.

She was at a loss of what to do as she waited for Chris to return. She had found a notebook in his room and doodled on a page. She began making a list.

*Roy—hit by car. Wanted free of "family."

*Family upset because of cremation... Did this matter?

*Her computer working slow before she left... Did that mean anything?

*Her apartment trashed—why?

*The guy at the club?

*Mark offering to take Roy's things for her while she was out of town. Why? He hadn't done all that much for Roy when he was alive. It seemed Mark was being overly helpful and kind.

*Roy not letting her know he belonged to the gym near her office.

*Roy's odd behavior before he died... making a few friends, insisting she get to know them. Had he been trying to tell her something?

When Chris still hadn't returned by four o'clock, she began drawing ivy, flowers, and patterned knots around her words. Even that quickly grew tiresome, so she threw opened the window feeling she could no longer breathe. He finally returned after six. He had been in a rush, handing her the suitcase he had retrieved from her car as he explained they had a dinner reservations with Jonathan at Jack's over on 7th Avenue for seven thirty. They would take a cab to the parking garage to retrieve the Tanya's car after dinner since they were still using Frank's Dodge Charger. Jack's was an upscale, Italian restaurant renowned for its low-key ambiance and the baby grand piano in the front window. Tanya enjoyed dining at a place offering real linen tablecloths, alternating in white and black, trimmed with red linen napkins, and heavy sterling place settings, good food, and great wine. Old world touches like black lacquered trim, large black and white ceramic tiles like a checkerboard, even the wait staff was appropriately attired. The wait staff was always discretely near at hand to refresh one's water glass, neatly dressed in white dress shirts, black slacks, apron, and shoes. They didn't seem to eavesdrop on private conversations over the din of the piano music or a soloist.

They had dined with Jonathan, who had spelled out his plan for her, and Chris to hide out for a few days.

"What if I don't want to hide?" Tanya asked. Jonathan shrugged.

"Tanya, it seems clear what happened to Roy, and who did it." He began logically. "What's not so clear is how I am going prevent them from killing you."

"Arrest them."

"We may *know*, but we have no proof."

"So they're going to get away with everything?"

"Tanya, can you give me a few days to do my job?" He had been contemplating what to do with Tanya when Chris offered up his family's cabin in upstate. It was apparent to Tanya that he and Chris had put their heads together earlier in the afternoon while she had been shut away in Chris' apartment.

"Don't I have a say? This is my life."

Jonathan shook his head. "Not right now. We need you to cooperate with us. We're trying to keep you safe."

The idea of hiding out with Chris considering her vulnerable emotional state didn't sit well with Tanya as she considered alternatives in her mind over dinner. It was the first time she had heard of Chris' family owning a cabin. She wondered, "How far away was your family cabin?"

"Several hours' drive northwest toward Albany," Chris offered.

Nodding thoughtfully, she asked, "So, will we leave from here?"

Sitting back in his chair, Jonathan shook his head, as he cleared his throat. "It's best if Chris shows up for work as usual."

"And what am I to do?"

"We'll slip you in Frank's office until I arrange for you and Chris to duck out." She thought of her suitcase sitting in Chris' room, of the journals she tucked away for her trip out west. She had not really gone through them while at her sisters. Perhaps they held a clue she had overlooked. "What about clothes? Food?"

"Taken care of," Chris assured her.

Jonathan looked intensely at her. "Did Roy have a safety deposit box? A locker, a friend's house outside the family he might have hidden something in?"

Tanya narrowed her eyes. "He belonged to a gym—Gold's I think—the one near my office in mid-town. He could have a locker there, I suppose." She chewed the corner of her lower lip thoughtfully. "Maybe he sent something to Beatrice."

"Who's Beatrice?"

"His grandmother. You met when she was staying with me. They were very close. Closer than he and his mother."

"Did she say anything while you were together about him sending her anything?"

She shook her head, as the waiter came to offer coffee and desert. Tanya asked for hot tea and a slice of chocolate decadence cake. The guys both asked for coffee. Jonathan requested a cannoli. When the dessert and drinks were served, Tanya offered to share her cake with Chris. He accepted her offer to spoon it into his mouth with a smile, as she leaned forward to kiss away a dab of chocolate from his lip. Jonathan's jaw dropped as he watched the intimacy play out between them as his girlfriend walked in off the sidewalk. He rose to greet her with a kiss, offering her coffee or something to eat as she took a seat next to him.

Tanya smiled over at Roseanna in her pressed white nursing uniform. "Sorry, I missed dinner," she said breathlessly. "The nurse on third shift arrived late." They all nodded their understanding. The waiter stepped forward. "Just a salad and coffee," she said matter-of-factly.

"Cream and sugar?"

"No. Just black." She reached out for Tanya's hand. "I'm sorry. Jon told me all about your plight over the last few days."

With a nod, Tanya thanked her for her sympathy.

By ten that evening, they were all at the club. Lucy awaited Tanya in Frank's office. "Do you want me to come with you, girl?"

Tanya shook her head. "I don't want you in harm's way too."

"Hey, what are friends for?"

Tanya smiled and impulsively hugged Lucy, she felt the return embrace, "stay safe," Tanya whispered in her ear before stepping back.

Lucy sniffed, she looked at Tanya with glistening eyes, "you too."

XXXXX

The bathroom door opened, pulling her from her reverie. The water was tepid; she must have dozed off in the tub. Tanya opened her eyes and sat up. Chris stood with a mischievous expression in nothing more than his towel.

She pulled her knees up instantly. "Need someone to wash your back?" He offered.

"I believe I can manage," she assured him as she blushed.

He shrugged. "Need help rewrapping your ribs when you're done?" She nodded. "I'm the man for the job." She smiled up at him, relaxing. It surprised Tanya to see it was already after three in the afternoon when she emerged from the bath. Chris had plates of sandwiches on the coffee table, the fire going, and music playing. She had borrowed a sister's bulky, sea foam green robe to wrap herself in after her bath. She struggled into a nightgown Jonathan had thoughtfully packed for her, and a fresh under garments. She never imagined how inconvenient and painful a couple of cracked ribs could be. They may not slow heroines down on television shows, but they had certainly limited her mobility. She knelt down on the bearskin rug next to him and smiled.

"A bit early in the day for a romantic dinner, don't you think?"

He shrugged. "Consider it a late lunch. Would you like me to wrap your middle before we eat?" She nodded her consent, and he got out a fresh roll of gauze as she slipped out of the robe. With his assistance she blushingly lifted her nightgown for him to wrap her ribs. They ate in silence before he pulled out the sandalwood oil and handed it to her; with a wry expectant smile and raised brow, he stretched out expectantly on his stomach on the rug. She rubbed a bit of the oil on her hands and slowly massaged his back and shoulders before the fire, as the spring sun drifted beyond the trees in the late afternoon. He turned toward her and reached one hand to loosen the robe she had tightly wrapped about her as she had worked all the way down to his lower back and up again. Easing up on the pressure of the massage, she smiled down at his face as his hand rested on the inside of her thigh. She felt her pulse quicken as his hand slowly slid down toward her knee. She leaned back against the coffee table, feeling intoxicated, and drifted off to sleep.

XXXXX

She awoke to dying ambers in the hearth, an ache in her side, and feeling the chill of the spring evening around her. She painfully rose quietly to her feet as Chris groaned beside her but remained immobile. She grabbed a throw from the back of the couch to toss gently over him and padded toward the stairs. Gratefully, she slid between cool, crisp sheets in the grand bed of his grandparents and drifted back to sleep. Sometime later, Chris had slipped in next to her; she didn't stir. When she rose early in the morning, she found him curled up around her; she cautiously extricated herself and rose. Down in the kitchen, she found a thermos and filled it with water and packed a sandwich and some snacks in a large handbag she had brought with her. She had her camera bag and two of her journals tucked under her arm; she felt ready to set out. Looking at the coats on the hooks, she pulled on a warm green pea coat that was undoubtedly Chris'. It felt like she had donned his coat before; she then pulled on a pair of black knit gloves before slipping out the back door. She left him a note on the kitchen counter.

Dear Chris,

I've gone for a hike. Be back later. T

As she closed the back door quietly, she recalled leaving a similar note for Aaron once. He had taken her away to the family cabin for a long weekend. His buddy, Roger Smith, had showed up and he called Aaron outside. Aaron claimed Roger wanted to go hunting or something. It made no sense to Tanya, as it was mid-morning when Roger arrived. Aaron asked if he could borrow her little sports car, as that's what they had arrived in. Tanya had agreed, and off the guys went. She watched them drive down the dirt road in her tan sports car and noticed the vibrant colors of the autumn foliage on the trees. She had thought to herself she would need to have the undercarriage cleaned after all the trips down the dirt road it had taken over the last few day as the guys drove away. A sarcastic smirk crossed her lips. *Lord, life is full of irony. I just keep traveling in circles and perils.*

Being at the Rosen's lodge made Tanya remember times at Aaron's family cabin. The last time she had given the place a through cleaning before wandering into the woods that surrounded it and gathering a handful of beautiful-colored autumn leaves one afternoon.

She had tucked them within the pages of a book on the bookshelf before sitting out on the porch awaiting their return. Not so unlike yesterday, when she had been cooped up in Chris' apartment. The Sand's cabin had been a good three miles walk back toward the small town of Spencer. She could walk it, but she had no inclination to do so. Eventually the guys would return with her car. While she sat on the porch, she wondered, how had Roger arrived at the cabin that particular morning? He had not come by car because they had taken hers. Someone must have given him a lift. How had he known they would be out there? Lisa, a cousin of Aaron's, showed up unexpectedly before the guys returned. Tanya was thrilled to see her. "I left my favorite jeans," Lisa admitted, "and my red hooded sweatshirt. Jake and I are supposed to go to the races tomorrow night, so I thought I'd drive out here and pick them up."

Tanya nodded at the time she hadn't given the information much thought Lisa went into Aaron's parents' bedroom off the living area to retrieve her clothes. "Lisa, do you mind giving me a ride home?"

Tanya asked nonchalantly as she grabbed a piece of lined notebook paper and a pen.

"Sure. Where's Aaron?"

"He left earlier with Roger," Tanya confessed. "I've no idea when they'll be back, and I have animals to feed."

Lisa looked around the room as she nodded. "Sure."

The note, similar to the one she had left Chris this morning, had been simple enough:

Dear Aaron,

I cleaned and waited. Lisa came by and gave me a ride. I couldn't stay any longer.

See you later. Love, T

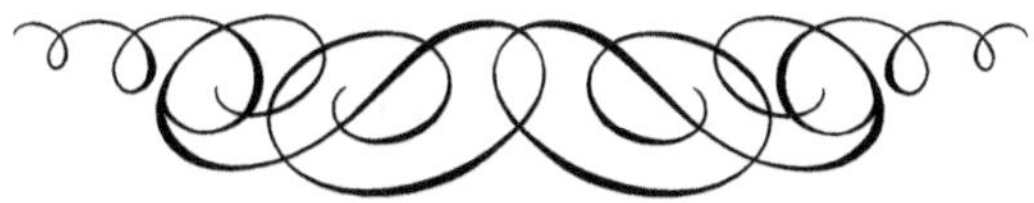

The dark, almost black lips and large, black eyes against sickly paper-white skin, was a phantom from her youth she readily recognized as M****, the Fuath in his boy form. He wore the same horizontal navy and white striped t-shirt, and dark denim jeans and worn black Converse high-tops she could still vividly recall. She stopped still in her tracks at the sight of his boy form rather than that of the black horse head she had grown accustom too in recent years. It'd been so long she had forgotten a fuath never ages its forms. He barred her path to Evald. *This time you may not enter alone, dear one. You have entered a crossroads in your heart. Remain where you are and find all you seek.*

Never before had he been so forward. Never had her heart blazed with such anger directed entirely toward him so that her entire body shook. Incredible sadness burned in his black eyes; sadness deeper than she had ever imagined possible in those dark orbs. He stood fast in silence; until she relented on the path, the mist swirled about him, and as quickly as he had appeared, both he and the mist were gone. She melted and wept with a flood of despair. It seemed there was no opportunity to escape the mess of her life; as a fairy, she was confounded. She needed not only direction; she needed someone to simply take her hand so that she may simply follow without thought or reason. What did the fuath mean that she could no longer travel the mist alone? Who would accompany her now that Roy was gone? She crumpled to the ground at his feet without sound. Surely, Lenora and Cecilia would not be expected to make the trip, long ago they had turned away. What could he mean? She was utterly alone. The path to Evald faded as quickly as she had conjured the mist. Slowly, she rose to her feet and walked to a large bolder near the edge of a cliff, to sit and contemplate.

She leaned back on the boulder and let her mind wander, drifting back to her return to Ithaca and a departing from her chosen path. Back to the absolute betrayal of Jan Sands that had sent Tanya over the edge. She struggled to face that dark abyss of memories long pushed far away from her conscious thoughts. Surprisingly, they were still raw and painful. The fuath was always right…he seemed to know her better than she knew herself. While living in the city she had lost touch with so much of herself. Hot tears cut paths down her cheeks in silent as her mind replayed the numerous painful events that lead her to sit upon this very cliff. Like Jan accusing her mother of having an affair with Mr. Sands long ago. Of her being the product of the affair. Had she only thought it all through back then she would have seen the error of Jan's thinking. But now that was all said and done, to marry Aaron would have bound her to a place and people she did not necessarily want to be bound too. Her mind rolled forward pass her college days to current tragedy. To events that led her to agree to run away with Chris Rosen in the wee hours of the morning like a fugitive. What had she ever done to warrant such emotional torment? Instantly, the fuath's face appeared in her mind's eye. He shook his head. *'You cannot enter in your present state.'* He warned, *'Too dangerous. You must work through this; follow your heart,'* he said in her mind. She knew he was right, but it didn't make her situation any easier. Her body took her back to Chris Rosen.

XXXXX

The semester in Brisbane with Auntie had been a Godsend. Now through her mind's eye, she saw it had been an escape, and she now longed for a similar such escape, and the fuath challenged her not to run. She had run to nurse her emotional wounds in security, and for a time, even imagined herself healed. She had lived as she could only live with her beloved aunt's unwavering affections. Auntie had always offered unconditional love and acceptance; that was truly special and unique about her. Tanya wanted to please her because she reflected the very best of herself. It had been heart wrenching to pack up and return to the States. She had even grown to like Neville because Auntie passionately adored him. "You could stay with us. Finish your education here," Auntie had generously offered.

Tanya had certainly been tempted. But in the end, she settled for an interlude in the south of France with Fritz and Natalie and Rich. They agreed to meet in Paris, and from there they had traveled to the Mediterranean for the remainder of her eight-day holiday. It had been glorious to reminisce of their first visit there together and to create new memories. It had been so enjoyable and relaxing an excursion, that in the end, Tanya hated to leave. She had only been away four brief months, and it had been so easy to shed the burdens of a lifetime. To imagine; the pain she carried around at Cornell had been only in her mind. The great weight never seemed to bear down on her when she was with Auntie; it had not returned while in France either, she realized.

As her plane glided into JFK airport in New York City, she inhaled deeply, and her mind raced to thoughts of returning to Cornell. Of dealing with family as she looked on the board for her connecting flight to Syracuse. Thoughts of how she would graciously avoid visiting Lockwood without hurting anyone's feelings flooded her mind. But perhaps Jan would make it easy on her. She prepared herself for the hour-and-a-half car ride from Syracuse airport to her boardinghouse just off Cornell's campus. Perhaps she and Jan could iron things out during the car ride, so that all could be well in some twisted way she couldn't imagine. She wished she had thought of someone from school she could have asked for a ride. Most of her school friends didn't have cars, and hers was garaged at the Sands barn with the hay and feed. She could have parked it at her mother's, but it would have sat out in the weather, and she preferred it hidden away in her absence.

Tanya looked around as she disembarked and headed toward the baggage claim; she didn't see Jan. Of all the people to greet Tanya at the Syracuse Airport, never had Tanya imagined Jan would send her darling son, Aaron Sands—the cause of Tanya's heartache and anguish. Tanya stopped in her tracks in shock. Where was Tessa? How had he driven all the way to Syracuse to pick up his longtime sweetheart without his new wife? Was she out of her mind, or was Aaron indeed standing up ahead waiting for her? Had she dreamed up the entire confession from Jan? Had she totally imagined the whole evening and all the events? Had Aaron actually married Tessa, or had it all been a twisted and pathetic nightmare?

Why was this man of all men standing at the gate, awaiting her departure with a smile of welcome? Was this some twisted, vengeful plan met to drive Tanya utterly insane? A smile crossed Aaron's lips as he saw her, and his arms spread in greeting. She moved toward him in the throng of disembarking passengers. He scooped her up off her feet, giving her no choice but to wrap her arms about his neck to steady herself. Searing pain scorched her heart as he squeezed her close before setting her down again. His eyes searched hers as her feet found solid footing, and she smiled up at him in disbelief as she collected her wits.

"What a welcome." Her cheeks blazed with color as she glanced about, her hair plaited down the right side of her face and chest. It was even blonder than Aaron could remember; her skin held a healthy glow. She seemed thinner, if that was at all possible, then when he had last seen her. Had it been at Easter time a year ago? He knew she missed him, had felt it in her heartbeat as they embraced; he could read it in her eyes. Why had she turned from him? What secret did she hide?

"Married life seems to suit you." She smiled up at him, admiring his lean, strong build, tan features, and dimples. Lord, how her body craved this man she could not have. The smile disappeared from his features. He glanced around. "Let's have a drink while we wait for your luggage to unload."

She nodded as he steered her by the elbow to a nearby airport pub. He headed for a small, corner table with lots of greenery nearby. He went to the bar after seating her; she looked out at the people as she waited. He returned momentarily with a Michelob in a bottle with a glass for himself and a tequila sunrise for her.

She smiled up at him as he set the drinks down. "Thanks."

He nodded as he slipped into the seat across from her at the small round table for two. "You ran pretty far from me, T." She grimaced and nodded as she sipped her drink. One mixed drink would hardly be enough. "I figured you wouldn't be coming back when I found letters between you and Tessa." She paled at the revelation but remained silent. He sighed at her silence, noticing how she clutched her glass and sipped from the thin stir. "But when I saw the album you made for our wedding, I knew your heart was still with me."

Tanya shook her head and sat back. "Aaron, my heart cannot be yours. You're married; you should be happy. Tessa loves Lockwood and the people there as much as you do. It's her home, as much as yours. It's not my home, it never was."

"It doesn't have to be mine, either."

Tanya sat back and gazed into his eyes for the longest time. The battle of wills had never ended; it had sojourned. How could Jan have sent him? Of all the people near at hand, Aaron was all she could do? Had she remained silent, Tanya and Aaron would no doubt be married instead of him and Tessa Goodrich. Tanya closed her eyes and took a deep breath, letting it out slowly. Perhaps when she opened her eyes she would realize it was all a bad dream. But when she opened them, Aaron sat across from her, watching her as closely as a cat. Tanya admitted she had eaten little on the plane, and now found herself feeling quite hungry.

"Okay, let's collect your luggage and find a place to eat." He finished his beer, put a tip on the table, and rose to offer her his powerful grip. She felt small and light next to him, and she skipped to keep up with his long strides.

"So did you stop over in France to hook up with Fritz?" Aaron asked as they were seated at Ruby Tuesday's. Tanya glanced over at him in surprise.

She smiled. "My, you are well informed of my movements."

He chuckled as the waiter came to take their drink order.

"I offered to go away with you, T. I'd have gone anywhere with you."

She shook her head. "Bodily, for a while, maybe. But I couldn't take you away from your joy, the farm Your family's farm is your joy, Aaron. Your heart's desire, not mine. You deserve to be with someone who can share your dream, your desires. That person wasn't me."

"Why couldn't it be?"

"Because Lockwood was never my home. I never felt accepted there. I never desired to remain there. I cannot live in Mother's dark shadow." She shook her head, "too many sad memories linger for me."

"Those memories are in your mind. They' ll be with you no matter where you go."

She shook her head. "No, they didn't follow me to Australia; they didn't invade my time with Auntie." She gave him a melancholy smile. "They're never there when I'm near Auntie. Not in Europe, not in Australia." She shook her head. "At Cornell, sometimes I escaped them; never did I escape in Lockwood."

Aaron sat back in his chair, throwing one arm over the back, and looked at her intently, as if he could look into her soul. "You and your sisters all ran away from Lockwood. You all have a deep-seeded secret that has wounded each of you differently." He shook his head and took a long swallow on a fresh bottle of Michelob before continuing. "I don't know what your secret is, T. I use to think you'd tell me when you were ready, but I guess you no longer trust me."

She reached for his big, tanned, callous hand with her small one and squeezed; how she longed to confide in him. "I've always trusted you, but you can't protect me from everything and everyone. You can't chase all the monsters from under my bed."

"You used to think so."

"We were children then."

"And now?"

"You're a married man. End of discussion."

He sat back and sighed. After a moment he nodded with a sad smile, the waiter brought their food. They ate in relative silence. On the way back to campus, Aaron stopped off at Stewart Park. They got out and strolled around the duck pond, and her mind drifted to happier times of growing up with him. He reached for her hand, and she took hold like old times. For a while she was swept up in a time when she felt no shame, when she had loved Aaron Sands with pure innocence. When they had picnicked in the park with Matthew and Cecilia and other friends. In the evenings, they would all go to someone's house for a round of cards before venturing home. For those few hours she could forget Jan's cruel innuendos that had shattered the fabric of her life. Back then she had seen a pleasant future in Lockwood or wherever Aaron Sands chose to settle down. They have a small ranch in the country, a couple of kids, and a dog under her feet. She had been able to visualize it as if it had already happened; Jan shattered that into tiny shards that could never be mended. How could she share such a burden with such a sensitive man like Aaron? It would destroy him as certainly as it had destroyed her. No, it was far kinder to listen to him and then encourage him to return to his wife. Tanya looked up as they walked back to his truck. She squinted as recognition dawned in her eyes, there in the parking lot was a creepy guy from the her college campus, she had not seen since before leaving for Australia. The guy had asked her out a number of times, and she had always turned him down.

"Hi, Tanya," he said as she passed hand in hand with Aaron. She nodded to him and kept on going. Aaron shot him a dangerous glare.

Aaron waited for her to keep up with his strides.

Who's the guy that gives you the shivers?"

She smiled up at him; they were so close their arms touched. "Some guy from campus," she admitted.

"Know his name?"

Tanya shrugged. "Forget him, Aaron."

Aaron glanced back. "Does he bother you? I'd be happy to have a word."

"No, Aaron. He's really not worth the time of day. I just ignore him. His name's Bobby; he lives between the Commons and my boardinghouse, but he's really no bother, honest." Tanya assured him as she gently tugged him toward his truck; he glanced back over her head at the guy they had passed. The guy leaned against a powder blue, older model Chevy Impala, watching them with a bemused smirk on his face. Aaron was as protective and jealous as ever. She opened her eyes to a clear mid-afternoon, lying on her back on the boulder where she had stopped to rest.

Tanya sighed deeply, as she rested on the bolder, with little motivation to go further. She let her thoughts linger on the creep at Cahoot's. She had forgotten about the guy from college so long ago until this moment of reflection. She let her thoughts of college continue to roll. The arguments she and Roy had usually involved Aaron or a member of her extended family. She let a flood of memories wash over her as she closed her eyes and dreamed. She could hear a woodpecker drilling a tree nearby as her mind took her back to a favorite hangout on University Avenue where the jukebox played, "Puff the Magic Dragon"…McDuff's Tavern? It was always hopping. She and her boardinghouse friends used to enjoy hanging out there. The place no longer existed; all that was left was a cornerstone. Tanya wondered why it had been torn down, but that was progress. She recalled falling in love with Cornell in the sixth grade while on an architectural field trip from school. The class had been studying columns: Doric, Corinthian, and Ionic. All were featured somewhere on the grand campus, they had stopped to examine the mega sculptures around the campus as well. Tanya had at that moment decided it would be a wonderful place to study and learn. She had no idea how she would pay for such a grand education, but somehow she would manage to make it happen.

XXXXX

Sitting up, tears freely flowed from her eyes as she recalled the great times she had with Roy riding around Taughanock Falls on his motorcycle, while at college. They had enjoyed casual picnics near the falls of Taughanock, Buttermilk and other places she had forgotten the names too. So many wonderful memories of moments with Roy, what had changed? Back in college it had been enough to simply enjoyed being with one. Sometimes he would be waiting at the mall entrance of Hill's when she would get off work at eight in the morning after pulling an all-nighter, just to give her a lift home. She often would eat with her coworkers at Friendly's before taking a bus back to campus. They double-dated with Janice and JB, Rick and Lisa, or Debbie and Bob. A smiled played on her lips as she remembered playing cards with high school friends and attending Colleen and Wayne's wedding. Tanya realized at the wedding reception that she really didn't fit in with her high school groups anymore. She was no longer dating one of them; she had chosen a different path. Most of them didn't attend college; some chose vocational school or considered themselves finished upon completing a two-year degree. They didn't see the benefits of going for the four-year degree or beyond.

I never really felt apart of the community growing up. I wasn't related to anyone there. Most of my classmates were somehow related to one another. Then I traveled extensively with Auntie in the summer and holidays. I don't even quite fit with my own sisters.

Ironically, I grew up on a farm but have no farmer's heart. I loved the wood around the fields, not the fields themselves. Most of my classmates rushed into marriage as if it would solve their problems and insecurities. I ran from it. I'll never rush in to having a family. Jan shattered my dreams. I loved Roy, but I couldn't legally bring myself to commit to him. My childhood was speckled with such pain until recently that I couldn't imagine having children to run and laugh with through the trees, as Father had once done with us.

In pairing up with Roy, I resigned myself to forget any maternal longings. Lenora was right; it wouldn't be fair for a fairy to bear the offspring of a leprechaun. Roy and I spoke of adopting, but we were never old enough for that.

And now? Now she was twenty-six years old, confused, and alone with a desirable human. If she wouldn't bare the offspring of a leprechaun and hadn't married the one human she had loved since childhood, why even consider a life with yet another? *Why has M**** turned me from the path? I don't want to love any more humans. I want to simply live and breathe as a fairy. Even if I am the last of my kind in Evald, and I never have a chance of mating. I simply cannot love a human like Cecilia.*

I cannot turn my back on our home, our heritage. I have no desire to own any nearby piece of land close to Mother. I'm thankful Beatrice entrusted me with the tapestry. I need never be reliant on the wood near Mother's as long as I have the tapestry.

Ever since Jan sat with Cecilia and me, I've never wanted land in Lockwood or anywhere nearby. The closest thing I've come to ownership in Lockwood is the tiny apartment over Aaron's garage. I'm sure that now Aaron would be thrilled if I never used that apartment again.

While in college, she rarely saw or spoke on the phone with her sisters, as she didn't have a phone of her own. To save money she used the house Mother's phone when necessary. She lay back on her chosen boulder near the cleft's edge where she was soothed by the sound of waterfalls as she pressed on and let her life play out as if watching a reel-to-reel movie against the sky overhead. She glimpsed herself in the past, when she used the payphone at work in the employee lounge of Hill's Department Store or the one on the Ithaca Commons after finishing up at Ritz Cameras just to hear the voice of one of her sisters. She realized she had been on her own for a long time. The loneliness had led her to Roy. He was away at school, alone, much like her. They moved in circles of students who came from money or had supportive parents or both. Both she and Roy seemed out of place, not truly having either. Roy had a loving grandmother; Tanya had dear Aunt June. Tanya was sort of local and had friends in town through her two part-time jobs off campus. Roy was at Cornell on the GI Bill after putting in his four years in the service. But neither seemed to have family encouragement. Friends were more important to Tanya than Roy. Once they started going steady, he confided in her that he didn't need anyone else. He didn't mind hanging with friends from time to time, but he preferred to simply spend all his free time with her or alone. Tanya told him she needed to hang with her friends from time to time.

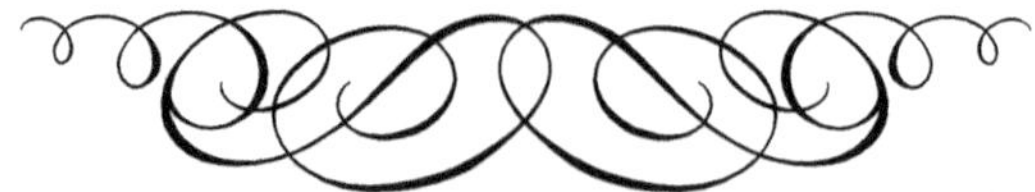

Tanya slung her pack over her shoulder as she got up from the boulder and looked for a direction to take. The day was fading if she did not hurry it would be evening before she reached the lodge. She turned to head back in the right direction. Confusion absorb her thoughts as they raced from M**** turning her away from the path, the immediate past, and her current predicament. Why was so much happening at once? Roy's death, the break into her home, the guy at Cahoots, and now being left alone with someone she found alluring. She stopped as her eyes darted around, looking for guidance that did not appear.

Tanya crumbed to the ground where she stood, and sobbed. Her mind took her back to a place of tranquility, a place different from all her other dreams. The apartment of the older couple; the couple that had been able to see her, there she had found comfort. She scrambled to retrieve a journal from the pack, and flipped through the entrances to find what she sought. With this couple she had felt there had been guidance. They thought she was the spirit of their daughter, and they were lovingly trying to lead her across to the other side to find eternal rest.

Immediately, I sensed she had caught me in my dream wanderings. She melted in a seat across the small table from me, her light blue-gray eyes never wavering from my face. Her husband stood behind her for some minutes, a hand resting on her shoulder. Until that very moment I never realized others could see me as I drifted through my dream state. I always imaged I passed unnoticed or as one of the characters. Roy had never actually seen me, not even when he felt me watching. Those times when I observed Roy, I always felt as light as a bird, high in a tree.

This was apparently not so, as I often enjoyed this couples garden. There was such a sense of hospitality in their garden, in their living room, I always felt welcomed. I looked deep into her eyes. "Forgive me," I heard myself speak in that strange, halting voice I didn't recognize as my own. "You've a lovely garden. I feel safe and welcomed there." I smiled sadly. I was curious as to how they could actually see me where so many others had not. "I never realized anyone could see me." I heard myself confess. "Even when you spoke to me, I imagined you were seeing someone you loved."

"How do you do it?"

"I dream," I replied matter-of-factly.

She nodded. "You began coming to us shortly after our daughter perished." She explained in a methodical fashion. With a wispy smile, she added, "Cynthia so loved the garden, as do I. Do you really enjoy our garden?"

"Oh, very much," I confessed. "It gives me such a sense of peace and joy just to visit." She sat back and sighed as I recalled their home through a multitude of repetitive dreams. Whenever I appeared at their home in my dreams, I would look down at myself to find I was dressed in a long, airy, white silky nightgown and robe that billowed behind me as I glided through the garden or the apartment.

"Where did you get Cynthia's nightgown and robe?"

I shrugged. "They appear on me whenever I'm in your garden or home," I explained. The lady nodded as if that somehow made sense to her.

She looked intently into my eyes. "Would you come with us now?"

I shook my head as thoughts filled me. Someone else's thoughts; I needed to share them with this couple. "Your daughter is content on the other side. She called me to comfort you; you must give her your blessing to go, Martha."

They both let out a gasp as I used her Christian name. "Did you see her? Talk to her?" I shook my head. "I'm sorry it doesn't really work that way. I sensed her desires. It allows me to travel to you when you were at your lowest. I'll not come again, as she wishes to move on. She's lingered for too many years." I reached out and rested my hand on her forearm. "She's waiting for you to let go."

The lady nodded. "I must let her go."

I nodded. I felt her feathery touch upon my hand her fingers were long and delicate, like her whole fragile being, and yet I sensed a deep inner strength. I was shaken to the quick by these revelations, and yet I remained calm, as if it were an everyday occurrence for me. Our eyes met and rested as she struggled to check her tears. They felt more of joy rather than sadness. After they left, I felt overwhelming peace and then the release. It was impossible for me to focus on reading. I rose to stretch my legs and wander about the library. I wandered out onto the sidewalk, in my stupor I bumped into an attractive man, near my age. We went up to the top of the Empire State Building together.

What am I?

By the time the lodge came back into view relief and hunger flooded through Tanya's body. She stepped up onto the porch and opened the front door. Chris swiveled around in his chair when he heard her come in. A smile played across his face as she slipped off her boots.

"Ready for a late lunch?" he asked nonchalantly.

She looked at him quizzically. "Isn't it closer to dinner?" she questioned as she sat her journals on the bottom stair and glanced toward a wall clock, which read four-thirty in the afternoon. She had left at six in the morning; Chris acted as if her behavior were normal. Where had the time gone? He rose as if he expected her to be gone most of the day, and they headed toward the kitchen.

"Sandwiches all right? Or would you like some soup as well?" Chris asked.

"Soup would be nice," she admitted. "I'm a bit chilled. Do you have hot chocolate?" He nodded as he went to the cupboard for the canister. "How's your programming going?"

Chris shrugged. "I'll have it worked out by tomorrow evening at the latest, I figure. I'll go to town to FedEx it out either tomorrow or the next day."

Tanya shot him an apprehensive look. "Chris…I…thanks." She swallowed a lump in her throat. "Thanks for coming to my rescue." How could she expect him to stop work just because he had come away with her? Silly, he still had deadlines to meet.

He moved closer, standing before her, as she leaned against the kitchen counter. "Not to worry," he assured her. "We'll figure this out." A wry smile played upon his lips as he nuzzled closer, giving her a few small kisses on her neck. He grinned pulling back as she turned toward the kettle; he moved behind her playfully leaning his head on her shoulder. "I brought something that might make you feel safer." She shot him a questioning look as he took her hand and turned off the kettle. He pulled her into the bathroom. Truly, over the last six months or so she had done well to avoid one on one time with Chris until now.

She realized she shied away because of an electric shock that ran through her body whenever they spontaneously touched. She was fine when she anticipated his touch, but the unexpected touches sent currents through her more intense than those she had ever experienced before. It was more intense than the currents Roy had rippled through her veins even in Evald. Chris seemed unaware of the current as he pulled her to the bathroom. She felt light headed as she followed behind him, drawn like a moth to the light. Standing her before the mirror, he smiled at her over her shoulder, just under a head taller than herself. He opened the linen closet and drew out a small bottle of hair color and pulled up a stool from the kitchen counter. "Let's wet your hair, I'll give you a trim, and darken it to a coppery red." She looked at him skeptically before bowing her head over the sink and wetting her hair.

"I've never dyed my hair before," she confessed as the tepid water ran through her hair in rivulets down into the drain.

"Don't worry." He assured her. She was unaccustomed to having her hair cut above her shoulders. He wrapped her shortened hairstyle up after being carefully colored. In silence she watched him as he worked, wondering where a man had learned to do a woman's hair. Chris expertly drew out an eyebrow comb, and colored her brows to match her new hair color. When all was said and done, she stood looking in disbelief at her reflection in the mirror, wondering who this stranger was.

She turned in surprise toward Chris; he smiled appreciatively. "What do you think?"

With a deep breath she slowly exhaled. "I hardly recognize myself," she admitted, steeling another glance at herself and reached up to touch her hair. "It's all right," she added with a nod of her head as she turned toward him. "But what of your appearance?"

"Me?" he asked.

She nodded. He smiled with a sigh. He bent over the sink, washed his hair, and combed it off to one side, trimmed the other side a bit shorter, and added a pair of owl shaped, brown-rimmed glasses. "Well?" He raised his eyebrows at her expectantly.

She smiled with satisfaction. "Hmm. I think that will do."

"Very well. Tomorrow we'll go to town together."

"What town would that be?"

"Selkirk." She nodded absently, as he gripped her waist and kissed her. She broke free from his embrace with a stunned look upon her face. Chris tilted his head to one side with a questioning look in his eyes. Clapping her hands together thoughtfully, she turned and ran upstairs. Chris followed at a much slower pace, curious. He entered her room as she rifled through the top drawer of the bureau. She rocked back as she opened her day planner and date book. She glanced at Chris with delight. "Chris, I must use a pay phone tomorrow in the afternoon or evening."

"Why?"

"To call Beatrice," she said as if he should have realized that by now.

"Beatrice?"

"Roy's grandmother in California. When it's noon here it's about nine in the morning there. I doubt Beatrice's up before nine or so." His face was puzzled; he didn't understand what had gotten her so excited. She went on excitedly as he stood with his hands in his pockets. "Don't you see?" she asked expectantly. "Roy may have sent her a letter of his troubles. Some clue she thought too trivial to mention."

He looked at her thoughtfully, and nodded in delight at his handiwork. What harm could it do to let her call and ask? "Okay. I'll check in with Jonathan first. I believe there's a payphone inside the lobby of the library. If not we'll find one that's inside." She nodded her agreement with the plan.

XXXXX

Chris rose early, close to seven in the morning. Tanya was already up and downstairs, singing softly as she pulled banana nut bread from the oven. Her journal sat open on the table, visible as he came down the stairs. Her journal was a thick, five-subject notebook with college-ruled pages. He could see her small, tight handwriting covering the pages that lay open as he heard the soft lull of her humming. Up until that moment, it had been his intention to finish his computer programming first thing. Instead he greeted her in the kitchen by wrapping his arms around her waist and kissing her cheek as he grabbed a piping hot cup of coffee. Glancing out the window over her shoulder, he caught a glimpse of the early morning. He ventured out onto the porch in his bare feet to take in the fresh air; the delicious smell of fresh bread wafted the air as he closed the door behind him. Quietly, Tanya joined him on the porch, smiling serenely. He smiled down at her and turned back to gaze out over the pond.

"It's so wonderfully peaceful here," she admitted dreamily. "I'd forgotten how much I enjoy the woods since moving to the city."

He nodded as he took in her profile; it was wonderful to see her looking so relaxed and rested. There were no longer any signs of the stress she had under gone over the last few days. The smell of fresh-baked bread stirred the hunger in his stomach. She stood near the railing with her face turned up toward the morning sun. As he stared at her profile, he had an idea.

"Let's go for a hike this morning." She turned and opened her eyes at him with a quizzical look.

"Seriously? I thought you were eager to get to Selkirk to mail off your work."

He shrugged with a smile and the wave of his hand. "That can wait. Let's enjoy the morning."

"Before or after breakfast?"

His eyes glittered with merriment. "Let's start off on a full stomach," he agreed. She smiled as she headed back inside before he changed his mind. She was dressed in faded jeans, a blue sweatshirt with a T-shirt underneath, and a pair of black knit gloves, and her brown hiking boots. She returned quickly with a backpack stuffed with food and a canteen of water, as well as his thermos of coffee strapped to the side of the backpack, her camera around her neck. She handed him a second pack; he glanced inside to see she had packed climbing tools and a blanket. He smiled at her as he zipped it up, and he ducked inside to grab a pair of socks and shoes. They headed toward a path behind the house that Chris explained would take them down to the falls. Tanya hadn't expected him to lead her on a hike that would most assuredly be strenuous both ways. She followed along without protest thinking how different he was as she got to know him. He was not the soft-palmed, city boy she expected at the club. So different from the persona she had painted of him, this outdoors man was an unexpected pleasure.

As they walked the wood, everything around them seemed surreal to her, as if she were walking through a dream while wide awake. There were times when she lost sight of Chris in a hazy mist, even though he was only feet ahead. She reached forward and took his hand; he glanced back over his shoulder toward her with a reassuring smile. They crossed a small stream, jumping from rock to rock to get to the other side. Looking about, she felt light headed, and she began searching for M****, but he did not appear. Her feet seemed to have a life of their own as she saw metallic wings appear on Chris' back; his clothes took on hues of darker blues and greens, trimmed in brown. A gasp escaped her lips in surprise. Chris hesitated on the path as he turned back toward her with narrowing dark eyes that glistened with pleasure at the transformation he saw in her appearance. Just as she was stunned as he transformed as she noticed his dimpled fairy smile that made his eyes twinkle with delight. He drew her close on the narrow path and looked down into her turquoise fairy eyes. "Do you recall years ago touring the Empire State Building with me?" She stood in shock as he continued in a gentle voice, "The girl I took up the elevator. The girl who disappeared before we exchanged names." Hmm, she loved his smile. She nodded and waited for him to continued, "You and I took a ride up the Empire State Building; we walked around, then you left me on the street without even a goodbye." She nodded her admittance as he turned, and they continued down a narrow hand in hand. The path was very stony along the cliff face not too far from the falls.

"It wasn't 'goodbye,'" she explained. "I saw you in dreams. Even before that chance meeting, you were in my dreams. I imagined we would meet up again." She could hear the rush of water as the damp scent of falls wafted through the air. Knitting his brow, he glanced over his shoulder.

"You're wrong, you know." She gave him a curious look. "Roy was not your mate, not your equal." He stopped before her. When she remained stunned and silent, he continued. "How could you have bonded with a trickster?"

How did he know that Roy was a leprechaun? She drew in a breath, staring up into his eyes. He meant her gaze with a dark storm in his smoldering eyes that startled her. Narrowing her eyes, she looked around and realized they were through the mist. M**** greeted them on the path; they were quite a distance from her beloved tree, Gosymonity. She smiled and shrugged, unable to speak. Chris laced his fingers through hers and smiled as they moved forward. Tanya furrowed her brow in puzzlement. How had everyone known save herself? How had she missed sensing Chris' true nature? She closed her eyes and tipped her face up toward the sky. She hadn't missed it, she realized, she simply hadn't accepted it. The memory of the electricity passing between them cleared her vision. There she was, in her mind's eye, a teen fairy. Running through the wood, laughing, as she ran, pursued by a dark, young, male fairy. Dropping her hands to her sides, she lowered her chin and stopped still. He turned around, the smoldering eyes of one fairy, looking into the eyes of her long-ago childhood pursuer.

"I've been so confused for so long," she mumbled her confession. He nodded as he offered his hand at arm's length. She looked toward M****. He smiled reassuringly and nodded. Extending her hand, she accepted his hand. Electricity flowed up her arm from his touch, filling her with delicious warmth she had never known could exist. He smiled at her as they stood still for some time. She once again felt the flutter of her wings, a feeling she had thought she would never feel again! His smile warmed her from within. Did he feel the current? Had he felt it all along? As they began to move forward side by side now that the path was wider, her wings fluttered despite the weight of her pack on her left shoulder, her feet scarcely touched the path. She had never felt such intense joy. Looking around, she felt at home in the wood after they crossed a narrow stream. Neither of them were walking now, they were both fluttering just above the earth, hand in hand. Excitedly, she took the lead and headed back toward her beloved Gosymonity, toward her room. There she could always feel the sun indirectly and lie in the shade of the roots in her grand four-poster bed.

She glanced over her shoulder twards Chris. "Why did you not speak before?"

"Didn't I. Hmm, I believe I commented that you and Grandmother were of the same colors?" Her mind flashed back to his grandparents' room when she first admired it. Why hadn't she seen?

"You, like your Grandmother, are water," she observed by his coloring, "but from deeper in the wood?" He looked down at his attire and back at her lighter shades of blue, green, and purple with a tinge of brown and nodded.

"Do you not remember me from our youth in the wood, Tanya?" Taking a deep breath and tasting the woodland scent on the air, she smiled as she looked up at the tall, straight pines. She nodded as a flood of buried memories poured forth as if a gate had opened.

"I recall a reunion." Memories began to flood her senses! She looked at him in awe. "We ran through the wood."

"I caught you," he reminded her.

She giggled. "Ah, but I escaped."

"I let you go," he insisted.

"Are we near your tree then?" She asked in utter amazement, "I'm sorry; do male fairies have their own trees?"

Amusement made his eyes dance and sparkle. "I live in my parents' tree." He pointed up the stream toward the thicker, older trees; they were so deep in the wood she could not see the fields of the local farmers that always seemed just beyond the stream near her home. Here, even in the height of the day, little sun trickled through the thick foliage to the ground beneath their feet.

She smiled and slightly tilted her head for him to take the lead. "Your cabin, your hike, your tree first," she demurred with a curtsy.

"Ah, but we are so close to yours." Still that calm smile and sparkling eyes in his face, silently he took her hand and brought it to his lips.

"Mine will keep," she assured him before turning off in a different direction heading up a narrow deer path into the tall old forest evergreens; the pine gave way to thicker, studier spruce, and hemlock, cedar and shorter yews. The low branches of a stand of spruce had been trimmed away, so that they could easily walk upright under them, through the soft brown needles on the ground below, these gave way to mossy ground and ferns. Tanya thought how soft a bed of pine and spruce needles must undoubtedly be. In Evald, her bed was of moss and dried leaves and sweet smelling lavender and mint. As they walked, she could no longer see fields; the light of the sun was blocked by the high thick canopy of trees; she was lulled by the soft babbling of the stream, twitter of birds high above, dapples of sunrays breaking through the branches above their heads. The thick canopy reminded her of the lattice of ivy that sheltered the front side of her room at Gosymonity. She felt the quiet serenity that only comes from walking in the thicker wood, of drawing from the coolness of the mountain water in the stream. Her mind wandered to images of yester years with her sisters. There had been cousins and others in the wood in their youth, elves, nymphs, and trolls. Where were they all now? Her mind drifted to a time in her youth when she had desired to bring Aaron into the wood. Lenora had counseled, "It is dangerous for man to enter the wood. Should you do so, he must not eat nor drink any of the food or water."

"Why?" she asked.

Lenora shrugged. "Do you wish him to cross back into his own world or remain with you?"

"I mean, why are we not trapped when we drink and eat of this dimension?"

Lenora grimaced. "Perhaps we are, and you simply do not yet know it." She had responded with a grin. Dear Lenora always spoke in riddles Tanya only half understood.

Tanya chuckled at her sister. "Right. I only dream of walking through the mist."

Lenora shrugged, as she offered Tanya a plate of cornbread, and cookies. "Does Mother venture here?" Tanya stopped eating a piece of cornbread she had just popped in her mouth in contemplation. No, Mother did not venture into the mist. She acted as though she did not know it existed. Would Tanya become like her mother? Lenora knew and understood so much more than Tanya ever seemed to grasp. Tanya blinked away the thoughts. The present came clearly into focus once more. Looking around she gave her head a shake. Instantly, she realized, Lenora was not with her today. She had returned to the moment at hand; surprised, here she was with a fellow fairy. A slow burning smile lit her face as her gaze rested on the back of Chris head. She couldn't contain the joyous laughter that bubbled up out of her. Chris turned to glance back at her as she closed the distance between them and wrapped her free arm around his neck to kiss him and know that all was real. Alas, she had found a true equal. Or more correctly, an equal had found her. Pulling free she dropped his hand and fluttered off through the trees toward his home tree as she shrieked with playful glee. He fluttered after her with peals of laughter.